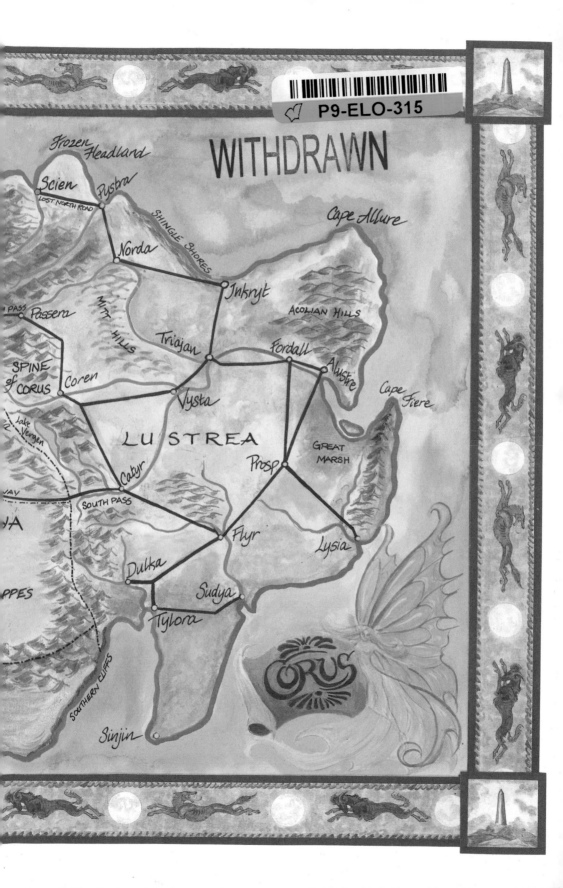

LADY-
⊹PROTECTOR⊹

L. E. MODESITT, JR.

LADY-
✳PROTECTOR✳

The Eighth Book of the Corean Chronicles

A Tom Doherty Associates Book
New York

LADY-PROTECTOR: THE EIGHTH BOOK OF THE COREAN CHRONICLES

Copyright © 2011 by L. E. Modesitt, Jr.

A Tor Book
Published by Tom Doherty Associates, LLC
175 Fifth Avenue
New York, NY 10010

www.tor-forge.com

Tor® is a registered trademark of Tom Doherty Associates, LLC.

Library of Congress Cataloging-in-Publication Data

Modesitt, L. E.
    Lady-Protector : the eighth book of the Corean Chronicles / L. E. Modesitt, Jr. — 1st ed.
        p. cm. — (Corean chronicles ; bk. 8)
    ISBN 978-0-7653-2804-5
    1. Corsu (Imaginary place)—Fiction.   I. Title.
    PS3563.O264L33 2011
    813'.54—dc22

                                                            2010036535

First Edition: March 2011

Printed in the United States of America

0 9 8 7 6 5 4 3 2 1

For my lady of the opera, who understands too well
the true cost of fairy tales

CHARACTERS

MYKELLA — Lady-Protector of Lanachrona

FERANYT — Lord-Protector [deceased]

JERAXYLT — Son and heir of Feranyt [deceased]

JORAMYL — Brother of Feranyt and Lord-Protector-select [deceased]

BERENYT — Son of Joramyl [deceased]

CHELEYZA — Widow of Joramyl

RACHYLANA — Younger sister of Mykella

SALYNA — Youngest sister of Mykella

AREYST — Arms-Commander of Lanachrona

CHOALT — Commander, Southern Guards

MAELTOR — Captain, Southern Guards

GHARYK — Lord and Minister of Justice; wife is Jylara

POROFYR — Lord, Seltyr, and Minister of Highways and Rivers

LORYALT — Forester of Lanachrona

KHANASYL — First Seltyr of Tempre

LHANYR — Chief High Factor of Tempre

ELWAYT — Palace Steward

SKRELYN — Prince of Midcoast

CHALCAER — Prince of Northcoast; older brother of Cheleyza

FIALDAK — Landarch of Deforya

SHEORAK — Envoy of the Landarch

SMOLTAK — Majer, aide to Sheorak

GHEORTYN — Seltyr of Southgate [one of the 12]

MALARYK — Envoy of Gheortyn

LADY-
PROTECTOR

1

. . . and that I will employ all Talent and skills necessary to do so, at all times, and in all places, so that peace and prosperity may govern this land and her people.

As the words of the ancient oath she had taken as Lady-Protector died away—making her the first Lady-Protector since Mykel the Great had created the office of "Protector of Lanachrona" hundreds of years earlier—Mykella stood for a moment looking out across the courtyard of the palace in Tempre. She had almost forgotten the remainder of the investiture ceremony. Almost. With only a slight hesitation, she walked down the steps past the bodies of her immediately deceased Uncle Joramyl and cousin Berenyt, their figures sprawled across the stone. Undercommander Areyst followed Mykella closely.

On the left side, at the bottom of the five low and wide stone steps leading up to the main entry of the palace entry, lay the body of Arms-Commander Nephryt who, less than a fraction of a glass before, had tried to cut her down with his saber. One of the Southern Guards had straightened his form and laid him out on his back, facing the palace. Beyond the body, a Southern Guard stood, holding the reins of the gray stallion that had been Joramyl's.

Before she mounted the stallion, Mykella turned to Areyst. "Have the bodies prepared for a quiet family memorial. There will be no procession and no honors for any of them." She almost added, *Traitors do not deserve honors of any sort.* She did not. That would have made her look weak before the still-assembled Southern Guards. "Have someone guide my sisters to the . . . Lady-Protector's study and provide a guard. I will see you there."

Areyst nodded. "Yes, Lady-Protector."

She could sense a certain amusement behind his words but also approval. She couldn't help but wonder what she had forgotten. With her Talent shields still tight about her, she swept the black cloak back over her shoulders, revealing the brilliant blue vest of the heir and the black nightsilk shirt and trousers she almost always wore. Then she mounted, wishing that she were taller and that she didn't have to jump to place her black boot in the stirrup. She wasn't about to ask for a leg up. She never had before, and now that she was the ruler of Lanachrona, she wasn't about to begin.

As she turned the stallion toward the east, before riding to the end of the palace, then north and out of sight to the rear courtyard, she used her Talent to extend her hearing, trying to pick up any words that might bode ill. Over the sound of hooves on the stone pavement that showed no sign of wear, even after thousands of years, she began to hear murmurs.

". . . rides like a guard . . ."

". . . never thought the daughter . . ."

". . . the one Seltyr looked to fill his britches . . ."

Had that been Malaryk, the envoy from Southgate, or one of the local Seltyrs from Tempre? Either way, that suggested problems, not that there wouldn't be scores of them in the days ahead.

Her eyes flicked to the massive oblong structure that was the palace. Not for the first time, she wondered what function it had served in the days of the vanished Alectors who had built it, because the interior was anything but designed for a ruler, even with all the additions, such as the kitchens, made over the years.

After she reached the rear courtyard, she turned the stallion toward the middle rear door to the palace. Two Southern Guards looked blankly from the stallion to her, clearly not expecting the daughter of the former Lord-Protector.

"A few things have changed," she said as she reined up. "Lord Joramyl was executed for poisoning my father and plotting the death of my brother. So was his son. That left me as Lady-Protector, and the Seltyrs and the Southern Guards have affirmed my succession."

The younger guard swallowed hard. The older and graying guard nodded slowly. "We have always served your family, Lady. We will continue to do so."

Mykella could sense the honesty behind the words. "Thank you." She dismounted gracefully, handed him the reins, stepped back, then turned toward the door.

". . . she do that?" she heard the younger guard say as she opened the door.

"She was named after Mykel the Great . . . for good reason, it appears . . ."

As she closed the palace door behind her, she certainly hoped so, but put that thought aside as she hurried along the wide interior corridor, following it west, then south, and finally east to reach the central stone staircase—wide as it was, the only staircase—to the upper level of the palace. At the base of the steps were two Southern Guards, both older rankers, rather than the interior palace guards she had known. That Areyst had made that change did not surprise her, but the speed with which he had acted did. It also pleased her.

The one on the left inclined his head. "Lady-Protector."

Mykella returned the nod and hurried up the stairs. Neither guard spoke again even after she passed them. Another pair of Southern Guards were stationed at the top. She nodded to both and turned to her left. In moments, she had reached her destination. For just a moment, she hesitated. Was it still Sexdi? Her father's memorial ceremony, just yesterday, seemed far longer than a day ago. She straightened and opened the door.

Chalmyr rose from behind the table-desk in the outer anteroom that guarded the entry to the study that had been her father's. "Lady-Protector."

Mykella almost smiled. "Who told you?"

"Undercommander Areyst sent a Southern Guard to inform me. He has also placed trusted guards in places in the palace."

"I know." She didn't mention how she'd discovered that. "The commander is quite able and very loyal." She paused and looked at Chalmyr. "How did you feel about my father's death and Joramyl's efforts to become Lord-Protector?"

"I was distressed, Lady. I cautioned your father about Lord Joramyl once. The second time I brought up the matter, he told me never to mention the subject again if I wanted to remain as his private scrivener." The gray-haired functionary smiled sadly.

Mykella could sense the truth of the older man's feelings. "Then you will serve me as loyally as you did him?"

"If you will have me, Lady-Protector."

"I will . . . but only if you remain honest and tell me of your misgivings about any action I may take or contemplate."

Chalmyr bowed deeply. "That I will, Lady." He straightened. "Your sister Salyna is already awaiting you in the study."

"Do you know where Rachylana is?"

"She is in her chamber. A pair of Southern Guards are posted there to keep others from intruding. The undercommander said that she was not to leave the palace without your permission."

"That is correct. Matters need to settle for a time."

When Mykella stepped through the inner door, Salyna was standing to one side of the desk in the study that had always been that of the Lord-Protector of Lanachrona, a study that had become Mykella's as the first Lady-Protector of the land.

Behind the outward poise of her tall, blond, and beautiful youngest sister, Mykella could sense confusion, apprehension . . . and even some fear. Given Salyna's expertise and training with weapons, that fear surprised Mykella.

"There's no reason for you to worry now," Mykella said.

"You can sense that, too, can't you?"

"When people are close."

"With what you did . . . why couldn't you save Father?" Salyna's voice was not quite accusatory.

"I couldn't learn what I learned fast enough." Mykella shook her head. "The . . . things . . . I did . . . today . . . some of them . . . today was the first time I did them." *At least in public.* But some of them she'd only tried once before, and all of them—except seeing the soarer, using the Table in the depths of the palace's lower levels, and beginning to sense what people felt—she had been forced to learn in order to survive after her father's poisoning by Joramyl. "Until I did them today . . ." She shrugged, a gesture between resignation and helpless-ness. "You know I tried to caution Father . . . and warn him."

"Did you have to kill Berenyt?"

"Yes. He was weak, and Cheleyza would have manipulated him. She might even have married him. She's that calculating."

Before Mykella could say more, there was a rap on the study door. "Lady-Protector, Undercommander Areyst."

"Have him come in."

The broad-shouldered and blond Areyst stepped into the study and immediately bowed. "Lady-Protector." As he straightened, his pale green eyes met those of Mykella. She could sense a firm resolve, as well as concern for her. That boded well, since she'd named him as both Arms-Commander of Lanachrona and her designated heir. She could also sense the thin strand of green amid the golden brown of his unseen life-thread, a thread that seemed more vital than that of Salyna's and far more than that of Chalmyr, whose thread was almost yellowish brown, stretching invisibly out to the east.

Areyst extended his hand, palm up. In it was a ring, golden with a large square-cut emerald set in the middle of the seal of Lanachrona. "This was your father's. The usurper wore it. It is yours now."

Both seeing her father's seal ring and hearing Areyst calling her uncle a usurper jolted Mykella, but she nodded as she took the ring. "Thank you." Because it was far too large to fit any of her fingers, she slipped it into her belt pouch.

"It is yours by right," Areyst said quietly.

"It is the Lady-Protector's by right," Mykella said gently, "not mine."

Areyst nodded.

Mykella sensed his approval of her words even as she thought for a moment. Although she had planned carefully the steps by which she had removed her uncle Joramyl and his son Berenyt after their all-too-successful efforts to kill her father and her brother Jeraxylt, she really hadn't planned beyond stopping her uncle from taking control of Lanachrona.

"Commander Areyst," she began, looking into his pale green eyes, "what sort of document or proclamation do we need to confirm you as Arms-Commander of Lanachrona?"

"A simple statement with the Lord-Protector's . . . the Lady-Protector's signature and seal, Lady Mykella."

"I'll also need your recommendations for the officers to take your place and that of Commander Nephryt in the Southern Guards."

"I would recommend Majer Choalt as Commander, but he will have to be recalled from Soupat." Areyst paused. "We should discuss the position of undercommander, now that Commander Demyl has . . . departed."

"For the moment, I assume you and . . . other officers you trust can handle the combined duties. Will that be a problem?"

"No, Lady." A faint smile crossed Areyst's lightly tanned face. "I will dispatch a courier to recall the majer immediately."

"I also need to deal with Cheleyza . . ."

"Confine her," suggested Salyna.

Areyst nodded.

Mykella looked to the Arms-Commander. "Would you have a squad escort her here to see me? Can you also spare a squad to keep anyone from removing anything from the villa? It's not personal property but belongs to the Lord- or Lady-Protector."

"Those matters I can and will attend to. Pardoning my forwardness, Lady, both would be good ideas. If you would excuse me?"

Mykella nodded. "If you would keep me informed as to your whereabouts after dealing with Lady Cheleyza."

"I will do so." Areyst paused. "I'll also have Captain Maeltor report here in case anything else comes up where you may need the Southern Guards."

"That would be good." Mykella smiled ruefully. She should have thought of that. At least, she'd been intelligent enough to involve Areyst. "You may go."

With a nod, the commander departed.

His brevity and haste told Mykella she should have thought of putting Cheleyza under guard even sooner, but it was less than half a glass after she'd become Lady-Protector, and dealing with her late uncle's wife hadn't been her highest priority. She almost shook her head.

Now . . . now . . . there could be no excuses. *Only mistakes when you fail to act as necessary.*

Once Areyst had left the study, Mykella turned back to Salyna. "I still need to talk to Rachylana."

"She won't want to talk to you," predicted Salyna. "She's convinced that she was in love with Berenyt and that he loved her. You've ruined everything for her. She thinks you did it out of spite and greed. She said that you've always wanted to rule after Father."

"I kept her alive. Cheleyza would have poisoned her again before long—or done something else equally fatal in order to keep Berenyt from marrying her."

"She won't believe that, Mykella. She never will."

"You do, don't you?"

Salyna offered a sad smile. "I wasn't sure for a long time. I *thought* you were right, but that was more because I trusted you. Now . . . people can't lie to you, can they?"

"They can lie all they want, and some still do."

"That's not what I meant. You've changed. Did you know that I danced with that Deforyan majer?"

"No. You didn't mention it."

"He asked a lot of questions about you."

From her one dance with Majer Smoltak, Mykella had no difficulty believing that. "And?"

"He said that no one could deceive you. He also said that such a trait was admirable and useful in a ruler, but for anyone else it led to great pain and chaos. It already has, hasn't it?" Salyna's voice was gentle.

"What else would you have had me do?"

"Knowing you, there weren't any other choices." A hint of bitterness lay behind the words, softly as they had been spoken.

Mykella walked toward the wide window that looked out on the front courtyard, still filled with the weak sunlight of a late afternoon in the middle tendays of spring, scarcely any warmer than winter. *Was Salyna right? Had all the deaths that she had already created, both directly and indirectly, been unavoidable, just because of who she was? How many others would there be?*

"You can't stop now," Salyna said. "Then all of it will have been for nothing."

Her sister's words brought her up short, with the suggestion that there was still more to do. Of course there was, but . . . *What have you forgotten? Who else was part of Joramyl's plots?* Abruptly, she stiffened. How could she have forgotten the lizardly Maxymt, who had replaced poor Kiedryn as the head Finance clerk? That reminded her that she needed to have someone track down Kiedryn's family and allow them to return to Tempre. She also needed to make sure they received the stipend Kiedryn would have received if Joramyl had not forced the poor clerk to suicide. As soon as practicable, she needed to talk to Lord Gharyk and all the other ministers who had served her father. And what about Treghyt, the healer? How much had he known, or suspected, about the poisonings?

She turned back to Salyna. "Have you seen Treghyt recently?"

"No." Salyna frowned. "Why?"

"I need to talk to him."

"Do you think . . . ?"

"I don't know. I need to find out." She turned as there was another knock on the study door. She sensed Chalmyr outside, along with another man. "Yes?"

The private scrivener eased the door open slightly. "Captain Maeltor is standing by, Lady-Protector. Do you have any orders for him?"

"I do. If you would have him come in." Mykella walked from the window back to a position before the carved desk that held so many memories, all centered on her father.

Chalmyr opened the door wider and gestured to the officer.

Maeltor was a captain Mykella did not recognize, barely half a head taller than she was, and that meant he was indeed short for an officer, but with broad shoulders and a muscular build. He carried his cap under his arm, and his face was olive-tanned under black hair. He inclined his head respectfully, then straightened, his black eyes alert. "Lady-Protector."

"Captain . . . I don't recall seeing you here before."

"No, Lady. I've just been promoted from undercaptain, and I was passing through before taking up a new post with Fifth Company in Dekhron."

Mykella nodded, then spoke. "There are a few other tasks that need to be taken care of. I'd like you to have some men take Maxymt into custody. He is the head clerk of the Finance Ministry, and that study is at the far end of the north corridor on this level of the palace. It should be open, but Chalmyr will have a key. I'd also like you to see if someone can locate the healer Treghyt so that I might talk to him."

"Yes, Lady-Protector. Is there anything else?"

"Not for the moment, Captain." *I'm afraid there will be, though.*

Maeltor nodded, then turned and departed, closing the study door behind him.

"Maxymt won't be there," Mykella predicted. "Neither will Treghyt."

"If either saw what you did on the steps," said Salyna, "they'll be on their way to the Iron Valleys, or taking a boat across the river to Squawt country."

"There are others I won't see again, either," mused Mykella, "and that alone will tell me who else was with Joramyl."

"Or those who believe you will think that," pointed out Salyna.

"That's all too possible. Some of them may even be guilty." Mykella took a deep breath. "For the moment, will you take over running the palace? I know that's not something . . ."

Salyna smiled. "I can do that. Chatelaine Auralya will be more than glad to tell me if I'm about to make a mistake." Her smile widened into a brief grin that quickly faded.

"Only for a while." Mykella paused. "In a few days . . . when the worst settles down, you can . . ." She stopped.

Salyna was shaking her head. "Things will settle down. They'll never be the same, though."

"You won't ever have to go to Southgate. Ever. Or anyplace else."

"Mykella . . . sooner or later . . . I'll have to go somewhere if I want to have a life of my own. We both know that."

"Later doesn't mean sooner. If you want to be matched, he will have to meet your approval, in person, and mine. You can also have the choice not to choose."

"Thank you. It would be nice to have some choice, or not be forced into choosing. What about you? You're going to take the commander, aren't you?"

"That's possible. I haven't said anything."

"He'd be a fool to refuse."

"That's why I haven't said anything."

Salyna merely nodded, but Mykella could sense a certain amusement behind her sister's pleasant expression.

Mykella paused. What else could she say? "Would you mind checking on Rachylana?"

"I can do that."

Mykella watched as her youngest sister slipped out of the study. *What if Areyst turns out not to care for me?* She didn't think she'd misread his interest, an interest that she had sensed months before . . . but . . . *What if it's only interest . . . and not much more?*

After she had set Chalmyr to drafting the documents promoting Choalt and Areyst, Mykella was still pondering over all the difficulties that lay before her when Salyna returned more than a half glass later.

"What did she say?"

"She didn't want to talk to me. She'd bolted the door. I talked to the door, and finally she let me in when I asked if she wanted the entire palace to hear what I had to say. She wasn't happy. She's been crying all the time since the ceremony."

"It's all my fault, of course."

"Mykella . . . what you did was necessary, but it is your fault."

"So it would have been better for Father's poisoning and Jeraxylt's planned 'accident' to go unnoticed, for Joramyl to seize the office of Lord-Protector, all so that she could marry Berenyt? So that I could be hurried off to Dereka, and you could be matched to the son of a spoiled Seltyr in Southgate?"

"She thinks she loves him. You killed him. That's all that matters to her now."

Mykella could only shake her head.

"Captain Maeltor, Lady," announced Chalmyr from outside the study door.

"Have him enter."

Maeltor stepped into the study.

"I take it that Maxymt has fled," said Mykella.

"Yes, Lady."

"That's not your fault. I should have sent someone as soon as I finished the investiture. What about the healer?"

"His study is untouched. It's very neat. He's not there. I sent several men to his home, but they have not returned."

"Thank you. For now, I'd appreciate it if you'd stand by in the antechamber until Commander Areyst returns."

"Yes, Lady."

Once Maeltor had left the study, Mykella turned and studied the desk, as well as the chair behind it. She'd need a higher chair if she were to use the desk, let alone not to appear dwarfed by it. She shook her head.

"What?" asked Salyna.

"So many things to do. Big things . . . little things."

"You can't do them all at once," Salyna said, her tone reasonable.

"No . . . but if I don't do most of them soon, matters will get worse."

"What do you want me to do?"

At that moment, there was another rap on the door.

"Commander Areyst, Lady," announced Chalmyr.

Salyna looked to Mykella. "He didn't mention Cheleyza."

"Have him enter."

Areyst stepped into the study. While he'd clearly blotted his face, it was still shiny, and his tunic was damp in places. "The Lady Cheleyza has fled Tempre, Lady-Protector. My men are attempting to discover which road she may have taken or whether she fled by the river."

Mykella couldn't say she was totally surprised by her aunt's departure. She did have to admire Cheleyza's speed of action. "Commander . . . if you would come with me . . ." As she sensed his concern, she added, "We're only going to the lower levels of the palace."

Salyna's eyebrows rose.

"You'd better come as well, Salyna," added Mykella, absently fingering the pouch at her waist that held the keys to all the locks in the palace, keys she had carried from the day of her mother's death years before.

Both Areyst and Salyna followed her as she walked swiftly from the study to the main staircase, then down and along the west corridor, not quite so far as to the rear door to the gardens, but to a locked door—one that looked like a closet door. It wasn't, but the door to the narrow staircase down to the lowest levels of the palace.

"What's down here?" asked Salyna.

"You know, but you'll see why." Mykella eased the proper key on the iron ring into the lock, turned it, and opened the door.

Three sets of boots echoed dully down the narrow stairwell to the small foyer at the bottom, where Mykella paused and glanced at the ancient light-torch in the bronze wall bracket before heading through the archway that separated the staircase foyer from the subterranean—and empty—hallway that extended the entire length of the north side of the palace.

"Mykella . . ." ventured Salyna.

"There's nothing down here that shouldn't be." Mykella wondered momentarily if she should have used her Talent to slip down to the Table chamber unseen. *But then, how would you have explained your absence? That's going to be a problem.*

Brisk steps brought her to the door set in the middle of the wall closest to the outside foundation, a door of ancient oak, with an equally antique lever handle. Yet that lever, old as it had to be, seemed newer than the hinges or than even the replacement stones that comprised the doorjamb. She pressed the lever down, and the hinges still squeaked as she opened the door.

In spite of herself, she shook her head. She had asked the palace steward three times to have the hinges oiled. Was the staff that fearful of the lower level? She turned to Areyst. "This is the Table chamber." Then she looked to her sister. "Did Father ever bring you here?"

"Just twice. It bothered me."

Mykella could tell that Salyna was uneasy although there was nothing overtly that strange about the windowless stone-walled space some five yards by seven, without furnishings except for a single black wooden chest and the Table itself—a block of blackish stone set into the floor whose flat and mirrored surface was level with her waist—her lowest ribs really, she had to admit. The faint purple tinge that had bothered her for the last several seasons and that in years, so far, she was the only one to sense, seemed to have faded since she had destroyed the Ifrit's creation that had emerged from the Table and tried to enslave her. It was hard to believe that the Ifrits were essentially the descendants—or perhaps cousins of sorts—of the legendary Alectors. "If you'd close the door . . ."

Areyst did so, not speaking as Mykella walked over to the Table and glanced down. Once she had doubted the old tales about how, before the Cataclysm, the Alectors and even Mykel the Great had been able to travel from Table to Table all across Corus. Then she had found that she could do so, although some Table chambers she had visited were blocked from outside, and one was located somewhere that was so cold that she'd almost frozen to death before managing to return to Tempre. Now, those Tables, a few buildings, the eternal and indestructible highways, the Great Piers, and the green towers were all that remained from that time.

Mykella looked at her own reflection in the mirror surface of the Table—short black hair, broad forehead with clear skin, green eyes with a darkness behind them, a straight nose, shoulders too broad for a woman as small as she was.

"Might I ask why we are here?" Areyst finally asked.

"To see if I can determine if the Table will show where Cheleyza might be at this moment. I don't know if you can see what it displays, but we might as well try." She did not look up as Areyst stepped up to her left and Salyna to her right.

Mykella concentrated, fixing an image of Cheleyza in her mind and projecting it toward the Table. Her own reflection faded, and the silvery black gave way to swirling silvery-white mists. Then, an image appeared in the center of the mists—that of a wide barge with ten men or so at the sweeps. Mykella concentrated on the barge, and the image in the Table enlarged enough that she could make out the dark hair and fine features of Cheleyza looking out from a hooded winter jacket toward the rear of the barge. Then she tried to get a better sense of where the barge was.

"It's all fuzzy . . ." murmured Salyna.

"She's on the river," said Areyst.

"Do you know where?" asked Mykella. "I don't recognize what's along the bank . . . the north bank, isn't it, from the light?"

"I can't be sure, but it looks like the stretch on the Vedra west of Tempre, no more than ten vingts from the Great Piers."

"That's not far," said Salyna.

"It might as well be a hundred vingts," replied Areyst. "There's no bridge across the river until Hieron, and that's more than four hundred vingts. The road on our side of the river isn't much more than a dirt track after the first thirty vingts, and there's no road at all on the Squawt side."

"She's going to get away? Just like that?" asked Salyna.

"Do you have a better idea?" asked Mykella evenly.

"No . . . but it seems so . . . wrong."

"Sometimes that happens. Unhappily, I doubt we've seen the last of dear Aunt Cheleyza." Mykella looked to Areyst. "I had Chalmyr draft the documents to promote you and Majer Choalt. We might as well go back to the study so that I can sign them." *And see what else has gone wrong.*

She turned and headed toward the door from the Table chamber.

2

Late that evening, after a modest supper by themselves in the family dining area, Salyna and Mykella sat in the family parlor, Salyna on the settee and Mykella in the armchair across from her. Rachylana remained closeted in her room, refusing to leave it except for necessities, and only when Mykella was nowhere close. Outside in the chill darkness, a light drizzle fell, and tiny raindrops coagulated and ran down the windowpanes in narrow rivulets. Only one wall lamp was lit, and Mykella noted absently that the mantle was soot-smoked.

"I can't believe Cheleyza left so quickly," observed Salyna. "She must have fled the palace right after the ceremony and packed her things immediately. She couldn't have taken that much. She hardly had any time at all."

"She thinks she'll reclaim whatever she left later. She's taking the river Hieron. From there, she'll make her way to Harmony, and she'll try to get her older brother and any allies he has to attack Lanachrona and overthrow me in order to make her child the heir and eventual Lord-Protector," said Mykella, recalling what her uncle's widow had told her about her background when Mykella had been forced to apologize to Cheleyza over the dress "incident."

"Her child? I didn't know she was expecting."

"She's carrying Joramyl's child. That was the reason she tried to poison Rachylana at that afternoon gathering—"

"How did you know it was poison? You've never said."

"I just knew."

Salyna looked at her older sister. "Knew or *knew*?"

"Sometimes . . . I can sense poison. It makes people look bluish. It was the same poison Uncle Joramyl used to kill Father."

Salyna paled. She swallowed. "Mykella . . . you're scaring me. . . . Again."

"You didn't think I'd have done everything I've done if I didn't know what was happening. I told Father about Joramyl. He wouldn't believe me." That wasn't totally true, Mykella knew. She'd told their father that Kiedryn hadn't been the one stealing golds from the Treasury, and she'd tried to point out that Joramyl had been the only one who could have, but her father had been adamant that he could totally trust his brother.

After a long silence, Salyna said tentatively, "But Rachylana didn't die." She paused. "You were alone with her. You did something, didn't you? To save her?"

"Yes. But she didn't drink as much of it, and I was there when it struck. I tried to save Father the same way . . . but he'd had too much, and it was too late. Joramyl saw that no one got to Father until he was almost dead." The last of Mykella's words dripped venom.

"I should tell Rachylana . . . about how you saved her."

"She won't believe you, and she'll want to know why I couldn't save Father. Then she'll be blaming me for that."

"Mykella . . . how did it all . . . happen? What changed you?"

Mykella thought. How much did she really want to say? Finally, she said, "It happened because of the soarer. She came to my room just before season-turn, and she touched my forehead and told me I had to find my Talent if I wanted to save my land."

Salyna shivered. "The Ancient said that?"

"She didn't speak. It's more like her words come into your thoughts. Things . . . they didn't happen all at once. I discovered I could see in almost-total darkness, and I began to sense what people felt. That was when I discovered that Joramyl was stealing golds, but I found that out by talking to traders and Seltyrs and comparing tariff receipts to the ledgers. When I showed the ledgers to Father, he just told Joramyl, and Joramyl forced poor Kiedryn to write a suicide note and drink poison. I even saw Joramyl, in the Table, riding somewhere with a man covered with a hood. Afterwards, I realized that it must have been Kiedryn. It was like that for weeks, all fall long, in fact. Everything I tried turned out wrong . . ." Mykella shook her head.

"But you looked so powerful and strong today."

"I made too many mistakes along the way, and people died. . . . Kiedryn, Jeraxylt, Father, the clerk who handled the Southern Guard accounts, the poor guard who was blamed for Jeraxylt's death . . . maybe others I don't even know about."

"Do you . . . kill . . . ?"

"No. I learned that from practicing on killing animals in the slaughterhouse just before they were about to be killed. No one saw me, and some of them dropped dead just before the hammer hit them. But I didn't figure out how to do that until after Father died."

Salyna's eyes were wide. "You still scare me, Mykella."

"Why? Joramyl killed more people than I have, and he used poison and treachery. So I can kill people with Talent. You've trained with arms, and you can kill them with a blade. I'd end up cutting myself to pieces if I tried that."

"It's . . . different."

Mykella took a deep breath. Nothing she said was likely to change her sister's mind. Not at the moment, anyway. Maybe once Salyna thought it over . . .

"Why did you designate Areyst as your heir?" Salyna finally asked.

Mykella offered a rueful smile. "Why do you think?"

"You wanted the support of the Southern Guards."

"That . . . and I didn't want to upset things any more than I had to." Mykella paused. "Right now, as things are, would you want to be designated as my heir?"

Salyna tilted her head. "No. At first, I was hurt. Then I realized that your decision protects both Rachylana and me . . . a little, anyway. We can't do what you can."

Mykella wanted to say that she couldn't do what Salyna could with weapons, but realized that saying it would come out as condescending. "That's only for now."

"Can you teach me what you know?"

"I don't know. Did you really see anything in the Table?"

"No . . . I didn't want to say anything." Salyna paused. "Areyst did, didn't he? Is he like you?"

"No. He has to have a trace of Talent, but that doesn't mean he could do what I can. The old records said that some of the followers of Mykel could see the soarer who appeared to him, during the Cataclysm, but most could not, and none of the others who saw the Ancient ever showed Talent." Again . . . that wasn't quite true. There was no record of any of them showing Talent; but if someone had wanted to conceal it, who would know after hundreds of years? "The soarer appeared to me in the walled garden the first time. That was several days before she touched me, and I could see her, but Rachylana was standing next to me, looking right at the soarer, and she saw nothing." Mykella could sense Salyna's disappointment, and added, "I didn't see her ever, before that. Maybe you will."

"You're just trying to cheer me up."

Mykella smiled gently. "Is there anything wrong with that?"

"I'm glad you tried." Salyna stood. "I'm tired. It's been a long day."

"It has." That was something on which they could definitely agree.

Mykella was tired. She'd spent the afternoon discussing the necessary changes in guarding the palace and other matters involving the

Southern Guards with Areyst, following his recommendations, except about supplies, where she had asked him to look into several matters before dealing with procurement. Salyna had been closeted with the chatelaine, trying to take over what Mykella had done for years.

Mykella rose and followed Salyna from the family parlor, then to her own bedchamber, the one that had been hers from the time she could remember, and the one she needed to leave, if she wanted any privacy at all, since its door opened onto the main upper corridor. That had never been a problem when she'd been the relatively insignificant daughter of the Lord-Protector, but now . . . with Southern Guards posted practically outside her door, unfortunately, with reason, it would be. She'd already asked Chalmyr and Chatelaine Auralya to remove any personal items of her Father's or Joramyl's from the apartments that had served them, and to clean the rooms thoroughly before she moved into the small suite that held a personal study, a sitting room, a wash chamber, and a bedchamber.

As she bolted the door to her bedchamber, she hoped she could sleep.

3

Septi morning, Mykella was up and in the family breakfast room early. She hadn't slept well. Salyna was already there, looking down at a mug of something, likely cider, and she had circles under her eyes. The two ate almost silently.

Not surprisingly, Rachylana had not yet made an appearance at breakfast, and, before getting up to finish readying herself for the day, Mykella instructed Muergya that on no account was Rachylana to be served in her room, and that no special meals were to be prepared for her.

". . . you can leave something here for her, but nothing more," Mykella concluded.

"Yes, Lady." The serving girl glanced toward Salyna, then back to Mykella.

"Just tell her that those were my instructions."

"Yes, Lady," Muergya repeated, before hurrying away into the serving pantry.

"That will just make her more angry," Salyna observed.

"I'm sorry if it does, but she'd rather have had us married off and enslaved and Lanachrona in ruins."

"It will be anyway. Your romantic dreams won't last long." The bitter words came from Rachylana, who stood in the doorway, attired in a long black dress, with a black shawl, and a set of polished black onyx beads around her neck. Her eyes were slightly bloodshot, and her mahogany red hair was swept back into two silver clips. "You won't be able to kill every armsman that the other lands send against you."

"You're assuming that all of them will attack," said Mykella, taking a last swallow of tea from her mug.

"You're assuming that they won't. Besides, just how many of the Southern Guards will follow your tame commander?"

"All of them, just about," replied Salyna. "He's anything but tame. He's the first commander in years with field experience, and they respect him."

"Oh . . . I forgot. You spar with the Guards. You think they'd tell you the truth?"

"They have so far," replied Salyna.

For a moment, Rachylana said nothing. Then she walked to the far end of the table and seated herself.

Mykella looked at Rachylana, wondering whether she should say more.

Salyna shook her head.

Mykella cleared her throat. "When you're up to it, Rachylana, we do need to talk."

"Why? You'll do whatever you want. You always have."

Salyna winced.

"Because," replied Mykella calmly as she rose from the table, "I'll only be guessing what you'd like unless I know what it is you want."

Even so, after we do talk, you'll still say that you told me what you wanted and that I ignored you, even when I haven't. "You know where to find me."

Rachylana looked away.

After glancing at Salyna, who gave the smallest of headshakes, Mykella left the breakfast room.

Back in her bedchamber, possibly for the last time, Mykella glanced into the mirror over the dressing table. She'd decided that she'd continue wearing what she always wore—the black nightsilk camisole and undertrousers, with a black nightsilk shirt that was really a tunic, and black nightsilk trousers over her black boots. The double layer of nightsilk was warm enough, if sometimes, in summer, too warm, and offered protection against all manner of weapons—even without her Talent shields. As formfitting as the nightsilk undergarments were, their protection was not absolute. The fabric woven from the wool of the nightsheep of the Iron Valleys stiffened harder than iron under a blade thrust or a bullet, but the pressure still caused some injury, especially given Mykella's tendency to bruise easily. Holding Talent-shields for a long time, she'd discovered the previous day, was also exhausting although she knew she'd need to do so whenever she left the palace. Hopefully, she could work out a compromise that protected her without wearing her down.

She turned away from the mirror and stepped from the chamber, walking toward the southwest corner of the palace that held the formal study-library. There were still two guards stationed in the main corridor flanking the outer study doors, and she nodded to both as she stepped past them into the antechamber.

Chalmyr stood waiting inside. "Good morning, Lady-Protector. A Majer Smoltak is waiting below. He requests that he be allowed to see you. He is—"

"The aide to Envoy Sheorak. At the moment, I'd prefer to see the majer rather than the envoy." Mykella had no doubts Smoltak knew that as well, which was why he was requesting the audience.

Chalmyr nodded. "There is also a written request from Envoy Malaryk."

"I'll see him tomorrow afternoon. Late in the afternoon." Mykella didn't feel like seeing the Seltyr from Southgate at all, but there was no sense in putting off such a meeting more than that, and there wasn't anyone else she trusted to handle the matter, not yet. "Oh . . . would you arrange meetings for me with Minister Gharyk, Minister Porofyr, and Forester Loryalt? I'd like to start with Lord Gharyk, if possible, but I'd like to see Commander Areyst after I meet with the Deforyan if the commander's around."

Chalmyr offered a slight smile. "I am certain I can do that. Will you see the Deforyan majer immediately?"

"There's no reason not to, is there?"

"I would think not. I will send for him."

"Thank you, Chalmyr."

The older scrivener inclined his head before leaving, and Mykella stepped into the formal study. The account ledgers she had requested were stacked on a side table, and she took the main ledger, the one that summarized the expenses by ministry. She smiled. Chalmyr had provided a thick square pillow for the seat of the desk chair.

She'd barely studied the first half page of the ledger when there was a rap on the door, and Smoltak, wearing the uniform of a Deforyan lancer, stepped into the study and bowed deeply. "Lady-Protector."

Mykella closed the ledger, eased it aside, rose from behind the desk, and gestured to one of the chairs before the desk. "Please sit down." When she had danced with Smoltak at the ball some tendays before, he had appeared to be some ten years older than she was, but seeing him in the study, she decided he was likely closer to fifteen, with a few silver hairs amid the light brown short-cut thatch. She reseated herself and waited until he looked at her, appraisingly. "What can I do for you, Majer?"

"You understand, Lady-Protector, that Envoy Sheorak finds himself in an . . . anomalous position."

Again, Mykella noted his heavy accent, but it scarcely bothered her, and that had to be the effect of her Talent in some way. "So he sent you to determine what that might be?" From the feelings she sensed, Smoltak was acting on his own, but she wanted to get his response.

"No, Lady. You already know I have taken that liberty because, with your accession to power, everything will change drastically, all across Corus. While I am but a simple majer and an aide to the Heir of Light, I am from Deforya. I have seen the power of the Ancients. You hold that power. I would not have it arrayed against the Landarch or his heir, and I would prefer a certain . . . understanding between Lanachrona and Deforya."

Much as she liked Smoltak's frank and warm directness, Mykella smiled coolly. "You want an understanding, rather than a treaty, because any formal alliance might cause others to act contrary to Deforya's interests, not to mention the fact that, if you or Envoy Sheorak proposed it, the Landarch would be offended, if not forced to repudiate it or discipline you both. Yet you also do not want Lanachrona to consider the Landarch as an enemy or as opposed to our interests."

Smoltak's smile was half-embarrassed, half-rueful. "Let me also say that the Heir of Light would have been greatly overmatched had you not changed . . . circumstances."

"In response to the question you did not ask, Majer . . . my sisters will be allowed to make their own choices in the matter of marriages, and I strongly doubt that either will agree to a match without meeting a prospective suitor. Nor will I agree to such unless I meet that suitor."

Smoltak nodded slowly. "That will make matters . . . difficult."

"You should also know that I have been more impressed by the manner in which you and Envoy Sheorak have comported yourselves than I have been with any other envoys."

Smoltak nodded. "Thank you. Perhaps we should return to Dereka to consult with the Landarch."

Mykella nodded. "You will need to inform both the Landarch and Aldakyr of the changes in circumstances, but, before you depart, I would suggest that you wait for a missive from me to the Landarch. It might be a day or so."

"I do believe we can wait for a day or so." Smoltak smiled. *Or even the ten long days of a week.*

Mykella could sense the last unspoken words as if they had been written on the air between them—and that the idea of waiting actually pleased the officer. She'd have to think about that. She was learning that, while she might sense what people felt, knowing how they felt often didn't translate into knowing *why* they felt that way. She rose. "Good day, Majer. I appreciate your initiative, and I trust you will convey my best to Envoy Sheorak."

The majer stood quickly and bowed. "That I will, Lady."

Mykella walked to the window and looked out on a morning that remained gray, though the clouds had lifted somewhat. The drizzle had stopped, but the stones of the courtyard still held the sheen of rain.

She wasn't totally looking forward to seeing those of minister rank who had served her father although there were not that many. Government in Lanachrona was comparatively simple. The Finance Ministry set and collected tariffs, served as depository and as a reserve holder for the commercial lending houses, and minted all Lanachronan coinage. The Ministry of Highways and Rivers maintained the ports and piers, including the towpaths and maintenance buildings on the Vedra, and the major irrigation canals of Lanachrona. It also set the standards for all canals and sewers and inspected the sewers and the midsize irrigation works across Lanachrona. The Ministry of Justice, headed by Lord Gharyk, supervised and set the standards for all local patrols throughout Lanachrona, operated all the low courts, and the court of review in Tempre, maintained the gaols, the workhouses and work camps for law-breakers, and administered the official standards of weights and measures. The Arms-Commander of Lanachrona was the head of the Southern Guards and responsible for all its men and facilities. If Lanachrona were invaded, and the Lord-Protector—or Lady-Protector—issued a proclamation, the Arms-Commander could also conscript able-bodied men to serve for the duration of the invasion. Lastly, there was the Forester of Lanachrona, responsible for all permits for logging on the Protector's lands and on all privately-held lands, and for inspecting and assuring that all logged lands were replanted. Five branches of government under the Lady-Protector, and one of them was vacant. *So far.*

The study door opened a fraction. "The commander is here, Lady."

"Have him come in." Mykella turned and walked back to the desk, waiting for Areyst.

The commander entered, wearing the cream and blue uniform of the Southern Guards and carrying a roll of paper, possibly a map. She surveyed him, both with her eyes and her Talent, almost smiling as she found his eyes appraising her. He was interested. That she could sense. He was also cautious. That was also good. She was in no hurry to match herself. Besides, not marrying immediately might hold off her enemies a little, particularly if they happened to think she might be available. *Let them think that for now.*

"Lady . . . you summoned me . . ."

She gestured for him to take a chair and seated herself.

"Before we discuss other matters," Areyst began, "I wanted you to know that I have assigned Captain Maeltor to duty here in the palace for the time being. He has a trusted squad at his command, and he answers only to you, or me, in your absence."

Mykella nodded. "You foresee . . . difficulties?"

"No one can force you to do anything, but it might be . . . more acceptable if you used the captain to deal with some situations rather than your rather formidable abilities."

Mykella laughed gently. "You're saying politely that I might otherwise be in a situation where I might have to slaughter some angry man and that having him escorted away by the captain would be politically more acceptable."

"Do you not think so?" Areyst smiled.

"In this, I accept your counsel and assistance, Commander."

"For today, he will be stationed in your antechamber with a guard for a courier." After a moment, Areyst went on. "There is one other matter with which I must trouble you."

"Only one?" asked Mykella gently. "Or merely the most pressing?"

"The most awkward, I fear. You had ordered that the bodies of the usurper and his son be tendered to his family, for cremation and placement in the family memorial . . ."

"Oh . . ." Mykella swallowed. With Cheleyza's flight from Tempre, Mykella was effectively the most senior member of Joramyl's family. Amid everything else, that aspect of matters hadn't struck. "Have Chalmyr and the steward arrange for the cremation this evening. Their ashes will go in the family mausoleum." *Traitors or not, they were family.* "There will be no ceremony."

Areyst nodded. "You did summon me. In what else might I be of aid?"

"You saw in the Table that Cheleyza is headed back to Northcoast, did you not?"

A quick flash of puzzlement flickered in his pale green eyes as he sat, the map still held in his left hand. "I saw her in a barge on the Vedra, as did you. The Vedra flows west and north from Tempre. That is in the general direction of Northcoast."

"You wonder why I asked that? Because not everyone can see what appears in the Table." Mykella paused. "I did not tell you that Cheleyza is carrying Joramyl's child."

"I had wondered, with the haste of her departure . . ." Areyst's lips, neither thin nor excessively full, quirked into a faintly rueful smile. "The envoy from Prince Skrelyn is still here in Tempre, you know?"

"I knew he was here. I assumed he hadn't left yet."

"You know why he is here?"

"Joramyl said he was seeking a match for his son, presumably with Rachylana. I haven't found any missives or papers." Mykella snorted, a most unladylike sound, but she didn't care. "I won't, either."

"It is unlikely. I have found none in the studies of either Commander Nephryt or Commander Demyl. When there are no records, that suggests matters are not as they should be." Areyst cleared his throat. "Prince Skrelyn is seeking a match, but not for his son. His consort died two seasons ago in childbirth. He has no sons."

Mykella could read the political currents. "Cheleyza's older brother is Prince of Northcoast. He and Skrelyn were already considering attacking Lanachrona, according to Joramyl."

"Doubtless they were . . . or would have if your father had remained Lord-Protector. By all accounts, Prince Chalcaer is most ambitious."

"If Skrelyn married Cheleyza . . . How very convenient." Mykella's voice dripped venom. *If Cheleyza offers herself as the tool for taking Lanachrona . . . she might end up the way she'd planned to deal with Berenyt . . . and then she might not.* Mykella had no doubts of just how ambitious and capable her aunt was.

"Precisely. That might be even more to his liking than a match with one of your sisters."

"Any suitor for my sisters will have to meet them—in person. They deserve that."

Areyst nodded.

"Your thoughts on the Lady Cheleyza, Commander?"

"She will exaggerate our weaknesses for her own interests," Areyst replied. "Many of those weakness are real enough without overstatement, and both princes are aware of them."

"Those weaknesses are?"

"I had thought we should discuss such matters. I brought a map."

"Go ahead." Mykella pointed to the clear surface of the desk and stood. Short as she was, that was the easiest way for her to see.

Areyst stood, unrolling the map. "We have too few companies, and some are not close to full strength, such as the two in Soupat, and the fourth and seventh companies in Hyalt. Sixth Company is at full strength, but Captain Suorl is ailing. He's ten years past the age for a stipend. The other three companies in Dekhron are also at strength."

"That's where Maeltor was being sent?"

Areyst nodded. "We can't count on the garrison at Indyor, either, loyal as the companies there are."

"Because of the distance from Krost? Or because the companies are armed and trained to deal with nomads and brigands?"

"All of that. Also, the removal of any of the companies would invite immediate attacks from the raiders and brigands in the Lower Spine Mountains." Areyst spread out the map, securing the corners with flat lead weights he extracted from a belt pouch. "This shows the northernmost regions of Lanachrona, those south of the Vedra and west from about two hundred vingts east of Tempre." He pointed. "Here is the road west to Hafin."

"That's the only way Skrelyn can enter Lanachrona, without taking lanes or marching through woods and fields, is it not?"

"At least until he nears our borders."

"Chalcaer would have to take the highway of the Alectors south from Harmony to Salcer. Is that not close to nine hundred vingts?" asked Mykella.

"It is more than eight hundred."

"Then he would still have several hundred vingts from Salcer to our border," observed Mykella, "unless he wanted to fight his way through the Iron Valleys or straggle along the north side of the Vedra and amass enough barges and boats to cross. That would be far longer and more difficult. Doesn't that make it more likely that Chalcaer would propose that Midcoast and Northcoast act in concert?"

Areyst laughed harshly, if softly. "Greed and ambition can forge an alliance of convenience, but mistrust will quickly dissolve it."

"But if Chalcaer offers his sister . . . ?" *More likely, she'll offer herself.*

"That might be inducement enough," admitted Areyst.

"Especially if they think we are weak." Mykella's eyes traversed the map. "How many Southern Guard companies could we transfer from south and the east? Could we base them in Viencet for a time?"

"We could pull two companies from Soupat immediately, and all of them for a time. We can wait a week to decide about how many companies to move from Dekhron. From farther to the east . . . ? There are three companies along the high road to Dereka. Removing them will weaken our eastern borders, Lady."

"We should consider shifting one or two companies. At the moment, we have less to fear from the Landarch than from Prince Skrelyn."

"Best we do so now. It will take a tenday for a courier to reach Eleventh Company."

"That's the one in the way-station fort on the high road due south of Emal?"

"Yes."

"You'd leave Thirteenth Company at the eastern borderlands station?"

"I would."

"What about conscription?"

Areyst's almost-hidden wince told Mykella more than the words that followed.

"It would take companies to train the conscripts . . . and time . . ."

In the end, Mykella and Areyst agreed on immediately shifting seven companies to join the two stationed in Tempre—and to basing all of them temporarily in Viencet. Areyst left to issue the orders, since it would take nearly a week for the orders to reach Hyalt and more than that Soupat. The only saving grace was that it would likely take at least two weeks for Cheleyza to reach Harmony. If need be, three companies stationed in Dekhron, and one in Borlan, could be barged down the Vedra to Tempre; but the more distant companies needed to be notified as soon as possible.

What if you're wrong? For a land the size of Lanachrona, the number of Southern Guard companies was far too few—twenty-three companies. The Guards should number at least twice that many. Areyst hadn't exactly said that, but it had been clear enough. Yet . . . from where would the golds have come to pay for supporting such a force?

Mykella shook her head, her eyes flicking to the ledgers on the table set in front of the built-in bookcases that dated to the construction of the palace. She needed to go over the tariffs paid by the Seltyrs and merchants, as well as the expenses—especially the expenses.

She retrieved the master ledger and began to study the fall summaries. In less than a quarter glass, she was frowning, noting that the Ministry of Rivers and Highways was spending almost as much as the Southern Guards was. That was something she'd noted in passing earlier, but, upon reflection, it seemed far too high. The indestructible eternastone of the Alectors comprised the main highways, as did the piers at Dekhron and Tempre. The river required little maintenance except for the towpath on the south side. But there were ten waterway inspectors . . .

She frowned again. She was missing something.

"Chalmyr . . ."

The old scrivener opened the door. "Yes, Lady?"

"Do you know all the kinds of inspections that Lord Porofyr's inspectors conduct?"

Chalmyr frowned. "They inspect the piers and the towpaths, the large irrigation channels . . . Oh . . . the sewers in the major towns and cities."

"Is there a list of their duties?"

"Why, yes. It's been a while, but . . . if you wouldn't mind." The older man scanned the shelves to the left of the desk. "Here. These are the compilations of duties. They haven't changed much since Mykel the Great wrote them out. Well . . . some say that the hand was Rachyla's."

"Thank you." *Why didn't you notice . . . or even look?*

Once Chalmyr had left the study, Mykella rose and pulled out volume after volume, quickly scanning them. While the books had been dusted, none had been opened in years, and over half were written in an older script that she had to struggle to make out. *Is that similar to what the Ifrit had spoken?* How would she know? She'd never seen it written.

A glass later, she sat back down at the desk . . . stunned. The most recent volume dated from the time of Rhystan, Mykel's son, and, from what she had skimmed quickly, it appeared to lay out the duties of the ministers of Lanachrona, and even the limits of the powers of the Protector. There was no mention of a Lord-Protector. Except for one book, she hadn't seen anything on military tactics, but there was a folio of maps that looked to be superior in quality to the map Areyst had used.

She wasn't surprised that she hadn't known the contents of all the volumes. Her father had largely kept her out of the study. He'd certainly never thought she'd become his successor; but Jeraxylt had never mentioned the books either, and most of them didn't seem to have been opened in years—except for those on the shelf at desk level directly behind the desk, consisting of a thin book of maxims, poems, and proverbs, apparently written by the first Feranyt; the single book on tactics, with a preface that noted it had been copied from an older version predating the Cataclysm; two books on construction and engineering; one apparently on the justicing system of the Alectors; and two histories.

Mykella was still trying to make sense out of what was on the study shelves when Chalmyr rapped on the door. "Lord Gharyk, Lady."

"Good." Mykella stood and waited for the slender, short, and balding Minister of Justice to enter.

Gharyk bowed, then smiled warmly at her. "Lady-Protector."

"I might not be except for you and your wife, Lord Gharyk." Mykella gestured for him to seat himself and did so herself. "And the portrait of Rachyla." She recalled how amazed she had been to see how closely she resembled the wife of Mykel the Great.

"You do look like her, even more so now." Gharyk seated himself, his eyes intent on her. "How might I be of service, Lady?"

"First, by continuing as Minister of Justice."

"I would be pleased to do so." Gharyk added, "I will begin immediately on the legalities of properties."

"Legalities of properties?"

"The Minister of Justice serves as the advocate for the Lord-Protector, or the Lady-Protector, and all the properties of the Protector, as well as any other interests, must be listed with the ascension of each Protector and published within a season. That includes all properties of a spouse. Annually, any new properties obtained or divested must also be listed each year by the turn of spring. This has been so since the later years of Mykel the Great. Of course, since you are the heir of both your father and your uncle, matters may be more complicated. Or they may not be." Gharyk smiled.

"I did not know that. Then, there are many things I may not know, and I would hope you will continue to enlighten me."

"I will do my best, Lady. I would beg your indulgence to suggest a few . . . reforms."

Mykella could sense only concern . . . and some worry. "Along what lines, Lord Gharyk?"

"As Minister of Justice, I do not receive reports, timely or otherwise, about the decisions made by city and regional justices and the sentences meted out. Nor do I receive reports on the numbers of offenses and offenders, and I do not have enough men trained in law to spend the days or weeks watching and reporting on what is happening in each hamlet, town, and city. Without such reports, it is difficult to determine whether justice in Soupat is even roughly equivalent to justice in Tempre or in Hyalt or . . ." Gharyk shrugged. "The older records indicate that such reports were once required."

Mykella nodded. "Perhaps you should draft a document that outlines what information is necessary and how it should be presented. Then you could explain them to me." She smiled. "If I approve of something, I will certainly have to explain it to someone . . . or many people."

"With your permission, I will draft just that."

"I would also like to see if you have any other observations that might be useful to me, or about various ministry positions . . ."

"The only vacant ministry is that of Finance, and you, Lady, know more about the accounts than does anyone I could recommend."

"That may be, and I will keep close watch on them, but a Lady-Protector"—she almost said "Lord-Protector"—"who tries to do everything will do none of it well."

"I do not do well at responding immediately to such, Lady. I would request that you allow me some time to consider . . ."

"I would be more than happy to have you consider those who might be able and honest in the service of Lanachrona." She paused. "You and Lady Gharyk, in fact."

"Jylara is a good judge of character, and you must have noticed that I do rely upon her."

"I would like to rely upon you both." With scarcely a pause, Mykella asked, "What do you think about Forester Loryalt?"

Gharyk tilted his head slightly before responding. "He is a good man. He knows the forests well. He is honest. He may be too trusting in his dealings with the large landholders, particularly in the east."

"You think that too many logging permits are being granted?"

"That I could not say. I do not know about forests except that they grow slowly, especially in the eastern hills and highlands. The Seltyrs of Southgate pay well for prime timber, especially for hardwoods, even though it takes almost a season to send a wagon to Southgate."

"How can they afford that?" asked Mykella.

"They have no choice. The hardwood forests of Midcoast have been largely over-cut, and it is even farther from the dark woods of Northcoast to Southgate. Also, the Prince of Midcoast imposes a passage tariff on all trade that does not begin or end in his lands."

Something else you didn't know. Mykella nodded. "What can you tell me about Lord Porofyr?"

Again, Gharyk hesitated before replying. "Lord Porofyr is well-respected. He is known to be astute in his dealings in fabrics and in carpets, and he is said to have many connections with all manner of factors and Seltyrs in Southgate. I believe that Envoy Malaryk has been enjoying the hospitality of Porofyr's Tempre villa. Other Seltyrs have as well."

"What of his time as minister?"

"Lord Porofyr has always been interested in maintaining what is conducive to profitable trade at the lowest cost to traders. The towpaths are well maintained, as are the way stations to the west and south. What else can I say, Lady?"

Mykella understood perfectly. "Tell me more about yourself, Lord Gharyk."

"Were my vanity greater than it is, I would say I am a simple man, gifted by birth and lands so that I could study the law. But no man is simple, much as he would like to believe that. My forebears were herders with the foresight to acquire land when it could be acquired easily, and they did. More recent ancestors managed it well, and I have had the fortune to be able to pay others to do the same so that I may live in modest comfort in Tempre. Our daughters are well and happily wed . . ."

Mykella listened to Gharyk's comparatively short autobiography, then asked a few questions before allowing him to depart.

She stood, stretched, and walked once more to the window, looking through the glass without really seeing anything. Gharyk's responses to her questions disturbed her, not because there had been any deception behind his words but because there had been none at all.

After taking a deep breath, she returned to the bookshelves beside the desk and searched through the volumes Chalmyr had pointed out until she found a thin ancient tome that described the government structure of Tempre—at least as it had been in the time of Mykel's son Rhystan, also sometimes referred to as Olent, although the histories never said why. She began to read. . . .

Less than ten pages later, Chalmyr rapped on the study door.

"Lord Porofyr is here."

"Have him come in." Mykella set the ancient manual aside and stood.

The hawk-nosed and black-haired Seltyr brushed past Chalmyr and into the study. He did not incline his head.

"Lord Porofyr . . ." began Mykella.

Before she could even gesture for the Seltyr to sit, Porofyr spoke. "I would like to tender my resignation as Minister of Highways and Rivers . . ."

"Might I ask why, Lord Porofyr?" Mykella remained standing.

"I do not feel that I can continue in the position to your satisfaction." Porofyr's voice was clipped, almost brusque.

Mykella could sense irritation, as well as anger and fear, but she continued to keep her voice even and pleasant. "My satisfaction, Lord Porofyr? I don't believe we've even discussed your ministry. Or has some action of which I am unaware led you to this conclusion?"

Porofyr looked at her coolly although anger surged within him. "The manner in which you . . . terminated one of my peers was rather abrupt."

"Arms-Commander Nephryt? I killed him only after he slashed me with a saber. Considering that he killed my brother as well, I think two such treasonous acts more than justified my action. You might note that I merely banished Commander Demyl although he was involved to some degree in my brother's death. Or did you feel that I was too lenient with Commander Demyl?"

"I wish you well, but I cannot in good conscience remain as a ministry lord."

"I do understand, Lord Porofyr." Mykella let her voice become almost sickeningly sweet. "I would not wish any man to act against his conscience, especially in serving a Lady-Protector. I do wish you well." She turned and projected her voice, "Chalmyr! Send in the captain."

Porofyr stiffened.

"I'm just giving you the honor you deserve, Porofyr," Mykella said in the same sweet tone she'd just used.

Maeltor stepped through the study door. "Yes, Lady-Protector?"

"Lord Porofyr has tendered his resignation as Lord Minister for Highways and Rivers. Since he has served loyally, I would like him escorted from the palace with honor. Have his personal study sealed until I can inspect it later today." Mykella turned to Porofyr and smiled. "Any personal items you may have left in the study will be sent wherever in Tempre you wish."

"You're being high-handed," Porofyr said coldly.

"Less than you, Porofyr. I'm heard not one word of respect, and you've seethed the entire time you've been here with anger and resentment at having to face a Lady-Protector. Since two others who served my father committed treason, I don't think sealing your study until I can examine it is anything more than a simple precaution." She smiled. "You did not wish to serve me and Lanachrona loyally, and I have accepted your resignation and released you from that obligation . . . as you wished. I trust you will serve Lanachrona well and loyally in your personal business." She nodded to Maeltor. "Escort him from the palace with the respect to which his past services entitle him. He is not to return to the minister's study, not until his successor is appointed, but otherwise he will have the same access to the first level of the palace as any other Seltyr does."

"Sir . . ." prompted Maeltor.

Mykella could sense the cold fury behind the stony face of the Seltyr before he turned and left the study with the captain. Given how strongly Porofyr felt, she doubted that she could have said anything— except perhaps begging him—that would have mollified him. *Even that probably wouldn't have worked.*

Several moments after the two had left, Chalmyr opened the door slightly. "Lady?"

"You can come in."

Chalmyr only eased the door open a trace wider. "I thought you would like to know that Forester Loryalt is somewhere east of Krost in the Vyanhills. His chief assistant, Cerlyk, doesn't expect him back for at least another four tendays."

"I'd like to have Cerlyk tell me about how things are going in the Forestry Ministry . . . the first glass of the afternoon tomorrow, before I meet with Envoy Malaryk. If that will be a problem, let me know."

"It shouldn't be, but I will, Lady." There was a pause. "Steward Elwayt is arranging for the pyre for this evening."

"Thank you . . . I do appreciate it."

Mykella walked back to the window and looked out. The day was still gray, and that, unfortunately, matched all too well how matters had gone.

4

After mulling over her meeting with Porofyr, Mykella occupied herself with studying the account ledgers and plodding through what appeared to be a manual on the law and structure of government, as well as refreshing her geography of Lanachrona and spending more than a glass with Salyna, going over the details of running a palace. Late on that Septi afternoon, Maeltor and two Southern Guards accompanied her down to the main level of the palace to the chambers occupied by the Ministry of Rivers and Highways.

Mykella was most careful in going through Porofyr's study. She found nothing out of the ordinary, not that she had expected to do so; but she did find a missive from a Seltyr Amaryk, suggesting that since Tempre was the principal beneficiary of trade on that route, Lanachrona should cut back brush along the ancient eternastone highway from Tempre to Zalt where it passed through the southern Coast Range. She tucked it inside her nightsilk tunic before instructing the clerks to send Porofyr's personal effects to him. Was that Amaryk a descendant of the one with whom Mykel had had such difficulties? *Does it matter now?*

After that, with some trepidation, she headed back to the upper level of the palace to see if Auralya and Salyna had completed moving her things and furnishings into the bedchamber that her father had occupied.

Salyna met her, as if she had been waiting. "I wondered where you were."

"Seeing if Seltyr Porofyr had left anything I should know. He resigned this morning. He said he couldn't serve me in the way I wished. What he really meant was that he'd almost rather die than serve a woman."

"He won't be the only one," predicted Salyna.

"I know, but Gharyk will stay, and I can probably handle the Finance Ministry for a while. I don't know about Loryalt." She shook her head. "Did you move out all of Father's personal things?"

"Most of them were already gone."

"Where are they?"

"Joramyl had them packed up and put in one of the storerooms. I took a quick look. I don't think anything's missing—except for the Lord-Protector's ring."

"Areyst gave that to me yesterday. You were there . . ."

Salyna flushed. "Oh . . . I was. I was . . . I thought . . . I don't know what I thought. You were so calm, both of you. I just thought it was a personal ring of Father's that Joramyl had taken. He was petty that way."

Even Salyna had seen it. Why didn't Father? Mykella wondered if she'd ever know the answer to that question.

"Just like you asked," Salyna went on, "I had them move Father's bed to your old room and your things to the apartment bedchamber. I did leave some bookcases. You had so many books stacked in the corner."

"The bookcases are fine." Mykella turned toward the rooms that would be hers.

There were actually two doors into the apartments, the main one leading into a hallway off which were the study on the right and the bedchamber on the left. In turn, both the private sitting room and the bath chamber were entered from the bedchamber. The second entrance to the main corridor was from the sitting room directly, but that door had almost always been bolted from inside. The arrangement of rooms was something Mykella would never have praised, but clearly a later adaptation to whatever the building had been before it became the palace.

Salyna opened the door to the hallway inside the private apartments. Mykella followed, her eyes roving over the paneled walls, bare except for the two tapestries that had always hung there and that depicted an idealized version of the private gardens, one in spring and one in the deep of winter.

Mykella sniffed. What was she smelling?

"I had everything scrubbed, and all the woodwork cleaned with lemon oil," Salyna said, before stepping into the study. "I left the desk and bookcase, but took out the stuffed red deer heads and brought in another nice armchair. It was Mother's favorite. You always liked it."

"Oh . . ." exclaimed Mykella involuntarily as she saw the pair of portraits hung on the wall above the modest writing desk. On the right was a formal portrait of her father, a copy of the one that hung in the gallery of Lord-Protectors on the main floor, and on the left was a portrait of her mother that had vanished years before.

"I hoped you'd like having the portraits here."

"I do. I wondered what Father had done with the one of Mother."

"He sealed all of her things up in a lower storeroom. I hope you don't mind that I brought some of them back."

"Oh . . . no." Mykella smiled, then turned toward the bedchamber.

Her old bed stood there, as did the area carpet from her room, and her other furnishings. In addition to her own armoire, there was a second near-identical one. Mykella turned to Salyna. "Mother's?"

Salyna shook her head. "Aunt Lalyna's. It was down in the storeroom, and when I saw it matched yours . . ." She smiled. "I think they were the set that Grandpapa and Grandmother used. You'll need more than one, now that you're Lady-Protector."

Mykella had to admit her sister was doubtless right.

From the bedchamber, she glanced into the sitting room, noting that the hearth had been cleaned and a fire laid but not put to flame despite the late-afternoon chill, and a blue and cream lambswool blanket had been folded over the back of the settee, as it once had been when she and Salyna had been children. She almost shook her head. The last time she'd been in the sitting room had been with her father after Jeraxylt's murder. She swallowed and looked at Salyna. "Thank you. Thank you so much."

"Wyandra helped me move your garments. I tried to put your things back the way you had them. You'll have to rearrange them, I'm sure."

Mykella stepped forward and hugged Salyna. "I can't tell you . . ."

For several moments, they hung on to each other. Then Mykella stepped back and blotted her eyes.

"Dinner should almost be ready," Salyna said

"What is it?" asked Mykella.

"Fowl. I told Auralya to fix the normal things, except that you'd never want river trout again." Salyna laughed. "Was that wrong?"

"No. I could barely choke down a mouthful of it."

"Neither could I."

Before long, the three sisters sat at the long cherry table in the family dining room. Mykella had decided against sitting at the end where her father had always seated himself but took the place she had always had since their mother's death years before.

She half-filled her goblet from the carafe, letting her Talent range over the white wine, but detected no trace of poison. She passed the wine to Rachylana. Her sister took the crystal carafe without a word.

Muergya hurried in with two domestic fowl, each sliced into halves, browned, and still steaming, accompanied by cheese-laced potatoes and apricot-walnut beans. To Mykella's surprise, the beans were actually warm and the potatoes hot.

"Muergya," she offered, after a mouthful. "You have my thanks, and please convey them to the cooks as well."

The serving girl inclined her head—surprised, but pleased—and retreated to the serving pantry.

The three young women ate in silence for a time. Mykella hadn't realized how hungry she had been, but then, she hadn't eaten since breakfast.

"I met with the assistant to the envoy from Deforya this morning," she finally said.

"What did he say?" asked Salyna.

"He wanted to know whether the envoy should return to Dereka and whether either of my sisters might be . . . available to be matched."

"To whom will you match me?" Rachylana's tone was quiet, but Mykella sensed the defiance behind it.

"I told him that anyone who wished a match with my sisters would have to meet them, and me, first. Then, you may choose whomever you and I can agree upon."

"No one will come to Lanachrona."

"They will." *One way or another. I just hope it's the way I want it to be.* "The majer did not seem terribly put off by those conditions. Envoy Malaryk has requested a meeting as well, and I'll see him tomorrow afternoon."

"He'll likely walk out on you." Rachylana's words were tart.

"He may not be happy," countered Salyna, "but he won't dare to walk out on you."

"I heard that you had that captain march Seltyr Porofyr from your study all the way out of the palace," said Rachylana.

"He tendered his resignation, and I accepted it. As I told him, he is as welcome in the palace as any other Seltyr who may have business here."

"None of them will . . ."

Between all the meetings of the day . . . and Rachylana's attitude and remarks throughout dinner, Mykella was more than willing to retreat to the private apartments. Yet once she closed the corridor door behind her and walked through the darkness that was no longer the barrier to movement it once had been, she was anything but ready to sleep.

She stood beside the writing desk in the private study, and questions tumbled through her mind. What had she missed? What had she already done wrong? Was she right to trust Areyst? Or were her doubts unreasonable, fueled by her reaction to her father's excessively trusting nature? How could she ever make Rachylana understand, and what was she going to do with her? What sort of public appearances should she be making? With whom should she be meeting? Exactly how should she deal with the Seltyrs of Tempre, who still held many of the same attitudes about women as did their peers in Southgate?

Some of those questions . . . some . . . she might be able to address by using the Table.

Thankfully, she no longer had to travel the corridors of the palace to reach the Table, not if she intended to go there alone. She walked over to the study window and pressed her hand against the stone next to the casement, reaching with her thoughts, her Talent, toward the greenish blackness beneath the palace. For a moment, she could not quite connect with the green before it extended upward and enshrouded her. Surrounded by the green that almost no one else saw, she willed herself into the stone and downward through it toward the Table and into the stillness of the Table chamber.

Almost by reflex, she let her eyes and senses traverse the Table for any sign of an Ifrit's presence; but there was none, save the lingering hint of purpled pinkness, and she stepped over to the Table and looked down into its mirrored surface. She concentrated on Areyst, worrying about what she might see, since her first uses of the Table had shown her brother and Berenyt in rather personal and compromising positions with various young ladies. The mists appeared, swirled briefly, and showed a silver-tinged and slightly faint image of Areyst sitting at a writing desk in a small stone-walled study that looked similar to the one where Mykella had confronted Commander Demyl. A single wall lamp cast light across the map spread before Areyst.

A goblet of wine stood at the edge of the desk, and the commander took a sip, then set the goblet down and picked up a pair of calipers, measuring a distance on the map, before writing on the paper to the side of the map. Another measurement followed, and another.

After seeing the concentration in Areyst's face, Mykella let the image fade. Whom else should she survey? *Rachylana?*

Her red-haired sister sat in an armchair in her chamber, an embroidery hoop in her hands, her cheeks wet. Mykella swallowed, then let that image fade.

Porofyr?

The Seltyr sat at a long oval table with three other Seltyrs, from their garb. Porofyr was talking intently, although his gestures were tight and controlled. Mykella recognized none of the three, and that was good because those at the table did not include Khanasyl, the First Seltyr of Tempre, nor Lhanyr, the Chief High Factor. Even so, it was clear that the four were not happy, and Mykella had few doubts that she was at least in part the cause of that unhappiness.

Maxymt?

All the Table revealed was that the former chief clerk was in a way station on one of the eternastone highways, his face shadowed as he stood back from a common cook-fire.

Treghyt?

The healer was eating at a rough trestle table in what looked to be a small cot that could have been anywhere at all.

Cheleyza?

Her aunt was still seated in a barge that appeared to be moving through rain and rough water. Mykella couldn't help but hope that Cheleyza was miserable indeed, even as she wondered just how much her aunt had had to do with Joramyl's efforts to become Lord-Protector.

She straightened and let the images in the Table lapse.

How long would she have to follow them? *Until you can do something about them . . . or know that they can no longer harm you or Lanachrona.*

At the moment, none of the those fleeing her were likely more than a day away on a fast mount, and she could travel far faster than that by using the Table . . . or, rather, the greenish darkness beneath the Tables. She'd already explored the other Tables she'd been able to sense, and all of them, except the one in Dereka, had turned out to be dead ends of one sort or another. But she'd traveled immense distances in a very short time, and she had been able to follow the blackish green lines where they lay beneath Tempre. Could she travel along them farther? How much farther? Far enough to be of use to her as Lady-Protector?

How would she know unless she tried?

She repressed a shiver, recalling how constricted and cold she had felt the first time she had dropped into the dark depths. Then she moistened her lips and let herself merge with the green and black and slide into the gray foundation walls and northward, trying to gauge her depth belowground—by a vague feeling, because she could not see, only sense.

The greenish-black lines or pathways seemed to branch . . . one heading westward, toward the Great Piers and the river. Recalling how the water weakened her Talent, she followed the branch eastward, which seemed to track roughly the Preserve. That made her more comfortable, despite the chill that crept into her body and bones, because she'd been able to sense the greenish-blackness on her more recent rides through the Preserve, a protected expanse of woods that bordered the banks of the Vedra and stretched a good twenty vingts northeast from the palace.

She was only guessing, but she thought she sensed the riverside hills that marked the northeastern end of the Preserve, and she willed herself upward, trying to sense her way to the clearing on the northernmost hill, from where she could see the river. As soon as she emerged from the ground, she raised her Talent shields. She'd learned the hard way that she couldn't travel the darkness holding shields, or use shields and a concealment screen, but she didn't want to stand unprotected in the darkness—even if the Preserve was supposed to be restricted to her use and that of those she permitted there.

She turned to the north, then glanced overhead. Asterta was a full but small green disc not quite at its zenith, while Selena, the larger and golden white moon, had just risen above the trees to the east. To the north, as she had hoped, was the silvered expanse of the River Vedra. *I can travel the darkness farther than just Tempre. I can.*

Her smile faded as, to her right, she heard a rustling, then sensed two figures walking along the riding path leading to the clearing. Both carried bows slung over their shoulders.

Poachers. Who else would be out there in the darkness?

"What are you doing here?" she asked, turning to face them and drawing strength from the green beneath the ground and letting it carry her voice.

Both men stiffened but kept moving toward her.

"Be meaning no one no harm," offered the smaller man, whose scraggly beard dangled above a ragged tunic, damp in places, doubtless from brushing against wet vegetation.

The taller man—a giant more than half a yard taller than Mykella—stepped forward. "Might be asking you that as well, little woman." He stopped a yard from her, peering at her. "Pretty little thing you are."

"You don't belong here," repeated Mykella, strengthening her shields. She hadn't brought weapons, and she really had no way to stop the men short of killing them. "Poaching in the Preserve is forbidden." Even as she spoke, she realized the naïveté of her words.

"Now . . . now . . . the Lord-Protector, he wouldn't be bothering himself over a red deer or so. Even if he did, he wouldn't be missing a deer or two, now and again." The poacher's huge hands reached to grasp her by the shoulders, tightening around the shields she held close to her—and still lifting her . . . but only for a moment before her shielded figure slipped from his grip.

Off-balance, she staggered, then stumbled backwards and landed on her buttocks and lower back, still within her shields. She immediately scrambled to her feet. Both angry and embarrassed, she strengthened her ties to the greenness deep beneath the ground and focused light around her, enough so that she could see the startled expression on the face of the bigger man and even on the smaller black-bearded poacher as well.

"You don't belong here," she said coldly. "If you don't turn and leave, you will never leave. Not alive." With that, she drew on the greenness slightly more so that her entire body rose from the ground, and her eyes were level with those of the poacher. "The Preserve belongs to the Lady-Protector . . . and the Ancients."

Both men backed away, slowly, then more quickly.

In moments, both were almost running.

Mykella let herself drop slowly until her boots touched the loosely packed damp soil and grass of the clearing. She took a last look at the Vedra, a shimmering silvery strip under the light of Selena, then reached down to the darkness.

She eased her way through the chill and the granite of the palace walls until she was back in the study. Her tunic was edged in frost, and she was shivering. After several moments, she walked toward the bedchamber.

She could already feel the soreness in her lower back and buttocks. She'd definitely have a large bruise there. The Talent shields might keep her from being struck directly, but she was so small, and her skin was so sensitive that falling would end up bruising her as much as getting hit would. Her shields would keep her from getting killed, but the way the night had gone, she could easily end up bruised all over her body. She'd have to figure out some way to anchor the shields to something . . . or they wouldn't be nearly as useful as she'd hoped.

Nothing is as simple as you think. Nothing.

She undressed methodically and pulled on a nightdress, then

climbed under the covers, still shivering occasionally. As she began to drift off to sleep, another thought slipped into her mind. Had Mykel the Great laid out the Preserve because of the greenish-black pathways? He'd never hunted, according to all the histories . . .

She had to get some sleep, and she pushed that thought away and closed her eyes.

5

Immediately after breakfast on Octdi, Mykella walked down to the main level of the palace, all too conscious of the soreness on her backside and of Southern Guards who followed her as she made her way to the lower accounting chambers, although the palace was not yet open to outsiders.

When she walked into the large main-floor room, Haelyt—the graying clerk in charge of the other clerks—bowed. "Lady-Protector."

Mykella could feel his apprehension even before she spoke. "Haelyt . . . I have not forgotten all the years you have served faithfully." She smiled. "And yet, I must ask more of you. Will you take up the duties—and the stipend—of the chief clerk?"

"I would be honored, Lady." After the slightest hesitation, he asked, "Maxymt?"

"The former chief clerk of the Finance Ministry left rather precipitously. For the time being, I serve as my own Finance Minister." She turned, and her eyes fell on the red-haired youth who was the most junior clerk. "As I believe you once murmured you wished, Wasdahl."

The young clerk paled.

Mykella smiled at him warmly. "Others might have held it against you. I do not, but you should be aware that anything you say might be heard and repeated." Then she turned back to Haelyt. "You will need to find two more clerks, I think. If you will walk with me back to my study, we can discuss those matters. I will need to provide you with the chief clerk's key and signet and a letter of passage that you can use until all the guards know you have access to the upper level."

"Yes, Lady."

No one whispered a word as Haelyt and Mykella left the accounting chamber. Once they were outside in the corridor and walking toward the center stone staircase to the upper level, Haelyt turned to Mykella. "Lady . . . I never expected . . ."

"I know. But you are accurate and trustworthy, and I value both. Can Vyahm take your place as assistant chief clerk? Should he, now that Minister Porofyr has resigned?"

"He is very accurate and most scrupulous in his duties, Lady. He served under both Lord Porofyr and old Lord Kuerlt."

Mykella sensed no reservations behind Haelyt's words. "Then he will succeed you. Do you know who could take Shenyl's place handling the Southern Guard accounts, or should I ask Commander Areyst for a recommendation from among his clerks?"

"If he would part with Jainara . . . She is most accurate."

Mykella repressed a smile. She hadn't known that there was a woman clerking for the Southern Guards. "Tell me about her." She started up the steps.

"Her uncle was Majer Allahyr, and she began by keeping the accounts for his battalion in Soupat. For several years, she dressed as a youth, and no one questioned. When the majer returned to Tempre, Commander Nephryt commended her work, not knowing Jainara was a young woman—she was listed as 'Jainar' on the pay list. Then he found out and made an order that, in the future, no women were to be clerks. She was moved to procurement accounts after the majer's death. After your father's death, the commander said she would be terminated, but Commander Areyst stopped that. Still . . ."

Mykella suspected the reason why Nephryt hadn't acted sooner was because the majer's daughter Eranya had been the mistress of Mykella's father. "It might be better for Jainara and the Finance Ministry if she became one of your clerks?"

"She is a good clerk."

"Then make her one of yours."

"I would be pleased to do so. . . ."

"I doubt Commander Areyst will complain, but if he does, I will explain to him."

"Thank you, Lady."

Once they reached the anteroom, Mykella outlined the situation to Chalmyr and left the two to make the necessary arrangements and draft the requisite documents for her signature.

She turned at the door to her study. "Would you also draft letters to First Seltyr Khanasyl and Chief High Factor Lhanyr requesting they meet with me next week, on Londi, if possible."

"Yes, Lady." Chalmyr smiled and nodded.

On her desk, Mykella found a short stack of notes and letters congratulating her on becoming Lady-Protector, most from more junior factors or Seltyrs, but among the missives from more junior traders were one from Khanasyl and another from Lhanyr. Mykella wasn't surprised. Both were astute, and felicitations cost nothing.

Areyst arrived at Mykella's study a glass before midday. He did not even seat himself before announcing, "The clerk Maxymt departed Tempre the afternoon you became Lady-Protector . . . healer Treghyt has fled Tempre. His daughter and son have not seen him since you became Lady-Protector. They said he was greatly troubled but would not tell them why."

"You could sit down, Commander," said Mykella with a smile. "Or have the demands I have placed on you kept you so busy that you've forgotten how?"

Her impish tone and smile seemed to touch Areyst, and he settled into the chair across from her. "There have been a few matters more than I had anticipated . . . including my losing one of the few clerks who seemed to understand the Southern Guard accounts."

"Jainara, you mean?"

"I just found that out less than half a glass ago. Seasons ago, she did reveal her doubts about some of the disbursements."

"Such as those to the nonexistent Berjor for tack that is not to be found in the storerooms? I believe I inquired about that sometime ago, did I not?"

"You did indeed, Lady." Although Areyst managed to keep his

voice level, Mykella could sense a wryness hidden behind his even tone and serene expression. "And I have learned over the past weeks never to discount what you tell me." He paused. "You did not seem perturbed by my report about those who fled."

"No doubt Joramyl threatened Treghyt with consequences to his family if Treghyt revealed his suspicions about how my father was killed. So . . . the healer said nothing and is fleeing for his life because he had not the courage of his convictions. Maxymt was in a way station somewhere last evening, and Treghyt was sheltering in a poor cot. Cheleyza was still on the River Vedra."

"You saw this in your Table?" Areyst frowned. "There were no reports of your leaving your apartments."

"That was not the fault of your guards, Commander. I have ways of reaching the Table that they cannot see."

"I have difficulty . . ."

Mykella called up the concealment shield.

"What—"

"I am still here, Commander." She released the shield. Better to let him see that than to learn of her other abilities.

"Might I ask a question, Lady?"

"You may."

"In the past few days, you have shown great abilities . . . ?"

"You would like to know why, if I have such abilities, I could not have prevented all that has happened?" Mykella let herself sigh. "I would that I could have. I knew Joramyl was taking golds. You know I knew because I asked you about Berjor. I had none of the abilities you see now—except that I could see and sense the ancient soarers and the Table. I would that I could have done something. But at first all I could do was to tell my father about the missing golds and show him the account books. Joramyl convinced him that Kiedryn was the guilty one. I protested, but I could not prove it to my father. I asked the soarer for help, and she touched me. Nothing happened at first, except that I learned how to conceal myself, the way you just saw, and I used that and what I saw in the Table to discover Joramyl's plot with Nephryt— but so far you are the only one who can see what I see in the Table, and no one would believe me." She smiled sadly. "I kept trying to learn, but

I could only learn the shields and how to kill after Rachylana and Father were poisoned."

"Your sister was poisoned?" Areyst stiffened.

"By Cheleyza, at an afternoon gathering, but I was standing right beside her when the poison attacked her, and I managed to save her. You can ask Salyna, if you want. I tried to do the same with Father, but Joramyl was clever enough that it was too late when I reached Father for anyone to save him." What Mykella said was not exactly the way things had happened, but she had no intention of talking about the Ifrit or certain other happenings. Not at the moment, at least. "I had never killed anyone until the day I became Lady-Protector."

"How did you know how?"

Mykella shook her head. "I learned from the soarer and the Table and hid in the slaughterhouse and killed animals just before they were struck with the hammer." Again, what she said was mostly true, if not in precisely the way she implied.

"Do you think this soarer, this Ancient . . . why would she help you?"

"She said I was the only one to save the land. I have not seen her in weeks."

Areyst was the one to shake his head. "Lady . . . I have seen enough to know that all this must be true, strange as it seems. But I beg you not to mention it to anyone else."

"You and my sister Salyna are the only ones who know. She saw enough to need to know, and you must know as Arms-Commander."

Areyst inclined his head. "I will not betray that trust."

Mykella already knew that. His honesty shone as much as the strand of green in his life-thread, that thread of green that doubtless allowed him to see what appeared in the Table. "That is why you are Arms-Commander and my designated heir."

"Lady . . . I am not of noble blood. I do not wish to be the heir."

"I know that is not your wish. For now, it is necessary. For me, for my sisters, and for Lanachrona. I will lift that burden as I can."

Although Areyst did not speak but merely nodded, Mykella could sense that he truly wanted to protect her, and she had to fight to keep her eyes from burning. After a moment, she spoke. "How long will we have before we see the armies of Midcoast and Northcoast?"

"It will be late in spring or early in summer . . . if they still choose to attack. I believe they will. The lady Cheleyza cannot reach North-coast for at least another tenday, and possibly twice that if the coastal rains are heavy. It will take a tenday for Prince Chalcaer to ready an envoy or his own entourage and travel south to Hafin. If . . . if his army readies itself while he is gone . . . and departs on word from a fast courier, it will be another two tendays before they could join Prince Skrelyn's forces at Salcer—that is what I would do, were I they."

"It's almost the end of the fourth week of spring, and by your count, they could not meet in Salcer for another five weeks, with a week's ride after that to our borders. That would be right after season-turn."

"We should not fight on the borders but just west of Viencet. They will have to travel four days farther, and there will be little forage, or anything else, on the lands west of Viencet."

"You will have to instruct me on how you plan to defend against them."

"Lady . . ." Areyst paused. "You are not trained in battle."

"I am not, and I do not plan to attempt to fight in that fashion, as my sister might. But there are things that I may be able to do to assist you, and so long as I am not in the thick of the fighting, I will be safe enough, as you saw with Commander Nephryt."

"Begging your pardon, Lady-Protector, but you must also rule."

"That's true enough, but Viencet is but a day's ride, unlike Salcer or Hafin." While Mykella had not ridden there in years, Jeraxylt had told her it was less than a day's ride. "Still . . . I understand your con-cerns, and because Viencet is not that far, whether I should be there is a decision we can discuss later. I would still wish to know what you plan . . . when you are ready to tell me."

"That will be several weeks, when I have reports on the companies I have summoned."

"Tomorrow, at midmorning, we will visit the villa that Joramyl occupied. I hope to find some golds sequestered there. Perhaps enough to pay for those supplies."

"That would be useful."

More than useful. Most necessary, given the state of the Treasury. "Tell me anything you think I should know right now . . ."

Areyst squared his shoulders. "As your sister has doubtless told you, the training of First and Second Companies has been adequate for parades and duties in Tempre, but little beyond that. I have ordered Captain Maeltor to set up the training system used in Soupat. . . ."

Mykella listened.

After Areyst departed, she picked up one of the old pens and drafted the body of a thank-you letter, then took it out to Chalmyr with the pile of letters she'd received. "Use this as the basis for replying to all these, except for Khanasyl and Lhanyr. Change theirs to use as much of what I wrote as you can but suggest that we should meet on Duadi or Tridi, rather than Londi, as I told you earlier. Don't use the phrase 'at your convenience.' You know this better than I do. If you can make my words more gracious, without showing weakness, please do so."

She did have Chalmyr send for some slices of cold fowl and bread before she met with Cerlyk. She had the feeling that she wouldn't last the afternoon without eating, but she accompanied the spare meal with cider because wine might have gone to her head—another disadvantage of being small, even if she did have muscles no one noticed because of her height.

Cerlyk arrived promptly at the chime of the first glass of afternoon. He was a slender man, lightly tanned, with wispy blond hair that was already receding although he did not appear to be more than a few years senior to Mykella. "Lady-Protector, you requested my presence."

Mykella gestured for him to sit. "Tell me about the state of the Lady-Protector's lands. I'd also like to know what the prospects are for timber harvests in the year ahead."

"In general, the lands are in good condition. There were several timber harvests last summer for several sections of land west of Hyalt." Cerlyk cleared his throat. "We do not plan any other harvests for several years."

"Why not?"

"Your father . . . well, through Lord Joramyl, requested we move up the harvests scheduled for this year and next to last summer, in order to raise golds so that tariffs would not have to be increased in order to meet expenses . . . of the Southern Guards, we were told. If we cut more timber this year or the next . . ." He held up several sheets of paper. "These explain the loss in future timber revenues if we do not reduce harvests for several years."

"I see. Would you have a copy of the revenues received from the harvests last year?"

"Oh, yes. We have the complete records."

"I'd like to see those for last year and the year before."

"I can bring them up shortly after I've answered any other questions you may have."

Mykella could sense no deception and nothing of ill ease in Cerlyk, only an almost-boyish enthusiasm as the Forester's assistant went on to explain about each of the major timber stands. After he had finished, then returned with the records she had requested, she began to study them, as well as to compare the revenues from the sale of the timber to the receipts in the master ledger. Nearly immediately, she realized that, of the three major timber sales, the receipts for only one appeared in the master Finance ledger, although the Forester's records had receipts from Joramyl for all three. Effectively, Joramyl had diverted or pocketed somewhere close to seven thousand golds.

Just where did all those golds happen to go? How long did he think he could get away with it? She hoped some of them were hidden in the villa that her father had allowed Joramyl to make his own; but if they had been, she suspected they were likely with Cheleyza unless Joramyl had hidden some from his wife.

"I will see her! Now!"

The angry voice—Rachylana's—penetrated the door so sharply that Mykella bolted up from the ledgers. She took a deep breath and walked to the door, opening it.

Rachylana's eyes were red, and she stalked into the formal study.

Mykella had barely closed the door when Rachylana began to talk, her voice surprisingly low, for the fury behind it.

"You didn't even tell me. You just did it. I can't believe that you were so cruel. But I can. It's always been you. Never anyone else. Just you. Always you . . ."

"What did I do?" *This time?*

"You had his body burned and the ashes stuffed into an urn and mortared away without a word to anyone. Not a blessing. Not a word . . . nothing! How could you?"

Mykella finally understood—Berenyt. "He was a traitor. He knew about poisoning Father and killing Jeraxylt. You may have loved him, but traitors don't get public memorials or ceremonies. He was family, and I didn't deny him a place in the family mausoleum. I didn't have his body left in the wild for the animals, and that has been done. I gave him a place. He didn't deserve a memorial."

"I read a blessing. I gave him what you didn't." Rachylana looked defiantly at Mykella.

"You had that right. I didn't say family couldn't mourn. I didn't say you couldn't grieve. I didn't say you couldn't give a blessing. I only said there would be no public memorial."

"You didn't even tell me."

"No . . . I didn't. I'm sorry. I should have."

"You should have."

"You're right. I should have." Even with everything plaguing her, Mykella should have told Rachylana. But she hadn't.

"You never wanted me to be happy."

"I want you to be happy." Mykella tried to project that feeling toward her sister, tried to put the feeling in her words. "I never thought Berenyt would make you happy, but I wanted you to be happy."

"It's too late, now. You ruined it all." With that, Rachylana turned and walked out of the study. She didn't slam the door, but she left it open.

Mykella just stood there. *What else could you have said . . . that was true?* Finally, she stepped forward and eased the door shut. Then she walked to the window, where she looked out across the courtyard and toward the green towers that flanked the Great Piers.

As the third glass of the afternoon on Octdi arrived, there was a knock on the study door, and Mykella looked up from the account ledgers dealing with forestry.

"Envoy Malaryk . . ." announced Chalmyr.

Mykella did stand and wait for Malaryk, but she remained on her feet only long enough to acknowledge his presence before taking her seat and gesturing him to the chair on the left.

"Lady-Protector, you are most gracious in acceding to my request so soon after such tragedies have befallen Lanachrona."

"I appreciate your solicitousness, Envoy Malaryk, and that of those you represent, but I am recovered from the tragedies. They came earlier, with the murders of my brother and father. Now, we must do what is right and necessary."

"In the midst of such . . . tragedies . . . one must admit that having a . . . Lady-Protector in Tempre is not something that anyone had contemplated. You must admit that never has a woman held power in any land in Corus."

"Oh?" offered Mykella. "It almost did happen here in Lanachrona. Mykel the Great named Rachyla as his heir and successor."

Malaryk smiled condescendingly. "It could also be said that the Alectors almost survived."

Mykella held back a retort—that some had survived, except that they had been changed by the Cataclysm—or changed themselves in reaction to it—into Talented humans. That was what the soarer had told her, and so far the Ancient had been correct in what she had conveyed. Instead, Mykella smiled politely. "All those almosts are in the past. Now, a Lady-Protector rules in Tempre."

"That is true. It is a great change. Any time that rule changes in any land is an unsettled time, and not all who become rulers remain rulers."

Mykella well understood that . . . and the veiled threat behind the words. "Perhaps you have a suggestion, Envoy Malaryk?"

"I can suggest nothing because the situation here in Tempre has gone beyond my instructions from Seltyr Gheortyn."

Mykella waited, then replied calmly, "I imagine you have some observations."

"Ah . . . observations. One may observe without understanding, and then, the one to whom one entrusts the task of observing may also fail to understand."

"Such possibilities always exist, Envoy Malaryk." Mykella paused before adding, "Without offering such an observation, one might lose potential advantages or useful information out of the mere fear of the lack of understanding."

"You are wise beyond your years, Lady; but wisdom, alas, is not all that decides what may happen in the world."

Mykella forced herself to smile again, tired as she was quickly getting of Malaryk's verbal games. "True. Wisdom without strength is limited, as is strength without wisdom, and knowledge does not always equal wisdom. You will note that I do indeed listen." *Not all that patiently.*

Malaryk nodded his wide and jowled head slowly and sagely.

Again, Mykella waited.

Finally, the envoy spoke. "You will understand that when I speak, I can speak only about what I observe and not about what may or may not occur in Southgate or even elsewhere here in Tempre, or in, say, Midcoast or Northcoast."

"I do indeed. You have made that most clear. You represent carefully and well the interests of Seltyr Gheortyn, and for those very reasons I would hear your observations."

"You are most patient for a woman so young, Lady Mykella."

I won't be if you don't stop weaseling and get on with saying what you have in mind to manipulate me. "I am looking forward to your observations, Envoy Malaryk."

"You are most kind to hear my words."

"I doubt that either of us believes the other kind, but the exchange of information is often mutually beneficial."

"Ah . . . yes . . . information. Information and ties based on mutual benefit, such as alliances. Alliances are often to the advantage of any new ruler, particularly in instances where the alliance is sealed by direct personal ties between those ruling adjoining lands . . ."

In short, you want me to agree to marry Gheortyn's idiot son and effectively turn Lanachrona into a fiefdom of Southgate, or failing that, to match Salyna to the idiot, then agree to every proposition Gheortyn makes. "That is most astute, Envoy Malaryk, not that I would have expected anything less from a man of your experience in the world. It is also a proposition to which I would have to give full and most serious consideration . . . were it to be presented to me with the full knowledge of such a ruler."

Malaryk nodded. "I could expect no more, and I request your indulgence while I return to Southgate and report to the Seltyr on the developments here in Tempre . . ."

"There is one other matter," Mykella said. "Before any match can be agreed upon, my sisters and I must meet such a suitor."

"That . . . that is most unusual. It is not . . . traditional . . ."

"It may indeed be a departure from recent practice, but if we are to speak of tradition, Mykel the Great met Rachyla—properly chaperoned, of course—several times before they were wed. I believe, from what my aunt told me, that such is still the practice for some in Southgate."

"Ah . . . yes . . . but . . . the distance . . ."

Mykella merely smiled.

Once Malaryk had left her study, Mykella just sat behind the desk for a time. She needed to talk to her sisters more about their desires. Except she had talked to Salyna, and her youngest sister really didn't know what she wanted, and Rachylana wasn't speaking much to anyone—especially to Mykella.

By the time she had read and signed all the letters Chalmyr had penned for her, and changed one or two, checked the master ledger of the Finance Ministry against the needs outlined by Areyst, and confirmed that the additional timber-sale funds had not been transferred to any other ministry account—or to that of the Lord-Protector—it was time for dinner, and her head was aching. So were her lower back and rear.

Salyna and Rachylana were already in the family dining room when Mykella entered and seated herself, if gingerly. Immediately, Muergya brought in a fowl casserole, along with lace potatoes. Mykella poured half a glass of wine and passed the carafe to Rachylana.

"You met with that envoy," said the redhead. "When am I going to Southgate?"

"You aren't. I told Malaryk that we would entertain any suitors, but that we needed to meet them before agreeing to a match."

"I'll never be matched. Never. Not after everything you've done."

Mykella suppressed a sigh.

"Don't look at me like that, either," snapped Rachylana.

"How was your day, Mykella?" asked Salyna brightly.

"Besides discovering that Joramyl pocketed something like another seven thousand golds from cutting timber that shouldn't have been, that the Southern Guard companies stationed here are undertrained, that Malaryk wants me to be matched to that idiot son of Seltyr Gheortyn and intimated that I didn't have the strength to rule . . . other than that, you mean? Oh . . . and that Porofyr was spending golds as it they rained from the sky?"

"That's what being Protector is all about," offered Rachylana blandly. "Among other things."

Mykella managed to smile sweetly although she bridled inside. "It is indeed." She took a larger helping of the casserole than she probably should have and eased the dish in front of Rachylana, then turned to Salyna. "How was your day?"

"Better than yours." The youngest sister laughed. "I didn't get in any arms practice, though."

"No one will want to practice with you anyway," murmured Rachylana. "Not now."

"Oh, they'll practice with me," replied Salyna cheerfully. "They just won't test me much, but I can improve my shooting now because no one will tell me I can't do it."

After that, conversation was minimal, partly because, Mykella suspected, she didn't make an effort to be outgoing, partly because she felt Rachylana would just make more snide comments. Later, following an all-too-quiet dinner, Mykella peered into the family parlor.

Salyna was seated on the settee, embroidering a design. She looked up. "Rachylana went to her room. She said she didn't want to talk to either of us right now."

"Did she tell you about Berenyt?"

"In great detail." Salyna shook her head. "She finally admitted that you didn't have much choice, but she won't ever tell you that."

"I know." Mykella stepped into the parlor, letting her senses range beyond the chamber, but no one else was near. She closed the door behind her. "I need your help."

"My help?"

"If you would . . . come here."

As Salyna set aside the embroidery and rose, Mykella concentrated on not only raising her Talent shields, but linking them to the heavy stone beneath her boots. "Try to knock me over."

"That's help?"

"It's the help I need."

"I could hurt you . . ."

"Not if this works, but make the first push gentle in case it doesn't."

The blonde raised both hands, then stepped forward and thrust them toward Mykella's shoulders. Her hands stopped just short of Mykella's tunic. "Oh!'

"Now . . . harder, but be careful. You could hurt your hands," cautioned Mykella.

Despite being more than a head taller than Mykella and a good stone or more heavier, even after several attempts, Salyna had no success in moving Mykella.

"That's enough.'

"I don't understand. What was this all about? When Commander Nephryt slashed at you . . ." Salyna shook her head.

"He slashed down and sideways at me. After that I discovered, since I'm so small, I can still be knocked over or backwards if I don't take precautions."

"Stirrups," said Salyna knowingly.

"Stirrups?"

"If a Southern Guard didn't have stirrups, he could get pushed right out of the saddle when his saber hit the enemy. It's the same thing, sort of, isn't it?"

Mykella smiled. "I hadn't thought of it that way, but you're right."

Salyna looked at Mykella. "You need some sleep."

"I need to study a few more things, but I won't be up too late."

"Promise?"

"I promise."

Stiff, sore, and tired as she was, Mykella wasn't about to make any more Table trips, not until she was more rested. Instead, she walked back to her formal study and went over the maps, the ones that showed at least some of the hills that lay along the eternastone highway that ran from Tempre to Hafin.

She had an idea . . .

6

Mykella did not sleep well and woke early on Novdi, while the sky was still lightening into featureless gray. She stretched and sat up in bed, wondering if she should slip down to the Table. She shook her head. So early in the morning, she'd see nothing of value. While she would also have liked to see what Skrelyn and Chalcaer were doing, the Table wouldn't display the images of people she hadn't met personally even if it weren't early in the day.

When she finished washing up, using cool water left from the night before, and dressing, she made her way to the breakfast room.

Muergya saw her and swallowed. "Just a moment, Lady." The serving girl rushed off, down the side serving stairs leading to the kitchens.

Mykella didn't want to sit down alone. She wandered into the serving pantry. All that remained was a half a loaf of dark bread, under a porcelain cover, and a small wedge of yellow cheese. *You will have to wait.* She walked back to the table and sat down.

Before that long, Muergya reappeared with a tray, on which was a teapot with steam curling from the spout, a plate of fried cakes, and what looked to be some sort of eggs covered in cheese. "I'm so sorry, Lady," said the serving girl breathlessly as she slid the teapot and platters in front of Mykella. "I didn't know you'd be up so early."

"Neither did I," replied Mykella dryly. "I had a lot on my mind."

"I'll be back with the ham strips in but a bit, and the stewed apples."

Salyna eased into the breakfast room as Muergya left and sat down across the table from Mykella. "What do you have planned for today?"

"Inspecting Joramyl's villa with the commander. I'm hoping dear Uncle hid some of those missing golds."

"If he didn't?"

"I'll see what personal items there might be that can be sold."

Salyna raised her eyebrows.

"Given how much he stole from Father and Lanachrona, I don't think that's unfair."

"Not unfair at all. Is it wise?"

Mykella nodded. "You're right. I'll ask Gharyk how to proceed, but I think we can gather them for safekeeping. I should have done that earlier although the villa has been under guard."

"You've only been Lady-Protector for something like four days."

Mykella smiled sadly. "How long doesn't count. Only how well."

Salyna snorted. "You *are* like your namesake."

"How would you know?" countered Mykella with a grin.

"The histories say that he left nothing to chance, not even his wife."

"Salyna!"

"You won't leave that to chance, either, will you? You've already planned that out, haven't you?"

"I have ideas," temporized Mykella. "Whether they work out is another matter."

"You'll work them out."

"We'll have to see," demurred Mykella, turning her attention to the tea and food that Muergya was placing before her.

Before long, she made her way down the side corridor, where she unlocked the door to the anteroom and slipped into the formal study. There she drafted a request to Lord Gharyk asking for an opinion as to the disposition of the personal property of a traitor who had embezzled from the Treasury and who had been executed without repaying the funds. Then she began to go over the expenditures made in the spring a year ago, hoping to see where she might cut spending in order to free golds for the Southern Guards. While she made her calculations and estimations, she heard Chalmyr arrive but did not go out and greet him.

Just before eighth glass, she rose from the desk and donned the black nightsilk riding jacket she had brought, but not worn, then stepped out into the anteroom. "You can leave for the day, Chalmyr. I won't be back until after midday. I'll see you on Londi."

"I could wait, Lady . . . if there's anything urgent."

"There's nothing that urgent." *Not that needs to be written right now. Other things, yes, such as finding out if any golds were left behind by Cheleyza.*

At that moment, Areyst stepped into the anteroom. "Third squad is ready, Lady."

"I haven't even groomed—"

"I had that taken care of," replied the commander with a smile. "You have more important tasks than grooming these days."

Much as Mykella knew that, she would have liked to groom her gray gelding. *Because you're afraid of becoming a prisoner of being the Lady-Protector? Where all the simple tasks are handled by others?* After the briefest hesitation, she said, "Thank you," then walked toward the door that Areyst held open for her.

Still thinking about all the changes in her life, she did not speak until they were on the main level and close to the east end of the palace, past the majority of the ministry offices, where various functionaries of traders and Seltyrs were gathered to finish whatever business they had before the ministries closed for the end-days at noon. "Have you had any reports from the squads guarding the villa?"

"They report that no one has tried to leave, except some servants. They had already fled. None of those remaining seemed surprised."

"I wonder how much has been taken."

"By the servants? I would guess very little. They have nowhere to go, and sooner or later they would be caught and punished."

That still left the question of what Cheleyza had taken with her, but there wasn't any point in speculating. Mykella pushed the east courtyard door open and stepped out into a gray day with low clouds that threatened rain. One of the guards held the reins to the gelding, positioned beside a mounting block. That did make getting into the saddle much easier. She and Areyst rode out of the palace courtyard at the head of the squad, then turned eastward, toward the main compound for the Southern Guards, located precisely two thousand yards—one vingt—from the center gate to the palace grounds. The entry road fronting the palace joined the older eternastone avenue that led to the Guard building, and Mykella guided the gelding onto the ancient road—although it appeared as though it had just been constructed.

That part of the eternastone avenue, which was also the high road that eventually ran south, then east out of Tempre, led to the villa that Joramyl had called his estate, although it belonged to whoever was Lord-Protector—or Lady-Protector. In less than half a glass, Mykella, Areyst, and the troopers who accompanied them neared the villa. It stood east of the road and back a good three hundred yards at the end of a paved drive that curved through low gardens. The two-story structure formed a V, with the open area between the two wings forming the entry courtyard, with the entry portico on the north wing and a walled garden filling the innermost section of the vertex of the V.

As she and Areyst rode up toward the entry portico, Mykella noticed the uniformed Southern Guards stationed at intervals around the villa and guarding the portico.

"Lady-Protector, Commander!" called out the squad leader who rode up. "We've let no one leave, as you instructed."

"I appreciate that, Jekardyn." Mykella was grateful she'd recalled the man's name.

She reined up before the portico and dismounted, then walked toward the doors, checking her Talent shields. Two Guards opened the doors and entered before her, as did Areyst, his hand casually near the hilt of his saber. Once past the oiled and shining golden oak double doors, Mykella took several steps, then studied the polished rose marble floor of the high-ceilinged entry hall, glancing briefly through the archway on the left into the small receiving parlor, where she'd once been forced by her father to beg Cheleyza's pardon. Her eyes went to the central grand staircase and the white marble walls, framed by darker rose marble columns. Besides the pair of archways, situated on both sides of the hall, there were also two doors of dark oak, both closed. One led, Mykella knew from her use of the Table, to Joramyl's very private study.

A man in a blue uniform, trimmed in gray, hurried up and bowed. "Lady-Protector . . . we have done nothing. Nothing, if you please."

Mykella looked at him. "You are?"

"Hrevor, the assistant steward, Lady-Protector."

"Where is the steward?"

"Paelyt came here with Lady Cheleyza. He departed with her."

Mykella nodded. "No one remaining here has taken anything?"

"Lady . . . I have not. I have told all the servants to leave everything as it was."

While Hrevor's forehead was damp, Mykella sensed the man was telling the truth. "You may escort us through the villa. We will begin with the private study behind the oak door beneath the grand staircase there." She pointed.

"I do not have the key to that chamber, Lady. Only Lord Joramyl did. Not even Lady Cheleyza did. The sculls could only clean it when Lord Joramyl was present."

Mykella looked hard at Hrevor, but the assistant steward was telling the truth. If the villa had been closer to the palace and the Table, Mykella could have reached out to the greenish darkness that underlay the Table and palace and slipped through earth and stone to enter the study from beneath; but she'd already discovered that only worked near the greenish black pathways that radiated from the old Tables—or had it been that the Tables had been placed on nodes in the pathways? Either way, that possibility wouldn't work in the villa.

Areyst cleared his throat softly, and held up a ring of keys. "One of these might suffice."

Mykella looked to the commander.

"Since the Lady Cheleyza fled before Lord Joramyl's body was recovered, we removed all personal items for safekeeping and placed them in the Arms-Commander's locked storeroom. There were no obvious valuables. You are the next of kin, Lady, except for Lady

Cheleyza. I thought the keys might prove useful and removed them from the lockbox this morning."

"You are prepared for everything, Commander, for which I am most grateful." Mykella smiled warmly at Areyst as she took the keys. *How many other things will you overlook?*

Hrevor followed, a step behind, while Mykella and Areyst crossed the entry foyer and came to a stop at the study door.

The fourth key Mykella tried was the one that unlocked the heavy door. She pushed it open, but did not step into the darkened chamber, instead letting her Talent probe the chamber.

Areyst gestured to one of the Southern Guards who had accompanied them. The ranker stepped past Mykella and into the chamber, looking around it.

"Seems clear, sir, Lady."

Mykella had not sensed anything either and eased into the hexagonal study, which looked to be exactly as she had seen it when she had used the Table. A round oak table, six oak chairs with padded seats and wooden arms drawn up to it, a single sideboard on which goblets were set on a tray, three bronze lamps in wall sconces, and two small and narrow windows high on the rear wall, both closed.

Areyst took a striker from his belt pouch and lit one of the lamps.

Mykella looked through the sideboard, but all it held were several sets of dice, some pasteboard cards, more goblets, a set of blue linens, and a halfscore of bottles of wine, all unopened. *There has to be more here . . . somewhere.*

She began to move along the paneled dark oak walls, occasionally tapping the wood, trying to feel what might lie behind the paneling. One part of the wall, the angled section between the rear wall and the left wall, felt different, almost empty. She studied it more intently, first with her eyes, then her senses, noting something like a cord or a wire that seemed to run behind the paneling and just . . . ended. Except, where it ended looked like a knot in the wood.

She pressed the knot. A narrow door swung open, revealing a small triangular room with three sturdy shelves. One each shelf rested an ironbound and locked wooden chest.

"It looks like the Lady didn't make off with everything," Mykella said dryly, fingering through the keys. None looked to fit the locks.

She tried them all, and none did. "We'll have to cut the locks, or break the straps."

"One of the armorers has tools to open locks," suggested Areyst. "That might be easier."

"We'll need a wagon to take the chests to the palace. I don't want to leave them here, but we need to see if there's anything else we need to take for safekeeping."

"I'll send for a Guard wagon."

"Thank you." Mykella stepped back and closed the hidden door.

She walked toward the study door, knowing she had much more to do. Even though the villa was hers as Lady-Protector, and even though Cheleyza and Joramyl had plotted the murders of her brother and her father, and stolen thousands of gold, she felt vaguely uneasy about rummaging through the rooms, necessary as she felt that was, but she needed to inspect every chamber . . . and that included cellars and storerooms.

7

By the third glass of Novdi afternoon, Mykella had returned to the palace, with the chests opened, their coins counted and stored in the Lady-Protector's strong room off the formal study. Mykella's search had turned up nothing that she might have called easily moved valuables, such as jewelry or coins—except for the three chests . . . and close to one hundred sumptuous dresses and gowns, none of which could have been sewn for less than five to ten golds apiece. There were also more than threescore ladies' riding outfits, thirty pair of leather boots, and over a hundred pair of shoes. *All that in less than two years?* Mykella had marveled.

A small chest in Berenyt's quarters contained fifty-seven golds, and forty silvers and some coppers had appeared in drawers and pouches throughout the villa. The three chests from the hidden study held one thousand seven hundred and eleven golds, a hundred forty-three silvers, and eighty-four coppers. That sum—and even the cost of Cheleyza's finery—left unanswered the question of what had happened to the larger part of the more than ten thousand golds, if not more, siphoned from the accounts of the Lord-Protector while Joramyl had been Finance Minister. She'd located three hidden chambers, one of which had held a score of ancient sabers, but found no other golds.

Mykella was sitting alone at the desk in the formal study when the door eased open and Salyna stepped inside.

"You didn't eat anything . . ."

"I didn't get back until a little while ago."

"Where were you?"

"At Joramyl's villa . . ." Mykella went on to explain what she had found—and what she had not, ending with, ". . . was just thinking about what to do next."

"You might think about eating." Salyna paused. "Over a hundred fancy dresses and gowns? She was only married to Uncle Joramyl two years. That's a new fancy dress every tenday—and there are five balls a year, something like nine if you count the Seltyrs' functions."

"I haven't counted," replied Mykella dryly. "Rachylana could tell us the number and how long each lasted to the glass."

Salyna winced. "You're being cruel."

"Cruel . . . but accurate."

"You need to eat. I had Muergya leave a warm plate for you. It's probably not warm now, but it's still good. I'll keep you company."

The two sisters walked back to the breakfast room, where Mykella sat down and began to eat a cooling fowl pie. A half loaf of dark bread and a beaker of cider sat on the table.

"What are you going to do the rest of the afternoon?" asked Salyna

"Study maps," replied Mykella after taking several more mouthfuls.

"You're not an Arms-Commander."

"No . . . but I want to understand what my Arms-Commander tells me."

"Mykella . . . do you trust anyone?"

"I trust you. I trust Commander Areyst." She paused. "Just because someone is trustworthy doesn't mean they'll make the right decision. The more I know . . ." She shrugged.

"You have something in mind, don't you?"

"I have an idea. The maps might help to see if it's workable."

"If not?"

"Then I'll have to think of something else."

"Do you really think Northcoast and Midcoast will invade La-nachrona?"

"I'd be foolish not to prepare for that, but I think they will. So does the commander. So, for that matter, does Rachylana. Envoy Malaryk and Majer Smoltak both hinted at it."

"What will you do?"

"Commander Areyst is marshaling the Southern Guards in Viencet. I'll study the maps and see what I can do."

"You said that before."

Mykella smiled. "I know."

"Sometimes, you're impossible."

"I won't know what I can do until I know more."

Salyna just shook her head.

After eating, Mykella finished the cider in the beaker, then rose from the table. "Thank you. I did need to eat. I'll see you later. Would you look in on Rachylana now and again."

Salyna nodded. "She's still brooding. Later . . ."

Mykella nodded. She understood that as well, even though she didn't want to have to worry about Rachylana on top of everything else. As she walked back to the formal study, thinking about Rachylana and her concerns about matching, Mykella wondered if she'd hear anything, directly or indirectly, from Prince Skrelyn's envoy. The odds were she would, if only so that he could report something back to the prince.

Once she returned to the study, after stopping by her quarters for her nightsilk riding jacket, Mykella pored over the maps, tracing the hills that bordered the southern bank of the River Vedra between Tempre and the Midcoast border, those that were closest to the north-ern highway. After a glass, she closed the folio and pulled on her rid-ing jacket, then walked to the window, where she could touch the granite. She reached out to the greenish darkness beneath the palace, let it enfold her, and slipped downward through the stone to the Table chamber.

When she emerged, she paused. Did the Table display a slightly brighter purplish pink than it had since she'd defeated the Ifrit or its creation? Strengthening her shields, she moved closer, but she could sense nothing that suggested the presence of an Ifrit, even one watching her through the Table from wherever it was that the Ifrits lived. Still . . . the pinkish purple seemed brighter, and she'd have to watch that as well.

Looking down at the mirrored surface of the Table, she focused her attention on Cheleyza. The mists appeared, swirled, and revealed her aunt still upon a barge, looking windblown and angry. Mykella couldn't help but smile. Cheleyza deserved whatever misery befell her. Quick searches through the Table revealed Areyst in an armory, Maxymt riding a horse westward along a dirt track rather than an eternastone road, and Seltyr Porofyr standing on a balcony, his face impassive.

Mykella stepped back, watching the mists vanish, and concentrated on the blackness below, letting herself meld with it and slip downward through the stone into the bone-chilling darkness. She pressed westward along the underground way, trying to judge how far she had come. She thought she felt the silver heaviness of the river to her right, and she tried to keep herself well within the blackness but not too far from the river. After a time, she sensed she was getting farther from the river, and she let herself rise through the earth and stone, only to find herself in the middle of a field. The damp earth was littered with limp tannish stalks, most likely of beans, remaining from the previous fall.

To the west, according to the sun, the field extended less than a hundred yards, ending at a low stone and earthen berm. South of her was a small cot with an outbuilding, and behind it a low line of hills. She turned and saw a line of trees to the north. Was that the Vedra?

Abruptly, she was surrounded by a mist that quickly dispersed. For a moment, she puzzled, but realized that the chill of her riding jacket had created a frost that had turned to mist. While the spring afternoon was cool, the air felt pleasant after the chill of the depths.

She raised a concealment shield. Could she soar any, drawing from the blackness beneath the field?

After recalling that feeling, which took several moments, because it had been weeks since the single time she had tried soaring, she rose from the ground and directed herself toward the hills beyond the cot. According to the maps, the hills curved more to the south just to the west of Viencet, but did the blackness follow the hills or parallel the eternastone highway or . . . ?

She had no idea. She was ruler of Lanachrona, and she knew so little of the land beyond Tempre . . . and less of the people.

She managed to travel across the field and past the cot and perhaps half a vingt toward the hills before she could feel her ties to the blackness weaken. She eased herself back down onto the winter-matted grass and studied the meadow and the scattered trees at the base of the nearest hill, estimating they were another vingt away. She wasn't about to walk away from where she could reach the blackness beneath the ground.

She turned back toward the cot, noting a thin trail of smoke rising from the mud-brick chimney. Whoever lived there could surely tell her where she was.

By the time she reached the narrow track that passed for a road, her boots were caked in mud, and she stopped to scrape the worst off on a stone. She glanced eastward toward several cots a vingt or so along the road, There was nothing to the west, except hills and woods. If those woods were part of the reserve woodlands held by the Lord-Protector . . . *Lady-Protector*—once she got back to the palace, the maps might help her figure out where she'd been.

She dropped the concealment and raised her shields tightly about her, then walked up the packed-clay path toward the cot.

A woman with braided black hair, clad in a shapeless gray garment that might have once been a dress, opened the door before Mykella reached it. Her face was worn and haggard. "Where did you come from, girl?"

"Where am I?" asked Mykella, not wanting to answer the woman's question.

"Standing in front of Tedor's and my cot, I'd be thinking." From inside the cot came the gurgling cry of an infant.

"How far is it to Viencet? Which way?"

"You'd be thinking of walking there?" The woman shook her head. "It'd be another day's walk. You'd best cross the hills to the old road first."

"The eternastone road that the . . . Southern Guards and the traders use?"

"The shiny stone one that never wears out. Aye . . . that'd be the one."

"How far is it across the hills?"

"As long as it takes. Half a morning, maybe less, ifn you walk quick-like."

"What's the nearest hamlet or town?"

"Meithyl . . . just up the way." The woman pointed eastward.

"Is there any hamlet to the west on this road?"

That got Mykella a headshake. "Them's the Lord-Protector's woods. Wouldn't want to be going there. Foresters'll flog you, they catch you."

Mykella fumbled in her belt pouch. Did she even have any coins? She felt one, two . . . They were silvers. She eased one from the pouch and extended it to the woman. "Thank you."

The woman's eyes opened. Then her mouth did. "What . . ."

Mykella felt embarrassed. "Please take it."

The woman finally did.

At that, Mykella dropped her shields. She stepped backwards from the stoop of the cot, then reached to the blackness and let it enfold her, sinking back to the chill beneath.

She looked so . . . old . . . tired . . . Yet, Mykella realized, the woman probably was less than ten years older than she was.

Pushing that thought away for a moment, Mykella pressed westward through the darkness for about as long, she felt, as it had taken her to reach where she had first stopped. Then she eased her way upward. It seemed to take longer. *Is that because you're getting tired?*

She emerged in the shadows of a wooded hillside, where the ground sloped upwards to the south. She decided on body-shields, rather than concealment, and began to walk, deciding that trying to soar through the woods would be unwise, given her lack of practice in avoiding things, because, while she could hold concealment while soaring, she could not hold body-shields as well . . . and sometimes not either, depending on how strong her ties to the blackness were. The trees were mostly evergreens, predominantly pines that seemed to top out at less than ten yards. The soil was dry and even rocky in places, and that suggested she was definitely more to the west, because Jeraxylt had mentioned how much drier the land was nearer the border with Midcoast.

After perhaps a quarter glass, she reached the crest of the hillside, but she could still hold her contact with the darkness deep below. More time passed before she could find a clearing from which she could look out to the south.

The trees ended at the base of the hills, a good two vingts to the south, over uneven sloping ground, and grasslands stretched farther southward, with widely spaced cots and one more substantial holding. She *thought* she could see a thin shimmering gray line in the distance, running east to west.

Could she soar above the low treetops and get a better view?

She dropped the personal shield and drew more strongly on the greenish darkness and rose, but as she neared the tops of the pines, she could definitely feel a shakiness to her control, and she quickly scanned the horizon from one side to the other. Back to the east was a town. That she could see clearly, and it was more than a hamlet. She guessed it was a good five, perhaps ten vingts away, and it looked large enough to be Viencet. She dropped slowly to the rocky ground, scattered with patches of grass and scraggly low bushes . . . and found herself breathing heavily.

For a time, she just stood there in the hazy late-afternoon sunlight, regaining her strength.

Why do you have to be so small? Why?

Complaining to herself wouldn't help, and once she felt more back to normal, she began to walk downhill, trying to see how far she could go toward the town before she began to sense a weakening of her ability to draw on the darkness.

She walked almost a vingt, and her feet were getting sore, her boots and trousers dusty, before she felt the attenuation of the darkness. The base of the forest was still more than a vingt away, and the road three or four times that. After taking a deep breath, she walked back uphill until she could feel the full strength of the darkness beneath, then called upon it.

The return to Tempre was far easier because she could sense the bluish point of light—that was what it seemed to be—that marked the Table, above the darkness of the path she traveled. Even so, she was shivering and light-headed when she emerged in the formal study.

That didn't stop her from going to the map folio and immediately studying it. Although she couldn't be absolutely certain, Viencet was the only large town located on the ancient eternastone road to the west of Tempre . . . unless she'd taken the black pathway along the more southern road to Zalt . . . but the flat showed no hills there, and the only town was almost to the border claimed by Southgate. Of course, the hamlet named Meithyl wasn't on the map, nor was the dirt road it was located beside. But the forest reserve was shown, and it seemed to match where she'd been.

Seemed . . . appeared . . . might . . . Mykella wanted to scream. The black paths underlying Corus didn't go where she hoped they would, and that was going to make everything difficult. *Again.*

She shivered and took another deep breath. She'd just have to keep trying . . . and she definitely needed something to eat.

8

Although all the ministries in the palace were closed on Decdi, leaving the lower-level corridors empty and quiet, except for the guards, Mykella didn't sleep all that much later than usual, possibly because she'd gone to bed early. She was up with the sun and in the breakfast room while the morning shadows were still completely cloaking the palace courtyards. She was finishing a cheese omelet, along with greasy ham strips when Salyna sat down across from her.

"You ate all of that?" asked her youngest sister.

Mykella nodded, then took a bite of dark bread slathered heavily with orange molasses preserves.

"You've never eaten that much," observed Salyna. "Ever."

"I was hungry." Mykella took a swallow of hot tea, and another bite of bread.

"From studying maps?" Salyna shook her head "You had Zestela clean your boots. They were covered in mud, she said. What did you do? Tromp around the gardens in the rain in the middle of the night?"

"I've had a lot of thinking to do." Mykella forbore to point out that it hadn't rained that much, especially on Novdi night.

"Things won't happen that quickly. Other rulers don't even know you're Lady-Protector yet."

"That's why I have to think now. If I wait to figure things out, it will be too late." *That's what happened with Father and Joramyl. By the time I understood, Father was dead.*

"You have to worry, but I think you're worrying too much."

"Do you want to go for a ride today?"

"I'm always interested in getting out of the palace. Where? In the Preserve?"

"No. I want to take the north highway toward Viencet and explore some side lanes."

"I can do that. Could I ask why?"

"I've discovered there are too many things I don't know about, except what I read and what people have told me. I need to see more."

Salyna raised her eyebrows.

"I am Lady-Protector for all the people of Lanachrona, not just of the factors and Seltyrs . . . and those with golds."

"If those with golds do not support you, you will not remain Lady-Protector."

"If those without golds do not support me as well, I will not re-main Lady-Protector that much longer. They are the ones who bring goods to market, who toil in the fields, who are servants in the palace and elsewhere, and who join the ranks of the Southern Guards."

"They don't count," said Rachylana from the door to the breakfast room. "They've always done what others have told them, and they always will."

"Like the women of Tempre?" asked Mykella gently.

"I suppose you'll have to find out for yourself, won't you?" replied the redhead. "As always. Except everyone else will keep paying while you try to make your romantic tales come true. They usually don't, you know?"

Salyna could not quite conceal a wince.

Mykella merely replied, "Some things each of us has to find out for herself, and they're often very different things. Would you care to join us on a ride?" She rose from the table.

"I think not. Even the common folk might find that . . . frivolous, so soon after so much tragedy."

Clad in black . . . I think not. But Mykella did not voice that

After she left the breakfast room, Mykella stopped by the two guards at the top of the wide stairway and asked one to convey a message to the duty section leader that she and Salyna would be taking a ride to the southwest. Then she returned to her quarters and finished dressing, not that what she wore to ride in was any different from her daily wear, except for a riding jacket and gloves, both of nightsilk.

Salyna met her in the main upper corridor, and they headed down to the lower level, then to the eastern door to the courtyard.

Mykella was more than a little surprised to find Commander Areyst mounted and waiting in the palace courtyard, but she concealed—she hoped—the feeling and smiled. "Good morning, Commander. I hope I'm not taking you away from other duties."

"On a Decdi . . . that I can manage, Lady." He inclined his head, then smiled at her.

The warmth behind his smile almost halted her, but she mounted the gray quickly. Behind her, Salyna mounted the big chestnut she favored.

As they rode out of the courtyard, with Mykella in the middle flanked by Areyst to her left and Salyna to her right, and toward the avenue fronting the palace, Areyst said mildly, "You didn't tell the duty-squad leader the purpose of this ride."

"No, I didn't. It's a ride of exploration . . . or of looking at Tempre and the highway and what lies beside and around it in a different way." That was certainly true, if on two levels. "I've doubtless been too sheltered, and I need to spend some time seeing things with my own eyes."

"On horseback, you'll still be sheltered in some ways." His voice was pleasant.

"That's true, but I'll have to try to look beyond that." She guided the gray to the right and westward onto the avenue that led to the Great Piers before it turned and angled southwest through Tempre. At the same time, she raised her shields. Given the reactions of the late Commander Nephryt, Seltyr Porofyr, and even her own father's feelings about women in power, she had no doubts that she offered a target every time she appeared in public.

Two Southern Guards rode around the three and took station a good five yards ahead.

"Commander . . . I have a favor to ask."

"Yes, Lady?"

"Do you recall Majer Allahyr?"

"Quite well. He was a good soldier, excellent grasp of tactics. Why?"

"I would like to request that his survivor's stipend—the stipend that should have gone to his widow—be reinstated and paid to his daughters. Until they are wed, of course."

"Do you intend to make that a practice, Lady?"

"I would think it should be in the case where both the Southern Guard and his widow have died, leaving sons or daughters too young to fend for themselves properly. I cannot imagine that this happens often enough to cause a drain on the accounts."

"It has not." Areyst nodded. "It might be more likely if the princes of the west attack."

"If we prevail, we can afford it. If not . . ."

"Then I will draft a change to the stipend rules for your signature, Lady."

"Thank you."

"It is a good idea. Many have felt that Majer Allahyr and Majer

Querlyt were forced to take early stipends because they had no choice after the deaths of their consorts."

"If there are other changes you think would improve matters with the Southern Guards, please don't hesitate to let me know."

"What about women in the Guards?" asked Salyna.

Areyst grinned before replying. "Lady Salyna, there are but a handful of women with your ability with arms, and that is far too few to comprise a squad, let alone a company."

"They could be trained," persisted Salyna.

"They could," agreed Areyst, "but not in time for the battles to come this year."

"What if . . . after we deal with the west . . . Salyna began to train women?" asked Mykella. "Couldn't they be used as auxiliaries . . . or for other duties, such as reinstituting the tariff stations on the highways?"

Areyst's eyes turned on Mykella. "That might prove useful, but only if you are successful in maintaining your rule."

In short, if you find a way to beat down and back Northcoast and Midcoast, you can do anything you want. But not until. Mykella smiled pleasantly and turned to Salyna. "I think the commander has given the most generous reply possible."

Salyna frowned, then nodded abruptly.

Mykella looked to her left at the park that fronted the palace on the other side of the avenue. Some of the trees were ancient, but their limbs sagged, and the borders of the walks were ragged. *Is all Tempre like that? If it's like that across from the palace . . .* She almost sighed.

Beyond the park and the palace grounds began the trading quarter of Tempre, with the crafters' shops and the buildings that held smaller traders. The size and exterior appointments of the buildings they passed improved as they neared the Great Piers, although the worn stone walks flanking the avenue were largely empty, as was normal for midmorning on Decdi.

A gray-haired woman quickly grasped the arms of a small boy and girl—possibly grandchildren—to keep them from running across in front of the horses. Mykella smiled and nodded to the woman. The only response was a stone-faced stare.

Are even the women dubious? Mykella almost snorted. Was there any doubt?

From the shoreward side of the Great Piers extended a stretch of pavement where, during the week, peddlers and itinerant merchants set up stands and tents—provided they paid a copper a day to the portmaster. Not a single tent was visible. Mykella glanced past Salyna to her right at the Great Piers, where she'd often stood beside her father and brother in the reviewing stand for the regular season-turn parades. The last time she had stood there had barely been a tenday ago, for her father's memorial procession. It seemed so long ago . . . and yet like yesterday.

At the end of the piers, the avenue turned to the southwest. From there it was so straight that not a trace of a curve was visible. Mykella could still sense the darkness beneath the piers, but that dark path felt as though it was diverging ever so slightly from the eternastone highway.

South of the piers, the dwellings on the north side of the avenue, those almost backing up to the towpath of the river, were all of two stories; but they were older, and worn, with the whitewash over the plastered stone showing a dinginess in places, and chipped areas where the less expensive dark stone and yellow brick showed through. In places, the shutters hung less than straight. Once the houses might have been the homes of smaller factors and more successful crafters. Now, each looked to hold several families.

From a sagging second-level balcony several blocks farther from the piers, four small children peered at the riders over a white railing whose whitewash was flaking and dingy gray. Their faces were gaunt, their eyes not quite vacant, and the wind from the west carried definite unsavory odors, presumably from the alleyways behind the slowly decaying structures.

"This isn't the best section of Tempre, Lady," offered Areyst.

Mykella knew that, but she hadn't looked quite so closely at the houses the few times she'd ridden past the piers. Most of the time she had ridden through the city, it had been on the other main avenue, the one to the east that led to the villa where Joramyl had lived.

In less than half a glass, they reached the low wall that had once marked the edge of Tempre—and still did, if not absolutely, since a few handfuls of huts and small dwellings dotted some of the fields to the southwest.

"I'd like to follow that lane to the right—the one short of the orchard," Mykella said.

"It probably doesn't go very far," said Salyna.

"It may not, but that's something I need to know."

Mykella did recognize the trees on the left side of the lane— apricots, one of the better orchard crops of Lanachrona.

Surprisingly, the lane did not end but curved westward around the back of the large orchard and over an old timbered bridge, under which ran an empty irrigation canal, diverging gradually from the eternastone road, so that Mykella could sense the darkness beneath although it was still too far to the north of her to be able to draw on it easily.

"You're trying something with Talent, aren't you?" murmured Salyna. "Is that why we're here?"

"Partly," replied Mykella in an equally low voice.

There were no more lanes that branched farther north toward the river, and in the end, they had to ride down an overgrown path to return to the main highway. Although Mykella sensed a greater divergence between the eternastone highway and the darkness beneath, she kept riding for another glass and a half before turning back.

In a few places, holders were beginning to work on fields and orchards, but most holdings looked barren and dreary, and despite just a slight chill in the air, Mykella saw no signs of spring growth. The return through the west side of Tempre was even more depressing than the ride out had been, most likely because she saw more and more signs of neglect in all-too-many buildings.

When they returned to the palace in early afternoon, it was clear to Mykella that she could not draw fully upon the deep darkness from the main highway, not unless her abilities improved, or unless there was a dark pathway nearer the highway farther to the west. The underground travel of the day before had suggested that, but she had needed to know more clearly.

When she reined up in the palace courtyard, she turned to Areyst. "Thank you, Commander. I do appreciate your company and solicitude. I will be taking more rides through Tempre this coming week, most likely one every day until I have seen more of what I need to see. While I appreciate your company, I would not wish to impose on you personally."

"I understand. I appreciate your concerns, but for the time being, either Captain Maeltor or I will ride with the squad accompanying you."

Mykella nodded, then dismounted, handing the gray's reins to the guard who had stepped up. She felt guilty in not grooming the gelding, but insisting on doing so at a time when it didn't matter would only have been an empty gesture. "My thanks, again, Commander."

"My pleasure, Lady."

Salyna didn't say anything until they were inside the palace and walking the empty lower corridor back to the staircase. "You're going to keep doing this? All over Tempre?"

"How else will I learn the condition of things?"

"What did you learn today?"

"That part of Tempre is very shabby, and that it didn't used to be." *And that the blackness doesn't follow the highway even close to Tempre.*

"That bothers you, doesn't it?"

"It does."

"Mykella . . . I shouldn't have to tell you this, but there aren't enough golds in all Corus to pay to keep everything painted and repaired."

"That part of town once was . . . If too much of Tempre is like that, something's wrong, and has been for a while. That's why I need to ride through all the city."

"If you find it too much that way, then what will you do?"

"That depends on what I see in the areas where the Seltyrs and High Factors live."

"Mykella . . ." Salyna broke off her words as she looked at her sister, shaking her head.

After several moments, as the two passed the guards and started up the steps to the upper level, Salyna spoke again. "The commander likes you, but he's very proper."

"He's cautious . . . very cautious."

"With you, that's wise."

Because he knows I can kill him without a weapon . . . or because he might feel something for me and doesn't wish to be rejected? Mykella hoped it was more of the second than the first, but she stifled a rueful laugh, brought on by the realization that, if Areyst truly felt the first, he was only experiencing what all too many women had felt for too many years. "With any ruler, that's wise."

"You took a long time to say that."

"I was thinking. I'm also hungry."

Salyna nodded.

Mykella headed for the breakfast room and the serving pantry, where there should at least be bread and cheese. Later, after she ate, she would need to scout the paths of blackness to the west and use the Table to check on people, especially Cheleyza and Porofyr, as well as others, at least until she was certain those others posed no threat.

9

Londi morning dawned bright and clear, but Mykella didn't feel that cheerful. On Decdi afternoon, she'd retreated to her apartments and slid into the darkness to explore farther to the west of Viencet. According to the maps and her own deductions, she'd covered perhaps another thirty vingts west of the town that held the Southern Guard's training base—and nowhere was there a black path closer than two vingts to the eternastone highway, and the closest she could get to the town proper and still draw upon the blackness was a good vingt and a half north, still in the wooded low hills. That wouldn't do at all.

When she had returned from her covert explorations for dinner with her sisters, Rachylana had remained as withdrawn as before, with occasional cutting comments, and Salyna was reserved, as if wary of a sister she wasn't certain she understood any longer.

Mykella had gone to bed early, but her sleep had been restless, and she was more than glad to get up. Breakfast conversation was not much better than that at dinner had been although she was pleasant. After she hurried through her food, Mykella returned to her chambers, ostensibly to wash up and prepare for the day. Those tasks completed, she did not immediately leave for her formal study but instead walked to the window, touched the granite, called upon the greenish darkness, and slipped through the stone down to the Table chamber. The first thing that struck her was that the Table was shrouded in a brighter and stronger pinkish purple, a color that only she, and perhaps Areyst, could see, although it was more that they sensed it within their minds than saw with their eyes. Raising her shields, she stepped closer to the Table. The surface remained a shimmering mirror, and she could not sense any Ifrits. Still, the color concerned her.

After a moment, she concentrated on Cheleyza. The image that appeared displayed her aunt in some sort of inn or public room, at a corner table, with three men, one of whom looked vaguely familiar. Mykella thought that he might be Paelyt, the steward who had come to Tempre with Cheleyza and departed with her as well, but she wasn't certain. Not for the first time, she wished she'd been more attentive in years past. Mykella couldn't tell from the public room in what town or city it was located, but the most likely wager was that it was in Hieron, because that was where one of the ancient bridges of the Alectors crossed the Vedra and from where Cheleyza could ride straight north on an eternastone highway to Harmony. That was a guess, but Mykella doubted that her aunt could have gotten any farther than Hieron in the five days since she'd fled Tempre. To have done even that would have meant paying extra for the barge to stay on the river at night.

The Table showed her nothing new or revealing about Maxymt or Treghyt, except that both appeared on their way away from Tempre, and Porofyr was seated in his counting room, a vaguely pleased smile on his face that troubled Mykella. After letting the former minister's image fade, she studied the Table again, convinced that it held a brighter shade. Yet . . . what could she do except keep checking?

She returned to her private study by the same stealthy method by which she had departed, then walked from her apartments down the corridor to the anteroom to her formal study.

Chalmyr was already there and waiting. "Good morning, Lady."

"Good morning. Has either Khanasyl or Lhanyr answered my notes?"

"Not yet, Lady."

"Are there any other missives? Have you heard anything from Prince Skrelyn's envoy?" Her own words reminded her of the promise to Majer Smoltak of a missive for Envoy Sheorak.

"No, Lady."

Mykella could tell that Chalmyr was skeptical about hearing from the envoy. *He might be right about that.* "Is there anything else I should know about?"

"Captain Maeltor left word that there was a fire in one of High Factor Hasenyt's warehouses."

Mykella thought. *Was that why Porofyr was smiling? Is there anything I can do about that right now . . . or at all?* "Is Hasenyt all right?"

"Captain Maeltor said that he was not injured and that the damage was limited to his smallest warehouse."

"Thank you for letting me know."

Mykella entered the formal study, closing the door. Hasenyt had been the first High Factor to support her, in the moments after she had executed Joramyl. Just how likely was it that the fire in his warehouse was coincidence? Especially after seeing Porofyr's face? *Not all that likely.*

Hasenyt was one of the few factors she'd met personally before her father's murder, but she'd only been to his villa once. *You should have paid more attention.* But she hadn't.

She eased the study door back open. "Chalmyr? I'll need the addresses of Hasenyt's warehouse, his factorage, and his villa."

"Captain Maeltor provided the address of the warehouse. I'll have one of the duty guards obtain the others."

"Thank you." Mykella closed the door and walked to the study window, looking across the courtyard, then at the park across the avenue. How could she determine whether Porofyr had acted against Hasenyt? Even if she could determine that, she doubted if there would be any real proof. *Is it always going to be like this?*

She took a deep breath and returned to the desk, where she opened the map folder, trying to plot out where she should make her next Talent trip. Abruptly, she stood. There was one other matter she'd forgotten.

Making her way to the end bookcase, she pressed the hidden catch, and the bookcase swung open to reveal an iron door. She unlocked it and opened it, revealing a second door, also locked. In turn she unlocked that and stepped into the small stone-walled and iron-paneled storeroom. From the small chest on the front shelf, she took twenty golds and twenty silvers and slipped them into her belt wallet. Then she closed the chest and left, relocking the doors and replacing the bookcase. She'd never carried that many golds, but, given what she was trying to do, having some coins seemed like a sensible precaution.

Recalling the missive she had not yet written, she pushed aside the map folio and picked up the pen, taking a deep breath. Writing and rewriting that short letter took three attempts, and almost a glass . . . and in the end she had a draft with which she wasn't exactly pleased. She ran her eyes over a very rough draft, catching the key phrases.

. . . we assure you that Lanachrona has every wish to remain friendly toward all, but particularly toward those, such as Deforya, who have treated with respect and courtesy, and certainly in the future, once matters are settled, we look forward to considering the matter of possible matches. . . .

Chalmyr can smooth this out and add more flourishes.

At least, it conveyed the idea that, once matters were settled in Tempre, she would consider matches. She took that to Chalmyr, asking him to redraft it in his elegant script. She had barely seated herself back at the desk with the map folio than there was a rap on the door.

"Captain Maeltor is here, Lady," announced Chalmyr.

"Have him come in." Mykella did not rise but merely waited for the captain to enter and close the door.

"The commander said that you would be making inspection rides through Tempre, Lady. Might I inquire as to when you would like to depart the palace?"

"A half glass. I'd like to begin by riding by where the fire destroyed High Factor Hasenyt's warehouse."

"Yes, Lady."

"We'll proceed from there, as necessary."

Once Maeltor departed, Mykella made another study of the maps, then sat at the desk, wondering to what degree she should consult Lhanyr and Khanasyl in the matter of appointing a successor to Porofyr. She shook her head. She had no one in mind. Even if she had, any decision should follow meetings with the two highest-ranking traders in Tempre.

She left the formal study before a full half glass had passed, but the gray gelding and Maeltor and the Guard squad were waiting in the courtyard under a hazy silver-green sky. Once she mounted, two guards led the way from the palace grounds, first westward on the avenue, then south. Hasenyt's factorage was less than two vingts away, roughly south-southeast of the Great Piers. Three warehouses stood forming three sides of a square around a central courtyard for loading and unloading. The trading building of the factorage formed the fourth side of the square and faced south.

Mykella and the captain had reined up before the porch of the building. While she had only been able to glimpse the fire damage from the gap between buildings as she rode up, she could certainly smell the odor of burned wood and other items in the damp spring air.

At that moment, a man stepped out from the double doors under the square arch in the middle of the building. Even though he was shaded by the overhanging eaves that formed the roof on the narrow porch, Mykella easily recognized him, a dark-haired and dark-bearded man some ten years younger than her father, she judged, and perhaps fifteen years older than she was.

"Lady-Protector . . . I did not expect . . ."

"The fire was not an accident, was it?" Mykella looked straight at the High Factor.

Hasenyt offered a rueful and sad smile. "It would seem unlikely, but none of the watchmen saw anything."

"Are they still here?"

"Ah . . . yes, Lady. I was just speaking to them."

"I would speak to them as well."

Hasenyt's eyes flicked from Mykella to Maeltor, then back to the Lady-Protector. After a long pause, he replied. "Of course."

"Separately," Mykella said, adding as she sensed Maeltor's apprehension, "with you and the captain, of course. They're in the building here?"

"Yes, Lady."

Mykella used the only mounting block in front of the factorage, then followed Hasenyt inside, followed by Maeltor and two Southern Guards. She didn't have to go far because both men were in the anteroom just inside the double doors. They sat on a bench against the side wall.

Beside them were two large men with truncheons. Both men looked puzzled to see Mykella.

Mykella repressed an ironic smile as she stopped some three yards from the bench, with Hasenyt to her right and Maeltor to her left. Clearly, Hasenyt had the same suspicions she did . . . or he just held the two responsible for not doing more to stop the fire.

"Naulyn, take Scerpio to my study. Close the door." The High Factor looked at the younger burly man on the bench. "Dionyl . . . the Lady-Protector has some questions for you."

Dionyl stood slowly, almost insolently, as Naulyn marched Scerpio through a door at the left rear of the antechamber.

"Were you the one who discovered the fire?" asked Mykella, trying to get a feel for the man but sensing little but contempt mixed with apprehension.

"Yes."

"Scerpio didn't see or smell it first?"

"No."

Mykella could sense the absolute truth of the responses. She could also see the frown on Hasenyt's face, as well as sense Maeltor's growing anger. She smiled and turned to the captain. "If you would, Captain . . . I'm certain Dionyl will reveal what really happened." Then she turned back to the watchman. "Why didn't Scerpio see it?"

"I don't know."

That was a lie. Mykella nodded. "Did you see the fire first or smell it? And where were you?"

"I was in the courtyard, walkin' from the west building to the north one, and I saw the flames coming from behind the big center door."

Another lie. "Just behind the door?"

"Close to it."

Mykella looked to Hasenyt. "I assume all the doors are on the courtyard side of the warehouses, and that there aren't any doors or windows on the street side. I didn't see any."

"That's correct, Lady," answered the factor.

"Dionyl . . . you didn't see anyone in the courtyard, except Scerpio, then?"

"I didn't see no one. Didn't mean someone wasn't there. It was a dark night."

Dionyl wasn't that bright because Selena had been full, and the night had been clear. But he had been telling the truth about not seeing anyone.

"How long did it take for the fire to catch after you set it—"

In a single flowing movement, the man drew a throwing knife and released it. The weapon struck Mykella's shields and half bounced, half dropped to the stone floor of the factorage. Hasenyt's mouth dropped open.

Absently, Mykella wondered why he was surprised since he'd observed Nephryt's futile attempt to decapitate her. At least, he'd been there. Or had he not believed what he had seen?

The man drew a long dagger from his boot.

This time Mykella was ready, and she took two steps sideways to place herself between Hasenyt and the attack, anchoring her shields to the stone. The attacker struck the shields with such force that he staggered back and went to his knees, dropping the dagger.

Maeltor stepped forward and clubbed the half-stunned figure with the hilt of his saber. The man sprawled facedown on the stone. The two Southern Guards pinned his still-struggling figure and began to tie him up.

Hasenyt swallowed.

In a few moments, Dionyl was trussed and held on the bench.

"Who paid you?" asked Mykella.

"I didn't do it."

"That's a lie." Mykella drew the faintest bit of light to her, just enough to make her entire figure seem brighter. "You can't lie to me without my knowing it."

Dionyl's eyes widened, and one of the Southern Guards gulped.

"Who paid you?" Mykella added Talent to her words, and the watchman shuddered.

". . . don't know . . . wore gray cloaks and hoods . . . caught me in the alley near Lhaed's . . . said if I said anything . . . turn my little brother into a woman . . . gave me two golds . . ." Dionyl shuddered again. ". . . what else . . . do . . ."

"He's telling the truth about that." Mykella turned to Hasenyt. "Someone might try to find his brother."

The factor nodded to the remaining man with a truncheon, who eased from the anteroom.

"I think that's a fair indication that the fire wasn't an accident," Mykella said dryly. "Let's see what the other warehouse guard has to say. Oh . . . and check Dionyl's purse although I can't believe he'd have kept what he was paid there."

Mykella questioned Scerpio in Hasenyt's study, a smaller chamber less than a third the size of the anteroom. Scerpio had little enough to say because he'd been asleep after drinking some of the wine that his compatriot had offered him.

Then Hasenyt's guard marched Scerpio out, and Mykella turned to Hasenyt.

"Who do you think paid Dionyl?"

"It could be one of several . . . or someone I do not even suspect."

"I would doubt that you do not have a good idea of who your enemies are."

"You are more formidable than many would believe, Lady-

Protector," replied the High Factor Hasenyt, "but there will be no proof at all of what I think and whatever you suspect."

Mykella was certain that he was correct about that. "For now, High Factor. For now."

Hasenyt nodded slowly.

Mykella understood all too well what he thought—that more of those thought to support her would suffer before anything remotely resembling proof would appear . . . if it ever did. While she wanted to promise to discover who was responsible, saying so would be unwise, especially since, even if she did discover the guilty party, it was more than likely she'd lack any proof to convince anyone but herself. "I am sorry for this, and I will not forget." *That . . . I can pledge.*

"Thank you, Lady-Protector." Even so, his eyes were sad.

After Mykella left the factorage and remounted the gray, Maeltor looked questioningly at her.

"Why?" she asked. "Because there are those who do not wish there to be honest and inquisitive rulers." *Particularly if they're women.* "We can ride south from here, can we not, then go east and take another boulevard back to the palace?"

"Yes, Lady."

"Then let us do so."

"That route will not be pleasant."

"Good."

Mykella could sense that her reply puzzled the captain, but she wasn't about to explain. Not yet, anyway. After riding a good six blocks south past other factorages and crafting shops, she turned the gray to the west, toward a small square, where another avenue ran north and south. The square was little more than a wide paved space where the boulevard and avenue crossed. From the pattern of stones in the center, once there might have been a statue in the middle. On the southwest corner stood an older inn, its stucco recently whitewashed, and the railings on the side porch shimmering with new varnish. The sign proclaimed TRAVELER'S REST.

Mykella turned north. After less than a block, she began to notice an unpleasant odor, clearly of human wastes. As she rode past an alley, she saw piles of night soil. *Why?*

Unfortunately, that odor was mild compared to the stench that began to seep into her nostrils after another three blocks, one that seemed to come from the west on the light breeze. After another block or so, looking down alleys and between gaps in buildings, mostly holding crafters, she could make out what looked to be a canal or the stone walls of a confined river.

"I want to look at the canal."

"It's the South River, Lady."

"It shouldn't smell like that," observed Mykella.

"It has since I was a ranker here ten years ago." Maeltor paused. "Maybe not this bad, though."

As she neared the river, still on the east side, they rode into the metalworking quarter, where smoke and haze air filled the air. While the buildings were set back from the river, and no open ditches led down the short slope from the structures to the river, two covered pipes led into the water, and an oily residue drifted downstream from the area of the pipes. That vaguely bluish shimmer on the water was not visible upstream from the pipes, suggesting strongly that some of the metalworks were letting wastes pour into the river.

Mykella shook her head but directed the gray onto the narrow lane along the east side of the water, little more than an alleyway that ran north from the bridge across the river that she had not taken. On the far side, Mykella noted two large walled areas within which stood several low buildings. Grayish smoke swirled upward from wide brick chimneys. As she looked more closely, she saw that protruding from the walls above the river were large clay pipes from which thin lines of brownish-grayish fluid flowed into the river.

"What are those?" she asked, pointing.

"Rendering yards, tanneries, where they turn animal fat into oils, skins and hides into leather . . ."

It was almost midday when Mykella ordered her escorts to head east to the next boulevard and begin the return to the palace.

Once she was back in her formal study, she wanted to look at the rules for metalworks, tanneries, and rendering yards. There was something she'd heard years before. . . . Had her father said that they weren't supposed to let their wastes flow into the rivers, or that they shouldn't be allowed to do that? He'd been talking with Joramyl, she thought, but . . .

Either way, she needed to know.

10

Once Mykella returned to the palace, after signing the recopied missive to the Landarch of Deforya, it took her only a fraction of a quarter glass to find the book that held the rules for sewers and rivers, but more than three-quarters of a glass to locate the sections dealing with rendering yards and tanneries. To her, at least, the wording seemed clear.

> . . . no liquid waste from carcasses, offal, or other sources used by a rendering yard shall be permitted to enter either the sewers of Tempre or its waterways. Such wastes shall be mixed with dirt and clay and carted to the old open mine to the south of Tempre, or to another locale as designated by the Minister of Highways and Rivers . . .

Similar wording applied to metalworking shops and facilities.

So why aren't they doing that? Are these rules out of date? Are there other rules? Except that Chalmyr had said that the rules hadn't been changed so long as he'd served—and that was more than fifteen years. Among other things, she needed to bring that up with Porofyr's remaining subordinates. She didn't have much time to think about that because Chalmyr brought in a sealed letter from Khanasyl.

"Just wait," she said as she broke the seal and began to read.

Dearest Lady-Protector,

Your kindness in immediately contacting us is most appreciated

and in keeping with the courtesy extended by both your father and
your late uncle . . .

Mykella's lips twisted at the mention of Joramyl, certainly a reference made to highlight without saying so the First Seltyr's displeasure
at having to deal with a mere woman.

. . . and we would be most pleased to call upon you at the first glass
of the afternoon on Duadi in order to discuss those matters of mutual concern and importance to the future of Tempre and its factors
and Seltyrs, in particular, since upon commerce rests the entire
foundation of the land. Previous Lord-Protectors have all benefited
from this understanding, as have the people of Tempre.

We look forward to meeting with you.

"We?" murmured Mykella. "Khanasyl sounds like he's the Lord-
Protector."

"Lady?" inquired Chalmyr.

"I was talking to myself. Khanasyl will be here at first glass of the
afternoon tomorrow."

"Very good. When would you like to meet with your ministers?"
asked Chalmyr.

Ministerial meetings—she'd forgotten about those. Her father had
mentioned them as tiresome necessities. "What about first thing in
the morning?"

"Eighth glass, Lady?"

She'd thought seventh glass, but nodded.

After he returned to the anteroom, she scanned the sewerage rules
again and the smaller volume that held later changes. She found
nothing that allowed liquid wastes in rivers or streams. She took out
the map folio again, but less than a quarter glass elapsed before Chalmyr again rapped on the door.

"A letter from High Factor Lhanyr."

I can hardly wait. Mykella took the envelope from Chalmyr and broke the green wax seal, extracting the single sheet of heavy paper and beginning to read.

Dear Lady-Protector—

I do appreciate your courtesy in writing. I must say that I was not totally surprised to receive your letter so soon after recent events because I was a great admirer of your father's honesty and of his concerns for Lanachrona. Your actions suggest similar concerns, for which I am grateful.

Unless I hear otherwise, I would be pleased to call on you at the third glass of the afternoon on Duadi, and I look forward to that personal meeting.

Mykella read the letter again. After the condescension in Seltyr Khanasyl's words, she was relieved at Lhanyr's approach. *It doesn't mean you can trust him . . . only that he's more civil. He could be more devious than Joramyl.* Still . . . she could hope for more.

She looked up at Chalmyr. "Lhanyr will be here at third glass tomorrow."

The scrivener nodded. "Your father was always pleased to meet with him."

"I hope I will be. I take it that his meetings with Khanasyl were more of a trial?"

"He never said, Lady. He did occasionally look weary afterwards, but that might have been my imagination."

"We'll have to see." She paused, then added, "Thank you very much, Chalmyr." She could tell that the scrivener was being polite, and that his impression was that those meetings had been more than a trial.

Later that afternoon, after dealing with letters of appointment for officials she had retaining, she "retired" to her chambers, but only to reclaim her riding jacket and gloves before she slipped down to the darkness and out toward the west once more. This time, from what she could determine, she managed to emerge from the darkness somewhere around sixty vingts west of Viencet. From there, it appeared she might be only a vingt from the highway, not that it would do much good when there was a gorgelike gully between the hillside where she could still draw on the darkness and the road. But . . . perhaps . . . if she explored even farther west . . .

She shook her head. She wasn't as tired as she had been when she'd first begun using the dark ways, but she was still cold and tired. *You can only do so much at once.*

She eased back into the darkness and back to her private study, where it took her almost half a glass huddled in a quilt before she stopped shivering . . . barely a quarter glass before dinner.

When she stepped into the family dining room, Salyna was waiting, just inside the door.

"What did you do today? I came by late this morning. You weren't there."

"I had to see High Factor Hasenyt. Someone set fire to one of his warehouses."

"That's because he supports you," said Rachylana from behind Mykella.

"We don't know that." Mykella moved toward her place at the table. "I did find out that someone paid one of his watchmen to do it."

"I didn't know you knew torture . . ."

"Rachylana!" snapped Salyna.

"I don't. He wasn't very bright, and I can be very persuasive—without force, unlike some." Mykella slipped into her seat, where she filled her goblet with the red wine in the carafe.

Her sisters sat quickly.

"What's for dinner?"

"A mutton stew," replied Salyna. "With onions and potatoes . . . and dark bread."

"That's a winter meal," said Rachylana.

"I need a heavy warm meal. I'm cold." Mykella's words were pleasant.

"You're not eating enough," Salyna said.

"Thank the moons you're both fortunate you can eat so much," commented Rachylana.

"Mykella's thinner. You can see it," persisted Salyna.

Rachylana looked closely at her older sister. "You are. I wish I had that problem."

Muergya appeared with a large casserole and a basket of steaming dark bread

"What did you do today?" Mykella asked, after serving herself, not directing the question at either of her sisters.

"I rode over to the Southern Guard headquarters and talked with the commander about training women for light duties. I pointed out that would free more guards to fight."

"Women won't do that," offered Rachylana.

"The ones without families or futures might prefer to be guards than harlots."

"The Guards shouldn't accept women like that," countered Rachylana.

"Why not? They accept men who've spent time in the workhouses and work camps so long as they haven't seriously injured anyone."

"What did the commander say?" Mykella interjected quickly.

"He said that it had to be more than an idea. Before he could think about it seriously, I'd have to plan it out carefully, and you would have to approve it."

"In practical terms, so would he." Mykella took a careful mouthful of the casserole, finding it very hot.

"You wouldn't think about that seriously, would you?" asked Rachylana.

Mykella finished swallowing and followed that with some of the red wine. "I'll look at anything that makes sense and might help Lanachrona. We're short of both Southern Guards and golds. If you have any ideas that will help with either, I'll consider them, too."

"You might sell all those dresses Cheleyza left," suggested Rachylana. "One way or another, she won't be using them."

"That's a possibility," replied Mykella evenly, "but there won't be many who could or would want to purchase them, and we'll likely only recover a silver on a gold. I'll need to talk to Lord Gharyk about the proprieties and legalities."

"You could close down her villa. Don't you have to pay everything now?"

"I do, but some of the grooms and servers have served the family for years, and I don't want it to fall apart. In time, someone else in the family may need to live there. Reducing expenses there is a good idea, though."

After spending another half glass with her sisters dining, and in forcing herself to eat more than she usually did, and another glass in the family parlor with Salyna, Mykella returned to her own quarters, locked the doors, and slipped down to the depths of the palace. As soon as she emerged, she immediately shielded herself before moving toward the Table. Warily, she eyed it. For a moment, she thought that the still-bright pinkish purple flicked, but nothing happened.

Should she try to see if someone watched from wherever that Alector had been? Efra—that was the name of the world. *Where in the heavens was such a world? One of the planets that circled the sun?* She shook her head. The old writings had said that the Alectors came from beyond the stars, and that had to be farther than the worlds that circled their sun.

She concentrated on the idea of Efra—and the mists appeared . . . and parted, but revealing only a seal of some sort with two crossed light-torches—except that they weren't quite that, but more like scepters that were also light-torches. She kept looking, but her head began to ache, and she closed her eyes and stepped back.

The Table flared brighter, then subsided. *Did I do that?*

She studied the Table again, but nothing changed, although it was a touch brighter than it had been before she had tried to reach Efra, wherever it was. After several moments, she began to search for people through the Table.

Areyst was at a desk in whatever quarters he had, since his surroundings were not those of Southern Guard headquarters, while Porofyr was studying a ledger and frowning. Cheleyza was in a tiny room, writing on a portable scrivening box by the light of a dim and smoky lamp. Hasenyt and his wife sat across a table as he shuffled pasteboard cards, while Lord Gharyk and Jylara sat before a hearth with dying embers.

Before long, Mykella eased her way upward through the stone and back to her private study. At times, most times, the Table showed little of value.

11

On Duadi morning, Lord Gharyk was the first to arrive, at a quarter before eighth glass, but Mykella had decided not to see any ministers—or those acting for ministers—before she met with them all. Next was Cerlyk, since Forester Loryalt had not returned from his inspection tour, followed by Duchael, the assistant minister for Highways and Rivers, and finally Areyst, who arrived just before eighth glass. Then Mykella invited them all in to sit around the old circular cherry table in the corner of the study that was also the southwest corner of the palace.

"Lord Gharyk . . . why don't you begin?" suggested Mykella.

"Ah . . . yes, Lady-Protector. We are working on the report to detail the changes necessary to return the justicing system to a more efficient and equitable system."

"If you could explain, in general terms, the problems I asked you to address . . ."

"There are several . . . the first is that the justices and civic patrols in other cities do not report on what offenses are taking place or what sentences have been meted out for what offenses. The second is, I have recently discovered, that certain offenders are being executed here in Tempre both before judgments are sent to the ministry and in some cases when those judgments are never reported." Gharyk moistened his lips.

"Thank you." Mykella could see why Gharyk was nervous. To her it looked very much as though executions were taking place as much to silence the offenders and keep the reports from the palace as to carry out justice. *But pointing that out at present would serve no purpose.* "I look forward to reading the report." She looked at Cerlyk. "Sub-Forester?"

"Yes, Lady-Protector. As I informed you earlier, Forester Loryalt is touring . . ."

Mykella kept a pleasant smile on her face for the nearly half glass that Cerlyk detailed the state of the Lady-Protector's forests and the decreased potential for immediate timber revenues.

When he had finished, she turned to Duchael, who had squirmed in his chair from the beginning of the meeting. "If you would begin by reporting on the condition of sewers in Tempre, Assistant Minister Duchael."

Duchael offered a smile and cleared his throat.

As he spoke, Mykella sensed apprehension and fear.

"Lady-Protector, the ministry's priorities under Lord Porofyr focused on the maintenance of waterways and the improvement of towpaths along the Vedra and the lower reaches of the Vyanna . . ."

"I understand that, and I'm most certain that those are in excellent condition. That is why I inquired about the situation with regard to sewers." Mykella smiled pleasantly.

"The situation in Tempre . . . is . . . uneven. The sewers in the eastern part and southeastern part of the city function well. There are few complaints about odors. . . ."

Mykella listened as Duchael explained the soundness of the eastern sewers, then held up her hand, and asked, "What about the sewers in the western part and center parts of Tempre, especially those bordering the South River?"

"There have been some complaints in the past, Lady, but not recently."

Mykella nodded. "I'd like to see the details when we meet next tenday. By the end of today, I would also like the names of the chief sewer inspectors in Tempre, and the name and position of whoever is in charge of sewer repairs and maintenance, the engineer." Her eyes fixed firmly on Duchael, then shifted. "Commander Areyst?"

"Lady . . ." Areyst inclined his head.

His pleasant smile vanished. "We have begun the repositioning of the Guards to deal with possible exigencies created by the unusual nature of your succession. It would appear that the major shifts in companies will be completed in two weeks, three at the outside. Stepped-up intensive training for the majority of First, Second, and Third Company will begin next Londi, but half a company will remain in Tempre. Different squads will comprise that half company as the others are rotated through the training in Viencet. . . . Commander Choalt will report directly to Viencet, most likely by next Duadi . . ."

When Areyst had finished, Mykella waited a moment. "As you know, the events leading to my succession began when I noted the diversion of more than two thousand golds in tariffs received from factors and Seltyrs. That is one of the reasons why, for the moment, I am also acting as Finance Minister. By checking records not previously available to me, I've discovered additional and significant diversions of golds by the previous Finance Minister. That might also be a reason why his widow fled Tempre. Needless to say, I am not pleased to find that such diversions took place, but I also understand the difficulties that would have been involved with trying to bring such matters up. Those difficulties no longer exist, and such diversions will not be tolerated." She smiled coolly. "You might wish to pass that on to any who might be tempted."

Behind his pleasant demeanor, Duchael was close to shuddering, his fear palpable to Mykella. Gharyk was apprehensive, but not in the same fashion as Duchael. Cerlyk remained attentive and concerned but not fearful. Areyst was attentive but definitely pleased.

"Now . . . do any of you have any questions of me?"

"When might you be appointing a Minister of Highways and Rivers?" asked Duchael.

"I will be meeting with several High Factors and Seltyrs over the next weeks. It would be premature to make a decision without hearing their views first. *If only to know whom not to appoint.* "In the meantime, I trust you will carry on." Mykella smiled again.

"Yes, Lady." Despair welled from Duchael, although it was well-enough concealed that only Areyst seemed to notice.

"Lady . . ." began Cerlyk, "there is a problem on some of the private lands along the Vedra between Borlan and Dekhron . . ."

"Yes?"

"Some have been reported to have planted water oaks instead of true oaks; most likely because the water oaks grow more quickly, but when they harvest, they are only harvesting the true oaks. In time . . ."

"We'll be short of true oaks. When?"

"Forester Loryalt calculated that it might occur as soon as the time of your children's rule . . ." Cerlyk looked slightly embarrassed.

"We have a little time for that. It shouldn't be neglected, but once the Forester returns, you should work out harvesting plans for those private lands that will address the balance."

"There have been plans . . ."

"If necessary, the Southern Guards and I will oversee those plans."

"Yes, Lady." Although his voice was polite, the subforester was pleased.

Mykella sensed that no one else wanted to ask about anything. She rose. "I'll see you all next week." Her eyes went to Areyst briefly, and she gave the smallest of nods.

The commander took his time gathering the thin leather folder he had not opened so that he was the last one in the study, but he did not speak until they were alone. "Yes, Lady?"

"I'll be riding out the eastern highway this morning. If you could join me . . ."

"I had planned to do so." Areyst inclined his head. "This was a short ministerial meeting from the reports I've heard before."

"They may be longer in the future."

"You will pardon me, Lady, if I doubt that they will be that much longer."

Mykella couldn't quite smother the grin she felt at Areyst's good-humored banter. "We will see."

"Indeed we will. If you will excuse me so that your mount and escorts are ready . . ."

Mykella gestured. Only after he left did she shake her head.

Less than half a glass later, she rode southeast along the avenue past the Southern Guard headquarters. Before her rode a pair of Southern Guards, and beside her was Areyst, with a squad following. The dwellings overlooking the avenue, while not villas, were well maintained, with whitewashed courtyard and structure walls, and kitchen gardens over whose walls rose well-pruned trees. At times, Mykella thought she heard the splash of fountains, and the air held aromas of cooking and spices and oils—but not any stenches or unpleasant odors.

Less than half a vingt farther southeast they began to ride past small villas set amid larger walled compounds.

"That is Seltyr Khanasyl's villa." Areyst pointed to a villa set on a gentle rise, whose lower reaches were enclosed by a shimmering white wall, breached only by a double gate—closed and presumably barred.

"It is rather impressive. It might even be larger than the palace."

"With the outbuildings on the back side of the hill, it doubtless is, as are several villas built in Tempre in recent years."

"That was built recently?"

"Comparatively. It was finished when I returned from my tour in Indyor." Areyst's voice was bland.

"That was not always the custom?"

"Seltyrs and High Factors have always had larger dwellings, but such . . . impressive near palaces have appeared but in the last ten years or so."

Since Mother's death . . . Had her father just given up . . . gone through the motions when she died? Would she ever know?

When she rode back into the palace, Mykella was somewhere between irritated and furious. The entire area along the eternastone-paved eastern avenue that became the highway at the outskirts of Tempre was filled with well-kept dwellings and clearly functioning sewers, and the waters of the smaller East River looked clear. Still . . . she'd need to cover other parts of the city before she made any final decisions.

She did manage to eat a quick but solid midday meal—cold fowl with pearapples in syrup and warm dark bread—before she returned to the formal study. Salyna and Rachylana had already eaten.

Lying on her desk was an envelope, sealed in reddish wax, but with an imprint she did not recognize. She opened it and read the brief lines.

Gracious Lady-Protector—
I offer my thanks, and those of Envoy Sheorak, for your timely missive

to the Landarch. We will be departing shortly. We wish you well in the coming season. We trust that Lanachrona and Deforya will remain fast friends, regardless of the machinations of others.

With the greatest respect.

The signature was that of Smoltak, Majer.

Mykella couldn't help but smile as she slipped the missive back into the envelope.

Just as the last of the grains of sand in the glass oozed out, and the first glass of the afternoon began, Khanasyl stepped into Mykella's study. He was the largest Seltyr Mykella had ever seen, and when he stepped through the doorway, he appeared far larger than she recalled although it had been several years since she had actually been close to him since he usually had avoided events, particularly balls, in the palace. Even standing behind the desk, she had to look up, and once they were seated, she was still looking up.

"Lady-Protector, you requested my presence." His voice was high, not quite a tenor, but thin and at odds with the touch of gray in his hair and his square-cut beard, and particularly with his broad shoulders and impressive physique, although a larger-than-necessary midsection suggested that with age he might have become slightly indulgent.

"You're most kind to see me so promptly," she began. "I understood you and others in Tempre might have some concerns, and I wanted to hear them from you, since, as First Seltyr, you certainly are the one to whom others will turn."

Khanasyl smiled warmly and broadly, but the warmth was skin deep, and his light gray eyes met Mykella's squarely. "You give me too much credit. I am but the first among equals."

Mykella looked directly back at Khanasyl, smiling faintly and projecting assurance. "I only give you your due."

For just a moment, the Seltyr blinked before smiling warmly once more. "You are indeed kind . . . yet there are concerns, I must say great concerns, over your acceptance of the resignation of Lord Porofyr. Some have suggested that might have been . . . a trifle unduly hasty."

"Seltyr Porofyr gave me little choice." Mykella offered a rueful smile. "Before I could say a word, he told me that he could not serve me. I attempted to suggest that such was not the case, but he insisted most firmly." She paused, as if reflecting, before going on. "It is possible that he might have deigned to remain had I begged and groveled."

"He felt that you had no interest in retaining him." Khanasyl fingered his beard, as if thoughtfully. "He also felt that you were not all that interested in continuing the successful and long-standing customs and traditions of Lanachrona."

"He may have intimated that to you or others, but he never gave me the chance to retain him. Those who believe I am upending things might note that I have retained the Forester, Lord Gharyk, and the highest-ranking officer of the Southern Guards remaining after the treachery of Nephryt and Demyl."

"Ah . . . yes. 'Treachery' . . . a useful word."

"I could have used 'murder' or 'theft' or 'deception.' 'Treachery' is just more inclusive." Mykella smiled brightly. "Might I ask you for any recommendations you might have that I could consider for a successor to Porofyr?"

"I had not thought . . ."

"You are known for your forethought, First Seltyr. Everyone knows you consider all aspects long before others realize there are even matters to consider. Pardon me if I express doubt that you have not considered who might be a worthy Minister of Highways and Rivers."

"Considered, yes. I have considered several, but without meeting with you, Lady-Protector, and learning what you consider of import, my considerations are just that."

Mykella gave a thoughtful nod. "My concerns are simple enough. I would like someone who understands rivers and the handling of sewers and waste as well as the need for sound towpaths and piers. I would like someone who is hardworking, knowledgeable, and honest, as well as one who understands the needs of both factors and traders and crafters and ordinary folk."

"You don't want much," replied Khanasyl with a high-pitched laugh.

Mykella laughed in return. "You asked. There may not be anyone who meets all those qualifications, but we might as well start with what would be best and work from there."

"Work from there . . . that is certainly possible. I will give the matter some thought and get back to you." The Seltyr nodded. "You know . . . I can remember when you were born . . . and when your brother was, too. Such a tragic death it was. I still can't see what they were thinking." He shook his head. "But things happen as they will, and we have a Lady-Protector, one who understands ledgers and costs, and who can provide an heir, and commerce and continuity are what underlie the prosperity of any land . . ."

Mykella nodded and listening, asking a question here and another there, for almost half a glass more, knowing that was the bare minimum before she could ease Khanasyl out. Only after the door was firmly closed behind the First Seltyr did Mykella take a long and deep breath. *The absolute and condescending arrogance of that . . .* She couldn't even think of an appropriate word.

She ended up pacing around the study for a time, just trying to settle herself for the meeting with Lhanyr. Then she went back over the ledger that held the expenditures of the Ministry of Highways and Rivers, but too many entries were large and general—and that suggested she needed to look at the separate ledgers for each subaccount.

"Chief High Factor Lhanyr," announced Chalmyr.

Lhanyr was close to the physical opposite of Khanasyl, a slender and wiry clean-shaven man, barely middle-aged, with short ginger hair and freckles, who stood but slightly taller than Mykella's sister Salyna. He bowed, then lifted his head with a shy smile. "Lady-Protector."

"Chief High Factor." She gestured to the chairs.

"Lhanyr . . . please." He seated himself quickly.

"You're kind to respond to my request," she said. "With all the changes that have occurred, I thought you and the other factors might have some concerns. I wanted to hear from you since you are the one to whom others will turn and to whom they will likely listen."

Lhanyr smiled ruefully. "They will listen, but there are always those who will not heed my words or the words of others. Both factors and Seltyrs have the habit of calculating their acts on the basis of what profits them in the current season. The wiser ones, who are fewer, calculate on the basis of a year or so. The wisest do what is necessary to survive the current times but calculate for the lifetime of their children."

"What are those concerns?" Mykella kept her voice even.

Lhanyr shrugged. "All know that you will likely have to raise tariffs. Most worry that you will raise them too high and too quickly."

"Why do you believe tariffs will be raised?"

"The Southern Guards is too small, and Lanachrona faces enemies to the west. Golds have been stolen from the Treasury, and not all the golds raised have been spent wisely. All know that you know these things. What else could we expect?"

While Mykella could sense calculation behind the factor's pleasant words and demeanor, that calculation felt almost honest and open, especially after listening to Khanasyl. "Some of these matters must be addressed, including the need for higher tariffs, but I have come to no decisions as to how to proceed. How do the factors feel about the amount by which tariffs might be increased."

"As little as possible, Lady-Protector." Lhanyr's words were delivered lightly and with an underlying humor.

Mykella just waited, smiling pleasantly.

"I cannot speak to the numbers, Lady, not for the others. We have not discussed such. Never have tariffs been raised by more than a copper on a silver, and I believe most would feel that a one part in five increase would be a heavy levy."

"I appreciate your candor, and I will consider your thoughts and observations." Mykella paused. "You have heard about the fire at High Factor Hasenyt's warehouse, have you not?"

"I have, and it troubles me greatly."

Lhanyr's words were backed by his feelings, more strongly than she had expected, and she asked, "Might you explain why?"

"Many saw that Hasenyt agreed to your accession as Lady-Protector. For him to suffer a fire set by others so soon after that . . . that begs coincidence, in my mind."

"Might that also be connected to my acceptance of the resignation of Seltyr Porofyr as Minister of Highways and Rivers?"

"I doubt that his resignation greatly concerned many factors."

"Oh?"

"You must know, Lady, that the relations between factors and Seltyrs have always been . . . strained."

"Does that date back to when Mykel the Great exiled Amaryk?"

"That did not make relations easier, but they were difficult before that because Southgate and Dramur offered coins and more favorable terms to the Seltyrs. Many factors and smaller traders suffered incidents such as befell Hasenyt. One of the reasons why the factors acceded readily to the Lord-Protector Mykel was because he was fair to all."

"I will certainly endeavor to follow his example."

"That is the wisest course, but it does present dangers. Fairness is seen as preferential by those who lose a previous and unfair advantage, as I am most certain you already understand."

Mykella unfortunately did, and she nodded once more before speaking. "Do you have a recommendation for a successor to Porofyr?"

Her question drew a crooked smile from Lhanyr, and a pause before he replied. "While many factors would prefer a factor as minister, such an appointment would only worsen matters at present. The appointment of a Seltyr of probity and fairness would better serve us all."

Are there any? Mykella did not ask the question. "That may be, but have you any suggestions of High Factors, as well?"

"There are several with both reputation and experience. Almardyn, among the Seltyrs, and Pytroven and Zylander have always shown those traits. There may be others . . ."

"If you think of such, will you convey those names?"

"I will indeed, Lady."

"Now . . . please tell me of the challenges that face the factors, Seltyrs, and the Lady-Protector in the matters of trade." Mykella smiled.

Lhanyr laughed, then shook his head. "You are disarmingly dangerous, Lady."

"I hope I am disarming. I doubt I am dangerous, but how can I address your difficulties if I do not know what they are?"

"Then I would say that the greatest danger is that the Seltyrs, as well as some factors, do not realize that their prosperity lies in your hands and in the strength of the Southern Guards. You must realize this already, for you are making changes in the Guards . . ."

Mykella listened for more than half a glass before seeing Lhanyr out.

Less than half a glass passed before the inevitable knock on the door occurred.

"Captain Maeltor has a report for you."

"Have him come in." Mykella stood and waited.

The captain bowed his head, then straightened. "Lady . . . Yesterday, you suggested that High Factor Hasenyt look for the watchman's brother. He's been found."

From Maeltor's expression, Mykella understood. "What was left of him, you mean?"

"Yes, Lady."

"What else?"

"The watchman was in the main gaol, awaiting his time before the justicer. He hung himself with his belt. The commander thought you should know."

"He was right. Thank you, Captain." She smiled politely and stood there until he left.

What could she do? She couldn't do everything. She couldn't even find out everything that had gone wrong, and every time she turned around, she learned something new, and little of what she learned was favorable.

Mykella walked to the window. She realized she was doing that all too often. She also realized that, one way or another, the next few months would be difficult, and if Khanasyl and Porofyr had their way, Tempre would be smeared with the blood of too many who might reveal too much. *But it's too early for you to act directly . . . yet.*

12

Mykella was not in any better a mood when she walked down the corridor toward the formal study on Tridi morning. Late the afternoon before, Duchael had arrived with the information about sewers. While his demeanor had been pleasant, behind that facade he had been anything but pleased.

Then, after that, Mykella's use of the Table had been similarly un-fruitful, showing her nothing new or of import. While the pinkish purpleness had not brightened more, neither had it diminished. Fi-nally, using the black pathways, she had finally located a low hill over-looking the eternastone highway, close enough that she could reach the blackness from the edge of the highway. Unfortunately, that locale, she suspected, was inside the border of Midcoast, although it was impos-sible for her to determine that exactly.

Dinner and breakfast had been quiet, with Mykella briefly explain-ing the problem of finding a new Minister of Highways and Rivers, then listening to Salyna's report on improvements to the palace that she'd discussed with Elwayt and on her ideas for training women Southern Guards. Rachylana had made few comments, not quite sulk-ing, and only asking if Mykella had heard from the envoy from Mid-coast. Mykella had not and said so.

"You won't," had been Rachylana's last words to Mykella at break-fast.

All those thoughts swirled through her mind as she stepped into the anteroom to her formal study.

Chalmyr stood. "Good morning, Lady."

"Good morning, Chalmyr. What new problems await us?" She kept her voice light.

"Envoy Vaerlon from Midcoast wishes an appointment with you this morning, if possible. He waits below."

Mykella offered a crooked smile. At least she could tell Rachylana that she met with the man. "Is there anything else more pressing?"

"Not at the moment, Lady."

"I will see him now. Please tell the duty guard I plan to ride out at a glass before midday."

"Yes, Lady."

Mykella nodded and entered her study, noting that Chalmyr had dusted the wood and closed the map folio, placing it in the corner of the desk, precisely aligned with the edges. She glanced toward the win-dow. Outside, the sky was hazy, with clouds appearing to the west. That confirmed her decision to ride through Tempre earlier in the day.

Before that long, Chalmyr announced Vaerlon.

When the envoy entered the study, he looked very much like he had stepped out of a tale of the coastal bravos, one of the romantic tales to which Rachylana had alluded more than once. He was tall and broad-shouldered, with sweeping black mustaches. His doublet was scarlet and worn over a shirt of a green so deep it was almost black, and his sword belt was of fawn-colored leather, as were his knee boots. Both belt and boots were oiled . . . and scarred.

"Lady-Protector." Vaerlon's bow was just shy of being dismissive.

"Envoy Vaerlon. I had wondered when you might make an appearance . . . after spending so many days in Tempre."

"When so much unexpected has occurred, one tends to be more . . . deliberate."

"Deliberation is always a wise course. What brings you here today?" Mykella gestured to the chairs before the desk before seating herself

Vaerlon paused, then slowly sat. "If I might observe, Lady-Protector . . . you do not wear the usual attire of a woman of state and position . . ."

"No. What I wear is similar to that worn by others of position and power. I always have worn this attire, except at balls."

"It is said you have powers like as to those of the Ancients." The dark-haired envoy's words were delivered in an offhand, almost-dismissive manner. "One never knows what to believe of such reports."

"Much is said, Envoy Vaerlon. One can choose to believe or not. While men act on what is said, often the outcome results from what is done . . . or what fails to be done."

"Determining what has been done, even when one views it when it occurs, is not always so easy as many believe."

So he saw the investiture ceremony . . . and can't quite believe what he saw . . . or chooses to think there was trickery. Mykella smiled politely. "There is always an explanation for what happens. Usually the simplest is correct, no matter how strange or unbelievable it may appear."

"I have found that to be true, yet explaining to those who have not seen can prove difficult."

"It can indeed, especially if those others have reasons not to wish to accept the report of one who has seen." *Or if, like your prince, they are considering invasions or attacks.*

"You have not answered my question, Lady," said Vaerlon, with a laugh and a glance designed as flirtatious.

"I don't recall your asking one, dear envoy."

Vaerlon smiled. "I thought I had."

"You made an observation. I offered a judgment on that observation. If your observation was a question, then my judgment was an answer."

"You have no guards close at hand."

"Should I?"

For just an instant, Vaerlon froze, and Mykella could sense apprehension. Then he smiled again although there was no warmth behind the expression. "You must know I had come to see for the Prince what the possibilities might be for a match."

"That I had heard. I had thought that, in your own time, you would appear . . . as you have. I presume it is the Prince for whom you inquire?"

"But of course. He is but a young man as sovereigns go, less than ten years older than you, I would judge."

"And he is intelligent, handsome, ambitious, kind, generous . . . and all the other terms that one must apply to a ruler?" Mykella spoke gently, leaving the sarcasm in her own mind.

"Not all who rule are so . . . but indeed he is."

"Then you and all of Midcoast are most fortunate. Most fortunate, indeed."

"Any woman who became his consort would be also most fortunate."

"I am most certain that would be so, for you would not be here were it otherwise." Mykella paused. "Because matters here have been so . . . unexpected, as you put it, I have not had much time to consider matters such as matching, either for myself or for my sisters. They are both beautiful, as you may have heard, far more so than me. I have decided one thing. Any suitor will have to meet the lady in whom he is interested before any match can be considered. Much of the difficulty here in Lanachrona might well have been avoided had the Lord-

Protector met the woman who became his brother's wife before the consorting." That was inaccurate, but true enough in spirit . . . and conveyed a message if Vaerlon were willing to accept it.

After another instant where something flashed through Vaerlon's thoughts and feelings, not that Mykella could sense anything but the fact that something had, the envoy nodded slowly. "I can see that you might wish such." He smiled. "If indeed Prince Skrelyn should be interested in a match, he might well undertake the long journey from Hafin to Tempre."

Mykella understood the meaning behind those words as well. "If he should, we will welcome him in precisely the spirit in which he comes."

"I will convey that as well, Lady-Protector, and your courtesy and directness."

Mykella smiled again. "I fear that I can be far too direct, dear envoy, but that is indeed one of my faults." She stood. "I do appreciate your requesting an audience, and I wish you well on your return to Midcoast."

Vaerlon stood and inclined his head. "I thank you, and offer my hopes that your rule will be all that it should be."

"You are most kind."

Mykella was more than relieved when the study door closed behind the departing envoy.

She had little time to recover, because in less than a quarter glass, both Salyna and Rachylana slipped into the study.

"I saw the envoy from Midcoast leaving when I was about to ride over to the Southern Guards," Salyna said. "What did he say?"

"Why was he here?" demanded Rachylana.

"To find out what he could although he did inquire, rather indirectly, about matching."

"He wanted to know about you, didn't he?" Rachylana asked.

"He was very indirect. He mentioned none of us by name. He only said that whoever was matched to Prince Skrelyn would indeed be fortunate."

Salyna snorted softly.

"What did you tell him?" asked Rachylana, her voice diffident.

"The same thing I told the other envoys—that my sisters would have to meet any suitor."

"You didn't mention your approval?"

"No. That seemed unnecessary." *Especially since he's not really looking for a match yet.*

"What did he say about that?" Rachylana looked directly at Mykella.

"He said something to the effect that if Prince Skrelyn were interested in a match, he would certainly have no problem making the long journey from Hafin to Tempre."

Salyna winced. "He only wants one kind of match."

"Why did you put him off?" demanded Rachylana.

"I was very polite, but Skrelyn has already made up his mind. Even before Father's death, he was thinking about attacking us. The only way that wouldn't have happened would have been if Joramyl had remained Lord-Protector. At least, he wouldn't have attacked immediately."

"What are you going to do? What will become of us?" Rachylana looked to Salyna.

"That depends on Mykella, doesn't it?" replied Salyna. "It's always depended on someone. Father feared what may come. Why do you think he wanted all of us matched and away from Tempre so quickly?"

"Now . . . what are you going to do?" asked Rachylana.

"Take a ride to find out more about what needs to be done."

"How will that help?"

"For the moment, Commander Areyst is doing everything he can to ready the Southern Guards. I cannot help there." *Not now.* "There are other problems in Tempre and Lanachrona that need remedying as well. So I might as well do them while I can."

"Such as the mundane and boring matter of selecting a Minister of Highways and Rivers?" asked Rachylana.

For a moment, Mykella couldn't believe what she'd heard. "Mundane and boring? Mundane and boring? As Finance Minister, Joramyl funneled thousands of golds from the Treasury, and Porofyr resigned immediately, and his assistant is acting guiltier than . . ." She couldn't come up with an adequate comparison. "It's too early to tell, but the ledgers suggest more thousands of golds are missing there. It could be more. We may not even have enough golds to get through the spring . . . because of corrupt ministers . . . and you're saying that choosing the right minister is mundane and boring?"

Salyna shot a glance at Rachylana that as much as said, "Now you've done it."

Mykella forced herself to lower her voice. "I'm sorry. I didn't mean . . ."

"You never mean," said Rachylana coolly, "but you still do it."

Salyna gently took Rachylana's arm and led her from the study.

How can she not understand? Ministers control tens of thousands of golds . . . and finding out that they've stolen them after the fact doesn't help—not when you can't find what happened to those golds.

Mykella forced herself to take several deep breaths. Finally, after donning her riding jacket and gloves, she walked down toward the courtyard. Given the sections of the city she had not yet ridden through, she doubted she would like what she was about to see. But she did need to see everything, at least from the saddle, because that would tell her what the words and feelings of men did not.

13

Quattri morning was comparatively quiet for Mykella, although it took more than a glass for her and Areyst to go over the manpower situation of the Southern Guards, the need for more mounts, and the shortages in Guard supplies, especially of gunpowder, because of the higher costs of brimstone. After that, she pored over the master ledger of the Ministry of Highways and Rivers before going to the upper-level study of the Minister of Finance to talk to Haelyt and to request the breakdown of figures in several places.

Still . . . by just before the first glass of the afternoon, Mykella and Captain Maeltor were riding southward on the eastern avenue toward the building that housed the sewer inspectors and the city sewer engineer.

"Might I ask the purpose of this ride, Lady? Besides granting you greater knowledge of the city?"

Left unspoken was a question as to why Mykella was concerned about sewers, and that was something she couldn't have answered logically. While the stench and the discharge into the rivers in central Tempre bothered her greatly, she felt that those problems were only the obvious ones. "Let us just say the more I know, the less likely golds will be spent unwisely, or, more important, the less likely that they will be diverted from where they are supposed to be spent. The Southern Guards did not receive hundreds of golds' worth of tack and other supplies that it should have received over the past year because those golds were diverted to Lord Joramyl's private purse. From looking at the accounts, I have other suspicions, but greater knowledge is necessary in order to know what questions to ask."

"Begging your pardon, Lady, but that does not preclude untruths by those you question."

"It does not, but I can usually tell when someone is lying. That ability does me little good, though, if I do not know the questions to ask . . . or whom to ask what." *Nor did it help in the past when I was not allowed to ask those questions or to be present when they were asked.*

Maeltor nodded slowly although Mykella could sense that he retained some doubts.

Mykella took a well-kept and stone-paved lane westward from the avenue and between two low hills covered with grass and trees. Beyond the hills at the end of the lane was the sewer building, a low one-story stone structure located on a flat area to the west of the East River. The ground in front of the building was paved with large slabs of the golden eternastone that also surfaced the Great Piers. *The Alectors thought that much of sewers?* That suggested to Mykella that she was perhaps not being so illogical. She glanced to her left, noting a large stone pipe emerging from the hillside, then slanting into the ground at such an angle so that it had to pass beneath the sewer building proper. *An aqueduct? From where? And why?*

As she rode toward the trapezoidal arch that formed the entrance to the building, she could see nine men, all attired in what looked to be clean gray coveralls, heading along the stone walk bordering the lane toward the avenue.

When they reined up before the entrance, Maeltor turned in the saddle. "Judyn . . . go find the sewer engineer Nusgeyl and tell him that the Lady-Protector is here to see him."

"Yes, sir."

As the ranker dismounted and hurried into the building, Maeltor glanced at the apparently departing workers. The captain said nothing, but his glance was more eloquent than words.

In return, Mykella nodded, then waited.

Before that long, two figures stepped through the angular columns of the entrance. The man who emerged with Judyn had longish wavy blond hair and bulging eyes dominating a pug nose and flat clean-shaven cheeks. He wore gray trousers and a dark gray jacket.

"Engineer Nusgeyl, the Lady-Protector has some inquiries for you," Maeltor said firmly.

"It would be my pleasure . . ."

Mykella sensed the affronted displeasure behind the cultured words and pleasant smile, but she said nothing, instead dismounting and stepping up onto fitted golden stones of the porch before the archway. "I've been riding through Tempre, and there appear to be areas where the sewers are not being used properly or where they do not appear to be used at all."

"Lady-Protector, as the chief engineer, I can assure you that we do everything to make certain that all is in good repair. What I cannot do, and what I do not have the authority to do, is to require that people use the sewers or use them properly. That is the task of the chief inspector."

Mykella sensed more than a certain amount of evasion but did not pursue that. "Where do the sewers discharge in the end? Or should I ask where they're supposed to discharge?"

"They all converge and flow into the underground collecting basin to the south and west of the Great Piers. From there, the main conduit carries the wastes farther westward, still underground, to the discharge point at the head of the western marshes. The waters flow through

the marshes, then into the west canal that empties into the Vedra after the waters flow over the last of the stone purifying sluices."

"How do the sewers all manage to collect these wastes in one basin
when there are two rivers flowing through Tempre that would separate the collection pipes?"

Nusgeyl offered a condescending smile. "The Alectors built stone
tunnels under the rivers with precise engineering so that the tunnels
all slope downward until they reach the marshes."

"Is not Tempre larger than in the time of the Alectors?"

"Only in the area to the southeast, and we have followed the same
plans in extending the sewers to serve those areas. The newer tunnels are higher, and that is why some of the more recent dwellings
are built on higher ground so that they can link to the sewers."

Mykella asked a number of other factual questions before she got
around to one of the other reasons why she had ridden to see the
sewer engineer. "I instructed the Ministry of Highways and Rivers to
look into and to make the necessary repairs to the sewers in the central part of Tempre. It is less than a glass past midday, yet when I rode
up, I saw workers leaving."

"We received the instructions from Assistant Minister Duchael
only late this morning."

"And your crews are leaving?"

"They work from dawn to early afternoon."

"Then you'll be having them start on the central area sewers tomorrow?"

"Ah . . . Lady . . . I'll have to develop a work plan . . . and see what
materials we will need, and where is best to begin . . ."

"And you will take care of those places where crafts or metalworks
are draining their wastes into the South River, of course."

"When we notice such, we will inform the chief inspector. Of that,
you can be certain, Lady-Protector."

"I'm sure that you will be most diligent, and I look forward to the
early commencement of your repairs." Mykella smiled politely, then
turned and remounted the gray. "Good day."

Maeltor said nothing about the engineer on the ride back to the
palace on a circuitous route that took them farther south and west

before wending their way through another part of Tempre, east of the metalworking area, where Mykella could not recall ever having been. There were areas where she smelled sewage, but she did not see what might be the source of the odors.

They were approaching the west end of the park across from the palace from the south when a Southern Guard galloped toward them. "Lady-Protector! Captain! There's trouble at the palace."

"What kind of trouble?" demanded Mykella, as the guard slowed his mount and turned to ride alongside Maeltor.

"Someone killed four guards while you were gone . . . from inside the palace."

"How?"

"It looks like the guards were sliced in half by a blade of fire . . . or something like it. These huge men with shiny black hair came up from the lower levels of the palace. They had weapons like pistols that shot beams of light. The blue light cut like a burning blade. They killed two guards by the rear door, and two more outside the palace stables. There were three of them, and they took six mounts."

"How did they saddle them so quickly?" demanded Maeltor.

"They were duty-squad mounts, sir. They cut down the two watching them."

"No one shot at them?" Maeltor sounded incredulous.

"Yes, sir. The two who were watching them shot at them, and so did three others in the courtyard. The bullets bounced off their tunics."

Maeltor glanced at Mykella.

"Keep riding. I need to get to the palace. Now."

Areyst rode in from Southern Guard headquarters as Mykella and her squad entered the courtyard. His face was grim as he eased his mount up beside her.

Mykella rode straight to the westernmost door at the rear of the palace, where she dismounted and handed the gelding's reins to the nearest ranker. "If you'd have him groomed, please." She opened the door, then waited for Areyst, who carried his rifle, before stepping inside and turning to the right.

Less than ten yards away, two Southern Guards stood at the top of the door to the lower levels of the palace. There was a hole in the wood where the lock had been. The lock and a semicircle of wood around it lay on the floor.

"Lady, sir . . . they came up this way," announced the shorter guard as Mykella neared.

"Has anyone been down there?" asked Mykella.

"Squad Leader Thanyr went down, but there's no one in the corridors. He didn't check any of the chambers."

"Thank you. You'd best stay behind me, Commander," Mykella said, opening the door.

"Lady . . ."

"If you don't want to get cut by a flame blade, that is." Mykella didn't actually know whether her shields would deflect such a weapon, but . . . if they didn't, Areyst was the one who needed to survive. She didn't know enough about strategies or combating strange weapons.

The staircase and the corridor were empty, but as Mykella walked deliberately toward the door to the Table chamber, she could sense a remnant of something purplish and ugly, like the last traces of an unseen mist, one that reminded her all too clearly of the Ifrit she'd fought off weeks before. The heavy oak door to the Table chamber had been forced in the same way as the staircase door, with the iron lock and a hand's worth of the wood that had surrounded it on the corridor floor.

Mykella paused outside the door, half-ajar. She could sense more of the purple, and yet she had no feeling of anything living. She stepped forward, taking a quick look into the chamber.

There, on the floor, sprawled a great misshapen form, the upper part with a massive male chest, swollen so much that the silver-gray tunic had no slack at all in it, and a bull-shaped head that had been charred into a shapeless mass, while the lower abdomen and legs were more manlike, and the trousers seemed overlarge.

"What is that?" asked Areyst, his voice restrained.

"I have no idea, Commander, except that it came through the Table with those who attacked the guards, and the attackers clearly killed it." Mykella walked over to the Table, which shimmered a pinkish purple, although the intensity seemed to have faded somewhat, still holding full shields, and looked down in the mirrored surface. She concentrated, trying to get the Table to show her the Ifrits who had slaughtered the guards, but while the mists swirled, they did not part to show a scene. *Is that because I've never seen them personally? Or for some other reason?*

She used the Table to check on her sisters, but both were upstairs in the family parlor, looking concerned but unharmed.

Mykella turned to the commander. "We'll need an armorer, or a smith. Someone who can forge steel plate across both sides of the door. Then we'll need a stonemason to wall up the corridor side."

"You know more than you're saying, Lady."

"The three who killed the Southern Guards are Alectors . . . or something like them. They're called Ifrits. They come from another world. It's named Efra. They use the Table, but they can only bring what they carry. This is the only Table in Corus—at least that I know of—that isn't buried or blocked. If we armor the door on both sides and wall it up, they won't be able to get back into the Table chamber, and anyone who tries to leave it won't be able to get out."

"Ah . . . what will you do if you can't use the Table?" he asked. "It's a valuable tool."

"Can your armorer fashion two heavy iron doors with locks that can't be smashed?"

"He's quite capable, Lady."

"You think I'm overreacting, Commander?" Mykella pointed at the figure on the stone floor, its tunic still shimmering, both with a silvery sheen that anyone could see and a purplish shade to her mind . . . and possibly to Areyst's. "Thrust your saber at that tunic. I'd wager that it's like armor to a hard blow. Then look closely at the burn cuts around the lock of the door." What she had already noticed was that the iron of the lock and the hinge straps had not been cut, nor had the stone of the door frame.

Areyst drew his saber and jabbed the inert form. The tunic gave slightly, but the blade did not cut through the fabric at all. He pressed more gently with the blade, then sheathed it. "The tunic gets harder the more force that's applied."

"It's like nightsilk in a way, except it's different." Mykella studied the body more closely, then frowned. Only the head and neck above the too-tight tunic collar were burned.

She looked to Areyst. "Only the head . . ."

"I'll make sure the Guards know that they can be killed with head shots."

"Or if they're hit with enough shots to the body, they might be bruised enough to slow them down . . . that is, if their tunics are like nightsilk."

He jabbed the dead figure's tunic harder. "I wouldn't want to rely on that tactic. I'll summon the armorer and have him set to work immediately."

"Dispose of the body, quickly, so that few see it."

"I had thought the same, Lady."

"Good." Mykella nodded absently, her mind already elsewhere.

Not only did she have to worry about a likely invasion by Skrelyn and Chalcaer, but now there were three Alectors, or Ifrits, loose somewhere in Lanachrona with weapons that could cut through anything but iron and solid stone . . . and for all her words about the Table's being the only accessible one in Corus . . . that was as much hope as anything, because she had no idea if there were other Tables elsewhere that she hadn't discovered. Three Alectors were a problem, but if there were more . . . with those weapons . . .

14

After leaving the Table chamber, Mykella made her way back to her formal study, where she spent the rest of the afternoon. She couldn't help but worry about the Ifrits, but there was little enough she could do without knowing where they were. So she concentrated on what she could address. She had received no recommendations from either Lhanyr or Khanasyl, but Areyst's suggested revision to the stipend rules was waiting for her, as were requests for decisions on spending from both Cerlyk and Duchael. Duchael's request was for another thousand golds to pay for the sewer repairs she had requested.

What are they doing with the golds they already received? With that thought, she went back to the Highways and Rivers master ledger, where, after almost two glasses, she could find no apparent reason why Duchael needed the funding. That meant another meeting with the weasel-like assistant minister . . . but not until Quinti, late as it was getting.

Cerlyk's request stated that maintenance expenses in the Vyanhills forests had been higher than anticipated, while revenues had been diverted, as he had discussed.

Another problem created by Joramyl.

When she finally walked down the corridor and into the family dining chamber, she was still fretting over the Ifrits and the sad state of finances.

"What is going on on the lower level?" demanded Rachylana from where she and Salyna stood at one side of the table. "Why weren't we allowed to leave the upper level earlier today?"

For a moment, Mykella said nothing. "No one was. Three men with some sort of fire-blades attacked the Southern Guards. The other guards were protecting you."

"How did that happen?" asked Salyna.

"They used an old hidden entrance to the palace on the lower level to bypass the guards."

"You didn't know anything about the entrance?" demanded Rachylana.

"How would she know?" countered Salyna. "I'd wager that no one else knew, either."

"I'm having it sealed," replied Mykella. *That's certainly true enough even if it isn't a conventional entrance.*

"Where is it?"

"In the Table chamber."

Salyna frowned. "Won't that . . ."

"The chamber will have double iron doors, with double locks," Mykella said easily.

"I never liked that place. It always gave me chills." Rachylana promptly shivered. "Why didn't Father just seal it off years ago?"

"He couldn't have known, or he would have sealed it," Salyna pointed out.

"What happened to the intruders?" pressed Rachylana.

"They killed several Southern Guards and escaped."

"Why would they break into the palace just to escape?" asked Rachylana. "That doesn't make sense."

"Unless they thought the entrance led to a strong room or something." Salyna frowned slightly. "Did they take anything?"

"It doesn't appear so." replied Mykella. "Nothing is missing."

"Who were they?"

"I didn't see them," Mykella said. "None of the guards saw them closely, but they were tall, dark-haired, and wore shimmering tunics."

"Who could they have been? Raiders from Midcoast?" speculated Rachylana.

"They were big," mused Salyna. "They could have been Reillies or Squawts from across the river."

"Most of the northerners are lighter-haired, and the biggest of the herders from the Iron Valleys have that funny gray hair," said Mykella. "We won't know for certain unless the Southern Guards catches them." She seated herself at the table, glancing to the windows, where scattered droplets of rain intermittently struck the glass.

"I wondered when it would rain. It's been clouding up all afternoon," offered Salyna, clearly understanding that Mykella didn't want to talk about the attackers any more. Her quick glance to her oldest sister did suggest she'd want more of an explanation later.

Mykella gave the faintest of nods.

Muergya immediately appeared with a platter holding three split and browned game hens and a basket of brown bread. She set the platter before Mykella and the basket in the middle of the table, hurrying out to the serving pantry and returning with a small casserole dish.

Mykella could tell that the dish held a mixture of potatoes, cheese, and prickle. She just hoped the cheese was strong enough to submerge the bitter taste of the prickle even though she knew she had to eat it because there were few other vegetables and no fruits available until

early summer. She served herself a game hen, then a moderate helping of the casserole.

The wine was a Vyan white she didn't recognize, drier than she
preferred, and slightly off, although her Talent showed no poison in it.

"Are you going to have a season-turn ball?" asked Rachylana after
taking one small bite of her hen.

"I hadn't thought about it, but there's no reason not to have one.
It's traditional." *And I shouldn't be upsetting any more traditions than I
have to at the moment.* "Would you like to make the arrangements?"

Rachylana brightened. Then she frowned. "There's really no one
special to invite."

"Sometimes it's like that," replied Mykella. "You'll have to make
do with whatever we have this time, except for the food."

"Your first ball should be special."

"We can't afford special. There may be even more golds missing
from the Highways and Rivers accounts, and that's in addition to several thousand more golds that Joramyl diverted to his purse."

"To pay for Cheleyza's gowns, no doubt," said Salyna acidly.

"I couldn't say," replied Mykella. "There's enough missing to pay
for ten times the gowns she left behind."

"I'll bet it's in jewelry," Salyna said as she sliced through a game
hen with a glittering knife that hadn't been on the table.

That just might be. Why hadn't she thought of jewelry? *Because you
don't have much use for it?*

"That might be," said Rachylana slowly. "Some of her necklaces
and bracelets were exquisite. I thought she'd brought them with her."

"Portable wealth Lanachrona paid for." Salyna turned her attention to the game hen.

Mykella took a bite of the fowl, still warm and with enough juice
not to be dry. After a moment, she turned to Rachylana. "I really
would appreciate it if you would arrange the ball. I've never been good
at that sort of thing."

"You, at least, should have a new dress," said Rachylana.

"Green, trimmed in black, and the same style as the last one. After
everything, it should be somber."

Salyna nodded.

After that, Mykella managed to keep conversation limited to the ball and food.

Later, Salyna followed Mykella back to her private study after announcing that she wanted to talk about how to add women to the Southern Guards.

Once they were in the study, Salyna announced, "You weren't telling everything."

"No. I wasn't. The attackers were Ifrits—Alectors. They came through the Table from the world where those who survived the Cataclysm live." Mykella thought that was right, from what the soarer had told her and what little she'd learned from the one Ifrit who had later attacked her from the Table.

"Through the Table?" Salyna looked shocked.

"That's what the Tables were for, back then. I didn't know they still worked that way."

"Will your iron doors . . . ?"

"Their flame blades don't cut through iron or stone. Commander Areyst has more men with rifles down there until the doors are in place. Their tunics . . ." Mykella went on to explain.

When she had finished, Salyna was silent for a time. Then she said, "What will you do?"

"Whatever I can."

"Oh . . . Mykella . . . if anyone knew just how bad things are . . ."

"They mustn't. What people know already is bad enough." *And Salyna doesn't even know it all.*

"If you survive all this . . ."

"*When* we survive all this, we can be grateful it wasn't worse." Mykella offered a rueful smile. She wasn't about to offer the all-too-trite saying that things could be worse, not when she knew that she'd find that they were even worse than she thought as soon as she discovered more.

Salyna shook her head. "Mother said no one would ever stop you . . . but I don't think she foresaw this."

Mykella wondered just how much their mother had foreseen, especially because it was unlikely her Talent came from her father . . . or not entirely, since none of the recent Lords-Protector had shown any.

"She must have seen something." She smiled again, if faintly. "I need to think."

"Of course."

Once Mykella was certain that Salyna had headed back to her chamber or the family sitting room, Mykella walked over to the outside wall and touched the stone of the window casement, reaching for the blackish green and letting it enfold her and carry her down to the Table chamber.

As soon as she emerged, she raised full shields, but the Table had almost returned to the duller pink-purple that it had displayed when she had first learned to sense it. She turned to the door, but it was shut, and boarded up somehow on the corridor side.

She approached the Table carefully, but the mirrored surface was blank, and she sensed nothing amiss. She concentrated on Porofyr.

The image that appeared showed the Seltyr across a polished table from Khanasyl, in what looked to be a private library. Mykella watched as the two talked, trying to make out what they might be saying although she suspected that much of it had to do with her . . . possibly even who Khanasyl might recommend for Minister of Highways and Rivers. She had no doubts she would not like whomever they proposed, but she had to ask, if only to stall for time while she struggled to understand more of what she faced in trying to put things to rights in Tempre and Lanachrona.

Next she sought an image of Cheleyza. Her aunt was seated at a long table in a large but dimly lit hall, between two men attired in a fashion similar to that of Vaerlon, the envoy from Midcoast. Mykella doubted that Cheleyza was in Midcoast. Since eight days on the river and road were unlikely to have taken her all the way to Harmony, even over the eternastone road from Hieron, she was most likely in a noble hall in Arwyn. Mykella watched for a time, but there was nothing she could see that indicated exactly where Cheleyza happened to be.

She made quicker searches for Duchael and Lhanyr, but saw nothing of interest, and—again—she had no fortune at all in finding an image of the Ifrits who had come through the Table. She did linger over a somehow indistinct image of Areyst, still at Southern Guard headquarters, studying maps, before she returned to her chambers.

15

On Quinti, Mykella was in the formal study early, so early she'd only seen Salyna at breakfast, and briefly at that. She was still irritated over Duchael's and Cerlyk's requests for golds. The fact that the day outside was gray and dreary didn't help her mood, either, but she immediately sent word to the duty-squad leader that she would be needing a spare mount for her morning inspection ride.

A half glass before midday, with Maeltor beside her and a squad of Southern Guards behind them, she reined up outside the narrow gray stone building beside the justicing building off the south-Tempre market square. Maeltor and one guard accompanied her inside to a small side chamber, where a slight figure dressed in a gray shimmer-silk jacket over black trousers and an ivory shirt rose from behind a spotless table-desk. His dark hair was slicked back from his narrow and clean-shaven face. His small deep-set eyes widened slightly as he beheld Mykella.

"Lady-Protector . . . I did not expect . . ."

"You are Chief Inspector Byrnyt?"

"Yes, Lady."

"Then you should not be surprised to see me." Mykella surveyed the inspector. "I see you have not been inspecting sewers recently."

"There has been no need, Lady-Protector."

"Why is that?"

"The sewers are performing as they were designed, Lady."

"Yet . . . in riding through Tempre, I have smelled odors that suggest not all is as it should be." She smiled. "I brought a mount for you to accompany me. We will see."

"Of course, Lady."

Behind his polite words, she could sense resignation and apprehension, but not fear or guilt. *Why no fear or guilt? If he has not been doing his duty, he should be concerned, and he doesn't seem to be a stupid man.*

In a few moments, they had all mounted and were riding toward the rendering area bordering the South River. As with the last time she had ridden along the South River, the array of clay pipes protruding from the walls on the west side of the river were still discharging thin streams of oily wastes. The smoke from the wide brick chimneys appeared darker, and the stench more pronounced.

She glanced at Byrnyt, noting that the inspector was working not to cough or choke on the fumes. Mykella decided not to pursue all her questions at that moment, not until Byrnyt had seen everything she had in mind, and they continued southward, entering before long the area filled with metalworks. There, the smoke and haze grew stronger and more acrid. The river still held a bluish shimmer downstream from the partly submerged pipes.

Mykella pointed. "Does that not appear to be oil on the river?"

"Yes, Lady, but oil is not permitted in the sewers, and I have reported this on more than one occasion."

"And what of the rendering yards?" she asked.

"Those . . . I have reported, but they are not sewer problems. They are river problems, and I have reported them."

Mykella could barely keep from lashing out at the supercilious Byrnyt by the time they had finished her reinspection of the area bordering the South River. Instead, when they finally left the metalworking section of Tempre behind, she continued to ride toward the inn and square to the south.

Before long, some two blocks north of the square and the inn, she began to scent the odor of human wastes. "Do you smell that, Inspector? Does that odor not suggest the sewers are in less-than-good repair?"

"It is not the sewers, Lady. Those are wastes that were not washed into the sewers. Some of those who own buildings have not refitted them with drains."

"And you have done nothing?"

"I have reported those failures, Lady."

Mykella did not pursue that . . . yet. The streets were not the place for a detailed questioning, at least not until she had completed conducting Byrnyt on her "inspection tour." So she turned the gelding westward, then back northwest toward the poorer section closer to the Grand Piers, where she had smelled rather pungent odors before.

When they reached the older houses holding too many families, she looked to the inspector, noting that his nose was twitching. "The sewers?"

"No, Lady. The sewers are not being used."

Mykella had had enough. She reined up and turned to Byrnyt. "I trust you can see why I am concerned about the sewers in all these parts of Tempre."

"Lady-Protector . . . the sewers are in excellent condition. Neither the metalworking facilities nor the renderers are allowed to discharge into the sewers, and they are not. Here, the owners have refused to change their buildings to use the sewers."

"Is it not your duty as chief inspector to ensure that they do not place wastes in the river? Or that people use them properly?"

"Begging your pardon, Lady-Protector, but my authority is limited to the sewers. The metal factorages know that all too well. So do the landlords."

Mykella wanted to scream. "Exactly who does have the authority to make them comply?"

"I do not know, Lady . . . only that I do not."

Mykella could sense two things—that Byrnyt believed he was telling the truth and that he was close to trembling with fear. She forced herself to wait for several moments and to speak calmly. "You said you have reported this problem. How often have you reported it?"

"Yes, Lady-Protector. I have reported it to the Minister of Highways and Rivers at the beginning and middle of every year since I became chief inspector."

"How long have you been chief inspector?"

"Six years at last year-turn."

Mykella forced herself to nod slowly, and say, "Thank you, Inspector. I appreciate your honesty in clarifying what your responsibilities are." She looked to Maeltor. "Captain, if you would have a guard accompany the inspector back to his place, then return to the palace with the spare mount."

"Yes, Lady." Maeltor turned. "Shultyn, forward!"

As Mykella rode back toward the palace, she considered what she had learned. First, she'd come perilously close to making a total fool of herself . . . and perhaps she had, all because she hadn't totally understood who controlled what. Second, she'd need to send a letter, not exactly of apology, but one expressing her appreciation of Byrnyt's patience and willingness to explain matters. And she *hated* making mistakes like that. The most depressing aspect was that all she'd wanted to do was to make things better in Tempre.

Once she was back in her study, still half-seething, half-brooding, she started to reach for the book that held the rules for sewers and rivers, then stopped.

Did she have to look up everything? She shook her head. In moments, she was headed down to the lower level of the palace to Lord Gharyk's study.

The diminutive Gharyk was there. Before he even finished standing, Mykella launched into her problem. "Lord Gharyk . . . I've been riding through Tempre and found a number of instances where wastes are being dumped into the South River and landlords are not connecting their buildings properly to the sewers. When I brought the matter to the attention of the chief sewer inspector, he informed me that he has been reporting improper handing of wastes from metalworks and renderers for years, as well as reporting on landlords who have not complied. He claims that under the Charter of the Protector, he has no authority to force the factorages to comply. Can you tell me whether that is correct, and, if so, what ministry has the authority to do anything about it?"

Gharyk offered a sad smile. "Lady . . . Minister Porofyr made the same reports to me. I requested that the local patrollers shut down the factorages. They did. Both the Seltyrs and the factors complained. Your uncle came and told me that your father had overruled me and said that I could not keep them from their business because we would lose their tariffs. I went to your father directly, and he said that he trusted Lord Joramyl's judgments."

Mykella just stood there. Gharyk was telling the truth. He regretted doing so, but what he said was true. She swallowed. *Will you ever get past all the problems Joramyl created?*

Except, she realized, her father had done little to stop Joramyl. *Why not? Because he didn't care, or because Joramyl told him that the Seltyrs would rebel and refuse to pay their tariffs? Would they now?* She would have snorted had she not been in Gharyk's study. Was there any doubt that they'd threaten her in the same way? *None at all, not the way Khanasyl is already acting.* But that didn't change the fact that she'd been wrong about who was responsible. It had been her own father, and that saddened her even more.

"Lady?" inquired Gharyk softly.

"I was just thinking. What other hidden threats have the Seltyrs made?" She turned her eyes on the Justice Minister.

"They conveyed what they believed, Lady. They would be most outraged if anyone called what they said threats." An ironic smiled followed his words.

"They seem to get outraged whenever they fail to get their way, and sometimes it appears that they can be rather vindictive. Did you know that someone set fire to one of High Factor Hasenyt's warehouses? And that the man who did so hung himself in the gaol within glasses, and his brother's body was dismembered?"

"I could not say that I am surprised. Lady . . . as I told you earlier, I do not receive the reports on what happens in the gaol and in the city and town justicing halls, but I have received enough information of the sort you have mentioned. I have been able to do little, for reasons of which you are aware. You are most impressive. They do not know just how impressive, and until they learn that, they will continue as they have done in the past—as their ancestors did until Mykel the Great forced them into line. It has been many years since the Seltyrs of Tempre have faced a strong Protector, and never one who is a woman."

Mykella's irritation faded as she listened to his calm words. Finally, she nodded. "Thank you. I needed that reminder."

"Lady . . . your father was a good man, but he was not as strong as he needed to be. Your uncle was strong, but neither good nor wise, and you have inherited a difficult situation."

Mykella offered a wry, if tight, smile. "I find I'm discovering that, more so every day."

Gharyk nodded.

After a moment, she asked, "Under the Charter, what power do I have to punish a lawbreaker?"

Gharyk smiled, pleased that she had asked the question, then said, "The Charter contains a most interesting clause in that regard. The Protector of Tempre has the right to pass judgment on anyone whose acts threaten or have threatened the well-being of Lanachrona, but any sentence the Protector carries out must either be meted out personally by the Protector without weapons in hand or carried out by others after a hearing before a justicer."

For several moments, Mykella was absolutely silent. "The Charter says that?"

Gharyk turned and stepped to the bookcase, from which he extracted a thin bound book. He opened it and flipped through several pages before extending it to her. "The second paragraph. This provision was added by Mykel the Great, but the Seltyrs all approved it. It has never been changed . . . for obvious reasons."

Mykella understood perfectly. If a Lord-Protector had Talent, no one would dare to change it, and if he did not, there was no need to. "Thank you," she said again, before turning and leaving.

As she hurried back to the upper level of the palace, she wanted to shake her head even as she considered what Gharyk had told her. She had almost reached the door to the antechamber when Salyna hurried up.

"I've been looking for you," began her sister. "I wanted to ask you . . . What is it, Mykella? You look terrible."

"The more I look into things, the more I discover how bad they are."

"What do you mean?"

Should I tell her? Mykella took a deep breath. "You'd better come into the study."

Chalmyr stood as the sisters entered the outer chamber. "Lady . . . when you are free, I have drafted some correspondence."

"Thank you. We won't be too long." Once inside the study, Mykella made sure the door was closed, then walked toward the windows, glancing momentarily beyond the palace grounds to the park, still bedraggled and shabby without the redeeming grace of spring's greening.

"What is it?" asked Salyna.

"You know all about the golds from the tariffs . . . I told you about those . . . before . . ." Mykella looked to her younger sister. "There's more . . . worse." She went on to explain about all the missing golds, about the timber sales, and about the sewers and what Gharyk had told her about the Seltyrs—but not the lord's judgments of their father and uncle.

"How could that be? How?"

Mykella just waited.

"It is . . . isn't it?" Salyna finally said. "Oh . . . poor Father."

"It explains more why Joramyl acted as he did." Mykella shook her head. "It was wrong. He should have tried to help Father."

"Maybe he did . . . until Cheleyza . . . She was evil. I never trusted her."

"That's possible." *Except that Joramyl was allowing the factors to break the law years before he married Cheleyza.* "I doubt we'll ever know for sure."

"What will you do?"

"Whatever I must. What else can I do?"

After Salyna left, Mykella walked to the window of the study. She couldn't help but still wonder why Duchael requested golds for sewer repairs if the problems didn't lie in the sewers. She turned to call Chalmyr. At least, she could deal with correspondence, and she needed to draft that letter to Inspector Byrnyt and have it dispatched quickly.

16

Standing beside her desk in the formal study, for the second time Mykella read through the missive that had arrived earlier on Sexdi morning, marveling at how much she disliked Seltyr Khanasyl after one short meeting and one set of words in ink.

. . . since you were so kind as to request our suggestions for a Minister of Highways and Rivers, we have discussed the matter with a number of others . . .

Other Seltyrs, no doubt.

. . . and have decided to offer several names for your consideration, believing that you will be able to select the one that best suits the needs of the ministry . . .

In other words, you'd better choose one of them.

. . . Seltyr Pualavyn, Seltyr Thaen, and Seltyr Klevytr all would bring exceptional qualities to the position, as well as a thorough understanding of the needs of all those in commerce in Tempre and Lanchrona . . .

They'll all do what you want, and if I refuse to name one of them, you'll make certain that everyone knows how stupid and willful I am. Mykella shook her head and extended the missive to Chalmyr.

"Do you wish to reply, Lady?" asked the scrivener as he took the heavy paper.

"If you would draft a suitably flowery response telling the good Seltyr how very much I appreciate his interest and his counsel and how he will be among the very first to know once I've made my decision as to whom I will appoint to become Minister of Highways and Rivers . . . Oh . . . and tell him that I am awaiting a response from the High Factors as well."

The scrivener smiled and nodded. "I will have a reply for you within the glass."

"The letter to Inspector Byrnyt was dispatched?" Mykella thought it had been, but wanted to make certain. She still hated admitting, even indirectly, that she was wrong.

"Yesterday, Lady."

"Thank you."

After Chalmyr had closed the study door, Mykella glanced toward the window, glad that the day was bright and sunny, even if her feelings were not. What was she going to do about the sewers? Should she do anything at all at the moment?

Probably not. They'll have to wait. You can't afford to get the Seltyrs more upset, especially when most of the Southern Guards from Tempre is in Viencet getting retrained, not that they'll actually resort to arms.

Still . . . it irritated her.

She took a deep breath. She needed to talk to Duchael and Cerlyk about why their respective ministries wanted more golds, but that could wait at least until she calmed down. Unless their requests were far more urgent than she suspected, they'd have to be deferred. With a possible invasion from the west, all available golds would need to go to the Southern Guards.

Her thoughts went back to the section of the Charter Gharyk had shown her. She'd checked the copy of the Charter in the study bookcase, and that wording was there as well, under the section entitled "Powers Reserved to the Protector."

That explained several things, including the lack of complaint at her means of becoming Lady-Protector . . . because by executing traitors without "weapons in hand," she'd effectively proved she was the Protector. While it was good to know she had that power under the Charter, it wasn't something to be used lightly.

Still . . .

The door opened, and Salyna stepped inside.

"I've been thinking, Mykella." The blonde slipped into one of the chairs before the desk.

"About what?"

"Training women to be guards. We wouldn't call them that. We'd call them auxiliaries or something like that . . . at first, anyway. If we started now, we could have a squad or two partly ready before summer, and that would free more guards if Skrelyn does attack."

"Have you been recruiting already?" Mykella couldn't help but offer the faintest of amused smiles.

"Not really. I have talked to some of the servingwomen and sculls. I asked them to see what their families and friends thought. Some of them thought it was a bad idea, and some didn't. This morning, Muergya and Zestela told me that they knew almost a score of women who wanted to know when it might happen."

"Would they be interested if they didn't get paid much until they finished training? The men don't, you know?"

"They don't make much now. Some don't make anything."

I should have thought of that, Mykella realized. "You're right. I'll talk to Areyst. We just might need every guard we can find. Is there anything else he should know or think about?"

"Size doesn't matter nearly so much if you can ride and shoot a rifle accurately."

"I think you've proved that, even to the commander."

"You might remind him."

Mykella laughed. After a moment, she asked, "How is Rachylana doing?"

"She's better. It was a good idea to have her organize the ball." Salyna stood. "I need to go. Commander Areyst will be here before long."

"How do you know?"

"He was on the first level checking on the duty guards." With that, Salyna headed out of the study.

As Salyna predicted, the study door did not remain closed for all that long.

"Commander Areyst, Lady." Chalmyr did not so much ask as announce and open the door for the officer.

"Lady." Areyst stepped into the study, bowed, then straightened and raised his eyes to meet hers.

As always, Mykella found herself slightly shocked when she looked into his pale green eyes and felt the warmth beneath the formality. Her own feelings of attraction vanished as she saw the gravity in his face and sensed concerns he had yet to voice. "Yes, Commander?"

"I regret that I must report that the Ifrits attacked and have taken over the summer villa of Seltyr Klevytr. One of the retainers escaped and ran to the highway. He waved down a Southern Guard messenger."

Although Mykella had just read Khanasyl's missive recommending Klevytr, other than a vague recollection of the Seltyr's name, Mykella knew nothing about the man although she thought he was younger and had recently inherited from an uncle. *After all the business with Khanasyl and the ministry, why did it have to be Klevytr's villa?* "Just three of them?"

"The villa is used little until summer, I understand, and much of the household staff was here in Tempre. With the weapons the Ifrits have . . ." He shrugged.

"Where exactly is the villa of Seltyr Klevytr?"

"Some fifteen vingts to the west of Tempre, in the rolling plains on the south side of the southwest highway."

Of course. They would choose a place where I can't draw on the darkness. She almost frowned. *But how would they know that? The other Ifrit didn't.* "What do you suggest?"

"Send out a squad to see what they can do. One equipped with sniper rifles."

"Do you have any marksmen?" Mykella smiled. "Besides Salyna, that is?"

Areyst grinned, if momentarily. "I had thought of taking her, but that would not be wise."

"I should go with you."

The commander shook his head. "There are but three of them, and they can be killed. The doors below in the palace are not finished, and if any others attempted to use the Table, you are the only one who could stop them. I told those on duty to aim for the head, but for one man to inform you immediately and with no delay."

Mykella didn't like it, but she could see the wisdom in his words. "You might want to find some iron-faced shields or something like that."

"There were five in the old section of the armory."

"There's one other matter."

Areyst raised his eyebrows but did not speak.

"Salyna was here earlier. She made the point that, if women were trained as auxiliaries, starting now, that might free more guards by summer."

"It well might . . . except it takes people to train them."

"What if she were in charge, and even did some of the training, but had to make them meet standards the two of you agreed upon before they could qualify for being paid?"

"The men wouldn't like it if barely trained women got paid the same as troopers."

"Salyna suggested that they be called auxiliaries. That way, their starting pay could be lower."

"I can't deal with that now."

"No. You need to go. What if I have her write up a plan for you when you return?"

"I could certainly look at it and see if it might work."

That means you're as desperate as Salyna thinks you are. "I'll have her do that. After you two talk, and if you can come to an agreement, then bring it to me."

Areyst nodded. "That would be best." His eyes flicked toward the window.

Mykella stood. "You'd better go and take care of the Ifrits."

Once Areyst departed, Mykella walked to the window, where she touched the stone, then reached for the greenish darkness and slipped down to the Table chamber. It was empty, but the Table appeared to be glowing ever slightly more brightly than it had been in the previous few days. She stepped forward and studied the Table more closely. She discerned nothing. Then she concentrated on Cheleyza.

The mists swirled across the silvered surface before revealing her aunt riding through a misty rain, the mount carrying her along an eternastone highway.

She's not to Harmony yet, and Chalcaer didn't come to meet her. Good.

Mykella sought out others of interest, but all were undertaking routine tasks—except that Porofyr was engaged in disrobing a young woman definitely not his wife, and Mykella quickly concentrated on Lhanyr, who was leafing though a ledger while talking to a younger man.

Once she finished her Table surveillance, Mykella stepped back and studied the Table once more. It had definitely brightened somewhat. Did that mean that another Ifrit or group of Ifrits was watching . . . or preparing to use the Table? How could she tell?

The appearance of the Ifrits concerned her far more than she had told either Salyna or Areyst. After all the years since the Cataclysm, why had they reappeared? What other weapons might they bring? Supposedly, according to the stories, during the Cataclysm the weapons of the Alectors had sunk the vaunted cities of Elcien and Ludar into the Bay of Ludar. But could the Ifrits bring such weapons through the Tables from where they were?

She shook her head. There was so much she didn't know, about the Table, about being a ruler . . . and most of all, she worried about not knowing what else she didn't know.

17

Because Mykella hadn't received any messages from Commander Areyst when she stepped into her study on Septi morning, she decided against riding through Tempre, even though there were still large sections of the city she hadn't seen recently—or with the eyes of a Lady-Protector. The only one she'd told about the Ifrits' taking over Klevytr's villa had been Salyna, and she had been very brief, despite her worries. Midmorning came and went, and there was still no word from the commander. So she had Chalmyr summon Duchael to her study.

Once the assistant minister for Highways and Rivers arrived, she immediately gestured him into a chair, and asked, "Would you please explain why you're asking for another thousand golds for the sewers?"

"You had indicated that repairs might be necessary, Lady, and there are not sufficient golds in the maintenance accounts."

Mykella opened the master ledger for the ministry and leafed through to the subaccounts. As she did, she concentrated on Duchael, sensing a growing nervousness. She glanced down the columns. "We are only a little more than three weeks into the year, and already three hundred golds have been spent on maintenance. That does not include the wages for the engineer's workers. On what, exactly, were those golds spent?"

"I don't know, Lady. Minister Porofyr made the transfers himself."

"Until I do know for what those golds were spent, do you really think it is wise for me to grant more golds to the ministry?"

"Lady . . . I cannot say. I only know that there are only two hundred golds left in the maintenance account."

"Last year, maintenance required one thousand two hundred golds. Please provide me with a listing of what maintenance was accomplished with those golds, as well as what maintenance was accomplished with the three hundred spent over the last three weeks. As assistant minister, surely you should be able to discover that."

Duchael swallowed. "Yes, Lady."

"Say . . . by Novdi morning. You can leave your report with Chalmyr if I'm not here."

"Yes, Lady."

Mykella stood. "That's all." Her voice was soft.

As Duchael backed out of the study, Mykella could sense a rising tide of fear and desperation. *Why? Because Porofyr has taken the golds, and Duchael fears for his life if he reveals that . . . and fears me if he doesn't?*

Once the door closed, she sat down with a sigh. Even when the numbers in the ledgers balanced, they didn't reveal what lay behind the entries. She had the sense that, for the most part, the Southern Guard entries were accurate. Otherwise, Joramyl wouldn't have had to fabricate false entries for comparatively smaller sums for tack from a nonexistent leather worker in order to obtain golds from the Guard funds. She hadn't sensed deception in Cerlyk, but that didn't mean Loryalt hadn't been diverting funds. *Or that he had,* she reminded herself.

She stood and walked to the study door, opening it partway. "Could you send someone to see if Cerlyk's in? If he is, I'd like to see him."

"Yes, Lady."

In less than half a glass, Cerlyk entered the study, bowing politely. "You requested my presence, Lady?"

"I did. I'm curious about your request for golds." Mykella motioned to the chair. "If you would explain it . . ."

"Yes, Lady," replied Cerlyk as he seated himself. "Most times, we wouldn't need to request anything at all. When the ministry does a timber sale or receives the overrides on approved private sales, the golds go into the Treasury, except for a portion reserved for the pay and maintenance of the local inspectors . . . and for running the ministry here in Tempre. Both those total one part in twenty, on average, and the Forestry Ministry keeps a reserve of between a thousand and two thousand golds for those wages and costs, including for the minister and me and the clerks. Even so, usually, we don't spend all of that over the year, because Minister Loryalt is most careful in approving expenses." Cerlyk paused. "Last winter, though, Lord Joramyl said that the Lord-Protector needed to draw on the reserves and transferred all but two hundred golds from us. We don't have any timber sales coming—I told you about that—and we won't receive any overrides on private sales until midsummer at the earliest."

"I see." What she saw was that Joramyl had been diverting thousands of golds more than she had already found. *But what did he do with them?*

"Do you know when Forester Loryalt will be returning to Tempre?"

Cerlyk shook his head slightly, as if puzzled by her change of subject. "Not precisely, Lady. Before he departed, he said that he hoped to complete his inspections by the end of the eighth week of spring, and that would be two weeks from next Londi."

"Does he usually return early or late from such inspections?"

"He seldom has been later. He is most careful in his estimations and calculations."

Mykella hoped that care also applied to the forester's estimations of revenues. She nodded, then said, "It appears that Lord Joramyl diverted large amounts of golds from a number of ministry accounts. Until Haelyt and I can determine all that is missing from various accounts, I'm reluctant to transfer golds anywhere. Do you need these golds urgently?"

Cerlyk tilted his head slightly, pursing his lips, replying after a few moments. "What we have *should* suffice for the next few tendays, possibly longer."

"That would be helpful. If matters become more urgent before that, please let me know. I hope we can resolve the discrepancies before then."

"Is that all you needed, Lady? Or is there other information you require?"

"Not at the moment." Mykella rose. At times, she felt like a string puppet, rising and sitting as required by the moment. "Thank you."

Cerlyk stood, bowed, and departed.

Would she ever get to the bottom of all the missing golds? Where could Joramyl have possibly put them? Or had Cheleyza taken most of them with her? The only thing Mykella had found hidden in the villa had been the antique sabers, and they weren't even the kind the Southern Guards used. That seemed to be her fortune, discovering more and more losses, and what little she did find seemed useless. She replaced the account ledgers in the bookcase although they'd have to go back to Haelyt before long.

The study door eased open.

"Do you have a moment, Mykella?" asked Salyna. "I wanted to ask you some things about the plan for the auxiliaries." She looked at her sister. "I can come back. You look worried. If I'm interrupting . . ."

Mykella shook her head. "Right now, I'm as much waiting and thinking as anything. I haven't heard from Areyst . . ." She motioned for her sister to come in and close the study door.

Salyna did so. "Is it about the Ifrits? They say that Seltyr Klevytr can be most intemperate. Has anyone told him?"

"I haven't told anyone but you. I'm not about to tell him until I have to. I hope we can get the Ifrits under control first." She smiled ruefully. "What did you want to ask?"

"I'd thought to train thirty women to begin with. I can handle that many, mostly, and if I could have the help of just a guard or two . . ."

"You're running the palace, aren't you?"

"I've asked Rachylana to help, and she's already doing some things."

Mykella should have thought of that. Keeping Rachylana busy might keep her out of too much trouble. "That's a good idea."

"They really ought to have training in sabers as well as rifles, but . . . with the shortage of arms . . . we could use wooden blanks, I suppose . . ."

Mykella frowned. There was something . . . "We found a score of antique sabers in Joramyl's villa. I thought they were useless. They're not what the Guards uses."

"They're blades! Once they get past the first stages, we can use them . . . Thank you!"

Mykella concealed an amused smile. She hadn't even agreed, not that there was any reason not to.

After more than a half glass, Salyna departed, and Mykella walked to the window and looked across at the park. Was there the slightest touch of spring green?.

"Captain Maeltor and a messenger, Lady," announced Chalmyr from behind her.

"Send them in." Mykella turned and walked back to her desk. She remained standing, not that such was required, especially for those who reported to her, but she was concerned and felt more composed on her feet.

The man accompanying Maeltor wore the blue uniform of the Southern Guards but with an embroidered insignia of a horse on the upper shoulder of his jacket.

"Slaedek has a message from the commander, Lady."

The Southern Guard extended a folded but unsealed sheet. "Lady-Protector, the commander asked me to tell you that the men who escaped the palace are trapped in a tower. They killed several retainers at the villa of Seltyr Klevytr, but they cannot escape."

"Thank you." Mykella took the sheet, unfolded it, and began to read.

Lady-Protector—
The attackers have barricaded themselves in the stronghold tower of the villa. They have several captives. One is the daughter of Klevytr. She is about the age of your youngest sister. The others are retainers. We cannot take the tower without risking her life.

They cannot be allowed to escape, but, for now, we will wait to see what happens . . . or for any instructions you have.

The signature below the words was a single "A."

Should she go to the villa . . . or not? Klevytr's daughter complicated the situation more than she would have liked.

"Captain Maeltor . . . if you and Guard Slaedek will wait in the anteroom for a moment, I would like to think over the commander's message. I will not be long."

"Yes, Lady."

Both Southern Guards looked slightly puzzled, but complied.

Once they were out of the study, Mykella slid the bolt, then walked to the window and touched the granite casement. In instants, she stood inside the Table chamber, raising her shields as soon as she emerged. The door was closed, but the inside was still the one of wood. *When will they finish the iron shutter doors?*

She walked to the Table, studying its brightness. So far, it was not pulsing a brilliant pinkish purple, and more than a day had passed the last time after the pulsing had begun before the Ifrits had arrived.

You'll have to chance it.

She glanced into the depths of the Table, seeking the Ifrits, but the Table revealed nothing. She hadn't thought it would, but it had been worth the effort. A second effort revealed Areyst in a white-walled corridor. The commander was talking to a Southern Guard. Mykella frowned. The guard's image was clear, but Areyst's was silvered and fainter. *Why would that be?* She watched for several moments, but nothing changed.

After reaching out to the greenish blackness, she transported herself back to the study, where she walked to the door and undid the bolt, then stepped out into the anteroom.

Chalmyr and the other two looked up. So did the messenger boy in the corner.

"Captain . . . I'll be riding to join the commander immediately. You will remain here as senior officer of the Southern Guards." She turned to Chalmyr. "If all goes well, I should be back sometime tomorrow."

"That's a hard ride in that time even . . ." Maeltor broke off his words.

"Even for a guard?" Mykella finished "It is, but that is what is necessary. If you would have my mount and a spare ready as soon as possible, I will join you."

"Yes, Lady."

She nodded to the two and walked from the anteroom toward her apartments to get her riding jacket and a few things.

Behind her, she caught a few words.

". . . she do that?"

". . . likely do more than any of us might wish . . ."

She certainly hoped so.

18

The sun hung just above the low hills to the west in the slowly darkening silver-green sky when Mykella and the squad of Southern Guards turned off the eternastone highway and covered the fifty yards of paved lane leading to the stone gates of Klevytr's estate. Mykella was somewhat tired, but more thirsty than anything, since she'd finished off her water bottle a glass or so earlier and hadn't wanted to stop. She'd been occasionally reaching out with her Talent, but the estate was clearly far enough away from the nearest of the underground paths of greenish blackness to be beyond her ability to reach and tap into it. She hadn't expected otherwise, but she had wanted to make certain.

The pair of mounted guards by the gate did not quite stare as they caught sight of Mykella riding beside Zhulyn, the squad leader.

"Lady-Protector!"

"Where is Commander Areyst?" She kept her voice calm but added just a touch of Talent, so that it carried.

"Up at the main villa, Lady," one guard finally replied.

The lane from the gates to the villa was less than half a vingt long and ran due south. It was not stone-paved, but covered in gravel, and still held ruts remaining from carts and wagons traversing it after the infrequent winter snows and too-frequent early-spring rains. On each side of the lane was a row of oaks, old enough that they would provide a canopy of shade once they leafed out, except in places where the original trees had died and not been replaced, and there were at least ten such instances, Mykella noted. The trees ended at a boxwood hedge that encircled what looked to be a garden, also circled by the lane.

On the south side sprawled the villa, a low one-story structure—except for the tower. As towers went, it did not seem terribly impressive, a square stone building that looked to have been stuck onto the east end of the villa.

Mykella didn't have to search for Areyst because he rode up immediately, his jacket partly unbuttoned. Although his face was shaded, with the low and late-afternoon sun behind him and in Mykella's face, she could see—and sense—a combination of strain, frustration, and worry.

"Lady . . . to the right! They occasionally try to strike anyone who approaches the tower with their weapons."

"To the right!" she repeated, guiding the gelding toward him.

As if understanding that the commander and the Lady-Protector needed space, Zhulyn gestured to the squad to hold back as Areyst and Mykella rode to the west around the hedged garden.

Areyst studied her, then nodded, as if to himself. "What about . . . ?"

"I have at least a day," returned Mykella. "Perhaps longer."

"Might I ask why you chose to come?"

"Because of the Seltyr's daughter." To forestall his objections, she held up a hand. "The Seltyrs of Tempre have suggested that Klevytr is suited to become Minister of Highways and Rivers. Let us say that I have my doubts. Also, I don't like having the Southern Guards tied up here for days and days."

"Can you do something we cannot?" There was a hint of a smile in his words although his face remained serious.

"We will have to see," she replied. "After I have something to eat and drink. Have they tried to say anything?"

"They've called out phrases, but none of us understood what they meant. They did hold up the girl, with one of their pistols pointed at her head."

"How many people do they have captive in the tower?"

"It's hard to say. Most likely between four and eight. None of Klevytr's retainers seemed to know exactly how many people were here because they didn't know how many came with the daughter. There are three retainers missing." Areyst reined up before the stables, a separate building set across a courtyard from the west end of the villa. "There are rations and other food in the chamber off the kitchen."

A guard scurried forward to take the gelding's reins when Mykella dismounted. As she followed Areyst across the uneven stones of the courtyard, she had to admit that she was sore in places . . . but not excessively so.

Two women in faded brown trousers and overblouses turned to stare as the commander and the Lady-Protector entered the kitchen from the courtyard.

"The Lady-Protector needs something to eat," began Areyst.

"Something that's ready now. Bread and cheese . . . cold meat . . ." offered Mykella, "and something to drink."

"Bread and cheese we have, Lady . . . but only a bit of cooked mutton."

"That will be fine."

"I'd feel . . . the master he might . . ."

"That's fine," Mykella repeated, "and I won't say a word."

Areyst moved toward a table on one side of the kitchen, where he stood at one end, his eyes fixed on her. "You're certain that will be enough?"

"I'm sure that will be all I need," she replied, settling gingerly into the wooden straight-backed chair at the other end of the table and unfastening but not shedding the nightsilk riding jacket.

Almost immediately, the older woman appeared with a platter on which was a small loaf of dark bread, a wedge of cheese, and several slices of mutton. Moments afterward, the other woman appeared with a beaker and a pitcher. Mykella studied all the food with her Talent but sensed nothing amiss. "Thank you."

"Being our pleasure, Lady."

Mykella hadn't realized just how hungry she was until after she had eaten all three slices of mutton, most of the loaf of slightly stale dark bread, and half the generous wedge of cheese, all accompanied by something that tasted like apple juice laced ever so slightly with vinegar, yet was not cider. Even her eyesight seemed clearer when she finished.

You need to eat more regularly if you going to rely on your Talent. But hadn't she reminded herself of that before . . . perhaps several times before?

By the time she and Areyst left the kitchen and began to walk along the main-floor corridor toward the east wing of the villa—and the tower—the sun had set, and the sky was fading into silver-green-purpled twilight. She could sense retainers in places, but no one actually stepped forward or looked directly at them. At the end of the east-wing corridor was a square stone arch. Behind it was narrow stone staircase leading up to a second-level entrance into the tower. Two Southern Guards with rifles flanked the archway, shielded by the stone.

"Stop behind the arch," said Areyst. "They'll fire at anything that goes beyond."

"Do you have something to stick out so that they will?" she asked.

Areyst pointed to a pole leaning against the wall. The last hand's length was blackened. "Will that do?"

"It should. When I nod, will you poke it out there?"

"I can do that, Lady." He smiled.

Mykella concentrated on extending her shields around the pole, as close as she could, because she didn't want the Ifrits to know what she was doing. She nodded.

Areyst extended the pole.

For several moments, nothing happened. Then the commander lifted it toward the second step. The briefest flash of bluish light flared around the tip of the pole. Following the blue flame came an exclamation from somewhere beyond the top of the steps.

Mykella could sense that her extended shields had blocked the flame, and she said, "Pull it back."

"Are you there?" she finally called out after easing over to the edge of the archway. "What do you want?"

After several moments, another string of words followed.

Mykella listened, then frowned. She *thought* she understood some of the words, but it had been easier listening through the Table

"What do you want?" she called again.

". . . submit . . . to . . . rightful . . . return . . . to . . . Alectorate . . ."

At least, that was what she thought she heard.

"You are outnumbered," she pointed out.

". . . not . . . long . . . you . . . harm   us . . . revenge . . . others . . . when . . . arrive . . ."

That didn't surprise her.

"What are they saying?" asked Areyst in a whisper.

"They want to be our rulers. More are coming, and we'll suffer if we harm them." She turned back toward the archway, and said loudly, "When will this happen?"

". . . before . . . you . . . think . . ."

"I need a large basket of food," Mykella said. "It would be better if it were a wide basket so that they can see what I'm carrying."

Areyst raised his eyebrows.

"The sooner the better," she added. "I doubt they're feeling patient, and I don't want to give them too much time to think about things."

The commander gestured to the trooper on the left. "Xander . . . you heard the Lady. Hurry back to the kitchen and have them put together a basket of food, then bring it back here as soon as you can."

"Yes, sir . . . Lady." The freckle-faced young man gave a quick nod and stopped, handing his rifle to Areyst. "You might need this, sir, and it will only get in my way." With that, he turned and hurried down the corridor.

"You're going to carry it to them, aren't you?"

"Of course. There's a good chance they won't shoot a girl bringing food who's carrying no weapons."

"Can't we follow you?"

"It won't do any good," she pointed out. "If I protect anyone who comes with me, you won't be able to shoot at them, and if you can shoot, then they'll be able to kill you with their weapons."

"What about you? If anything happens to you . . ."

Mykella shook her head. "You know how to kill them, and you

know how to seal the . . . entrance." She'd almost said "Table," but she didn't want to reveal that aspect of matters to others. *Not yet.* She lowered her voice. "If I can deal with these Ifrits, before others show up, I'll have learned more, and we won't have our forces split. Besides, if anything happens to me, just seal up the tower and post snipers."

"What about the Seltyr's daughter?"

Mykella smiled coolly. "If I'm killed, no one is going to care that you sacrificed some retainers and one unfortunate young woman." *It's only if I sacrifice her and survive that everyone will be upset, not that they really care that much about a younger daughter, but they'll do anything to discredit me.*

It seemed as though a glass had passed before Xander returned with a wicker basket a good half yard across and little more than a hand deep, on which were piled several loaves of bread, cheese wedges, a small ham, and several jars sealed with large corks and melted wax.

"Good." Mykella took the basket, then called out, "Food . . . we're bringing food."

After waiting for several moments, she concentrated on strengthening her shields, then stepped away from the side of the archway and moved forward in the dim light from the high side windows, holding the basket before her. She stopped and waited, then took another step, waiting again before she took the third. Slowly and carefully, she made her way up the stone stairs. Finally, she stepped through the archway at the top of the steps and into a small room or foyer. To the left was another set of stone steps leading upward to the third level. The steps were against the outside wall, but there was not even a railing on the inside edge. Directly before her, against the back wall of the chamber, was a flat table. To the right was one Ifrit.

She had to look up at the Ifrit, who stood several yards away, his pistol-like weapon aimed at her. She concentrated on making out his life-thread, a purplish cable that extended, unseen, in the direction of Tempre, linked in some fashion, she expected, through the Table there. It took her a moment to locate the node that held all the threads of his being together, and from what she could tell, he possessed only light shields, if any at all.

". . . one . . . with sense . . . at last . . ." A cruel smile creased broad features set in a pale white face beneath bluish black hair. His shimmering tunic and trousers were of a dark gray, as were his boots.

Mykella did not see the other two Ifrits, nor any of the captives. "Where are the others?"

". . . they . . . here . . . up . . ." He pointed to the table.

She carried the basket to the table, setting it there gently, but kept her eyes and senses on the Ifrit the whole time. Then she took a step back from the table, positioning herself so she could take in both the steps and the Ifrit.

A voice called down the steps.

A set of interchanges followed between the Ifrit who watched her and the one she could not see, but who, she sensed, was at the top of the next set of steps. After a moment, she realized that both of the other Ifrits were on the next floor of the tower. The gist of the conversation was that the locals had sent a girl with food but that they had not yet acknowledged the superiority of the Alectors. Mykella kept her face impassive, revealing nothing.

After several moments, the second Ifrit appeared, walked down four or five steps of the staircase. He held something like a pistol, and it was pointed at Mykella. His eyes raked over her as if she were a piece of meat. *Or one of the cattle. That was what the first one called me.*

Mykella shifted her concentration from the first Ifrit to the one on the steps, seeking out with her Talent the node that held his life-threads knotted together. She felt clumsy, but the Ifrit did not seem to even note her Talent efforts until she jabbed and twisted the node apart, with life-threads spraying apart. A single short scream preceded a large body pitching off the steps.

By then Mykella had turned back to the first Ifrit.

For a moment, his eyes had darted to his falling compatriot, but they dropped to Mykella, and the pistol flared blue fire. Although the bolt of flame sheeted off her shields, a needle-knife of pain went through her shoulder, and she winced, then concentrated on the Ifrit's node. That was made easier because he did not move, but kept flaring flame-bolts at her.

Abruptly, he collapsed, sinking more than falling onto the stone floor.

Mykella turned and hurried toward the stone steps, but had only climbed three when the third Ifrit appeared at the top of the steps. He was huge, perhaps almost three yards tall, and he came down the steps, two or three at a time, moving so fast that she could not focus on his life-thread node. Instead, she anchored her shields to the stone and waited. The blue flashes from the pair of weapons he flourished flared against Mykella's shields. While the fire again peeled away from the shields, each flame still felt as though a knife had been thrust through her, each blast more intense than the last.

The Ifrit's mouth opened in a snarl as he realized she was not going to move. Then he crashed into her shields and staggered back, his long legs losing their purchase and straddling her shielded legs as he rebounded back against the stone steps. In that moment, when he was relatively still, Mykella reached out with her Talent and ripped apart his life-thread node.

"The Ancients . . ."

Then the massive form lay still. Mykella released the link of shield to stone. For several moments, possibly longer, she found herself shivering as the residual needles of pain began to subside. *Even when you stopped the fire, you couldn't stop the pain. Is that so that their weapons work against each other?*

Hoping she didn't have to discover the answer to that question, she bent and shoved and dragged the dead Ifrit to one side of the steps before slowly trudging up to the third level of the tower. There, she could sense people behind a closed oak door. There was no lock, and she lifted the lever.

"It's all right." Mykella held her shields as she opened the door.

Inside, five women huddled in the corner. A tall girl—or young woman—wearing a stylish yellow and brown quilted jacket over shimmersilk trousers looked at Mykella. Her eyes widened.

"Lady-Protector?"

"I came as quickly as I could," replied Mykella. "They're all dead."

"Did the guards kill them?"

Mykella paused. *What do I say to that? If I say I did, it's boasting, and I'm a terror. If I deny it, I'm lying and undercutting myself.*

"You killed them? Like you did the usurper?"

Mykella nodded. "You're Seltyr Klevytr's daughter?"

"Yes," admitted the tall young woman nodded. "I'm Kietyra."

Behind them, the servitors were talking.

"They killed some of the Southern Guards . . ."

". . . they killed Rani . . . and Byhylt . . ."

One of the women remained huddled in the corner, sobbing silently.

Mykella raised her voice. "All of you need to come with me. There aren't any more of them. They're all dead," she said again, feeling that some of the servingwomen had not really heard what she said. Then she stepped out into the open area that served as both a chamber and the top landing.

"You came personally," said Kietyra, following her.

"Yes." Mykella wasn't about to say exactly why. She started down the steps.

Kietyra's eyes dropped to the giant form still sprawled on the steps, then the two on the floor below, taking in the shiny tunics and trousers. "They were Alectors, like from the old days, weren't they?"

"Yes, but I'd appreciate it if you kept that to yourself for now."

"Are you really an Ancient?"

Mykella laughed, if ruefully. "No, Kietyra. I was born and raised in Tempre, and I'm very much not ancient. I just have a few of the talents of my ancestor." That was fair enough.

She stopped and picked up the pair of pistols the last Ifrit had carried, and once she was on the level that afforded access to the stairs down into the villa, she recovered the other two weapons, slipping them into the pockets in her riding jacket. Every time she bent, needles of pain went down her back. She just hoped they'd fade before long.

Kietyra said nothing about the weapons but remained close, as Mykella went to the archway at the top of the steps, and called out, "I'm bringing Kietyra and the others out. The attackers are dead."

Not trusting that someone might fire accidentally, Mykella held her shields as she led the women down and into the east corridor of the villa.

After several moments, Areyst stepped into the archway at the bottom. Mykella could sense his relief . . . and the fact that it was more than just that she had taken care of the Ifrits.

". . . Lady-Protector . . ." offered Kietyra from beside Mykella, "Thank you."

Mykella felt embarrassed. "I did what I could."

The young woman lowered her voice. "I can see it wasn't that easy. It hurts for you to move, and there are flat welts all over your face. I won't say a word."

"The attackers?" asked Areyst.

Mykella finished descending the narrow stairs, so close that she and Kietyra were elbow to elbow. "I left their bodies there. Moving them would have been difficult."

"Xander!" called Areyst. "See that Lady Kietyra and her women are escorted to their quarters."

"Yes, sir."

Before she stepped away, Kietyra looked again at Mykella, and mouthed, "Thank you, Lady."

Once the women were farther down the corridor, Areyst turned to Mykella. "You have bruises all across your forehead and face." Behind his words was far more than concern, yet those feelings were as if locked away. "You need to sit down. This way . . ."

Is it that obvious? Mykella let him lead her to a side chamber, a sitting room of some sort that looked out on a walled garden lined with miniature trees of various kinds.

"I think I need to work on my shields." Mykella sat down in the nearest armchair. "How many men did the Ifrits kill?"

"We've found ten bodies so far."

Mykella nodded. After a moment, she said, "I need your help, Commander."

Areyst smiled ruefully. "You need my help? After that?"

"I need to get back to Tempre, and I'm going to ask a favor. I want you and half the guards that accompanied me to ride out of here and travel a vingt or so toward Tempre. Then I want you to send that half back to Tempre with the gelding, while you and I ride north for several vingts. Then you'll return to the villa with the spare mount. After several glasses, dispatch the remaining guards from my party, with the spare mount, and send them directly back to the Southern Guard barracks."

"Lady . . ."

"Trust me. I need to get back to Tempre. You'll see."

Areyst concealed an exasperated sigh. "As you wish, Lady. I must say that I do not understand."

"You will," she promised. "We need to go."

"We cannot do this in the way you wish. I will need to dispatch those who came with me. The men and mounts you brought, especially the mounts, need fodder and rest. I will return with them tomorrow."

"I should have thought of that," she said with a rueful laugh.

"Let me have my small victories, Lady." He smiled. "I insist on one other matter. You need to sit and rest for a while. Were you my sister, I would demand that you not return tonight. Since you are my Lady-Protector, I can only beseech you to rest for a time. A short nap would be better. I will post guards outside so that no one will disturb you."

Mykella opened her mouth, then closed it. After another pause, she said, "I have their weapons. Their bodies should be buried quickly. You might wish to save their clothing."

"I had thought that."

Mykella glanced to her left. There was a large couch, and she was yawning. "You may be right, Commander, but do not let me sleep more than a glass, or we both may regret it." She stood and walked to the couch, where she sat in the middle. *It's not too soft.*

For a moment, Areyst's face stiffened. Then he shook his head. "There are times I still see you . . . as you were, not as you are."

Mykella almost wished he could have seen her as she had been . . . for a few moments longer. "Thank you, Commander. No more than a glass, please."

"One glass only." Areyst turned and left the chamber, closing it behind him.

Mykella eased the four weapons from her jacket and placed them on the side table before she stretched out. She wasn't even certain she heard the click of the latch plate before she was asleep.

19

Mykella woke with a start, and needles of pain ran through her back. Her face felt sore as well, but she struggled into a sitting position on the couch. Outside, it was pitch-dark, especially in the walled garden beyond the window and the pair of glass doors. Slowly, she sat up.

Do you really want to do this? After a moment, she answered herself. *What will happen if you aren't in the palace, and more Ifrits arrive? With more weapons like those? Or ones even worse?* She straightened and slowly stretched.

At that moment, a soft knock echoed from the closed door.

"Lady?" The voice was Areyst's.

"I'm awake." She struggled toward the side table and replaced the weapons inside her riding jacket, then straightened. "You can come in."

The door opened. The commander stepped inside, carrying a lantern. "Did you sleep?"

"I did. You were right."

"Is it wise for you to travel tonight . . . even in whatever way you must?"

Mykella found a crooked smile on her face as she stood, trying not to wince. "Wise? No. But it is even less wise to remain here."

"Your spare mount is saddled and ready, and a half squad of those I brought will accompany us, then proceed to Tempre . . . at a measured pace."

"I hope we do not need them, but I cannot say what else may emerge from the Table."

"Lady . . . there is one thing. About the bodies."

"They should be buried. Quickly."

"We cannot. Their bodies turned to dust, Only their garments and tools remained."

Mykella frowned. "Did that happen with the body in Tempre?"

"No."

She had no answer. "Keep the garments and tools. They might be useful. Tell the guards they're to say that the bodies were removed."

"I already did so."

"Thank you." She paused. "I need to take care of a few matters before we leave."

"There is a . . . just two doors down."

"Thank you."

Once she had dealt with the necessities, and even washed her face and hands, she rejoined Areyst. They walked to the west end of the villa and out into the courtyard. Mykella forced herself into the saddle without help, and it took more effort, even with a mounting block, given the stiffness in her back and calves.

They rode down the lane to the eternastone highway, with two guards before them, and the remainder following, the only sounds those of hooves on gravel, the occasional *whuff* of a horse, and low murmurs. The sole moon in the sky was Asterta—a half disc of green overhead.

Does that mean anything?

Again, the troopers gave Areyst and Mykella space to themselves once the party was on the highway and headed northeast toward Tempre.

"Do you think these . . . Ifrits are allies of Chalcaer or Skrelyn?" asked the commander.

"No. They think we are little better than cattle." Even as she finished speaking, Mykella realized her words had shocked Areyst. "That is the way they have talked of us in the few times I have overheard their words," she said quietly, easing her mount over closer to his so that they were almost stirrup to stirrup.

"You understand their words?"

"Not all of them, but enough to hear that they wish to return and rule."

"Yet . . . we could not build the highways or the Great Piers or the green stone towers, or the bridges that last forever. People talk of how wonderful times were before the Cataclysm."

"I have no doubt that times were wonderful for the Alectors." Her voice held only the slightest trace of irony. "We cannot build what they did. Nor can we make the weapons they use. Yet those three Ifrits killed four of your troopers and ten of Klevytr's retainers without a thought. They would have killed me if they could have. Acts speak louder than words or legends."

"You do not trust words, Lady?" he said lightly.

"After all those I have heard that turned out to be false? When I hear a man say one thing . . ." She broke off her words quickly. She'd almost said *and knew he thought another.* She *was* tired, and not thinking so well as she should have been.

"And?" he asked.

"And found that he was lying all the time. When it is your uncle, it makes one . . . less trusting."

The commander nodded.

They rode on for a time before he spoke again. "I made a few changes in your plan. There are four troopers waiting ahead. They will wait there, and we will ride with those returning until we are out of easy sight of the four. The squad has been told that they are needed in Tempre, but that you have insisted on riding partway to see them off. Then we will turn as if to ride back before heading north on one of the lanes. How far must we ride?"

"I cannot say exactly. It might be as little as a vingt or as far as four." *I hope that's close to correct, but it should be, this close to Tempre and the hills bordering the Vedra.*

"I heard you say you were not an Ancient, Lady, and I have seen you from a distance over nearly ten years." He paused. "Yet there are tales about the Ancients returning, and those tales all mention strange appearances in the past two seasons."

Mykella laughed, softly. "I am not an Ancient, but one of the Ancients has appeared. I have seen a soarer several times. She warned me that the Ifrits might try to return. She could not tell me when, only that it would happen." While that wasn't quite the way it had transpired, it was close enough not to be a falsehood.

"Seeing one is said to be a blessing and a curse."

"I could not argue with that, Commander." *Not at all.* "Where are the four guards?"

"Less than three hundred yards ahead, just past the pond on the north side."

To Mykella, riding the distance to the patrol seemed to take another glass, but before long, she could sense the mounted figures . . . and then see them.

The lead riders exchanged passwords and kept riding.

"Koammyd," Areyst said loudly to the rightmost rider of those waiting, "I might be a while before I return. Just hold here."

"Yes, sir. Good evening, Lady."

"Good evening," Mykella returned.

Once they passed the four, Mykella began to use her Talent and her eyes to search for a likely lane that extended far enough to the north toward the deep greenish darkness to her left, still well to the north.

"It would be best if we did not ride too much farther," Areyst said calmly.

Mykella understood. "There is a lane ahead. We could pull out into it and let the others pass."

"That would be good."

Mykella could tell that the commander did not see the lane because he waited until they had ridden almost a hundred yards farther before he called out. "Squad leader! This is where you leave us." He guided his mount into the lane.

Mykella followed and reined up beside him.

The two of them remained quiet as the rest of the troopers rode past. Then Areyst asked, "How far along the lane?"

"I won't know for a bit." Mykella turned her mount.

The lane was little more than a dirt track, but it stretched almost straight northward for at least a vingt. As they neared a rise, Mykella began to feel that the darkness beneath was much closer but not quite close enough to touch. Still, they rode over the rise and close to another vingt before she could actually sense and link to the darkness. At that point, she reined up and dismounted, awkwardly, because, if anything, she was even stiffer than she had been immediately after dealing with the Ifrits.

Areyst reined in his mount, and asked, "Now what?"

"You'll tell the guards at the villa that I returned with the half squad."

"I think I will just say that you are on your way to Tempre."

"That's better. You'd best return Kietyra to Tempre with you."

"I'd thought that."

Mykella led her mount closer to the commander, then extended the reins. "Take them. I will see you in Tempre."

With that, she drew the darkness around her and began to sink into the ground, toward the chill depths below. For a timeless moment, she searched for the blue marker that was Tempre, then focused on making her way there.

The chill seeped through her nightsilk jacket and trousers, and she felt as though she were motionless, suspended in greenish darkness. The four weapons were like blocks of ice inside her jacket. Then, abruptly, she was almost beneath the blue angularity that radiated from the purple shroud above the dark ways. She concentrated on easing herself upward and finally emerged in a corner of the rear courtyard of the palace.

Absently, she realized that she would likely be in her chambers long before Areyst returned to Klevtyr's villa. She took a step toward the rear of the palace, raising her shields around her . . . and winced. The cold of the darkness had momentarily numbed some of her aches, but it had also stiffened her, creating yet other aches.

Holding both a body shield and raising a concealment shield, Mykella walked toward the rear entrance to the palace, dropping the concealment shield as she neared the pair of sentries.

One turned, his mouth opening. "Lady! We thought you had gone to join the commander."

"I did. I borrowed a Southern Guard mount to return quickly."

The two scrambled to open the iron night gate.

"There you go, Lady."

"Good evening." Mykella smiled as she stepped into the palace, still holding the body shield.

She made her way past two more sets of guards, all surprised, then up to her apartments. Once there, she walked to the window of her bedchamber and touched the granite of the casement to slide down to the Table chamber.

The Table was brighter, but not brilliant. She wished she knew what else she could do, besides watch, but her eyes were burning, and she was stifling yawns with practically every breath. More than anything, she needed sleep.

You need to do something. You just can't wait and watch.

Yet, standing there in the darkness, sensing the lambent unseen pinkish purple, she could think of nothing. Nothing at all.

You're too tired to think.

After using the darkness to return her to her chamber, she disrobed and collapsed into her bed.

20

Octdi morning, at the first hint of gray in the morning sky, Mykella bolted awake. Her eyes went to the window, where the hangings were still slightly parted. It had been dark when she'd gone to sleep, and she hadn't even thought of pulling them all the way closed. She shivered, not from the cold but from the sense of menace that had pervaded dreams she could only recall vaguely, save that Ifrits had been everywhere, and with each one that she had somehow bested, two or more had appeared.

You have to find a better way to deal with them . . . she told herself. *You have to.*

She made her way to her private wash chamber. The pitchers of water were cool. She really wanted hot water, but she also didn't want to wait for it. So she did her best and dressed in clean undergarments and nightsilk blacks. She then concealed three of the Ifrits' weapons in the armoire that held most of her garments, slipping the fourth into a side drawer of the desk in the study. After breakfast, she intended to study it.

When Mykella approached the breakfast room, Salyna stepped out into the doorway. "When did you get back? From the look of you, you rode all night."

"I didn't, but it feels as though I did," Mykella admitted.

"There are bruises on your face."

"I had a little trouble with the Ifrits. They're dead . . . and Seltyr Klevytr's daughter is all right. They killed some of his retainers before I got there."

"Who killed what?" demanded Rachylana from behind them.

"The men who broke into and out of the palace tried to take over Seltyr Klevytr's summer villa and took his daughter hostage. That's where I was yesterday." Mykella was glad her sister hadn't heard the word "Ifrits." Mykella needed to be careful about what she said although she suspected she couldn't keep the Ifrits hidden from Rachylana much longer.

"Why did you have to go? The Southern Guards should have taken care of that," Rachylana pointed out.

"The First Seltyr recommended Klevytr for the post of Ministry of Highways and Rivers. I'm unlikely to appoint him. Exactly how would it look if I let those . . . bravos kill her or demand a ransom from Klevytr or me? And then refuse to appoint him?"

Rachylana winced. "How did you manage it?"

"I pretended to be an unarmed servant girl bringing them food. They were big, and I'm not. When I got close enough, I did to them what I did to Commander Nephryt."

Rachylana looked at Mykella. "You look terrible. You can't keep doing things like that."

"I wish I didn't have to, but . . ."

"You need to eat," insisted Salyna. "No more talking until you have tea and a hot breakfast."

Mykella took her place at the table, and Muergya immediately brought out a mug of still-steaming tea, followed by fried ham slices that were warm but not hot, and warm eggs scrambled with cheese— and dark bread. Mykella ate, thinking as she did about the Ifrits and the Table.

What can I do? What did the soarers do before? She stopped for a moment, took a swallow of tea, then nodded. *Why not ask?*

After that, she finished off two large helpings of eggs and ham without saying a word.

"When exactly did you last eat?" Salyna finally asked.

"Yesterday afternoon when I got to the villa. Then I had to come right back, and no one was up when I returned."

"You are the Lady-Protector. You could have asked someone to get you food," Rachylana pointed out.

"I was so tired, I didn't even think about it." Mykella stood. "I need to finish getting ready for the day. Sooner or later, Klevytr will show up, and he'll be upset."

"For saving his daughter?" Rachylana frowned.

"No . . . for failing to stop the attackers that I didn't know were going to break into the palace, then go to his villa. I still have to figure out where to get more golds for the Southern Guards and see if I can find what Joramyl or Cheleyza did with the rest of the missing golds."

"Where are you going today?" asked Salyna dryly. "To Viencet? Or Krost? Perhaps Dereka?"

"I have no travel plans." *Not on horseback.* Mykella forced a grin. "I'm too stiff to ride anywhere today."

She walked back to her own apartments, where she removed the weapon from the desk drawer. It appeared almost like a caricature of a pistol, with a black oblong grip large enough that her hand could barely fit around it and still be able to squeeze what seemed to be a trigger, although it looked like a smaller plate that would recess into the grip. There was nothing that looked like a firing chamber, and the barrel appeared to be a solid cylinder of a material similar to that used in the ancient light-torches. The barrel and the grip flowed together seamlessly.

Mykella concentrated on studying the weapon with her Talent—and almost recoiled—so angry did the purpleness within the weapon seem.

From where does it draw power? There isn't anyplace to insert cartridges . . .

She did have one idea. She donned her riding jacket, sliding the weapon into the side pocket, then used the darkness to drop herself through the stone and to the Table chamber. The Table was slightly brighter than on Septi, but it had not started to pulse.

She took the weapon from her jacket and laid it on the Table, trying to link Table and weapon. The mists swirled, and the weapon glowed more purplish for a moment. A line of script appeared in the middle of the mist. Mykella could not decipher the characters, and shortly they vanished.

While she could not be certain, she had the sense that the weapon had been repowered in some fashion. She replaced it in her jacket..

Now . . .

She concentrated on reaching the soarer through the greenish darkness. After a time, she stopped.

The soarer did not appear.

What next?

She thought. The soarer always left a brief trail of green. Could she seek out traces of green amid the deeper darknesses that ran beneath all the lands of Corus? She took a slow deep breath and reached out to the greenish darkness, then let herself sink through the stone and into the depths, her senses reaching out, trying to find traces of green . . . somewhere—ignoring the sense of stone around her, smothering her.

For a time, she sensed nothing. She willed herself farther from the Table and its comparatively glaring purpleness. Then, in the distance, an icy distance, she caught a glimmer of a greenish thread, one with a tiny line of amber or gold within it, and she willed herself toward it, even as she felt oh-so-cold, and so sluggish.

. . . have to . . . have to . . .

As often before, suddenly Mykella was in the midst of the narrow green, flashing . . . somewhere . . . until she found herself standing in a strange room, an empty chamber with a single wide window before her. She looked down, to find she was standing on what seemed to be a silvery mirror. Shards of ice shattered off her nightsilk jacket, and she was wreathed in fog, so much so that for several moments she could only discern the outlines of the chamber around her.

As the icy fog faded away, and as her shivering subsided, she could see that the walls were of an amberlike stone, holding depths of light beneath their surface—and a shade similar to the yellow golden thread embedded in the green path she had traced through the darkness. On the wall to her left was a row of amber pegs seamlessly attached to the walls.

Slowly, she walked to the window, seeing beyond it the silver-green sky of Corus. The glass of that window was flawless and set in a silver-like metal, and she could sense the chill beyond the glass. After stepping up to the window, which had no hangings at all, a strange thing, she thought, she looked out, realizing she was in a round tower. Below were other buildings, all of them curved in some fashion or another, and so many that they extended a good vingt or so from the tower to a circular wall of the same amber stone that composed both the tower and the other buildings. Beyond the wall, the ground was white, but she could not tell whether that whiteness was sand or ice or snow.

A greenish radiance rose behind Mykella, and she turned toward the door, solid golden wood without windows, or peepholes, and a single-lever handle, of the same metal as the window casements. The radiance flared, then vanished to reveal a soarer—the soarer. Mykella found herself, for the first time, looking into brilliant green eyes that were clear, and deep—and very old. She shivered at the chill of ages she sensed behind the soarer's eyes. "Where am I?"

The hidden city. It is not for you or your people.

"The hidden city of the Ancients? On Corus?"

Where else?

Mykella detected a hint of humor—she thought—behind the words.

Why did you seek us out?

For your help. The Ifrits are coming. I fear they bring weapons greater than what I can do.

It is possible that they will bring in a . . . device . . . that will activate the scepters . . .

What the soarer said made no sense to Mykella, none at all. How did one activate a scepter? "I don't understand. What is a scepter?"

It is a device that allows them to remain as they are and not as they should be. Once they reactivate the scepters . . . they create more . . . strength in the Tables . . . and even you will be hard-pressed to resist them.

"But most of the Tables are blocked . . . except the one in Tempre."

Those that are inaccessible can still lend strength to the others, and you cannot be everywhere at once. They will wear you down . . . and they could once again build the weapons that destroyed cities.

Sore and aching as she was, Mykella already felt worn down. "Elcien and Ludar?"

Worse than that . . . Do you know of the Great Black Lake? It was once a city, and nothing remains.

The bottomless black lake that was more than four vingts across . . . there had been a city there? Mykella shivered, even as something else the soarer had said struck her. "There are other Tables they can use?"

There are Tables in Alustre and Blackstear, and it would not take much to use the power of those in Dulka and Lysia. Dulka is blue and maroon to you, and Lysia is yellow and orange.

"None of those are close to Lanchrona," Mykella pointed out.

Once more than a few Ifrits appear in Corus, more and more will come, and they will be able to bring weapons that will destroy even iron doors.

"What can I do?"

You must link yourself fully to the deepest of the green, that depth you barely touched to find the hidden city. Only that will give you power to stop them. You must not let it touch your being when you confront them, but only channel it against them and their devices.

"Only channel it?"

Go! The soarer vanished.

Mykella stood there for a moment. *That's all you're going to get.* Then she concentrated on finding the darkness.

Returning from the hidden city was far easier than finding it, and Mykella made her way back directly to her private study, where she removed the nightsilk riding jacket, stiff and ice-cold, and wrapped herself in a quilt to warm herself up enough to stop shivering.

Weapons that turned cities into bottomless lakes? and she was supposed to stop them? How? *Link to the deepest green . . . channel it? How? When?* As if she had the time to sit and wait and monitor the Table every moment of every day until something happened. She sat on the edge of her bed and shivered . . . and thought . . . and shivered.

In time, the shivering subsided, and she made her way to her official study, carrying the riding jacket, the strange weapon still inside it.

"Good morning, Lady," offered Chalmyr.

The messenger boy nodded but said nothing. But then, messenger boys seldom did unless spoken to or instructed to speak.

"Good morning. Is there anything I need to address?"

"Assistant Minister Duchael left a missive. I put it on your desk. Chief Clerk Haelyt would like a few moments at your convenience."

"Is there anything from High Factor Lhanyr?"

"No, Lady."

Mykella went into the study and closed the door behind her. She took the weapon from the jacket and eased it into the second drawer, dragging out a sheet of writing paper and easing it over the weapon. Then she folded the jacket and set it on an empty space in the bookcase. Only then did she pick up the document from the desk, and, still standing, begin to read what Duchael had written on the maintenance accomplished with his ministry's funds.

The maintenance commenced after year-turn was that of ongoing upkeep and repair on existing structures and facilities in order to assure continued flow of sewage through the entire system serving Tempre . . .

All well and good, but taking half a page to say that you spent the golds on required maintenance doesn't tell me how you spent them.

Finally, halfway down the second sheet, she found the actual listing.

. . . repointing mortar on facing of exposed sewer conduit in southeast sector, adjoining estate of Seltyr Thaen . . .

. . . repairs made on eastern conduit, east of First Seltyr's villa . . .

. . . replanting over repairs made on eastern conduit . . .

. . . oiling of woodwork and casements of sewer inspection building . . .

. . . excavation and repair of sewer conduit adjoining warehouse
of Seltyr Thaen . . .

The listing of repairs—all comparatively minor—went on for
almost two pages, and all except the work next to Thaen's warehouse
had been in the eastern part of the city. Were all the references to
Seltyrs Duchael's way of trying to show that Porofyr had been the
one making the choices, or had Duchael just been copying the former
minister's words?

Over the remainder of the morning, she spent more than a glass
with Haelyt, and most of that time was devoted to detecting, as best
they could, additional questionable entries, all made at the direction
of Joramyl, and questionable payments. After taking a quick midday
meal in the breakfast room, with Rachylana, since Salyna was over at
Southern Guard headquarters obtaining measurements and information for her training project, Mykella returned to her study.

She was still pondering the advice from the soarer, wondering if
she should immediately attempt to undertake such a linkage, when
Chalmyr knocked softly on the door.

"Yes?"

"Seltyr Klevetyr would like to see you. He says it is most important."

"I'll see him." Mykella stood. She didn't want to be sitting when
Klevetyr barged in.

The door opened, held by Chalmyr, and a short and stocky dark-
haired figure with slightly olive skin strode through it. Chalmyr
quickly and gently closed the door.

"Seltyr Klevytr." Mykella smiled politely and gestured toward the
chairs.

"No, thank you. I will not be long."

Mykella merely nodded.

"Lady-Protector . . . I have just discovered that your failure to se-
cure the palace has resulted in grievous harm to my villa. Your negli-
gence has cost me ten valuable servitors and endangered my daughter,
and you did not even have the courtesy to inform me."

How does he know that? Mykella could sense the fury infusing the

Seltyr and realized that words alone would do nothing. Instead, she used her Talent to bend light, so that her entire being became luminous. Then she infused each word with Talent.

"You will not come in here and attack me. Sit down, calm down . . . and listen." With the last word, she extended her Talent, as she had done in fighting the Ifrit, and half threw, half pressed Klevytr into the chair, holding him there.

Fear and rage warred within the Seltyr, but fear—and a growing realization of the power he faced—won out. He swallowed. "Lady-Protector . . . perhaps I was too hasty . . ."

"You were." Mykella released the Talent pressure and let the light die away. She remained standing. "I understand your concerns, especially about your daughter, but you acted without knowing what really happened. The three bravos who attacked the palace managed to obtain ancient weapons that cut men apart with flame. No one has seen such weapons in hundreds of years, and the three attacked here when I was not in the palace. They stole the mounts of the Southern Guards they killed, and they rode off down the avenue. Once they left Tempre, no one knew where they had gone until Commander Areyst received word from one of his men. I immediately dispatched him with a force to deal with them. At that time, we did not know that your daughter was at the villa."

She paused for a moment to let her words sink in.

"As soon as I found that out, I left and rode there personally. I dealt with the bravos, despite their weapons, and I made sure that your daughter was safe. I returned here late last night. Exactly what else would you have had me do?" That was a dangerous question, she realized once she had asked it, but she couldn't take back the words.

"Bring the malefactors back and rip them to pieces on the Great Piers." Klevetyr's voice was low and intense.

"That is not possible. I killed them in rescuing your daughter before she was harmed."

"You . . ."

"You doubt me . . . even now?"

After the briefest hesitation, Klevytr asked, "Lady-Protector . . . why did no one know about such weapons?"

"People find relics of the old days now and again. Some are useless. Some are like the highways and the towers—or the light-torches that still look as when they were created. I cannot say where they found such weapons, only that we killed them and recovered the weapons."

"I must ask if this could have happened if most of the Southern Guards assigned in Tempre had not been moved to Viencet."

"It would have. Most of the Guards are always at their compound, and that is a vingt away. The brigand-bravos attacked and left before word even reached the commander."

"And now . . . who will protect us with those few away from Tempre?"

"There are Southern Guards in Tempre, and the remainder of those engaged in reclaiming your villa from the brigands will be returning late this afternoon. Commander Areyst will be bringing your daughter."

"Why did you—"

"I returned nearly alone through the darkness. That would not have been suitable for her, especially after what she had been through." Mykella smiled politely. "Now that you know what occurred in greater detail . . . you might wish to return to your villa and inform everyone that your daughter is safe . . . and that we held her safety most dearly."

For a moment, Klevytr looked as though he might question his dismissal, but then rose and bowed. "I appreciate all your clarifications, Lady-Protector, and I thank you."

In short, you've suddenly realized that it might not be wise to defy me in person, no matter what Porofyr and Khanasyl tell you. "You're most welcome, Seltyr Klevytr. I have been forthright with you, and I appreciate those who are equally forthright. As you may recall, I care little for deception and plotting, for they undermine a land, and I care too deeply for Lanachrona to allow such any longer. I would that you would convey my best wishes to your daughter."

"I will do that, Lady." Klevytr eased himself from the study, not quite backing out, but not turning fully away from Mykella.

Little more than a glass later, Maeltor arrived, and Chalmyr ushered him in to see Mykella.

"Lady-Protector." Although the captain's face was pleasant, she could sense a certain unease and curiosity.

"Captain." Mykella did not rise from behind the desk.

"Lady, the remainder of third squad has returned to Tempre, with your gray. You obviously outpaced them. Squad Leader Shaert reported that you had remained at the villa, but the duty-squad leader reported you arrived late last night, alone."

"Sometimes, it is faster to travel alone, Captain. What else?"

"Commander Areyst will be returning with fourth squad early this evening. He is escorting Mistress Kietyra and her . . . maids."

"Thank you. Did Shaert say how the ride back went?"

"An easy ride, Lady, as easy as any fifteen vingts."

"Good. He didn't run into any more brigands?"

"No, Lady."

"I'm glad he did not, and I appreciate all that you and the Southern Guards have done."

"They appreciate all you have done, Lady."

Once Maeltor had departed, Mykella returned to her own quarters, with her jacket and the Ifrit weapon. From there she slipped through the darkness to the lowest level of the palace, noting that the inner iron door had yet to be installed and that the Table did not seem brighter than earlier. Most important, it was not flashing.

Then, standing well away from the Table, she extended Talent tendrils toward the blackness below, concentrating on trying to reach with her Talent the "deeper" green that the soarer had claimed would allow her to best the Ifrits. Yet with each extension, she could sense that the green retreated. That was how it felt.

She redoubled her efforts, and the tendrils brushed the brighter and deeper green, and, for a long moment, she felt as though she had almost linked with that deeper green . . . before the links she had extended frayed away and she stood, breathing rapidly, as though she had run hundreds of yards, shuddering and shivering within the chill stone walls of the Table chamber.

For a time, she just stood there, recovering from her first effort. Then she tried once more, extending herself toward the depths. That attempt was even less successful and left her even more exhausted.

Yet she suggested that such an effort should not have been that diffi-cult.

How else could she link herself to that green?

After a moment, she shook her head, accepting reluctantly that she was too tired to make another effort immediately. *But what if the Ifrits arrive before you can learn how to do that?*

She had no answer for that question.

Using her Talent and the darkness, she returned unseen to her apartment, donned the riding jacket, made sure that the Ifrit weapon was well hidden, and made her way down to the main level, empty except for guards, since the palace was cleared of those with business after fourth glass, and then out and into the walled private garden. With all of her other concerns, she had yet to study firsthand the weapon the Ifrits had brought through the Table from Efra.

When she reached the corner of the garden farthest from the palace, where she had first seen the soarer so many weeks before, she eased the weapon from her jacket and, using both hands, lifted and aimed it at the corner of the wall to the left of the broken statue, a distance of some ten yards. She squeezed the plate that she'd thought was a trigger.

The plate did not move, and nothing happened.

After lowering the heavy pistol-like weapon, she studied it again, closely, finally noting a lever flush against the metal back of the firing plate, she eased the lever from the downward position to one that pointed forward and raised the Ifrit pistol once more. She squeezed the plate, and it moved . . .

A line of bluish fire flared from the end of the weapon and kept flaring . . . until she released the firing plate.

"Oh . . ." she murmured, realizing that there was a spring or something behind the plate and that it would keep discharging energy so long as pressure was applied, at least until that energy was exhausted.

She quickly moved the safety lever, for that was what it had to be, to the nonfiring position and stepped forward. The blue fire had scoured the lichen away from the stone of the wall in a space about the size of her palm, and heat radiated from the impact point. The surface of the surrounding stone was blackened, and she could smell an acrid odor, most likely burned lichen and moss. As she'd surmised, the weapon had not had much effect on the stone itself although it looked to her as though the stone in the center of the area that had been scoured had lost perhaps a fingernail's thickness compared to the surrounding surface.

With enough time and energy, they could cut through stone.

That thought scarcely cheered her.

She turned and paced off what might have been fifty yards, then tried the weapon again, aiming at a tree branch overhanging the wall. The blue flame sliced through the limbs, and the branch sagged onto and over the wall. After several more attempts, she put the pistol on safe once more. From what she could tell, the weapon was extremely effective up to fifty yards, but the flame became less focused beyond that and was almost ineffective at a hundred yards.

Between her worries and the effort to link with the deeper green, by the time she headed back toward the palace for a quiet glass or so before the evening meal, she felt exhausted. Yet she knew she'd have to put on a cheerful front for dinner . . . somehow.

The only problem was that Salyna was waiting at the top of the palace's main staircase. "Mykella . . . we need to talk." The blonde looked toward the formal study.

"It's important?"

"You should know. I don't think you want too many others knowing."

"There are always too many who know . . . unless no one else knows, and sometimes that's worse." Mykella turned toward the front of the palace.

Salyna took two quick steps to move up beside her older and smaller sister.

Chalmyr nodded but said nothing as the two sisters entered the anteroom.

"I didn't expect you to be here so late," Mykella said.

"It's no problem, Lady. I thought you might need me to be here for a while."

"Thank you." Mykella offered a smile, then led the way into the formal study.

Salyna followed and closed the door—firmly—before she stepped up to the side of the desk, turning to face her sister. "Mykella, I had some of the guards go out to the villa with me. We took a cart to get those sabers. They were dusty, but they weren't old at all."

"They weren't? They looked old. They weren't like the saber you use."

"They aren't. According to Ghalyan, they're the kind of sabers issued to the Northcoast heavy cavalry. They've never been used, and there were twenty-one of them."

Mykella frowned. "What else?"

"According to the villa servants who are still there, that's about how many retainers Cheleyza brought with her and how many left with her when she fled."

"She had a squad of Northcoast troopers at the villa?"

"We can't be certain . . . but it is rather strange."

"Why did they leave the weapons?" prompted Mykella.

"I'd guess they weren't for them. No cavalryman would willingly leave his blade, especially if he thought the Southern Guards might come after them."

"Joramyl planned to bring in Northcoast troopers secretly? Is that what you think?"

"I don't know what to think—except no one gathers twenty-one new sabers without reason. I also found one empty cartridge box."

Mykella glanced toward the window. *Had Joramyl been planning an armed coup before deciding on murder? Or had Cheleyza and her "steward" had something else in mind from the beginning?* "I need to think about this, but Cheleyza's involved more than we thought."

"You never trusted her, did you?"

"No, but I honestly didn't think she was planning to take over Lanachrona by force. Even two squads wouldn't have been enough to take the palace, let alone the Southern Guards."

"She could have been coppering her wagers."

"In case Father discovered?" asked Mykella. "She was probably making sure she could escape if things went wrong . . . and she did just that." After a moment, she added, "I'll tell Areyst, but I'd just as soon you just keep it to the fact that you found the sabers in a storeroom."

"I can do that. And they will help in training the auxiliaries." Salyna paused. "I'll see you at dinner?"

"You will." Mykella smiled.

The study door hadn't even closed behind Salyna before Chalmyr announced Areyst.

The commander stepped into the study. "Lady."

"Commander, do sit down." Mykella settled herself behind the desk, taking a long look at the officer, from short-cut blond hair and pale green eyes to his trim, but muscular figure. "I'm glad you've returned safely. You look concerned, though."

"So do you. I saw the Lady Salyna depart as I was entering the anteroom."

"I let her recover the old sabers I discovered in the hidden room in Joramyl's villa—I told you about them. You were checking something else, I think."

"Empty cartridge boxes." Areyst's voice was dry. "And?"

"The sabers weren't old . . ." Mykella explained. ". . . and that is why, I believe, Cheleyza was so prepared to flee when I acted against Joramyl."

"The sabers were not there solely for her protection."

"I don't believe so, either, but I don't know exactly what else she might have had in mind. There were not enough arms to foment a rebellion or attack the palace."

Areyst nodded. "There is another difficulty . . . of sorts. Klevytr's retainers saw the bodies of the Ifrits before they turned to dust, and some were claiming that they were Alectors that had been returned to life. I suggested that was unlikely since they had been killed, but . . ."

"Before long word will be all over Tempre," Mykella finished. "That can't be helped. We have another problem." *Among many.* "Klevytr knew about his daughter by early afternoon. By then, only the first half squad had returned to Tempre."

The commander nodded, slowly. "Khanasyl has an informant within the Guards. I may even know who he is."

"Someone who is always at headquarters and friendly to all the men?"

"Who else could it be? The first half of third squad returned to

Tempre about a glass after midnight, and they were required to stay at headquarters. They did not return to duty status until a glass before noon. Seltyr Klevytr did not approach you until early afternoon, but before the remainder of third squad had returned. Word will always get out." Areyst shrugged. "Was Seltyr Klevytr polite and civil?"

"Not at first. I had to display some Talent to calm him down. I don't think he saw what happened when I became Lady-Protector."

"Or he chose not to believe it."

"Or Khanasyl suggested it was some sort of trickery." Mykella tilted her head. "Didn't the Seltyrs have a higher position under the Alectors, especially on Dramur?"

"You're thinking that he knows that the attackers were Ifrits and that he'd rather have them as rulers than you?"

"I was thinking more that he believes that the First Seltyr should be Protector of Lanachrona, rather than a woman."

"From what I've seen, Lady, most Seltyrs feel that way. So do many High Factors."

"And you, Commander, what do you feel?"

Areyst met her eyes. "If you do all that you are capable of, you will be one of the great rulers." His lips quirked. "Unhappily, you will have to do all that in order to maintain your rule."

"Then that is what I will do." Mykella managed to keep her smile wry although a part of her was warmed by the feelings she sensed behind Areyst's cool assessment.

21

Novdi morning, Mykella slept later than usual, if only by a half glass, but immediately upon waking, she washed up and pulled on clean trousers and shirt, boots, and jacket, carefully laid out by Wyandra the night before, then slipped down to the Table chamber. She was gratified to see that iron plating totally covered the inside of the door. A quick inspection revealed that no wooden surfaces could be seen. The Table radiated a slightly brighter shade of the pinkish purple, but was not pulsing.

Not yet.

Mykella walked over and looked into the mirrored surface, concentrating on Cheleyza. When the swirling mists cleared, she could make out her aunt, in a morning dressing gown, standing beside a low and long divan of some sort and facing a man attired in a dark green shirt with yellow piping, mostly covered by a worn leather vest—most likely a hunting vest, Mykella thought. Both Cheleyza and the man were talking and gesturing—vigorously.

Mykella studied the man, a good head taller than Cheleyza, who was not only elegantly proportioned, and anything but short. He was not only taller, but had broad shoulders. Still, there was something about him . . . his neck and features, and the same black hair, if cut short. Abruptly, she saw the similarity. In all likelihood, Cheleyza was arguing with her brother Chalcaer, and Chalcaer was anything but pleased.

Not for the first time, Mykella wished she could hear the words.

Mykella didn't see much point in looking for most of the others she'd used the Table to follow, not so early in the day. Instead, she focused on trying to reach the deep green, but, as with her last attempt, she could not reach or connect to it.

What if I have to go to it . . . or almost to it?

With that thought, she let herself flow downward and into the stone beneath the chamber, sinking deeper, until she was surrounded by the blackness. Only then did she begin to seek the deeper green. Even so, she could approach it but not link to it, or even control it in any fashion.

What am I doing wrong?

She attempted another approach, that of following the green thread, trying to find the line of amber . . . but the amber was gone, as if it had never been. As the chill crept more deeply into her bones, she finally rose back upward, straight to her own apartments. There, for close to a quarter glass, she huddled in a quilt, warming up, trying to think about how else she might be able to control that deeper green . . . and whether she would have the time before the Ifrits appeared with greater weapons.

Finally, she made her way to the breakfast room, where both her sisters were already eating. She slipped into her place quietly, waiting for Muergya to pour tea into her mug.

Rachylana looked up from the tiny omelet on her platter and stared at Mykella. "Are you all right?"

"I feel fine." *At least physically.* "Why?"

"You're . . . there's a green shade to you . . . but there's not . . ."

Salyna stopped eating and looked at Mykella, then at Rachylana. "She looks more rested to me."

In turn, Mykella studied Rachylana with her senses, not just her eyes. Was there just a hint of a thread of green in her life-thread? While she half hoped not . . . there was. Not so much as with Areyst, whose green line, while narrow, was thick enough to be easily sensed, but a definite green thread.

"What is it?" snapped Rachylana. "Now you're looking at me. Why?"

Mykella offered a laugh. "You definitely don't look green."

Rachylana glanced at Mykella, then shook her head. "You do . . . and you don't."

"Maybe you're the one who didn't get enough sleep last night," suggested Salyna.

"I was thinking about the season-turn ball . . . It will be rather dull with all the envoys gone. They all have departed, haven't they?"

"The Deforyans and the southerners have left," Mykella replied. "I don't know about Vaerlon. He's Skrelyn's envoy."

"I saw him when he came to meet with you," said Salyna. "He looked full of himself. He was also looking at every wall in the palace like he was counting up what everything was worth."

"Cheleyza said the coastal princes were envious of us," Rachylana added.

"She's doubtless trying to get her brother to attack us," Mykella said.

"They won't, will they?" asked Rachylana. "I know you said you thought they might, but do you really think they'll attack?"

"Rachylana—" Salyna's voice contained equal parts of exasperation and incredulity.

"I'd wager more than all of Cheleyza's ball gowns on it," said

Mykella quickly. "Cheleyza wants her child to rule Lanachrona. The coastal princes want what we have. Southgate wants more power for the Seltyrs and advantages in trade. The only way for all of them to get what they want is for the coastal princes to conquer or weaken La-nachrona." *Where the Seltyrs are already unhappy with a woman ruler.*

"You never said she was pregnant," replied Rachylana.

"She did. You just weren't listening," declared Salyna.

Muergya entered the breakfast room with an omelet and ham slices for Mykella, who took a sip of her tea in the welcome lull in conversation.

After taking several bites of her omelet, Mykella asked, "How are you coming with the arrangements for the ball?"

"It's hard because we don't have many golds . . ."

Mykella nodded and listened while she ate.

Salyna glanced to Mykella and raised her eyebrows, but Mykella just smiled and continued with her breakfast. In less than a quarter glass, she had finished, returned to her chamber, washed up, and headed for her formal study.

When Mykella stepped into the antechamber, Chalmyr rose, as always, and nodded. "Lady, there's a message from Commander Areyst on your desk. His messenger said it wasn't urgent. So I just left it there for when you came in. You're never that late."

"Thank you." Mykella entered the study, opened the sealed missive, and began to read.

Lady-Protector—
We have just received word that Commander Choalt has arrived in Viencet. He is increasing the training schedule. He has brought another three squads of recruits. Two more squads of recruits are coming from Borlan, and three from Dekhron and Krost. With those recruits already raised in Tempre, by rotating troopers and mixing the recruits into existing companies, we will have two more companies available by summer.

Even with two more companies, what Areyst had not mentioned was how likely the Southern Guards was to be outnumbered. *And how many more golds would be required to pay the additional troopers.*

Always, always, the golds bothered her, especially the puzzle about what Joramyl—or Cheleyza—had done with the thousands and thousands of golds diverted from the Treasury. Had she missed something at the villa? Mykella didn't think so, but it was worth another search.

With that thought nagging at her, and nothing urgent for the moment, she sent word to the duty-squad leader that she would be riding out to the villa.

Then she got out the ancient maps of Corus and began to check the actual locations of those Tables named by the soarer. While she knew Alustre was far to the east, the map confirmed just how far— and that Lysia was even farther. The Table where she had almost frozen so many weeks before had to be Blackstear, because none of the others was that far north.

Little more than a glass later, she dismounted at the villa that had been Joramyl's and launched into a thorough search, beginning at the uppermost levels and going through every room and every piece of furniture and every drawer.

Along the way, she did find ten golds hidden in a wallet discarded or forgotten by Cheleyza, as well as a bundle of letters to her aunt, but all were various thank-you notes. Mykella kept them for future reference, to see who appeared to have been overly friendly to Cheleyza. The only new hint of what might have happened to the golds was a scrap of paper, caught in the side of the drawer of the small writing table in the hidden study. That section looked to have been torn up, as if to have been burned, since one corner was brownish and fragile. Had Joramyl been interrupted and let that small scrap slip down into the table?

As soon as she found it, she immediately read over the words.

. . . . chest contains the golds . . . .
. . . . cavalry needed to sustain . . . .

He sent the golds to build a cavalry force! The conclusion was inescapable. But to whom? And why?

Mykella shook her head. There was only one possible answer.

After that, she went through the small study again but found nothing else. Nor did she discover anything else in the remaining rooms on the main floor or in the cellars below that might have shed more light on the missing golds. Once again, she had just enough proof to be certain of what Joramyl had intended but not enough to convince anyone else. In fact, if she revealed what she had discovered, most people would immediately have decided that there was far less danger to Lanachrona—rather than more.

When she could find nothing else to search, she sat down in the small once-locked study with Hrevor, the former assistant steward and now acting steward for the villa.

"The villa steward came to Tempre with Lady Cheleyza, you said? Were you the steward before?"

"No, Lady. I was assistant under Elwayt before he became the palace steward when old Tunstyl's heart failed. I thought I might become steward here . . . but then Paelyt arrived . . ."

"What can you tell me about him?"

Hrevor swallowed.

"Go ahead."

"He didn't know what he should. Not what any steward or assistant steward should. He knew horses and stables, and victualing, but he didn't know about wines or overseeing a kitchen. That didn't bother him, either. He'd just ask me or tell me to do it in the usual fashion."

"Didn't that surprise you?"

"At first, I just thought it was because he was an outlander. When he gave orders to the grooms and ostlers, and the hunters, though, they jumped. I heard things. I think he used to be a cavalry officer in Northcoast . . ."

"You didn't say anything?"

"I told Elwayt, and he said he'd mentioned it to the Lord-Protector. The Lord-Protector said that the Lady Cheleyza needed her own people, and if that made her happy, and Lord Joramyl happy, then that was fine with him—that's what Elwayt told me, Lady. He truly did."

Oh . . . Father . . . Mykella barely managed to keep from shaking her head. "What else was different about Paelyt?"

"Sometimes, a wagon would arrive from Northcoast. He insisted that only he or his men would unload it. It was the same when the wagon was sent back, and the men who guarded it I'm fair-on sure were cavalry or soldiers."

"When was the last wagon sent back to Northcoast? Do you remember?"

Hrevor frowned, then tilted his head. "Couldn't have been more than a day or two afore your father died, Lady. Might have been three. No more than that. Only a chest or two and maybe three kegs of good Vyan wines. Still had almost ten guards, though."

Mykella had a good idea why.

In the end, she learned little more from Hrevor, and it was close to twilight when she finally rode back to the palace.

22

By early Londi afternoon, Mykella was standing at the study window, fretting again. While she and Haelyt had been able to figure out most of the Treasury ledger entries that had been falsified, neither of them had been able to determine all those who had physically received the golds. She had also received a note on behalf of Kiedryn's family, thanking her for the provision of a stipend; but Kiedryn's widow had declined the chance to return to Tempre, writing that Vyan was much better suited to their circumstances. Mykella couldn't say that she blamed the woman. In a way, it had been Mykella's fault that Joramyl had forced Kiedryn to suicide. *But it wouldn't have happened, either, if Father hadn't trusted Joramyl so much.*

Her lips twisted. Rachylana would have told her that she was trying to make everything right and that in real life things didn't work out as well as in romantic tales. Mykella knew that all too well, but she still had to try.

After the midday meal, before she returned to her formal study, she eased down to the Table chamber. Outside in the stone-walled corridor, crafters were hammering and working, most likely installing the locks on the outer door, and the sounds echoed everywhere.

The Table did not appear any brighter, and, in a way, that also worried her. Still, she had work to do. Her first effort was to focus on Cheleyza.

For a moment, Mykella thought she had inadvertently concentrated on someone besides Cheleyza because the figure that had appeared once the mists had vanished appeared to be that of a young cavalry officer . . . except it was not. Cheleyza wore a dark green uniform and had reined up beside the hard-faced man who had accompanied her on the barge and riding northward. *Most likely Paelyt.* He also wore the same uniform, with an insignia that appeared to resemble crossed gold axes on his collar. The two appeared to be on a rise, with another line of tree-covered hills in the distance. *Reviewing troops? Plotting?* Mykella couldn't tell and let the image lapse.

Next she thought about the healer who had let her father die.

Treghyt lay on a pallet, motionless. Mykella had no idea where, except that he looked to be in a humble cot, and two younger people stood looking over him. The woman, older than Mykella and worn-looking, was sobbing. Mykella couldn't feel much sympathy for Treghyt, but could understand how a daughter, if the woman did happen to be his daughter, would feel grief, especially since she doubted the woman knew of Treghyt's betrayal.

Next came Maxymt. The former chief Finance clerk was wearing a jacket that had once been almost finery but was stained and dirt-smudged. He appeared thinner as he walked along a dirt road, glancing back over his shoulder, a worried expression on his face. *I hope you worry for the rest of your miserable life.*

Mykella decided she should also check on what Commander Demyl was doing. She should have done that earlier, given the commander's anger when he'd left Tempre. The Table promptly displayed an image. Demyl was riding between two other men—troopers in white uniforms, officers from the silver insignia on their collars. White uniforms? She had to think for a moment before realizing that the white was the color of Southgate. *That makes sense.* Demyl was the sort to land on his feet anywhere, and doubtless he intended to act against Lanachrona as he could from his new position.

Porofyr was in his study, poring over a ledger, while Khanasyl was walking through his factorage, talking to another man, who kept nodding at the Seltyr's every word.

Mykella let the Table clear and took a slow deep breath. She still needed to learn how to control and channel the green that lay so far below. She slipped into the nearer darkness, then moved deeper until the black gave way to a green so dark it was close to black yet not black at all. For an instant, the green wrapped around her, swathing her in an aliveness that was both bracing—and chilling. But when she extended her Talent to gather the green, it slipped away from her.

After a moment—or what seemed a moment—she used her Talent to form a basket of blackness that she extended around the green. That tactic seemed to work, except that the green squirted out of the basket before she could "close" it. She tried several more times but could not quite englobe any of the green before it slipped way.

Still, she had learned something.

In the end, she had to leave the green-dark depths and return to her apartments, then walk to the formal study. No sooner had she entered it than Chalmyr followed her, extending a heavy paper sealed in maroon wax. "A missive from High Factor Lhanyr, Lady."

"Thank you." Mykella broke the seal and read, even before Chalmyr had left the study.

Most honored Lady-Protector—
In as much as you requested my thoughts on the matter of a factor who might be suited to the position of Minister of Highways and Rivers, I have mulled over the matter to the best of my ability. In my opinion, and it is only my personal opinion, either High Factor Zylander or High Factor Pytroven would make an excellent choice for the position. I must caution you that I have not talked to them. I could not say whether either would consider the post. Zylander might

be more inclined. His eldest is already respected in his own right as a factor . . .

Mykella nodded as she finished the lengthy explanation. She had to admit that she trusted Lhanyr's recommendations far more than those of Khanasyl.

Is that because he's more trustworthy?

Unfortunately, trustworthiness had its limits because being trustworthy didn't necessarily equate to good judgment. Still, she appreciated Lhanyr's effort, and she had some thinking to do.

"The Lady Salyna and Commander Areyst," announced Chalmyr.

Mykella had almost forgotten that she'd agreed to talk over Salyna's plans for training women auxiliaries for the Southern Guards. "Have them come in."

Before the last words were out of her mouth, Salyna had opened the study door and was walking in, followed by Areyst. The commander offered a warm, but rueful, smile to Mykella.

Salyna handed two sheets to Mykella. "Commander Areyst has already received a copy."

After the two were seated before her desk, Mykella read through the first page—a rationale for the auxiliaries and a proposed budget and pay structure—and then the second, which contained an outline of a training schedule. When she finished, she looked to Areyst. "Do you have any comments on the proposal, Commander?"

"The schedule would appear rather ambitious," he said with an ironic smile, "but I have learned in recent weeks that one must be careful in judging what a talented woman can do."

Mykella wasn't about to acknowledge the potential pun in his reply. "That is true, but there is a difference between the possible and the impossible." She looked to Salyna. "Do you really think you can meet this schedule?"

"I don't see why not. Most of the Southern Guard companies are in Viencet. That leaves much of the headquarters facilities unused. That way, we won't interfere with normal activities. Also, I've found two stipended squad leaders who are willing to work with me and with Squad Leader Shaolyt. I already have over fifty women who are physically able and want the chance. Once they're trained, they can do duties that the guards don't like. Some could be clerks. Three have experience with horses . . ."

Mykella listened, impressed by the lengths to which Salyna had gone. She could also sense that Areyst, despite his professionally pleasant expression, was also impressed.

When Salyna finished, Mykella looked to Areyst. "Your thoughts, Commander?"

"It is a well-thought-out plan, but it has one obvious flaw."

"That is?"

Areyst offered a slightly embarrassed smile. "Lady Salyna is likely the only person, saving yourself, who could make this work. Once it is established, say, for several years, it offers enough to the Southern Guards that it will continue."

Mykella understood and turned to her sister. "Are you willing to commit to directing this for the next two years?"

"I am. Longer if necessary."

"If we agree to this," Mykella continued, "I will hold you to that commitment."

"I understand."

"Then," added Areyst, "there is one other necessity. The Lady Salyna must be granted the rank of undercaptain."

"How will the Guards take a woman officer?" asked Mykella.

"In the immediate term, I would request that Undercaptain Salyna give direct orders only to women and the three squad leaders reporting to her. If she needs other assistance, she is to come to me or to an officer delegated to represent me. Likewise, no male officer can give her orders but must go through the same procedure. The sole exception, which I hope never occurs, would be in battle."

Mykella thought for a moment, then nodded.

"So long as this is for the immediate term, I would agree," said Salyna. "If and when the women guards prove worthy, I would ask that you reconsider that procedure."

"That would seem reasonable," replied Areyst. "When would you plan to begin training?"

"On this coming Londi. The sooner we start, the better."

"You can actually assemble those women and the necessary supplies by then?"

"I already have," replied Salyna.

Neither Mykella nor Areyst could totally conceal smiles.

23

The first task Mykella undertook after breakfast on Duadi was to check the Table again, apparently no brighter a shade of pinkish purple than the day before, then attempt once more to find a way to control the deep green that seemed to lie so far beneath the palace.

Wearing her riding jacket and gloves, Mykella dropped into the depths and just let herself be surrounded by the deep, deep green. As she did, she began to sense more of the "markers." The black one she had earlier visited—and nearly frozen in doing so—was much brighter, as if black could be brighter. Another marker she had never sensed before, one of orange-yellow, also was brighter. That had to be Lysia, from what the soarer had said. Even the "trace" marker in Dereka seemed somewhat brighter, with its crimson and gold. Why would it be brighter, when there was no Table remaining there? The nearest marker was the bright blue of Tempre, yet it did not seem any brighter than the orange-yellow marker, or especially the black one, and she sensed that the orange-yellow marker was the most distant, as it indeed was.

Did the brightness signify that the Ifrits were trying to activate those Tables or that the brighter Tables were near where the so-called scepters might be? How could she tell which was which? Or if brightness meant anything at all besides some actions by the Ifrits? She wrenched her thoughts back to dealing with the problem at hand—trying to channel and control the deeper green.

Again, she could immerse herself so that she was surrounded by the green, but any attempt to control it by extending her Talent scattered it, and none of her attempts to surround it with shields or the equivalent were successful.

When she returned to her own chamber, both frustrated and angry, she wasn't so chill as she had been on previous occasions. Had that been because of the gloves—or her anger?

There was something else as well . . . something she'd noted and almost forgotten. When she had emerged in the hidden city of the soarers, she'd been standing on a silver mirror . . . and no one put mirrors on the floor. The only other place she'd seen anything like that was the Tables themselves. Were there other silver mirrors . . . those used by the soarers?

For the moment, investigating that speculation would have to wait because she needed to hurry to the study for her weekly ministers' meeting.

The first of ministerial representatives was Cerlyk, but Duchael, Areyst, and Gharyk entered the study almost immediately thereafter and took their places around the old table.

Mykella began. "As Commander Areyst already knows, and some of you may have heard, the brigands who attacked the palace left Tempre and attempted to take over Seltyr Klevytr's villa. They carried ancient flame-cutting pistols. In the end, they were killed, and Seltyr Klevytr's youngest daughter was rescued. There will doubtless be various rumors, but the important point is that, even with powerful weapons, they were unsuccessful—and we now have those weapons." She looked to Areyst. "If you would continue with a report on the Southern Guards, Commander?"

Areyst smiled politely. "Thank you, Lady. I will not go over the matter of the brigands, except to say that the successful resolution of the matter would not have been possible without the Lady-Protector."

As he spoke, Mykella could sense veiled amusement, not at her but at the understatement of his words. She did manage to maintain a pleasant smile.

". . . Commander Choalt has arrived in Viencet . . ." From there Areyst went on to expand upon the report he had earlier sent to Mykella.

"Thank you, Commander." Mykella turned to Duchael. "What do you have to report?"

"Lady-Protector, the chief engineer is undertaking a thorough inspection of the sewers in the western and central parts of Tempre . . ."

A quarter of a glass and many words later, Mykella looked across the table. "Cerlyk?"

"There is little to add at the moment, Lady-Protector, save that Forester Loryalt did send a message indicating that he is likely to return as he planned. . . ."

When the assistant forester finished, Mykella nodded to Gharyk.

"Lady . . . as a result of your inquiries, we have been looking into why a number of offenders have died in gaol before they could be brought before a justicer. This has turned out to be a greater problem than I had known. You may recall that Justicer Juasyn suffered a riding accident last summer and died. His family reported that the girths on his saddle had been mostly cut through, but who had done that was never discovered. What is unfortunate is that his death occurred less than a week after he had sent a missive to Gaoler Huatyn asking about the deaths of three offenders who had all died of various causes in gaol before they were able to be tried . . ."

Mykella was anything but surprised by what Gharyk reported. "Would you recommend that Huatyn be removed as head gaoler?"

"That would appear prudent, Lady."

"Then draft the proper document for me to sign."

Gharyk nodded. He didn't seem relieved, but even more concerned. Mykella wasn't about to pursue that in a meeting.

Once the four had left the study, Mykella walked back toward her desk. She looked at the open-topped wooden box set on the second shelf of the study bookcase. The top missive of those stacked there was the short letter from High Factor Lhanyr. Its very presence reminded her that she would have to make a decision on whom to appoint as Minister of Highways and Rivers. No decision she made would be well received. The Seltyrs would back a Seltyr for the post of Minister of Highways and Rivers, and the factors would want a factor. Was there anyone who looked at both sides? Mykella nodded slowly. Almardyn—one of the few Seltyrs in Tempre who also held the lesser title of High Factor. *Does he belong to both groups so that he can learn more . . . or just obtain better trading terms?* Absently, she realized she never would have considered that question, let alone asked it, a year earlier. Still . . . Almardyn had seemed honest and objective enough the one time she'd met him personally and face-to-face.

His views on filling the position couldn't help but be instructive. *And that way you can also claim you talked to other factors and Seltyrs.*

She walked to the door of the study and opened it enough to look out at Chalmyr. "Would you send word that I will be riding out in a quarter glass?"

"Yes, Lady."

"Thank you."

She closed the door and withdrew into the study, stopping halfway between her desk and the bookcase. *Who else should you talk to about it?*

In the end, she made no decision except to talk to Almardyn first, and less than half a glass later, accompanied by a half squad of Southern Guards, she was reining up outside Almardyn's warehouse, a block to the south of the Grand Piers, an older two-story stone structure. Two wagons were pulled up to the loading docks on the west side, and the two men rearranging barrels in the rear of the far wagon glanced up at the sound and sight of the riders.

Mykella dismounted and handed the reins to the nearest guard, looking at the squad leader. "Zhulyn . . . please wait. I doubt I'll be long."

"Yes, Lady."

Mykella walked up to the front entrance, a simple doorway set within an ornate but older faux-marble arch.

A youth opened the door before Mykella could reach out to lift the black-painted horsehead knocker. His eyes took in Mykella with puzzlement, then widened as he realized she wore nightsilk and the riders waiting on the street were Southern Guards. "Lady . . ." His voice trembled.

"I'm here to see Seltyr Almardyn."

The youth just stood there and swallowed.

"What is it, Jhesyt?"

"Sir . . . sir . . ." The boy stepped back as the Seltyr appeared.

Almardyn's eyes narrowed for a moment as he beheld Mykella, but he smiled politely. "Lady-Protector, I would not have expected you . . ."

"Might I come in? I would like a few words with you."

"Please do." Almardyn stepped back, opening the door wide.

Mykella concentrated momentarily, assuring herself that her shields were in place, then stepped through the doorway and followed the Seltyr to the warehouse study, a small white-plastered chamber with a table-desk, and wooden file boxes stacked neatly to the right. There, after closing the door, Almardyn turned. "First you come to see me on behalf of your sire . . . and now as Lady-Protector. Should I be honored or worried, Lady?"

"Both, I would judge," replied Mykella with a smile. "I was impressed with you the last time we met, and I wished to have your thoughts. I also felt that, if I came to see you with a squad of Southern Guards, you could certainly point out to others that meeting with me was not your choice."

"Your choice of words, Lady, is worrisome. You imply that others might not feel I should meet with you."

"There are always some who feel that meeting freely with a ruler is unwise. I came to see you and seek your thoughts. As you may have heard, Seltyr Porofyr chose to resign rather than continue as Minister of Highways and Rivers. I consulted with First Seltyr Khanasyl and Chief High Factor Lhanyr. Each recommended possible successors to Seltyr Porofyr. You are, so far as I can determine, the only one who is both a Seltyr and a High Factor. Because you are, I felt talking to you before making a decision would be wise." Mykella smiled politely.

"You are most kind to think of me, but I doubt that I can add much to what others might already have told you."

"Seltyr Khanasyl, with the advice of Porofyr, has suggested that I appoint one of several Seltyrs to the post of Minister of Highways and Rivers. Has he consulted with you on such matters?"

"Lady . . . I would not wish to reveal confidences . . ."

"I am not asking you to reveal the subject of any talks you may have had on the matter with either Porofyr or Khanasyl. I merely would like to know if either sought your counsel. Did he?"

Almardyn smiled sadly. "That is a confidence as well . . ."

Mykella could read the answer even without using her Talent. "At this time, would any Seltyr of capability be interested in such a position?"

"I would think it unlikely. If I might speak freely, Lady, those of ability would not wish to have to act against the interests of their houses, and to accomplish what is necessary for Lanachrona might well require such."

"They would prefer not to support higher tariffs, although tariffs have been too low for too long, you mean?"

"That would be one example."

"What might be another?" Mykella asked, hoping her words were guileless.

Almardyn's eyes twinkled for a moment. "I am certain you can think of a few, Lady Mykella."

"And some might not prefer greater oversight of the justicing system?"

Almardyn did not reply, only smiling politely, but Mykella had sensed his internal wince, and she said, "It is somewhat unusual that, upon occasion, those who might testify against a Seltyr fail to live, even in the gaol, to make it before the justicer."

"There have always been those with great power and position—and their confidants—who make their own rules, Lady. I can only say that I am not one of them. That way is too dangerous for a Seltyr with but a single son and four daughters, none of whom has the attributes of a child of the Ancients."

Mykella decided not to refute or acknowledge his description of her. "I appreciate greatly your conduct, and my door will always be open to you, as yours has been to me."

Almardyn inclined his head.

Mykella nodded in return, then straightened. "As always, thank you very much, Seltyr and High Factor."

"I could do no less for a Lady-Protector of such diligence," replied Almardyn.

"Nonetheless, I do thank you," Mykella said, before turning to depart.

The ride back to the palace was without event, as Mykella considered what she had learned from Almardyn . . . and what she had not. He had as much as told her that her problems did indeed lie with Khanasyl and Porofyr and not to accept any of their recommendations, but he had not offered any alternatives . . . except perhaps, by lack of reference, to accept Lhanyr's recommendation.

Once Mykella was back in the palace, as she walked up the staircase to the upper level, she saw Salyna standing at the top of the steps.

"Mykella . . . do you have a moment?"

"Of course." Mykella stopped next to the topmost stone balustrade post.

"Could we go to your study?" Salyna glanced down the corridor, then back to Mykella.

Mykella nodded but said nothing until the two were inside the formal study. "What is it?"

"It's not much. It's nothing compared to everything." Salyna paused, then went on. "The auxiliaries need uniforms . . . I've already arranged for the cloth, and the thread and needles. I've paid for it. There's more we need. I hate to ask. I know how few golds are left in the Treasury, but they'll also need boots. I've talked it over with Areyst. They won't get boots until they complete their training and agree to serve for three years . . ."

"You paid for all the fabric?" asked Mykella.

"It was my idea."

"How much? Everything you had?"

Salyna nodded. "Twenty-one golds."

Mykella shook her head. "It must run in daughters."

"What?"

"Pride. Unwillingness to ask for things. Of course I can spare golds for that. How many? When do you need them?"

"I need twenty for a deposit . . . and if all sixty make it through, I'll need another thirty."

"Sixty? You have sixty women who will do this? Every time I ask, there are more."

"Well . . ." Salyna flushed slightly. "Seventy wanted to, but some of them couldn't do the tests that the squad leaders and I worked out."

"You'll have your golds." Mykella turned and walked to the book-case on the left and pressed the inlaid goldenwood, then pivoted the bookcase out from the wall, revealing a locked iron door. After unlock-ing the door and sliding it into the stone recess, she stepped into the chamber and opened the smallest chest of those set in the recesses in the stone. She counted out a hundred golds into one of the leather pouches with the Lord-Protector's seal on it, then walked out of the strong room, closing and locking the door and replacing the bookcase.

She handed the pouch to Salyna. "There are a hundred golds, for whatever else you need, too."

"I didn't mean . . ."

"A hundred golds are nothing compared to the good of releasing a company to fight."

"In time, it will mean more than that," Salyna promised.

It will . . . if I can find a way to stop the Ifrits and their devices and weapons and defeat the coastal princes . . . and keep the Seltyrs in line . . .

But Mykella smiled.

24

By Tridi morning, Mykella still had no good ideas as to which Seltyrs or High Factors she could talk to on the matter of possible ministers—not without making matters worse.

As she walked toward her study, she almost stopped.

You're doing what Father did. Why does it have to be Seltyrs or High Factors? With a rueful smile, she turned and headed the other way—toward the study of the Finance Minister.

Chief Clerk Haelyt looked up from a ledger as Mykella stepped into the Finance study and brushed a wispy strand of gray hair back off his forehead. "Yes, Lady?"

"I need your observations about some of the factors and Seltyrs."

"My Lady . . . you must know that I seldom encounter any exalted persons."

"I do." Mykella smiled. "I also know you encounter their golds and their functionaries, and you know who pays on time and who does not, and I am certain that there is much that you have heard. I'm not asking you to guess or gossip. I'm just trying to learn about certain Seltyrs."

"I can only tell what I know and what I've heard, and some of that may not be true. Not everything one hears is as it should be."

"I understand. I've met with Seltyr Klevytr, and his daughter seems quite thoughtful. What have you heard?"

"I wouldn't know the daughter, Lady, nor the Seltyr himself. His account clerk was always the first here to present the Seltyr's rendering of what was due. Twitchy, nervous fellow, name of Bastulyt, the kind that's always looking over his shoulder." Haelyt shrugged. "Might be the way he is. Might be who he serves. Couldn't rightly say."

Mykella nodded. "What about First Seltyr Khanasyl?"

"Him? When I was first clerking, he used to present billings for his sire. Spoke very well . . ." Haelyt chuckled. "Spoke so well that he once got Kiedryn to agree to a change in a billing. Kiedryn told me to deal with him after that. Didn't speak so well to me. That was after I didn't agree with him and told the Finance Minister—that was Lord Felkyn—not to change the disbursement. Never saw Seltyr Khanasyl after that, but his fellows never argued, either."

"High Factor Lhanyr?"

"Friendly quiet fellow. Very prompt in settling, not pushy in receiving . . ."

"Seltyr Thaen . . . ?"

"Younger Seltyr. Only seen him once. Full of himself and snapped at his clerk . . ."

"Seltyr Pualavyn . . . ?"

"Can't say as I know anything at all, Lady."

"What about High Factor Pytroven?"

"Never seen him. His men are most polite, well dressed, and direct. Not full of themselves, though."

"Zylander?"

"Seen the most of him. He handles more himself than most factors do. Careful, but sharp. Never raises his voice."

"Seltyr Thaen?"

Mykella caught the hidden wince.

"Not the most retiring sort, that one. Yelled at old Kiedryn more than once. Yells louder when he's wrong. Doesn't think he ever is. Your uncle had to dress him down more than once . . ."

When Mykella had finished with Haelyt, she made her way down to the lower Finance study, where she posed similar questions to Vyahm. The only Seltyrs or factors with whom Vyahm was acquainted—of those in whom Mykella was interested—happened to be Lhanyr and Hasenyt, and he knew little except both were honest in their billings and prompt in paying their tariffs.

When she had finished talking to Vyahm, Mykella looked to the newest Finance clerk, at the table in the corner. Jainara was close to what Mykella had anticipated in most respects. She was short and boyishly slender, with hair barely longer than that of a youth. What Mykella hadn't expected was the carrot red hair and the spray of freckles across her face.

"Jainara . . . if you'd come with me?"

"Yes, Lady."

Mykella detected no apprehension and only minimal curiosity as she led Jainara out of the study. For all Jainara's apparent youth, Mykella had no doubts that the clerk was at least several years older than Mykella herself.

The two walked to the end of the corridor, where Mykella stopped. For the next quarter glass, the hallway would be empty—and then the palace doors would be open to all those who had business with the various ministries.

"Jainara . . . you've been a clerk for the Southern Guards and now for the Finance Ministry, You've posted accounts for factors, crafters, and Seltyrs for years, haven't you?"

"Yes, Lady-Protector."

"I'd like your opinion on several of them."

"Might I ask why, Lady-Protector? I am but a clerk."

"That's exactly why. I have opinions from those, as Haelyt puts it, of exalted rank. Several of them have been recommended for a ministerial position. I've discovered the way men handle people and golds, especially when their peers are not looking, can tell a different story."

Jainara smiled, faintly. "Did you ask for me to be promoted to the Finance Ministry, Lady?"

"Only after Haelyt recommended you."

Jainara offered a puzzled look. "I scarcely ever saw him."

"He saw your work. He sees more than most realize. Now . . . about the Seltyrs and factors. What do you know about Seltyr Klevytr?"

"Personally, I know nothing. Of those who I know who have encountered him, none would wish to again."

"First Seltyr Khanasyl?"

"Nothing, Lady."

In the end, Jainara had favorable impressions of both Pytroven and Zylander although she thought Zylander cool. Of Thaen, she said, "He's loud and rude. He's a bully, and he doesn't even know what's in his own accounts." She had no impressions of the others about whom Mykella asked her.

Mykella barely made it back to her study before the palace opened to outsiders. There she spent a glass going over correspondence and missives—as well as Rachylana's suggested invitation list for the season-turn ball. By the time she had finished signing, changing, or approving all the documents, she was having trouble keeping her mind on them since her thoughts kept going back to the Ifrits and the coastal princes, but especially to the Ifrits.

Could she really afford to ignore what might be happening at the other Tables, especially after what the ancient soarer had told her might happen? How could she discover what might be happening if she did not travel to those Tables? Where should she travel first?

Blackstear—that had to be the black-marked Table that had seemed to be the "brightest" the last time she'd checked. She almost shivered when she recalled just how cold it had been when she had emerged there weeks earlier. Although it had been winter, she doubted that it would be that much warmer in midspring, not as far north as Blackstear was.

After leaving the study and walking back to her apartments, she donned a heavy winter coat over the riding jacket, which caught momentarily on the haft of her small belt knife, as well as nightsilk gloves and felt-lined winter boots. She also retrieved two of the pistol-like Ifrit weapons from where she had concealed them in the armoire, slipping one into each side pocket of the coat.

Then she reached out to the darkness and dropped into the depths, directing herself toward the shimmering black marker, far "brighter" than she had realized, possibly because the blackness understated the brightness. That worried her.

Mykella emerged in a dark chamber—one with no light at all except for the pink-purple glow of the Table. Her breath steamed, but she could only see that as she looked/perceived the Table. The Table appeared to be a dimmer purple-pink than the one in Tempre, but there was something about it, almost as if some sort of unseen cable threaded away from it, a cable perceived only by her senses. Did that mean Ifrits had already used the Table?

She nodded slowly as she studied the chamber, but, other than the Table, it was empty of all furnishings.

Through a doorway to her left she could make out a ramp heading upward. She walked toward it, stopping when she stepped through the doorless archway to the foot of the ramp because, in the dim light filtering down the ramp, she made out bootprints in the frost that covered the green stone—large prints that were fresh. They had to be from Ifrits. Immediately, she raised both shields and concealment. She also eased one of the ancient flame pistols from her coat before slowly easing her way up the ramp, careful to keep her steps amid the welter of bootprints. From somewhere above, she heard murmurs, but then she realized that the voices were coming from a distance.

Once she reached the open archway at the top of the ramp, she gazed out and down a long wide corridor, flanked by columns of amber gold stone, seemingly the same as that comprising the Great Piers or the ancient buildings of Dereka. The hallway—empty of decorations or furnishings—was brightly illuminated by light flooding through translucent clerestory panels in the high roof.

The voices seemed to come from the far end of the corridor, and Mykella moved slowly along the columns on the right side. While she hoped that whoever was speaking would not see her, her shields had not proved to be totally effective against Ifrit weapons, and she wanted to be able to duck behind a column if necessary.

As she neared a set of archways to side chambers, she slowed, then looked into the one on her right. It was empty, and dim, because the ceiling was solid stone of some sort, and where there had been windows were oblong sections of the wall covered by rough-cut gray stones fitted and mortared in place. The polished stone of the floor was lightly covered in frost and dust and showed bootprints.

Mykella moved onward, noting that she had to be nearing the voices because they were louder. The next pair of chambers she passed were also empty, but the voices were far louder, and she eased up to the next archway. She could sense purplish figures—Ifrits—inside the chamber to her left, and she walked quietly across the corridor and stood behind the golden stone column flanking the side of the archway, listening and trying to better use her Talent to discern more about the Ifrits.

Four Ifrits stood in a semicircle, facing toward the outside wall, doubtless toward what had once been a window, and the voices stopped for several moments. Since the Ifrits were looking the other way, Mykella peered around the edge of the column, wanting to see them with her eyes and not just her senses. With her eyes on the Ifrits, she eased one of the Ifrit pistols out of her jacket and thumbed the safety lever to the firing position.

The four all wore the silvery garments, uniforms of some sort, but the colors were different, as if they belonged to armsmen of four different lands. The colors also appeared almost washed-out, unlike the uniforms worn by the Ifrits who had attacked the palace. Their life-threads also were dark and twisted purplish cords that ran from each to an oblong box that rested on the floor in the middle of the semicircle. From that box, a single larger cable snaked downward through the stone in the direction of the Table chamber.

What struck Mykella the most was that despite their size, all four carried an impression of gauntness and tiredness.

With a string of words Mykella did not understand, the tallest Ifrit turned and leveled what looked like a rifle—except that it had the same crystal barrel as did the flame pistol Mykella carried. The rifle spewed firebolts directly at Mykella.

Even as the grayish blue flames smashed into her shields, she could sense an outpouring of what she could only have called intense hatred. She staggered back for a step, then straightened against the hail of fire that both reflected from her shields—and also burned, but not nearly so much as had the fires from the Ifrits at the villa.

She could understand a few of the words from one of the Ifrits who carried no weapon.

. . . Green! . . . the green . . . vileness . . .

Mykella almost fired the pistol, before realizing her own shields would like send its bolts back at her and stuffing it into her coat. She Talent-reached for the life-thread of the Ifrit with the rifle and twisted his life-thread apart.

He stumbled and crashed to the stone, and the rifle bounced from his lifeless hands and skittered away.

The second Ifrit leveled a wide-barreled pistol of some sort at Mykella and fired, yelling, *. . . green . . . ancient bitch! . . . halt . . .*

Something crashed into her shields, rocking Mykella back, but she took a step forward and concentrated on his life-thread. As it frayed and exploded apart, another assault impacted her shields. She turned to see the third Ifrit wielding a saw-edged blade that glowed yellow beginning somehow to cut his way through her shields.

Each stroke of that blade, shorter than a saber, but longer than a dagger, created lines of pain radiating down her neck. She mentally fumbled but forced herself to concentrate through the pain, locating his node and finally tearing apart the threads.

A last, vicious swath of yellow raked through her mind and skull.

For a long instant, Mykella stood stock-still, trying to see and sense through pain-fogged eyes and thoughts. As both cleared, she saw the last Ifrit, ignoring the weapons but scrambling toward the device on the stone floor, picking it up and doing something to the metal box-like oblong.

Mykella sensed a swelling purpleness rising from around the device and struggled to create another a Talent probe to send toward the remaining Ifrit.

The Ifrit lifted the device, as if using it as a shield, but Mykella snaked her probe round the metal box and ripped at the life-thread node. The box dropped, and Mykella looked into the eyes of the dying Ifrit—a woman, she realized, whose eyes held total despair in that instant before they went blank.

Mykella's eyes dropped to the metal device and to the unseen thread or cable that wound back down to the Table below. The cable was swelling in a way she didn't comprehend, only that the purpleness flooding down it toward the device threatened . . .

She tried to strengthen her shields before a wave of blackish purple slammed into them . . . and blackness hammered her into darkness as the entire ancient building shuddered and shook.

Mykella woke to find herself sprawled against the far wall in the chamber on the other side of the corridor from the room where the Ifrits had been. She slowly moved to a sitting position, then stood. She could sense no other living things around her, as if the Ifrits had never been.

Had they even seen her, or just a green mist—or something like it?

She moved out to the corridor and looked to her right, where the corridor seemed to end in a gloomy recess less than fifteen yards ahead. There was an exit—or there had been one—but it had been walled up, with square sections of golden stone mortared in place. Mykella moved to the last set of archways. She studied them closely, noting grooves in the stone. Had they once held doors?

After a long moment, she turned and retraced her steps back to the chamber where the Ifrits had been. There she stopped in the archway, feeling slightly light-headed, and as if cold liquid oozed through her short hair.

The entire structure was empty of all furnishings, and every outside window had been mortared closed. She had seen nothing except the bare structure, not even any light-torches or their brackets. Just walls and columns and floors and ceilings, all of cold stone. There wasn't even a scrap of parchment or a fragment of metal. She didn't pretend to understand how the structure had come to be as it was. All the tales of the Cataclysm had indicated it had happened suddenly. Why and how had the Table building been sealed so carefully? Who had done it? How long ago? It certainly hadn't been accomplished recently. And why? To protect the Table? Had the Ifrits come back at some time and done so to protect it?

She took a step into the chamber.

The only sign of the Ifrits was four sets of silvery garments and four pair of boots. *How long were you unaware? The bodies of the other Ifrits had stayed for a time.*

As she finished the thought, a greenish glow appeared beside her, followed by the diminutive figure of the soarer. *They were not from the same Ifrit world. These were the last survivors of the world that brought the Cataclysm to Corus. They had a . . . device . . . that hoarded every bit of lifeforce left on that poor world . . . When they died . . . only the lifeforce locked within their garments remained.*

"The device . . . that was what exploded?"

That was what called me. You have done well . . .

The soarer's words explained why the Ifrits had looked so different, even to their weapons and garb. Lifeforce locked within their clothing? There was something . . . Yet . . . Mykella couldn't help remembering the look of total despair in the face of the female Ifrit just before she died. But Mykella had done well?

"There were two worlds of Ifrits?" she finally asked. "Two?"

There have been many, each one sucked dry of life . . .

"How do they do that? Why?"

From where do you think the great eternal highways and buildings come? Their strength is from bleeding lifeforce from a world.

"I stopped these and the ones who came before them."

That will only make those from the other world more cautious and more angry. It may take them more time to prepare, but they will come with greater numbers and greater weapons. The world will be bled dry of lifeforce, like all the others, unless you stop them.

"Me? What about you?" Mykella couldn't help it. Why was the soarer putting everything on her?

I cannot do what you can. Once there were many of us . . . and we did stop them . . . at a cost you would never know . . . now . . . An impression of a sad shrug followed.

"Your advice hasn't been all that helpful. You told me I needed to use the dark, deep green. How? I've surrounded myself with it. I've tried everything. Nothing works."

You cannot capture it. It must capture you.

"You said I couldn't let it touch me . . ."

That is when you use its power. Before that, you must become one with it. That is the only way in which you can separate yourself from it when the time comes.

"How do I let it capture me?" Mykella tried not to snap. She was worn out, both from fighting the Ifrits and from trying to understand too many things she'd never had to think about before.

By being like it . . . I must go . . . this . . . was . . . almost too far.

The green glow—and the soarer—vanished, leaving Mykella alone amid chill and lifeless stone.

She looked for the weapons used by the Ifrits but saw nothing. *Because they were powered by the lifeforce of a dying world?*

Why are the Ifrits coming back to Corus now? Why not earlier? Father couldn't have stopped them. Neither could Grandsire.

No one and nothing answered her questions.

Would she ever know the answers?

Mykella shivered. Lines of ice covered her skull. That was the way she felt, and the light coming through the translucent glass or stone had dimmed, whether from oncoming twilight or clouds, there was no way for her to tell. She began to walk toward the ramp down to the Table when she felt a chill wind gust around her. Where had that come from if the building had been sealed so tightly?

The gusts strengthened as she neared the ramp, and the ramp looked lighter. She saw why even before she reached the archway at the top of the ramp. A massive tree trunk had smashed through a section of the roof, falling so far that, halfway down the ramp, she would be able to touch the trunk.

Had the Ifrit device reached beyond the building? It must have. What that might have been, Mykella had no idea, only that coincidence couldn't explain the fall of such a huge tree.

She shivered again, more of a shudder, and she realized that she needed to get back to Tempre, that despite the heavy coat and gloves and felt-lined boots, she was far too cold.

As she eased down the ramp, she paused as more fragments of stone shifted and slithered down through the openings on each side of the massive tree trunk. On the upper side, there was a gap between trunk and golden stone—a gap perhaps half a yard in width and a yard long through which frigid air gusted. Should she investigate?

Mykella shook her head. *What good would that do?* Besides, she was more than a little exhausted and getting colder by the moment

She frowned as she looked at the trunk, a good three yards in breadth. It had just fallen, crashing through the side or edge of the building, with gouges in the bark. Yet the bark shimmered. She reached up and touched it. Even through the nightsilk gloves, the trunk felt warm but somehow lifeless. She eased out one of the unused flame pistols, and tapped the trunk. The crystal of the barrel *clanked* . . . as if the trunk had turned to stone. She replaced the pistol and eased out her small belt knife from under her coat. The blade did not even scratch the barklike stone. Slowly, she replaced the knife.

How did that happen? From that device? Had it sucked the life out of the tree, trying to defeat me? Or had it tried to suck lifeforce all the way back to the dying Ifrit world?

Again, she had no answers, and she put one boot in front of the other and made her way down to the Table chamber, if only because it was closer to the dark pathways that would take her back to Tempre.

It took all her strength to travel those green-black paths, and she staggered when she emerged in her palace bedchamber. All she wanted to do was collapse on her bed, wrapped in warm quilts.

"Mykella! Mykella!"

The shouting seemed so far away . . . so far . . .

Mykella slowly walked, or staggered, toward the door of her apartment and slid the bolt, letting the door open. She couldn't even open her mouth, let alone speak.

Salyna stood there in the palace corridor. Her mouth dropped open. "Oh . . . what . . . happened to you . . ."

Mykella could feel the world wobbling around her.

Then she didn't feel anything at all.

25

When Mykella woke up, she was sweating. That wasn't surprising given the comforters piled around her. From the hazy light filtering through the gauzy window hangings and from the dark velvet night drapes being drawn back, she could tell it was still day. Her head ached, and her eyes burned, but she could make out Salyna sitting beside the bed in a chair brought in from Mykella's private study. So was Rachylana, except on the other side.

"What glass is it?" Mykella asked, struggling with the comforters to sit up and escape the excessive warmth.

"Fourth glass of the afternoon. Tridi afternoon. You've slept for two glasses," said Rachylana.

"*What* were you doing?" Salyna demanded. "There were narrow slashes across your head, but none of them cut any hair, and there was blood frozen in lines across your scalp. There are bruises on your arms and back, and a lump on the back of your head. There are more welts on your face." She rose, leaned forward, and lifted two pillows.

"You're still greenish, too," added Rachylana as she stood. "Not so much, though."

Salyna frowned as she slipped the two pillows behind Mykella's back.

Mykella tried not to wince when Salyna touched her left shoulder. "Fighting . . . Ifrits . . ."

"Ifrits?" asked Rachylana.

"They attacked the palace again?" Salyna's words were but a fraction of a moment after her older sister's.

"What are Ifrits?" demanded Rachylana.

"Like the old-time Alectors," said Salyna impatiently. "They use the Tables to come here from another world. They caused the Cataclysm."

Rachylana looked from Salyna to Mykella.

"No," replied Mykella. "These Ifrits came through the Table at

Blackstear. What's worse is that they weren't even the ones from Efra. They were the last survivors of the old Ifrit world . . . and when I killed them, I finished killing that world . . . I think, or it died because they'd taken the last of the lifeforce to get here. I didn't mean to, but they attacked me . . ."

"Mykella, you scare me," replied Salyna. "At times, it's like I don't know you. You were my little older sister. I was trying to look out for you. Now . . . you're . . . you're someone I barely glimpsed before. It's like . . . the world's not the same. You know I never had rosy ideas about things, but . . . they're darker . . ."

Rachylana glared at Salyna. "You didn't tell me any of this." Then she turned to Mykella. "You didn't, either." She paused. "I knew you were doing something. You've been doing it for weeks. You aren't in your study. No one knows where you are, and you've never been one to hide in your rooms. I don't care what anyone else says—you look, maybe feel, greenish to me. Why didn't you tell me?" With her last words, the edge on her voice turned into sadness.

"Because . . . you've been so angry with me," Mykella admitted. "You wouldn't talk to me for days."

"I was angry," Rachylana said. "But you're my sister."

Salyna opened her mouth, then closed it.

Mykella waited.

"I'm . . . sorry," Rachylana said slowly. "I hurt so much . . . about Berenyt. It seemed liked you wanted to lash out at everyone and take everything away. But . . . I . . . well, I'm not stupid. I can see now; that bitch Cheleyza was manipulating Uncle Joramyl and Berenyt. Berenyt only thought he loved me. None of them even saw it. Father didn't, either. She tried to poison me, didn't she?"

"Yes," Mykella admitted.

"You saved me." There was another silence. "Why couldn't you save Father?"

"I tried. I didn't get there in time," Mykella said. "Joramyl didn't let anyone know Father was ailing until it was too late."

"Treghyt suspected, didn't he? He knows you know. That's why he fled. Why didn't you do something?"

"I could follow his movements through the Table," Mykella said, "but that didn't tell me where he was. The last time I looked, on Londi, he was dying. I think he might have taken poison himself. I don't know, but I think so."

"Why can you do all this?" Rachylana asked. "Why you?"

"I don't know. Two seasons ago, I saw the soarer in the garden. I asked you if you saw anything . . ."

Rachylana's brows knit. "I remember. I thought there was a green mist around the broken statue, but then it was gone. Is that why you look green?"

"She doesn't look green," interjected Salyna.

"To me she does. It's like a mist around her. In a way . . . anyway, why does that allow you to do all this?"

"I don't know," Mykella said. "The soarer just came to me and told me that I needed to save my world and my land. Every time I think I've managed to figure something out, something else happens."

"Why did these other Ifrits go to Blackstear? It has to be cold there. Is it because there's a Table there? The only one they could find?" asked Salyna.

"I don't think they knew which Table was what, and they were too tired to do anything else. I went there because I was afraid they were the Ifrits from Efra that the soarer warned me about, the ones who want to take over Corus."

"The ones you killed . . . they didn't want to conquer us? Then why—?" pressed Salyna.

"Their world was dead—almost so. They were trying to escape. The moment they saw me, they attacked. They had weapons I'd never seen before, but they all went to pieces, I think, when the box that kept them alive, it must have been something like that, exploded." Mykella swallowed. "It was awful. The first one attacked me, and then the others . . . they called me the green vileness . . . something like that. But . . . afterwards . . ." She gave the smallest of headshakes. "You don't know what it was like. I can still see the desperation . . . the agony in her eyes just before she died . . . like all hope everywhere had vanished."

"Her?"

"Some of them are women."

"How could they?" asked Salyna.

"Do what? Kill a world . . . kill our world?"

Salyna nodded.

"They use the lifeforce of everything that lives to make their grand buildings and highways, like the Great Piers and the green towers and the highways . . . even power their weapons, I think."

"That's . . . awful . . ." Salyna shuddered.

"How did you know they were there . . . how did you even get there? The Table chamber is locked and ironbound," pointed out Rachylana.

"I don't need to be in the chamber," Mykella said. "Not anymore. I can do it if I'm touching the stone walls of the palace." That was true enough if not the entire truth. She shivered and pulled one of the coverlets up around her. She'd felt so hot before, and now she was chill again.

"I'm going to have Muergya bring up some hot broth and bread for you," said Salyna. "You need something warm, and you need to eat more. Your face is thinner than I've ever seen it." She turned to Rachylana. "Make sure she stays in that bed."

Rachylana lifted her eyebrows.

Mykella could sense the unspoken question, and she almost laughed, except she was too tircd. "I'll stay. I'm not going anywhere."

"Not until you feel better, a whole lot better." With that, Salyna turned and left the bedchamber.

Not until the outer door to the main corridor closed did Rachylana speak. "She can't see the green, can she?"

"No."

"Could I use the Table?"

"You might be able to use it to see things," Mykella said, "but you shouldn't. Not now. The Ifrits can use it to take over the mind and body of anyone who cannot shield herself. One almost did that to me at first."

"When you can . . . when it's safe . . . will you show me?"

Mykella nodded, tiredly. "Please . . . please don't try now. I don't want to lose anyone else."

"I won't. I promise." The redhead looked at Mykella. "You're green, and pale, and so tired you're almost yellow. You need to rest." She sat down in the straight-backed chair. "I'll be here."

As she lay there, sore in more places than she wanted to count, Mykella couldn't help but wonder. *Those four were fleeing with what little they could bring, and you barely managed to defeat them? And the soarer said that the other Ifrits had even greater weapons?*

Except she hadn't "defeated" them. She'd killed them, and the raw despair in the eyes of the last Ifrit woman gnawed at her heart. Yet . . . what else could she have done? If she'd turned her back on the situation, she'd have been fighting two groups of Ifrits before long, and the ones in Blackstear wouldn't have stayed there, and they would have recovered and gotten stronger. And they hated her . . . just for what she was. They hadn't tried to talk or do anything but attack her with every weapon they had.

At the same time, she had only herself to blame for her injuries. She hadn't even drawn on the green darkness to help her. Was that because she'd been surprised at the speed and anger of the first Ifrit? She'd been fortunate to discover them . . . just because one Table marker was a little brighter than the others. That scared her, too. What else might she miss?

Not for the first time, she felt she didn't know enough. But where and how could she learn more . . . before it was too late?

26

On Quattri, Rachylana told Chalmyr that Mykella was slightly indisposed. That was Rachylana's suggestion, one that Mykella was happy to take, especially since she was even more bruised and sore than she had been on Tridi. She only left her chambers to eat and, once, to check the Table, just to make certain that it was not flashing. In fact, it seemed slightly duller. Mykella hoped that was an indication that another Ifrit attack was not imminent, but there wasn't much she could do about when or if more Ifrits might arrive . . . and she did need the rest—and food.

When she was stronger, though, she needed to investigate about the silver mirrors Would they help her with the deep dark green? Or were they even usable anymore?

Quinti morning, she took her time getting dressed, insisting for one of the few times in her life on using the porcelain tub filled with near-steaming water. While the warm water soothed her while she was washing, it cooled too quickly, and she was still sore when she made her way to her formal study. Tired as she had been on Quattri, by Quinti, the thought of remaining cooped up in her quarters seemed like con-finement. She had taken Rachylana's advice and used powder and a touch of unguent to cover those welts on her face that had not faded.

Chalmyr offered his usual pleasant greeting when she stepped into the anteroom, then cleared his throat.

"Yes, Chalmyr?"

"Lady . . . the envoy of Prince Skrelyn has requested a few moments of your time . . ."

"Is he here . . ."

"He awaits below."

"I'll see him." *Why is he still in Tempre? As a spy?* "Also . . . would you send word that, if he's in Tempre, I'd like to see Commander Areyst."

"Yes, Lady."

Mykella entered the study, and, for a moment, the very walls felt as though they were pressing in on her. Had her father felt that way? She shook her head. She'd been Lady-Protector for something like half a season, and she was feeling hemmed in? Did all rulers feel that way?

She laughed softly and ruefully. *Those with any intelligence do . . .*

Before long, Vaerlon was entering the study and bowing. "Lady-Protector, you are most kind to see me on such scant notice."

Mykella gestured to the chairs, waiting until the envoy seated himself in the chair farthest from her. "I see little point in making someone wait to prove that I can do so. If ever you must wait, it will be because I am already engaged. On what matter did you wish to speak?"

For a moment, Vaerlon was silent.

Mykella could sense that her directness had caught him off guard. She waited.

"Lady-Protector, you must realize that it is most unusual . . . most unusual . . . in dealing with matches . . ."

"I fail to understand what you find unusual, Envoy Vaerlon. Would you care to explain?"

"This . . . business of having outside matches meet . . ." For all of Vaerlon's apparent uneasiness, beneath the words was calculation.

"It might be considered unusual by some, but is it not equally unusual to think that a man and a woman who will spend years together should be matched without ever seeing each other?"

"That is always the way it has been done."

"Not always. Mykel the Great had certainly met Rachyla before they were matched. So have others."

"Those were different times."

"Are not all times different times?"

"Indeed they are, Lady-Protector, and in times that are different, there is often great stability in relying upon customs tried-and-true. That is a maxim I have often heard from Prince Skrelyn."

"He must have many maxims. Does he guide his conduct by a few that are tried-and-true?"

"He is an accomplished ruler, Lady-Protector."

Mykella almost sighed. "Surely, you did not wish merely to tell me, once more, that my desire that the prince see any of us he might consider matching, is unusual. Or is there some other matter we should discuss?"

"You did say that the times are unusual . . ." replied Vaerlon.

"I did, and I believe you agreed, Envoy Vaerlon. Yet I have the feeling we may not think the same matters are the ones that are unusual."

"Or we may." Vaerlon smiled. "In one instance, I do believe that we might well agree. Some have said that the brigands who attacked the palace and Seltyr Klevytr's villa were not brigands at all but Alectors who wished to bring back the old ways. That would be a most unusual occurrence, would it not?"

Where did he hear that? "When anyone attacks the palace, that is unusual. When it occurs soon after a new ruler takes over the palace, that is also unusual. But anyone who attacks the palace and the villa of a noted Seltyr is a brigand. Brigands are not unusual. They have been around since there have been cities. These brigands did have ancient weapons, and that is less usual, but weapons do not make a brigand an Alector any more than claiming a title makes a man a Seltyr." Mykella paused. "How did Seltyr Klevytr come to tell you this?"

"I do not believe I said that."

Mykella gained the impression that Klevytr had not been the source, and said, "Thank you for the clarification. As you must know, Seltyr Kelvytr was not at his villa when the Southern Guards dealt with the brigands. He is a cautious man, one unlikely to make a judgment without being present or without the word of someone equally trustworthy."

Vaerlon smiled pleasantly but did not reply.

"Do you not think so?" pressed Mykella.

"I could not say, for I have but met the Seltyr in passing."

"But you have met First Seltyr Khanasyl, have you not."

"How could one not encounter such a presence?"

"*Indeed.*" *He's more than met Khanasyl.* "When do you expect Prince Skrelyn in Tempre?"

"I do not know if he will consider coming to Tempre for the purpose of a match. He has certainly not had time enough to receive my last message and to reply. And, as I indicated to you, he believes most firmly in the old ways."

"You did indeed suggest that. I have indicated how I feel, and he will doubtless take that into account in deciding whether to proceed or not."

"He is a most discerning man."

"As are you, Envoy Vaerlon. I take it that you will be leaving us to return to Hafin?"

"That is my plan and my charge, Lady-Protector."

"Then I wish you well, and may you have a safe journey." Mykella stood. "Perhaps you will be fortunate and meet Prince Skrelyn in Salcer, so that your travels will not be unduly long."

Vaerlon rose in response and bowed slightly. "One can never tell, Lady-Protector. One can never tell."

Once the study door was firmly closed, Mykella rose from behind the desk and walked to the window. The spring sunlight offered little reassurance.

From Vaerlon's internal reactions, she doubted he would be traveling all the way to Hafin, but did he even know what Skrelyn planned? And why was Vaerlon dealing with Khanasyl? According to what she'd overheard years before, Skrelyn had effectively banished all but a few Seltyrs from Midcoast and restricted the holdings of the remaining High Factors. She doubted that had changed.

"Lady?"

"Come in."

Chalmyr opened the door, inclined his head, then stepped forward and handed her a folder. "Minister Gharyk brought this up. He said you were expecting it."

Expecting it? Oh . . . the document dealing with the head gaoler. "I am, thank you."

When Chalmyr closed the door, she sat down and slipped the large envelope out of the folder. There were three pages, and each was filled with precise and detailed script. She began to read. By the time she had finished, she was shaking her head. Huatyn certainly needed to be removed . . . yet . . . was that something she should do immediately?

After a time, she replaced the document in the envelope and the envelope in the folder and placed both in the open-topped box on the bookcase shelf. She wanted to consider that more fully. Then she took out the map folder, laying it on the desk and settling down to study the map that showed the border between Lanachrona and Midcoast—the area around the west highway.

She was still trying to memorize details when Chalmyr rapped again.

"The commander is here."

"Have him come in."

The study door opened, and Areyst stepped inside. He bowed, then straightened.

Mykella took in his short blond hair and the pale green eyes that seemed to look through her, but not cruelly or coldly, but warmly, yet as though he understood something about her. She held in a soft laugh. He did. He was ten, if not fifteen, years older than she was, and he had far more experience with women than she did with men. "Commander." Mykella did not stand. That would only have betrayed her soreness. She motioned to the chair nearest her.

"Lady-Protector. I had heard that you were . . . indisposed . . . yesterday." Concern and curiosity lay behind the polite statement. He seated himself gracefully.

"Indeed I was . . . but not in any normal manner. We'll get to that in a moment. I have a question for you. I want an honest answer. Do I appear green or shrouded in a greenish mist to you at times?"

A wry smile crossed the commander's lips. "I had not expected such a question as that. Yet I should have."

"And?" pressed Mykella.

"I would not put it quite that way. It is more like you are enhanced by the faintest of green lights." He paused for the slightest moment. "That light casts no shadows, and I do not think others see it. I have said nothing to anyone. Might I ask if that is because you can do things as do the Ancients?"

"Why should you have anticipated the question?" asked Mykella, deliberately ignoring his.

"I saw the figures in the Table. Your youngest sister did not, although she was careful not to say that she failed to discern them."

"What did you see when you looked at the Ifrits at Klevytr's villa?"

"An ugly purple-pink glow around them."

"Exactly. Some people can see as we do although I think we sense it more than see it."

"Is that why you picked me as Arms-Commander?"

"No. I picked you as Arms-Commander because I thought you were capable, as did others, and because I know you are honest. What I have revealed to you is because I know you can see what others do not."

"Thank you. I would not wish to hold my position for reasons other than what I can do for you and for Lanachrona."

"It is likely, although I do not know for certain, that the more I learn how to do in the fashion of the Ancients, the brighter that green light or glow will become. More people will likely note it, and I fear that I will need to be . . . circumspect. However . . . the reason I was 'indisposed' yesterday was because on Tridi, I found myself fighting four more Ifrits. . . ." Mykella went on to explain what had happened, if as briefly as she could. ". . . and when I returned, I was . . . shall we say, not fit to be seen . . ."

"You are wearing powder. Is that . . ."

"To cover some of the bruises and welts? Yes."

"Lady . . ."

Mykella shook her head. "There's nothing to say. There's no one else to do what must be done. It's our ill fortune that we must face the coastal princes and the Ifrits at the same time."

"It may not be ill fortune," offered Areyst. "If they can use the Tables as can you . . ."

Mykella almost used words she never uttered with anyone else around, then caught her tongue. "They might well have chosen this time for exactly that reason."

"That . . . or it could be ill fortune. I have found that, for all the sayings about fortune favoring the good, it always seems to favor the evil who are bold."

"Why do you think that?"

"Because that is what I have seen." Areyst smiled. "I do not believe that fate or the world conspires against the good. It is that those who are good look to avoid unnecessary fighting or bloodshed. They will wait, knowing that fighting kills more good men than evil, because, I believe, most men and women are at heart good. Those who are evil and seek to gain goods or power have no compunctions about acting and letting others die to achieve their own goals. So . . . fortune appears to favor the evil." He shrugged. "Was not that part of what led to your father's downfall?"

Mykella nodded. "He wanted to believe the best of those close to him."

"Hope for the best but never close your eyes or mind to what is."

"Will you be leaving soon for Viencet?" she asked.

"I had thought to leave on Septi. That is when the next two squads return, and I will accompany those now here in Tempre to Viencet and their increased training. I will leave Captain Maeltor and Undercaptains Jionyl and Bursuin here." He paused. "Will you need their assistance in dealing with . . . Ifrits?"

"They cannot help there. I may need their help in dealing with other matters. I hope not."

"Other matters?"

Mykella offered a crooked smile. "I cannot be everywhere."

"No one can be, not even a Lady-Protector with the skills and gifts of the Ancients. Captain Maeltor will do whatever you request."

"Thank you."

"Is there anything else you require of me?"

"Not at the moment, Commander." *Not at the moment.* She stood, managing not to wince.

"Moving still hurts, does it not?" he asked gently as he rose.

"Not so much as yesterday."

"Lady . . . I would not be untoward . . . but as you can, I would that you consider your own health."

Mykella detected the slightest flush . . . and a certain embarrassment, and she wanted to reach out and take his hands. She did not. "I will do my best, Commander." Her eyes met his. "Thank you," she added softly.

Areyst bowed. "Good day, Lady, and do take care." He turned, careful not to look back.

He really does care.

That thought warmed her through—until she started to sit down, and a line of pain flashed from her shoulder down her back.

27

On Decdi night, the three sisters gathered for the evening meal in the family quarters. The remainder of the week had passed . . . if not quickly, neither as slowly as it might have. Mykella had not left the palace. She'd been unable to find Treghyt using the Table, and that meant the old healer was dead. Maxymt was still on the run and appeared more gaunt than ever, while Demyl was now an officer in the Southgate forces, or so it appeared from the white uniform and the other officers apparently obeying him. Of greater import, Cheleyza was still in Northcoast, and she and Paelyt were definitely supervising troopers, or cavalry. Chalcaer wasn't around his sister all that much. That also bothered Mykella.

Areyst had departed for Viencet on Septi as planned, and Mykella had to admit she did miss him, but she knew the Southern Guards would need all the extra training that Areyst and Choalt could provide and that there was little point in Areyst's remaining in Tempre.

When Mykella had called up the darkness in the Table chamber, just enough to sense beyond Tempre, she had found that none of the Tables or the colored markers were any brighter, and the one at Blackstear had faded noticeably. She had not attempted to seek and control the dark green of the depths because, until Decdi, she had not felt fully recovered from her skirmish with the Ifrits. That delay bothered her, even though the Tables seemed to give no indication of an immediate Ifrit arrival or attack. Even so, as she settled into her place at the table, she resolved to make another attempt later that evening.

She took a large helping of the crust-covered fowl, then eased the hot casserole dish to Salyna. Before sampling the steaming mound of fowl, vegetable, and potato chunks, Mykella poured herself a full mug of tea. Then she broke off a large chunk of the dark bread she preferred.

"I'm glad it's hot," said Salyna. "It was chill out this afternoon."

Mykella took a sip of tea and nodded although she hadn't been outside.

"You've been quiet, Mykella," offered Rachylana. "Are you all right?"

"I'm fine."

"You look better, but the green hasn't faded much."

"She isn't green," insisted Salyna.

"I probably am," Mykella said. "It comes from using the Table and traveling the way the Ancients did. Not everyone can see it. It doesn't have anything to do with how I feel."

"Why can she see it, and I can't?" asked Salyna.

"I don't know." That was only partly true, because so far as Mykella knew, no one who did not have at least a trace of green in her life-thread could see the green. She just didn't know why that was so. "You might as well ask why some women have blond hair and some black."

"Was Mykel the Great the oldest?" asked Salyna.

"It can't be that," pointed out Rachylana. "Father and Grandfather and Great-grandfather were the oldest, and they couldn't see anything in the Table, and none of them believed there were soarers still alive."

"They didn't even believe in the Table," Mykella said.

"They should have," muttered Salyna.

Mykella could sense a certain frustration and desperation in Salyna. "You've got a very busy week ahead." She lifted her mug of tea and looked to her youngest sister.

"Many tendays like that to come. It's better than doing some things."

"You mean, like arranging balls?" replied Rachylana edgily. "Do you really think these women auxiliaries will help—except by reducing the number of harlots near the Southern Guard barracks?"

"Most of them aren't harlots," Salyna replied. "There are more sculls and sweeper women, and third and fourth daughters from laboring families who don't want to be harlots and sculls."

"The guards will look down on them," predicted Rachylana.

"There aren't many guards in Tempre right now. They won't look down on them by the time I'm finished with them."

"I'm certain of that," replied Mykella. "Do you think many will finish your training?"

"Not all of them will. That's why I'm starting with sixty-five."

"Will those stipended-off squad leaders be that much help?" asked Rachylana.

"They're not in charge. I am."

"Will they listen?

"They will. Majer Smoltak said that Salyna was better than most Deforyan mounted troopers," Mykella said. "Commander Areyst said she was better than most Southern Guards."

"Women aren't as strong as men."

"Most women aren't. That's true," admitted Salyna. "It's as much about training and technique as strength. You have to have strength. That's why we've worked out some special exercises with weights for the women. But strength isn't everything. Besides, they just have to be good enough with weapons to be able carry out Guard duties that don't involve fighting. Unless, they're attacked, of course. Or if there's no one else left to fight."

"If they try to collect travel tariffs, they'll be in for trouble," suggested Rachylana.

"Not necessarily," said Mykella. "If Lanachrona is viewed as strong, no trader or factor will refuse, even those from Southgate. They may not like it, but they won't refuse." What she didn't say was that such strength depended on Areyst and the Southern Guards . . . and on her. "When will you have the season-turn-ball invitations ready to be dispatched?"

"On Duadi or Tridi," replied Rachylana. "Your new gown isn't quite ready."

"Do you think . . . a new gown? I know I agreed, but . . ."

"Some appearances need to be kept up," Salyna said.

That surprised Mykella. "I'll try it on when it is ready," she said to Rachylana. "Thank you."

After a lengthy dinner, Mykella pleaded tiredness and retired to her apartments. From there, she slipped down through the granite of the walls to the Table chamber. She studied the Table, but it remained as it had been for the past tenday. She hoped it remained that way, at least until she could figure out a way to master the darker green of the depths.

Remembering what the Ancient had told her, she took a deep breath, not that she really needed to, and dropped downward through the stone, directing her course toward the dark green that appeared to her senses as both brilliant and lightless, yet conveyed the essence of "green." She came to rest, or so it seemed to her senses, in the middle of the dark way, an underground conduit that was of the darkest and yet brightest green in the center, sheathed by a brighter green, then cloaked on the outside by a green that was almost black.

Let it capture you, she reminded herself.

As the chill began to seep into her flesh and bones, Mykella tried to "feel" green. How else could she let that underground torrent capture her rather than just flow around her?

Tendrils of the darkest green caressed her, swirling around her, then began to pass through her, leaving a path of both chill and light . . . chill and light. After a time, Mykella began to touch with her Talent, ever so lightly, the tendrils that swirled around and through her. While some of those filaments edged away, others did not. Before long, she could sense when to touch a filament and when not to. Then it did not seem to matter.

She realized, abruptly, that she was so tired . . . so tired . . .

It took enormous effort to pull herself free of the depths, and yet, once she was free, the return to the palace was almost effortless, or so it seemed.

When she again stood in her bedchamber, it was dark outside the palace. Surprisingly, she was not chilled. Cool . . . but not chilled to the bone. *Is being outside the deeper green what causes the chill?*

That was another question she could not answer.

She walked to the window and looked out to the west, in the general direction of the Great Piers. Those she perceived as outlined in a golden green. *Did you ever see them that way before?*

While she wasn't absolutely certain, she didn't think she had. Had she done something to change the Great Piers? Or had letting the green depths capture her changed how she perceived things? One thing she did know. The journey to the depths had exhausted her, and she still hadn't done anything about the mirrors.

She turned back toward her bed.

28

On Londi, Mykella awoke before dawn to the sound of rain pounding against the windows, with gusts of wind rattling the panes. She rose quickly but stopped after several steps away from her bed, feeling as though she walked in a green haze or mist. She looked around, trying to determine the source of the haze, then made her way to her dressing table, where, when she looked into the large mirror, she saw nothing out of the ordinary, just the reflection of a too-pale, black-haired, green-eyed woman who looked too young to be a Lady-Protector.

She took her time washing and dressing, but the sense of the green haze did not dissipate, and she left her quarters and walked to the breakfast room. Both her sisters were already seated at the table. Rachylana looked at Mykella, then smiled faintly before looking down at her platter.

"What was that look for?" asked Salyna.

"Nothing," replied the redhead.

Mykella understood the look all too well and gave the tiniest head-shake when Rachylana looked her way.

Rachylana nodded slightly.

"That just means you don't want to tell me."

"There's nothing to tell." Rachylana paused. "I could have said that Mykella still looked a bit green, or I could have said that she wasn't about to go riding through Tempre today, no matter what she'd said last night about needing to see more of the city."

"I could still go riding," said Mykella ruefully, "but I wouldn't see anything. How will this affect your training?" She looked to her youngest sister.

"I'd already figured that out. We can use the stables, since most of the horses are in Viencet. Besides, guards have to do what they do in the rain and the snow." Salyna took a swallow of tea, then added, "Most of the trainees are used to foul weather, anyway."

"What if more show up?" asked Mykella.

"I've planned for that. We could take another ten, and I'll just work them harder and take the best. If most of them last, there will be jobs for them. There are thousands of guards. What difference will ten more women auxiliaries make, except that they'll end up doing tasks the men find boring or demeaning."

Rachylana raised her eyebrows.

"You know as well as I do," Salyna said, "that the men like to prove they're strong, that they're good with weapons, and that they're irresistible to women. Most of them don't like tasks that require details or learning numbers or more than basic reading."

"You're going to teach them that?" asked Mykella.

"At night. Why not? It'll keep them busy, and it will keep the guards at headquarters away from them."

Mykella ate and listened, adding a few words here and there, and wishing Salyna well when her younger sister hurried off to the Southern Guard barracks. Then she rose, returned to her quarters, and finished readying herself for the day.

Less than a quarter glass later, she left her quarters. She couldn't help but worry as she walked swiftly along the upper-rear hallway of the palace toward the Finance Minister's study. She knew that the Treasury was perilously low, and she'd asked Haelyt to calculate how much would be needed over the next two seasons and how many golds in tariffs and fees were likely to be paid. From her own study of the master ledgers, she had the feeling that she wasn't going to like the figures Haelyt should have waiting for her.

When she stepped into the study of the Finance Minister—hers until she found someone else she trusted—she looked to the graying clerk. "Good morning, Haelyt."

"Good morning, Lady."

"Do you have the calculations?" Mykella walked to the side of the wide desk where Haelyt had several ledgers laid out.

"I do." The chief clerk handed her a folder. "The expenses are fair-on close to what you'll need to disburse. The tariffs and fees . . . they're my best judgment of what you might expect, based on past years. Might be lower, given all that's happened."

A great deal lower, since many of the Seltyrs won't want to pay a Lady-Protector. And some few, she knew, always delayed payment until the Finance Minister was ready to arrive at their warehouse with a squad of Southern Guards. "Give me a summary, if you would."

Haelyt nodded. "The total of the golds held by the Treasury directly at the moment is nine thousand seven hundred thirty-six golds. Each of the ministries also has golds in its own strong room. The Southern Guards holds six thousand three hundred and three golds; the Forestry Ministry has but two hundred; and the Ministry of Rivers and Highways has five hundred ten golds—"

"Assistant Minister Duchael claims they only have two hundred. He reports, and the ledgers support, that they've spent three hundred since the beginning of the year. That's a discrepancy of three hundred and ten golds."

"And three silvers, actually," added Haelyt dryly.

"Can you and Vyahm reconcile that for me?"

"We will see what we can do."

"Go on," prompted Mykella. "What are the likely expenditures?"

"The largest are those of the Southern Guards. The weekly payroll is just over nine hundred golds. It was close to twelve hundred a week two years ago . . ."

Down a quarter? Seven companies' worth?

". . . food and supplies run almost as much, some eight hundred a week . . . and another hundred or so for other items . . ."

"Close to two thousand a week. That means they'll need more golds after the turn of summer."

"Yes, Lady. As you may recall . . ."

"We transfer every season." She almost shook her head. "We can't transfer even enough for half a season . . . unless . . ." *You raid the three thousand or so in your strong room, and there's no point in that.* ". . . we have some more revenues. What about river tariffs?"

"There have been very few barge tariffs. There never are in early spring."

"How much has the portmaster turned in?"

"A little over a hundred golds since the turn of spring, fifty last week."

Mykella nodded. "What can we expect from the spring tariffs?" With what was left in the Treasury—and what she had in the strong room—there was enough to meet the Lord-Protector's obligations into the third week of summer, possibly the fourth . . . and just maybe the fifth. The question was whether the spring tariffs, due in a little less than three tendays, would provide enough golds to get the Treasury close to when the summer tariffs were due, although the river tariffs should increase with the summer barge traffic on the River Vedra.

"Usually, there are some timber revenues and private-land timber-sale override tariffs . . ." ventured Haelyt.

"There won't be any timber revenues," Mykella said. "Joramyl overcut the Protector's lands the last two years. There may be some private-land tariffs. I won't know until Forester Loryalt returns later this week or next week."

"Ah . . ." Haelyt cleared his throat. "The winter- and spring-turn tariffs are always the scantiest. I looked them up for the past years. The worst year was seven years back, when the total was seventeen thousand, three hundred. The best was five years ago, when there were extra timber sales, and that was twenty-two thousand six hundred."

Mykella nodded. She'd thought that Joramyl would have figured out to leave enough to rule if he had remained as Lord-Protector, but . . . if anything at all went wrong . . .

It will. The way matters are going, it definitely will. "I've told all the ministries to avoid any new spending without checking with me first."

"Minister Porofyr used to claim that he'd already spent golds when he hadn't," Haelyt said quietly.

"Do you think Duchael might have that habit?"

"I couldn't be saying, Lady-Protector."

Mykella smiled. "I think you just have. I will have a talk with Assistant Minister Duchael . . . after we finish here."

Mykella opened the folder and read through the columns. The

figures were clear, and she only had a few more questions before she left Haelyt and headed to the lower level of the palace.

When Mykella stepped into the Highways and Rivers Ministry study, her eyes swept the chamber, taking in the two clerks in the smaller front desks, and the rear desk that was Duchael's. Even from the entryway, Mykella could sense that someone was in the minister's private study with Duchael. *Who could that be? The palace isn't open to outsiders yet.*

"Not a word," she commanded in a low voice.

The two clerks exchanged glances, but neither spoke.

Mykella could sense that the older clerk was worried, and that the younger was somehow almost pleased, but she slipped toward the closed door to the inner study—most properly the chamber of the minister—which Duchael was not. Using her Talent, she could catch part of the conversation.

". . . can't do it . . . she watches everything . . . worse than Lord Joramyl . . ."

". . . what's a hundred golds? Don't want stenches for my spring festival . . . Khanasyl . . . upset . . ."

". . . can't . . ."

". . . could you use . . . say ten golds?"

". . . could, indeed, but not now . . ."

". . . who would know . . . ?"

Mykella opened the door and stepped into the inner study.

Duchael looked up from where he sat behind the minister's desk. So did the older man seated across from him.

The assistant minister turned pale. He stood quickly. "Lady-Protector . . . you may know Seltyr Pualavyn."

The slender ferretlike Seltyr rose, if with what Mykella thought was a languidly disrespectful manner. "Lady-Protector."

"I do know of the Seltyr. By reference." Mykella's smile was cool. "You are here early, Seltyr Pualavyn."

"By the courtesy of the assistant minister." Pualavyn's smile was oiled with insincerity.

"He can be most courteous. I am most certain you can finish whatever matters you were discussing at a later time."

"Of course. Of course. I would not intrude upon the business of the Lady-Protector. It certainly takes precedence over mere commerce."

"Not commerce, Seltyr, just festivals." Mykella smiled again, stepping aside and glancing toward the open door. "Good day."

For the merest instant, Pualavyn's eyes turned hard and cold, but he continued to smile as he inclined his head. "Good day, Lady-Protector."

Mykella said nothing until the Seltyr had left the outer study. Then she closed the door to the inner study and turned to Duchael.

"Lady-Protector . . . he was most insistent. I did nothing."

"I know. I saved you from that choice. I'm about to save you from another. There will be no more expenditures from your ministry's accounts, except for payroll, without my personal approval. Any expenditures that you 'discover' that supposedly occurred before this moment will be deducted from your pay—and from the chief engineer's if he makes them. Is that clear?"

"Yes. Lady." Duchael swallowed.

"The engineer can use his normal crews and any material in his storerooms. He may not purchase anything except with the golds he already has in his possession—unless he has my written authorization. You will make that known to him immediately."

Duchael glanced to the window and the gusty downpour besieging Tempre.

"Immediately," Mykella repeated.

"Yes, Lady-Protector."

"You can report on your meeting with him at the minister's meeting tomorrow." Mykella smiled once more, then left the study, heading to the upper level of the palace. Had Haelyt known Duchael was meeting with Pualavyn? Had someone told him? Why that particular morning?

Mykella found it all too convenient that every single one of the Seltyrs that Khanasyl had recommended had demonstrated serious flaws within weeks of being recommended. Khanasyl was anything but stupid, and that indicated where he stood. It also indicated that he had at least some sources of information within the palace, not that Mykella expected anything else.

29

Mykella looked from the window of her formal study out across the palace courtyard to the park across the avenue. After two days of violent storms, Tridi was bright and clear. Green was everywhere. Unfortunately, that meant much of the "green" consisted of recently leafed-out branches ripped from trees, bushes flattened onto stone walkways, and general vegetative carnage. The steward's men were busy sweeping leaves out of the front and side courtyards, but no gardeners had appeared to clean up the park.

She turned from the window, thinking. The ministers' meeting on Duadi had been short, with little discussion. Gharyk had not brought up the matter of the removal of Gaoler Huatyn. Mykella appreciated his tact because there was something about the document that bothered her.

Or is it the problem of replacing Huatyn?

She just wasn't certain, and yet she didn't want to end up like her father, not making decisions until she had every possible fact in place—and then being wrong anyway. One way or another, she needed to come to a decision before long.

"Lady . . . Assistant Minister Duchael."

"Have him come in."

The door opened, and a slightly disarrayed Duchael stepped in, bowing hurriedly and deeply. "Lady-Protector . . . I regret having to bring this matter to your attention, but . . ."

"But what?"

"The storms were so violent that the East and South Rivers overflowed their banks, and the Vedra washed out the towpath in several places." Duchael's eyes flickered toward the windows, then back to Mykella.

"Then we need to inspect those areas immediately."

"They need to be repaired, Lady-Protector."

"I'm certain that they do, but there is almost no barge traffic at the moment. A glass or two will not make much difference."

"They are metaled paths," murmured Duchael.

"Indeed, and what lies under that stone and gravel? Come. We will go see."

"Yes, Lady."

"Where is the worst damage?"

"It is a half vingt west of the oxen pens south of the Great Piers."

"We'll start there, but make sure you know all the locations. I'd like to see every break in the towpaths near Tempre."

"Yes, Lady."

Although Duchael's reply was firm and direct, Mykella could sense more than a little concern hidden behind his words. *Why? Storms happen.*

Still, his worry suggested that something was not well, and Mykella suspected she knew the cause, but she was better off not dashing to conclusions until she inspected the destruction.

Less than half a glass later, Mykella, Duchael, and Maeltor, accompanied by a squad of Southern Guards, rode westward on the avenue toward the Great Piers. A warmish breeze blew out of the southwest, and as it swirled around Mykella, she found herself riding through pockets of cool moist air, then warm dryness.

"Captain Maeltor . . . directions to that . . . location will be waiting when we return?" Mykella did not wish to be more specific about the request she had made earlier, not with Duchael riding to her right.

"As you ordered, Lady."

Duchael frowned but said nothing although worry continued to radiate from him.

The avenue had been cleared—mostly—except for a few larger downed trees they had to ride around, but the paving stones and sidewalks were littered with leaves and smaller branches.

"Mostly the old water oaks that the wind took down," said Maeltor conversationally.

"They're not supposed to be planted in Tempre," Mykella pointed out.

"Some still are. They grow quickly and provide shade."

Mykella turned to Duchael. "Don't their roots try to clog the sewer tunnels?"

"We cut down any near the tunnels, Lady, and we charge the landowner. The ones beside the avenue—most were planted by Seltyrs and factors for shade . . ."

Mykella repressed a sigh, looking ahead to the Great Piers. There, the golden stones were clear of leaves and twigs, and the River Vedra had subsided, although it was still high enough that Mykella could have reached down and touched the water from the piers. That was a level she'd only seen a few times in her life.

As Mykella rode past the piers and toward the end of the towpath and the ox pens beyond, she saw that dirt and sand had washed into most of the pens, but the comparative handful of oxen waiting to be barged downstream had all been moved to the easternmost pen, which appeared undamaged.

"Where exactly is the first damaged section?" she asked Duchael.

"Beyond the pens . . ."

I know that! How far? But she only nodded and guided the gelding around the last pen and onto the stone apron that marked the space between the end of the towpath and the piers, then along the apron on the river side of the ox pens. She rode almost a full vingt on the towpath, past two hills, until they reached a point where a creek ran from between the hills and under a stone bridge into the river. On the far side of the bridge was a small ravine that the creek had cut through the towpath.

Mykella rode onto the stone bridge, a sturdy structure, if partly covered in dirt and mud, where she reined up. The foundation under the paving stones of the approach to the west side of the bridge had been eroded by the storm waters so that about a third of each of the stones protruded out over emptiness. On the far side of the new ravine, several planks protruded from the clay, although two had been smashed and twisted by the force of the water. She could just make out the ends of far larger timbers, to which the smaller planks that had been broken or swept away had been attached. Paving stones lay storm-tossed in the ravine. She glanced to her left, up the creek, then at the hill side of the bridge, where a web of branches and vegetation had matted together into a dam of sorts that blocked the brick and stone arches under the bridge.

No one's been clearing the creek bed, and the last repairs were done with planks rather than timbers.

She turned in the saddle and looked back at Duchael. "The records for towpath repairs are in your study, are they not?"

For a moment, the assistant minister said nothing. "They should be."

"Maintaining them has always been your responsibility, has it not?" That was a guess on Mykella's part, but she couldn't imagine Porofyr taking care of those details.

"Yes, Lady."

"I will need them when we return." She turned the gelding, carefully.

To get to the second break in the towpath required retracing their path almost to the Great Piers, then taking the avenue and side roads to the west, and finally a narrow lane to the river. There, runoff from the hills had eroded the base of the towpath, leaving a slumped mass of earth and displaced paving stones. Again, Mykella could see the signs that the area had been repaired shoddily, apparently with dirt and clay and thin timbers rather than the heavy timbers that flanked the washed-out area.

The third break was less than half a vingt farther west. It, too, had been caused by excessive runoff eroding a previously poorly repaired area. Mykella studied it briefly, then turned to Maeltor. "I've seen enough, Captain." She flicked the gelding's reins and started back.

Once they were on the avenue, she turned to Duchael. "As I said earlier, I'd like to see the records on when those sections were last repaired. As soon as we return to the palace."

"Lady . . . it might be difficult to tell when . . ."

"Oh . . . we don't get that many storms like the one yesterday. All three breaks look to have been repaired at about the same time with the same size timbers and methods. I'd wager that it happened three years ago in late summer, or five years ago in the fall. You can look there to begin with." She smiled politely although she was seething inside, and keeping her voice level took a certain concentration.

By the time they reached the Great Piers on the return ride, in some ways, Mykella actually felt just slightly sorry for Duchael. As assistant minister to Porofyr, he was limited in what he could do—or say. Even as the daughter of the Lord-Protector, she'd found it almost impossible to prove corruption, let alone have anyone believe her or what she discovered. At the same time, she was getting tired of finding evidence of corruption everywhere.

How long has all this been going on? Since Mother's death . . . or did it start long before? She doubted that she'd find a good answer to all that, but she'd discovered enough to know that it all couldn't have started in the past few years.

When they reached the palace, Mykella rode directly to the rear courtyard—on the west side, reining up by the private entrance there. "Captain . . . wait here. We will likely be riding out again quite shortly. If we do, the ride will not be that long." She turned to Duchael. "I expect the records of those repairs in my study in less than a quarter glass."

The assistant minister paled.

Even Maeltor took a quick glance at Mykella before she dismounted and handed the gelding's reins to the nearest Southern Guard. Mykella hurried up to her quarters, from where she dropped through the blackness to the Table chamber. The Table did not appear any brighter, not that she could tell, and she stepped up to it and concentrated on Porofyr. In instants, his image appeared. The Seltyr was wearing riding clothes and talking to a man dressed in worn pale blue trousers and shirt in the courtyard in the center of his warehouses. The sight of the supercilious and arrogant former minister made her blood seethe, but after studying the image, she let it lapse.

Since she had a little time, she also quickly looked for Cheleyza and Areyst. Cheleyza still wore the cavalry uniform and rode with several Northcoast officers. Areyst was also mounted and looked to be conducting some type of mounted maneuver.

Mykella blinked. Unlike the figures of those around him, the commander was again shaded a silvery green, and appeared hazy and even less visible.

Why is that? Because he has a trace of Talent? Is that why you couldn't track the Ifrits with the Table? Or was that because you didn't know them? That was another question she wouldn't be able to answer soon, she suspected.

She used the darkness to return to her quarters, from where she walked to her study.

"Lady," offered Chalmyr.

"Has anything happened of which I should be aware?"

"You have several missives from Seltyrs. I believe that they are urging you to use your resources to repair various . . . difficulties created by the storms."

"I'm certain they are." Mykella laughed harshly. "I'm still working on the towpath problem. Did any of their messengers indicate particular problems?"

"I believe the sewers have backed up in the southeast . . ."

That didn't surprise Mykella. Some of those tunnels and pipes had been added later, and she doubted they had been installed with the same care as those built in the time of the Alectors. "I am certain Chief Engineer Nusgeyl can deal with those problems. Is there anything else?"

"Your sister, Lady Rachylana, had a question, but she said that she would see you later, and Minister Gharyk came by . . ."

Mykella listened for a time, wondering how long it would take Duchael to find the report on the towpath repairs—or if there even happened to be a report.

Close to a quarter glass later, the assistant minister arrived, hurrying into the outer anteroom and coming to an abrupt stop as he saw Mykella standing there. "Lady-Protector . . . here is the report you requested." He handed her an envelope.

"Thank you. I appreciate your effort to find it quickly." She smiled politely. "Now that I have seen the damage, you may make arrangements for the proper repair of the towpaths, but every single disbursement for timbers or goods I will see, and no new men are to be hired. Use the engineer's crews. If he complains, I will see him. Is that clear?"

Duchael swallowed. "Yes, Lady."

"Good. You may go."

Duchael did not quite flee.

Mykella carried the report into her study and read through it carefully. She'd been correct. All three repairs had been accomplished five years before by the same crew in the third week of fall. More interesting was the observation that the repairs had been accomplished according to the specific directions of Minister Porofyr with the normal charges for such repairs. The report was signed by an Assistant Minister Stefyl, in the same cursive as that in which the report had been written. Mykella had no recollection of him, but she wouldn't have.

Mykella took several moments to open the strong room and place the report on a shelf beside one of the chests. Then she locked the door and slid the bookcase back into position. She stopped in the anteroom. "I'm riding out again, Chalmyr. I don't know when I'll be back."

The aging scrivener nodded. "Yes, Lady."

Mykella hurried back down to the rear courtyard, where she jump-vaulted into the saddle of the gelding—necessary because there was no mounting block nearby. At least she did so gracefully. Then she turned to Maeltor. "We'll be heading to Seltyr Porofyr's warehouse. Your men should have their arms ready once we're there. We are going to deal with a corrupt traitor."

Maeltor's eyes widened, but he only said, "As you command, Lady-Protector."

"You saw the bridge and towpaths. Would you have repaired them with just dirt and thin planks, and covered the packed earth under the paving stones with that thin a layer of gravel?"

"No, Lady."

"Would you have charged the same amount as required for the right kind of repair and pocketed the difference?"

Maeltor smiled ironically. "One way or another, Lady-Protector, Tempre's going to be very different in a year."

Mykella nodded. She understood what the captain meant all too well. She flicked the gelding's reins and turned him toward the east end of the courtyard.

The ride to Porofyr's warehouse complex—less than a half vingt to the southeast of the Great Piers—took less than a quarter glass.

As they neared the iron gates, Maeltor called out, "Ready rifles. Four man front!"

The two tough-looking men at the gates to Porofyr's warehouse courtyard looked at the Southern Guards as they reined up with their rifles ready.

"The Lady-Protector is here to see Seltyr Porofyr," announced Maeltor.

"He's not here, Subcaptain."

"Oh, did he leave in the last quarter glass?" Mykella concentrated on sensing the two sentries, immediately catching their unspoken re-action.

"He's not here." Neither man would look at her.

"He is here. Please open the gates," Mykella said politely.

"We can't open them unless the Seltyr or the warehouse boss says to."

"Then ask the warehouse boss," replied Mykella coldly, extending her senses.

"He's not here."

She peered through the iron bars of the gates, catching sight of a black-haired man mounting a horse. The man was Porofyr, wearing the same riding clothes. She also could see that there was a rear gate. "Maeltor, send some men around to the left. There's another gate there, and Porofyr's trying to leave."

"Gheryn and second rank! Around to the left! To the other gate! Don't let anyone out! On the double!"

"Second rank! On your orders, sir!"

Four troopers wheeled their mounts as one and left, not at a gallop, but at good speed.

Mykella looked to Porofyr's sentries. "It appears you were mistaken. The Seltyr is here after all. For the moment."

At that instant came a series of whistle blasts, and the two sentries pulled out pistols.

"Fire! Fire at will!" snapped Maeltor.

Mykella extended her shields to cover the captain as shots filled the air, and most came from within the warehouse compound, some from men in dark green who appeared on balconies and roofs. No bullets struck the shields, none that she felt, anyway.

Both sentries went down, and one of the guards vaulted off his mount and searched the two, coming up with a heavy key that he inserted into the lock. The lock opened, and the heavy chains dropped away. Then the guard pulled the gates open, and Mykella immediately rode into the courtyard, urging the gelding toward the other gate—and Porofyr.

The Seltyr had ridden toward the rear gate but had turned when he'd seen the Southern Guards approaching. He saw Mykella and spurred his mount directly toward her, raising his pistol and firing. Mykella didn't even feel the impact on her shields even after Porofyr tried to charge his mount into hers, but the Seltyr's stallion lurched off-balance and tumbled, throwing the Seltyr to the ground. Without hesitation, Mykella reached out with her Talent and wrenched his life-thread apart.

Only then did she glance around. The remaining workers in the courtyard, those who weren't sprawled on the ground, were being rounded up by the remaining guards. She still didn't understand why Porofyr had ordered his men to open fire at the guards unless the Seltyr had known Mykella or the Southern Guards were coming . . . and he had something to hide. Since she did not see any guards in difficulty, now that the shooting had stopped, and not knowing how to be helpful, she just waited beside the stallion that had struggled back up and Porofyr's body.

In time, Maeltor rode across the courtyard to her.

"How many men were shot?" Mykella asked.

"We only lost one," replied Maeltor, "but three are wounded. They look to recover, I'd judge. That's not bad. The Seltyr had what amounted to half a company of armed men. We surprised some of them, killed four. Two or three got away on foot."

"Don't worry about them for now," replied Mykella.

"Lady . . . there's a special wagon they were readying to leave," said Maeltor mildly. "You should take a look at it."

Mykella rode across the courtyard beside the captain, reining up in front of the open doors to the center warehouse.

The high-sided and roofed wagon had four black dray horses in the traces, held in place with leads by guards. The side panels of the wagon glistened with green paint, and the black lettering on the side proclaimed POROFYR, S&F. Mykella dismounted, handed the reins to a guard, and walked up to the wagon, then around to the open rear doors. Maeltor followed. Inside the wagon were four locked chests. She probed them with her Talent. While she couldn't be absolutely certain, she felt that all contained golds, and perhaps gems in smaller chests within the larger chests.

"Look at the wagon itself," suggested Maeltor.

Mykella did. The side panels were actually planks covered with thin iron sheeting, and there were three concealed rifle ports on each side. Those features explained why the wagon needed four dray horses. She turned to the captain. "The wagon's well maintained, but not new."

"That was my thought."

"Is the driver around?"

"My men have him by the doors."

Mykella left the wagon, located the teamster, and walked across the shadowed warehouse to the man, using her Talent to gather the faintest outlining of light around her.

The teamster's eyes were wide when she stopped in front of him.

"When did you get the orders to ready the wagon?"

"Only a glass ago, Lady-Protector." The teamster's eyes did not meet Mykella's.

"Did the Seltyr tell you where you were headed?"

"He just said we were leaving Tempre and wouldn't be back for a time."

"How many men were going to accompany you."

"Ten, like usual."

"How many trips have you made to Southgate since the turn of spring?"

"Just one, Lady. That didn't count the one coming back right around spring turn."

"Did you have chests like those on that trip?"

"They were the same chests. They came back empty, I'd guess. The wagon rode lighter, anyways."

Mykella spent almost half a glass questioning the man, but while his replies added details, she didn't learn much new. Finally, she turned to Maeltor. "We'll need to search both the warehouse and countinghouse, and we will take the wagon back to the palace. Do you have enough men to put a guard on the Seltyr's villa?"

"We have enough to keep anyone from driving out with wagons . . . but once it gets dark, we might not see anyone who tried to get away."

"That will do. Send the other squad, or as many as you need, out there. Once we get the wagon back to the palace, and the chests stored safely, I'll join them. Right now, I need to go through the buildings here. It shouldn't take very long.

"We'll finish securing matters. Where do you want the prisoners held?"

"At the Southern Guard headquarters, for the moment."

"We're not . . ."

"Have Subcaptain Salyna's auxiliaries help with food and the like. If you send the prisoners to the gaol, anyone who knows anything will either die or vanish."

Maeltor nodded.

As Mykella had suspected, a quick search of the premises, aided by her Talent, revealed nothing of easily transported wealth. The warehouses themselves were largely empty, confirming that Porofyr had been planning to depart for some time.

Then Mykella, Maeltor, and the remaining troopers accompanied the wagon back to the palace, where the chests with their golds were carried into the Treasury strong room and set to one side for actual counting later. Mykella did have one lock forced, and that chest looked to have several thousand golds.

Missing golds, but not the ones I'd started out to find, she thought.

She'd sent a messenger boy to find Duchael, but he returned to report that the assistant minister had left the palace much earlier in the day. Mykella had no doubt that Duchael had fled Tempre. Finding him was a luxury that could wait, indefinitely if necessary.

The sun was low in the sky, well past the fourth glass of the afternoon, when Mykella rode from the palace again and out the Eastern Avenue to Porofyr's villa, a large structure set on an artificial hill and located but half a vingt from that of Khanasyl, she noted. The outside gates, set back some twenty yards from the Eastern Avenue, were iron glazed with white enamel and anchored by massive gate towers of whitened stone.

Squad leader Zhulyn rode toward Mykella and Maeltor, reining in his mount as he neared them. "Lady-Protector, Captain, there aren't many people here, just retainers."

That didn't surprise Mykella, either. "I'll still need to look around."

"This way, Lady."

Mykella followed the squad leader up the stone-paved lane from the gates to a circular drive around a hedged garden. The base of the raised garden was held in by a white marble wall, sculpted with an elaborate floral frieze all the way around, it appeared. On the far side of the garden was a covered entry rotunda with mounting blocks and steps of white marble leading to a set of three arches. The two arches flanking the double doors of the entry arch were filled with gold and green stained glass that fanned out from the base. The doors were of gleaming brass.

Mykella said nothing as she dismounted, but her previous anger was nothing compared to what she was feeling at the moment. She walked up the steps, and the ranker stationed there opened the door for her.

The circular main entry hall was high-ceilinged and twice the size of the entry hall in the villa that had been Joramyl's. The floor was polished green marble, and inlaid in the center, under the dome, was a mosaic depicting Porofyr and his wife. The faces had been created in detail, out of semiprecious stones that remained in place and showed a younger Porofyr. Mykella stepped back from the mosaic. While pedestals were set in alcoves regularly spaced around the hall, all were empty although they had apparently held statues or other art of value. The brass brackets that had held hangings remained in place, but the hangings were gone.

"Most things of value have already been taken, it appears," she said to Maeltor.

"I would judge so."

She stepped toward the archway at the back of the entry hall. She might as well see what there was to see . . . and make her own judgments as to how much Porofyr had stolen.

How can you tell what came from his factoring and what he stole?
She shook her head.

In the end it didn't matter. All she could reclaim were the golds she'd captured and the property and whatever else was left.

So much for the merely mundane and boring business of dealing with ministers.

30

By midmorning on Quattri, Mykella's head was aching with all the questions swirling through her mind, but one kept coming back as she stood by the window looking out across the avenue at the park that had yet to see gardeners cleaning up the broken branches and debris.

How could all of this have happened?

How? Just one look at a villa like Porofyr's should have told her father something was amiss. Hadn't he ever really looked? *She* should have guessed, if only from the faintly amused expressions and words when the Seltyrs attended the balls at the palace and the condescension concealed behind their polite words. *Except that you could only speculate about the reasons until you began to master your Talent.*

But . . . she seemed to face the same problem all over again. Each improvement in her Talent and her understanding seemed to reveal problems of which she'd had no idea before, and while her Talent had increased, so had the scope of the problems before her. She was facing a possible invasion and the likely desertion of at least some of the wealthiest Seltyrs, but to keep the Seltyrs from running off, she'd need almost all the Southern Guards—leaving nothing to fight the coastal princes. Yet if she fought the coastal princes, if she beat them back, or even destroyed them by some way she hadn't figured out, she'd still have problems with the Seltyrs.

The first thing before she had gone to her study, after a long breakfast where she'd explained to her sisters for the second time—the first being at dinner the evening before—exactly what Porofyr had done, was to find Haelyt. The two of them had counted the golds in the chests taken from Porofyr's wagon. There were almost seven thousand. In addition, there was a pouch containing gemstones that were probably worth more than the golds. She'd kept the gems and two thousand golds and had them stored in her personal strong room.

He had already shipped most of his wealth to Southgate. Mykella shook her head. She could and would seize the villa and grounds, but she needed golds more than lands and buildings at the moment. *Why did he wait so long before trying to leave? Was that because he wanted to take everything he could before I discovered what he'd done?*

After that, she'd drafted and sent short messages about Porofyr to the head clerk in the Highways and Rivers Ministry, to Cerlyk, to Lord Gharyk—and to Areyst, knowing the commander would not receive her missive until late in the day. She'd also dispatched a message to Chief Engineer Nusgeyl to begin repairs on the towpaths, under the conditions she'd outlined to Duchael earlier, although she chafed at having to spell them out again. Then she'd used the Table to check on Khanasyl and others. The First Seltyr had not appeared overly distraught as he had been sitting in a rather ornate study. After that, she'd returned to her formal study and drafted letters to High Factors Pytroven and Zylander, requesting that they call upon her at the palace at their convenience.

Then Rachylana showed up with Elwayt so that the three of them could go over costs of running the palace and discuss the season-turn ball. When they left, Mykella sat there for several moments, realizing that most of the morning had vanished.

More than once, she'd tried to figure what took all of her time. There were the various letters she had to read and reply to . . . and the constant references to the master Finance ledgers, the meetings with the clerks about expenditures, largely because she had so few ministers, and that didn't include her "scouting missions" through the darkness, her time using the Table . . .

If she had more people she could trust . . . if she could find such . . .

and that took more golds and time to train them, and she already didn't have much of either left over

"Lord Gharyk, Lady," announced Chalmyr, stepping into the study. The old scrivener raised his eyebrows just slightly.

Mykella understood. Gharyk was agitated, or less than happy. "Thank you. I'll see him." She turned and walked back toward the desk.

Gharyk hurried in. "Lady-Protector, I just received your message. This is most . . . disturbing."

"About Porofyr?" Mykella gestured to the chairs, then settled behind the desk.

Gharyk sat down, except it was more like perching on the front edge of the chair. "Lady-Protector, you certainly have the right to take a Seltyr into custody, and even to demand and carry out an execution, but the method . . . a writ for his detention would have created less concern."

"Lord Gharyk . . . I do understand that. But exactly how do you propose that I could have found Porofyr once he rode off? It's not as though I have thousands of Southern Guards that I can dispatch to hunt him down every road. I caught him just before he left Tempre for good. He had an armored wagon filled with chests of gold, and he had already sent the wagon to Southgate several times, filled with even larger chests. His family had already departed, along with most of the valuable items from his villa, and I have no doubt that the golds he siphoned off from the Ministry of Highways and Rivers are largely in Southgate. Duchael warned him that I was going out to see him, and now he has fled as well."

"Oh . . . dear . . ."

"Exactly. Everywhere I look, someone has been siphoning off golds. The Southern Guards is understrength. The Treasury is depleted; the coastal princes appear to be raising an army to attack." She paused. "And I have to worry about greedy Seltyrs who have essentially plundered the land. If I kill them all, and that's what most of them deserve, I'll have no commerce and even greater ruin. Yet this can't go on." *And that doesn't include what the Ifrits will do.*

Gharyk said nothing.

"Can it? If Lanachrona is to survive? Or had they all planned to dismember the land and have one of the coastal princes or the Seltyrs of Southgate take over?" Mykella paused. Was that why Joramyl had sent all the golds to Northcoast? To build a force to repulse Southgate without alerting the Seltyrs of the southwest? Did that mean that Cheleyza and Chalcaer would merely point out that they were going to take over a corrupted Lanachrona from a weak Lady-Protector and greedy Seltyrs?

"I do not know what the First Seltyr and others may have planned." Gharyk's voice turned wry. "I am not exactly in their graces."

"I doubt that we will ever know what they had in mind. Not now. They will either flee or protest that they are loyal, and for those who remain, there will be little evidence to the contrary by nightfall today." *Not that there was much of that to begin with.*

"You understand much, Lady."

Mykella offered a crooked smile. "I think what you're suggesting is that there's still a great deal that I don't understand. You're right about that." She paused. "We do have to act to make it clear where I stand. I want a proclamation that states that any Seltyr or factor who has committed a crime and leaves Tempre will have all assets and land seized and held for public sale at the discretion of the Lady-Protector."

"You can do that, Lady, but will that not tempt many Seltyrs to leave?"

"It probably will tempt some, but I'm certain that there are High Factors who would very much appreciate gaining warehouses and other trading assets at a comparatively low price. I also don't want someone or their heirs complaining that they didn't know or didn't understand." She paused. "I also haven't forgotten about the other document. The problem there is that I don't know that replacing one gaoler is likely to change anything at all."

"That is true, Lady."

"I'd appreciate any ideas you may have on that as well."

"I would suggest turning the operation of the gaol over to the Southern Guards for a time and have Commander Areyst train a new gaoler and those who work for him. Any other option would not accomplish what you have in mind."

Mykella nodded. "Then doing so will have to wait. We scarcely have enough Southern Guards to deal with the threats from the coastal princes. In the meantime, I would like you to put down your thoughts in writing as to how the gaol should be operated and who should have what duties and what responsibilities. That way, when we do make the necessary changes, everyone will know what those changes are and why they are being made."

"That may be for the best."

"It's not for the best, Lord Gharyk, but as you have pointed out, at times not everything that should be done can be done." Mykella wasn't certain he'd actually said that, but the sentiment lay behind much of his advice.

She smiled and listened to more of his advice for almost half a glass, then, after he left, slipped back to the family quarters to eat. She'd barely returned to the formal study after gulping down cold lamb and warm bread and a mug of passable lager before Chalmyr rapped on the door.

"The First Seltyr is here to see you."

"Good. I need to see him." Mykella stood. She didn't want to be sitting.

The physically impressive and broad-shouldered Seltyr stepped through the door, which Chalmyr closed quickly and quietly behind him. Both Khanasyl's gray hair and square-cut and equally gray beard were slightly disheveled. He barely bowed before beginning. "Lady-Protector, I have received most disturbing news . . ." His high voice was controlled, but there was great emotion behind that control.

"There have been a number of most disturbing events recently, First Seltyr. To which are you referring?"

"The manner in which you . . . dealt with Minister Porofyr. There were no justicing procedures, no writs . . . You have that authority, but it has not been used in generations and for good reason, particularly against an honorable Seltyr—"

"A Seltyr, yes. An honorable one?" Mykella's voice dripped scorn.

"No Seltyr who diverts tariff-raised golds from the Treasury to his own coffers is in any way honorable. No Seltyr who has his men open fire on the Southern Guards is either loyal or honorable."

"He did those things? Truly?"

Surprisingly, Mykella could sense honest shock behind Khanasyl's even facade, but she suspected that shock was more at Porofyr's stupidity . . . or his getting caught. "He did indeed, and he corrupted his assistant minister as well. Porofyr knew full well what he was doing. He had already emptied his villa of all valuables and sent his family to Southgate. He has on at least two occasions sent an armored wagon filled with golds to Southgate as well, and the first of those trips took place before I became Lady-Protector."

The disclosure of the timing shocked Khanasyl more than the revelation of Porofyr's actions. For a moment, his eyes flickered, and his jaw started to drop. "That is most interesting."

"I am certain that it is, because it means that he has been deceiving you as well. Do you think that such is the mark of an honorable Seltyr?"

"Lady-Protector, I cannot speak to what this man has done . . . or failed to do. I can only speak for the honorable Seltyrs who remain. They are worried greatly, and they have asked whether Tempre remains a good place for trade." Khanasyl's voice was mild.

Behind the smooth words, Mykella sensed calculation. "Why would you say that?"

"It would appear, or so some have said, that Tempre is less safe than it once was. For trade to be profitable, a land must be safe." Khanasyl's smile was condescending. "I do not approve of what Porofyr has done, if it is as you say, and I have no reason to believe that it is otherwise. Yet . . . why would a Seltyr uproot himself and leave so much of value behind if he did not feel that such steps were necessary?"

What can you say to that? Mykella nodded politely, thinking. *You can't use Talent force on everyone. They'll just be angry and fearful and offended once they leave your presence. And they're not already, after what you did to Porofyr? Besides, it's most likely that they all regard me as a powerful child, who can destroy them and fails to understand the complexities of their world.* "Less safe, First Seltyr? In what manner? Compared to what and when?" She kept her voice pleasant.

"In the recent past, we did not have brigands attacking the palace and the villas of Seltyrs. Nor did we have the Lord-Protector taking the law directly to a Seltyr, regardless of the cause."

"In the past, no Lord-Protector needed to take the law directly to a Seltyr because Seltyrs did not deceive and corrupt, then attempt to flee before their offenses were discovered." That was unlikely to be true, Mykella knew, but there was no way that Khanasyl was about to say that Seltyrs had always been greedy and self-centered. "As for the brigands . . . they had powerful ancient weapons. Yet they were brought down quickly."

"Most assuredly." Khanasyl smiled openly and falsely. "But one might ask why they felt it necessary to make such an attack?"

"One might indeed. One might also ask why they fled the palace and attacked a Seltyr's villa. One might even ask if that might be because so many of the golds that flow into Tempre go not to the palace Treasury or to the people, but to the Seltyrs. I have noted that many of the villas of Seltyrs are far grander and expansive—and more well-appointed—than the palace. Also most interesting is the fact that those villas are the ones most recent in their construction and furnishings." She smiled, as falsely as had Khanasyl. "If Tempre is not so safe as it might be, could that just possibly be because my predecessors were too preoccupied with pleasing the Seltyrs and less concerned about maintaining order and justice within Tempre? Might it be that some of the threats we face from the coastal princes might have arisen because they feared to collect tariffs adequate to maintain the Southern Guards?"

Khanasyl's eyes narrowed slightly. "There are implications behind your words . . ."

"Indeed there are, but you might note, First Seltyr, that I did not say a single word that could be taken as less than complimentary about anyone but my predecessors. My goals are to improve justice and order and to strengthen Lanachrona. Surely, from your own words, you and the other Seltyrs would not wish otherwise . . . would you?"

Khanasyl was silent for the briefest of moments. Then he laughed. "You do well with words, Lady-Protector. You are personally very powerful. But a land is nourished by golds. Golds are gathered and multiplied by those who combine skill and trade and factoring."

"And by the hard work and labor of the crafters and the tillers and many others," Mykella added. "If too great a share of those golds is gathered up by too few, the land suffers."

"If too great a share is spread to the many," countered Khanasyl, "there is no way to collect enough in tariffs to maintain order or to pay the Southern Guards."

"You are absolutely right," agreed Mykella. "But a proper share of those golds gathered by those with the skills you praise must be used by the Protector to keep Lanachrona strong. We have men being killed while awaiting justicing, and when I became Lady-Protector, the Southern Guards was smaller than in generations. As I said, the errors were not those of the factors or the Seltyrs, but of my predecessors. But they were errors, and I have begun to remedy them. Surely you would not wish to see Lanachrona continue to be weakened by a failure to return to the wise customs and rules established by Mykel the Great, would you?"

"Lady-Protector, I cannot refute your words. Yet I must point out that no man would willingly see his patrimony diminished to rectify the errors of the past."

"I can appreciate that, First Seltyr, even when such patrimonies were increased in the past by the unwillingness of Protectors to tariff as much as necessary. At the same time, failure to change matters might well leave many with no patrimony at all—if the coastal princes have their way. That is why matters must return to the wiser ways of the past. With such threats facing Lanachrona, how can I not insist that we do so?" Mykella looked directly at Khanasyl, using her Talent to project a sense of honest inquiry.

"What might you mean by a return to the wiser ways of the past?" Although his words were seemingly open, there was concern and apprehension behind them.

"A justicing system where offenders survive to testify might help.

So would tariffs high enough to maintain a Southern Guards large enough to discourage other lands from threatening Lanachrona. More solid repairs of towpaths and bridges damaged by bad weather. An understanding that treachery by Seltyrs or High Factors could result in not only execution but confiscation and sale of property and other goods . . ."

"Treachery is often a matter of words, Lady-Protector." Again, Khanasyl's voice was mild.

"Speaking against my decisions is not treachery, First Seltyr, but stealing thousands of golds from the Treasury is. Voicing concern about increasing the size of the Southern Guards is not treachery; but offering aid, advice, and comfort to the rulers of other lands is." Mykella smiled. "You and I know the difference between words of concern and treachery. I will listen to words of concern, as I have listened to yours. I will not countenance treachery."

"You make that obvious, Lady-Protector, but some might not see matters so clearly."

"Then I would hope that you could see your way to making them clear to those who have difficulty seeing that opposing the good of all Lanachrona for the sake of a few extra golds, even a few thousand extra golds, is not good trading but treachery."

"Your words are harsh, Lady-Protector."

"The times are harsh, First Seltyr, and I will do what I must to keep Lanachrona strong. I will be no harsher than necessary because that serves no one well, but I will do what I must."

Khanasyl inclined his head slightly. "I do not know that we agree on all matters, but I also would see a strong Lanachrona."

You just don't care much who rules so long as you can trade and hold on to what you have. Mykella did not voice that thought. Instead, she stood. "I appreciate your directness and your coming to see me about Porofyr. You asked me why I acted, and I told you. So long as you ask, I will answer."

Khanasyl stood, gracefully, especially for so large a man, and offered a bow slightly more than perfunctory. "I will ask, as necessary, and look for your answers."

After Khanasyl had left, Mykella couldn't help but note to herself that the First Seltyr had never mentioned the position of Minister of Highways and Rivers. That tended to confirm her suspicion that his written recommendation had only given the names of unsuitable candidates, possibly to see if she would take those recommendations and reveal herself as having poor judgment.

31

When Mykella reached the family quarters for the evening meal, only Rachylana was waiting.

"Salyna said she'd be late because of what she had to do with her sculls and loose women."

"If she can make something greater of them, and if anyone can, she can, so much the better. I thought she'd be late. That's why I asked you to have Muergya ready everything a glass later."

"She's still not here." Rachylana shook her head. "She thinks she has to do everything."

"She does," Mykella said, settling herself across from her sister. "That way, no one can complain when she gives an order. No one can think they don't have to do what they do because she's the Lady-Protector's sister. She also proves that a woman can do whatever it is. That's important. No one's trained women in arms since the time of the Alectors, and the only women trained then were Alectors."

"They were more like men."

"Who was?" Salyna hurried through the archway into the family dining room.

"Alector women," said Mykella.

"No . . . the Alectors were smarter about using women . . . or we're stupider." Salyna slipped into her chair. "I'm sorry I'm late. I'll have to eat in a hurry. I need to get back and make sure that they're all doing their studies."

"Why did you even bother to come to dinner, then?" asked Rachylana.

"I needed to talk to you both."

"You mean you needed to talk to Mykella."

"No. I need your help, too."

"My help?" Rachylana raised her eyebrows.

"Yours," repeated Salyna. "I've got the auxiliaries in working grays. They'll do for now, but once they're trained, they'll need real uniforms. The guards have what they call undress and dress uniforms. We can wait on dress uniforms, but they'll need something that looks official and like the regular Guard uniforms—except they have to be alike and not too different, and they can't look like they were stuffed into a man's uniform. People will just laugh at them, and we can't have that. They need something that works for women and looks good . . . and doesn't cost too much to have sewn. You're better at that, and I just don't have enough time. I was hoping . . ."

"You want me . . . ?"

"Why not?" asked Mykella. "You have good taste, and you know what looks good. Salyna knows how it has to work. Between the two of you, I'm sure you could design an undress uniform that's comfortable, workable, and looks decent. I'm going to need the auxiliaries more than I thought because there are going to be more duties for the Southern Guards. Commander Areyst will need every fighting man he can muster."

"If you put it that way . . ." ventured Rachylana.

"You'd really be helping us both out," Mykella said.

"Things are that bad?" asked Rachylana

"I'm effectively Finance Minister, Minister of Highways and Rivers, and Lady-Protector. Three of the candidates for Minister of Highways and Rivers are totally unsuitable, and I have to meet with two others to see if they're even interested. At the moment, anyone who has the status, ability, and the integrity to become Finance Minister isn't going to be interested."

"Do you need all three qualities?" asked Salyna.

"Without status, I'll end up having to spend more time supporting the minister. Without ability, we'll lose more golds we don't have, and without integrity, things will get even worse." Mykella poured hot tea into her mug almost to the point of overflowing, then had to lean forward and sip it before daring to lift the mug. She took a mutton chop off the serving platter, then poured hot apple gravy over it and over the mashed potatoes she'd served herself first.

"Maybe that was why Father settled on Joramyl," said Salyna. "He thought he could trust him, and anyone else was worse."

"I still say that Uncle Joramyl wasn't all that bad until he married that bitch Cheleyza," interjected Rachylana.

"She didn't help matters. She's working to train cavalry troopers in Northcoast now," said Mykella. "Her steward here—did I tell you that he's a cavalry officer?"

Salyna nodded. Rachylana shook her head.

"At least they haven't started riding toward Lanachrona yet."

"They won't until the crops are in," suggested Salyna.

None of the three spoke for a time.

"The First Seltyr saw you today. Did he mention the ball?" asked Rachylana.

"The ball?" Salyna almost choked on the mouthful of mutton chop she was chewing.

"I thought he might, just to be polite," said Rachylana. "Or was he playing at being upset over what you did to that worthless Porofyr?"

"He couldn't believe that Porofyr was that stupid. He didn't exactly say that, but that was behind his words. He did suggest that Tempre wasn't a very good place for trade, and he was hinting at the idea that some of the Seltyrs might pack up and leave the way Porofyr tried to do. He also left the hint that some of them weren't too pleased with me."

"That's hardly a surprise," said Rachylana ironically.

"They won't dare to oppose you," Salyna said.

"Not directly." Mykella took a mouthful of mashed potato that tasted slightly bitter, despite the gravy, possibly from having been stored in the cellars for too long. "What if they just pack up their more valuable goods and golds in wagons and leave for Southgate?"

"The Southern Guards could stop them," Rachylana pointed out.

"Not if I don't know that they're leaving. I can't post sentries on all the roads leading to the southwest highway."

"Let me see what I can do," Salyna said.

Mykella could use any help her sister might be able to provide. "I would appreciate that."

The three ate and talked briefly before Salyna hurried off. Then Mykella retreated to her chambers, where she donned her nightsilk jacket and slipped a pair of gloves into the jacket before sliding through the stone down to the Table chamber. The Table remained relatively muted in color, but . . . something about it bothered her. Yet she couldn't even put a finger on what that might be.

She started to reach out to the dark green, knowing she had to gain better control of the green at the heart of the depths, when she sensed a line of amber and green . . .

. . . and the ancient soarer hovered before her.

"What is it? I've been trying to master the deepest green."

You cannot master it without first guiding it. Your time is growing short. You must find the scepters before the Ifrits arrive and keep them from using them.

"Can't I destroy them? Or hide them?"

The sense of the negative flowed from the Ancient. *If you move them, they will be easier to find. They cannot be destroyed unless you would travel between worlds. The scepters cannot be destroyed on our world.*

"Why do you always suggest I do the impossible?" Mykella didn't bother to keep the anger out of her voice.

No one else can. Holding a scepter would destroy one of us. For . . . other reasons . . . it will not destroy you. It would not destroy any of your people, but you are the only one with the Talent to travel to find them.

"I'm the only one with Talent . . . in the whole world?" That seemed improbable.

No. The nightsheep herders have the Talent, and so do others, but none have mastered what you have.

There was something left unsaid, and Mykella ventured, "They can't sense you?"

They flee and will not listen.

"Why?"

They will not hear the truth.

"What truth?"

That the Ifrits were not all destroyed and that all who have Talent are either part Ifrit or part soarer . . . or both.

Was that an insurmountable problem? She almost laughed at the question when she realized she just hadn't had any other choices but to listen to the soarer.

You have not seen the others. They are dangerous to those without Talent, and they frighten the northerners. Lanachrona is too warm for them. You must find and guard the scepters. You must . . .

"How do I find them?"

They should make the Tables glow more brightly . . . for you.

"Not for you?"

The purple blinds us to certain . . . kinds of light . . .

With that the soarer shrank into a greenish mist . . . and then vanished into the depths.

Mykella did have the feeling that the brief conversation, if it could have been called that, had exhausted the Ancient. After a moment, she fastened the black nightsilk jacket all the way up, pulled on the nightsilk gloves, and reached out to the darkness below the Table chamber, seeking as she did the somehow muted and yet brighter crimson and gold marker that was located in Dereka. As had often seemed to happen before, even as she sought out the crimson and gold, for an endless instant, nothing seemed to happen. Then the faded but strangely bright marker rushed toward her and surrounded her.

Recalling the soft sand in the pit that had once held a Table, Mykella bent her knees as she emerged from greenish blackness, catching her balance before stepping toward the edges of the stone depression. Using both eyes and senses in the near darkness lit by only the faint glimmer of the sole light-torch, she discerned no one near. The antique door was still closed, a door that led to a staircase and the upper levels of a building now little more than a warehouse.

Mykella used her Talent to lift herself out of the pit until she stood on the ancient floor. The chamber was as deserted as it had been before, with no furnishings, just bare stone walls, but walls that held the faintest illumination of a gold that she sensed, not saw, walls bearing not a single gouge or scratch—gold eternastone, similar to but not exactly like the golden stone of the city of the soarers. Had they had something to do with building Dereka?

If she remembered, if she ever saw the soarer again, she should ask.

For a moment, she entertained the idea of appearing before the Landarch, then shook her head, for all the irony of the fact that she hadn't wanted to be matched and married to the Landarch's heir and live in Dereka . . . and yet she kept coming back to Dereka. At the moment, doing something like that would only complicate matters, and she needed to see if she could discover the scepters that the ancients so feared.

She could sense a faint purpleness . . . somewhere near, yet it was not in the chamber where she stood. She concentrated. It did not lie behind the door with the ancient lever handle, but it was more on the north side of the chamber. She moved around the sand-filled pit to study the wall there. At first, it appeared unbroken and solid stone, but to the left of the light-torch bracket was the faintest line. She eased farther left, where there was another line—some sort of stone door?

How could she open a door with no handles? She smiled, ironically. She didn't have to. She concentrated on the blackness below, letting herself flow through the stone and into the room or passageway beyond. The narrow passage had seemingly been cut from the stone itself, and only the faintest light oozed from an open doorway little more than five yards away. Mykella walked carefully to the doorway and stopped, peering into a square chamber—one that looked to be precisely five yards square. Unlike the Table chamber, the room looked untouched since it had been abandoned.

A table-desk stood in one corner, and a chair with longer legs than most. Beside the desk was an oddly proportioned settee. Against the wall to the left was a wide chest of drawers, unlike any Mykella had ever seen, somehow both broader and taller. The light-torches above the table-desk shed an even glow across the chamber. Mykella looked down to see clothes lying on the floor, just inside the doorway—a green tunic trimmed in brilliant purple, with matching trousers, and black boots. The fabric held a silvery sheen. The garments were laid out as if someone had been lying down and vanished, leaving the clothing behind. Mykella frowned. There was something about the garments, similar as they were to those worn by the Ifrits who had attacked the palace. She extended a Talent probe toward them, then recoiled. They felt like the eternastone of the roads and the remaining Ifrit buildings. Why? She shook her head. Like the Tables, and like the green towers, the garments bore an infusion of lifeforce. Was that why the one world had died, because the Ifrits had squandered lifeforce to preserve everything, including mere clothing . . . just so it would endure for eons?

Her eyes went to the light-torch bracket in the far left corner, twisted or wrenched downward. On the polished gray stone floor below lay the remaining pieces of the light-torch and beside them lay a silvery jacket, a pistol-like device, and a pair of boots on their sides. The pistol-like device was like the one the Ifrits had used, but Mykella could tell that its power had long since dissipated.

She stepped over the clothing in the doorway, not touching it, and moved toward the source of purplish power—a chest or casket in a niche carved more than head high from the wall behind the table-desk. The casket was over a yard in length and of black and a metallic silver that held a purplish sheen. A key with a triangular head remained in the lock of the casket although the lid was closed.

Mykella pulled the chair over to the wall and stepped onto it to get a better look at the casket, since she could see that it was not placed on the ledge, but actually embedded several spans into the stone so that it could not have been moved without breaking the slab into which it was set. She tried the lid. It lifted, showing that the key had been left in the open position. As she raised it, her mouth opened. A wave of deep purple too brilliant to look at swept over her, and she had to squint, barely making out that within a set of heavy metal brackets lay what could only be one of the scepters the ancient soarer feared—a thick rod of silver and black, two metals exuding light and intertwined, topped with a massive blue crystal. The crystal glimmered with energy, the source of that deep and brilliant purple that was almost too intense to view or sense directly. A smaller purple crystal was set at each end of the casket, and the metallic base of the scepter rested against one crystal and the larger blue crystal against the other. A silvery bar ran from the base of each crystal down through the bottom of the casket and into the stone.

Mykella reached out with her Talent, trying to explore just what it was about that scepter . . . and found herself being hurled from the chair across the room into the stone wall opposite the casket. She half staggered, half slid sideways on the wall, then ended up with her boots sliding out from under her and landing in a heap on her rear on the floor.

While her shields absorbed much of the impact, her eyes blurred for a moment, and she found herself breathing hard. She just sat there until she could see straight. Then she slowly forced herself erect, looking to the casket set in the wall. The lid had fallen shut, cutting off the worst of that purple radiance.

And I'm supposed to be able to hold that? She definitely didn't want to touch that scepter without using Talent, and it was all too clear that whatever powered the scepter or whatever controlled it reacted violently to Talent. She could also understand why the soarer had said that moving the scepter would make it easier to find. The casket or box that held the scepter clearly muted its power, so much so that it was barely detectable with her Talent from more than a few yards away—except that it did "brighten" the gold and crimson of the purple web nexus where the Table had been.

Was there anything else around that might make it easier to handle the scepter? After moving the chair away from under the chest and back toward the table-desk, Mykella approached the too-tall chest and opened the top right-hand drawer. Inside were two greenish crystals that held an ugly lambent purple. Mykella touched neither, nor did she brush the sheets of what looked to be a shiny parchment with her gloved fingertips. Although she could see that the top sheet was covered with strange symbols, each symbol written exactly in the same size as the next, she could read none of the symbols. That could wait.

She closed the drawer and opened the other one. It contained some coins, a pair of shears, and a thin coil of wire. She opened the double-width drawer below to discover a long shimmering garment of some sort, all a golden silver, with large strange symbols down the front.

Even touching the fabric seemed repugnant, and she quickly closed the drawer.

Turning back to the table-desk, she opened the single wide drawer, but there was little inside—a miniature knife with the purpleness she disliked, an oblong block of jade with an enameled and unfamiliar seal upon it, and some sort of stylus in the form of a leafy branch. There were also a number of sheets of the eternal parchment, all blank. She closed the drawer, standing there for a time, trying to think.

She agreed with the soarer that taking the scepter was unwise, assuming that she could even have found a way to touch it, but she couldn't exactly stand around and guard the scepter, either. Finally, she made her way from the chamber, well aware how unsteady her steps were.

At the end of the passageway, she decided not even to return to the Table chamber that no longer held a Table but concentrated on the darkness beneath, reaching out to the greenish black and letting herself drop into the depths. As the blue marker of Tempre hurtled toward her, she sensed "behind" her the increased brightness of the yellow-orange marker. Was that where the other "scepter" was hidden? Lysia, was it?

Even if it happened to be there, what could she do? Whatever else she could do, even checking to see if her surmise was correct would have to wait until she recovered her strength. Not for the first time, she wished that she'd been taller and stronger, like her sisters . . . but there was little she could do about that now.

Mykella slipped back through the granite of the palace to her chambers. Her entire body was shaking as she emerged in her bedchamber, and her legs were so weak that she immediately sat down on the edge of the bed.

She'd found one scepter—for all the good it had done her—and she was getting more and more tired and angry at finding out the more that she learned and did, the worse matters seemed to get.

Except . . . she was so tired that she wasn't going to be awake long enough even to stay angry.

32

On Quinti morning, awakened by Uleana's firm rapping on the apartment doors, Mykella was stiff and sore all over, a state that seemed to be happening more than she'd like, but she made it to the breakfast room only to find herself there alone. Crumbs at Salyna's place suggested that her youngest sister had eaten bread and cheese early and left for the Southern Guard complex and her auxiliaries and their training. Mykella finished most of her own breakfast—an omelet of sorts with warm dark bread and ham strips—and was working on a second mug of tea when Rachylana appeared.

The redhead settled into her chair and looked at Mykella. "What happened to you? You're purplish as well as green."

"I ran into a nasty relic of the Ifrits in dealing with the Table."

That got her another look.

"What? Isn't the Table door locked?"

"It is, but being Lady-Protector does have advantages. These days, I need to use the Table to see things."

"What sorts of things?"

"What Cheleyza is doing, what some of the Seltyrs are doing . . ."

"Can you tell what Skrelyn is doing? Or the Landarch?"

"I can only look for people I know personally," Mykella admitted. "And I can only see what's happening close to them at the time I'm looking."

"That's better than nothing."

"Sometimes." Mykella's voice turned wry. "Most of the time, people aren't doing much that tells you anything, and I can't spend every moment watching them." Not to mention that it was difficult to distinguish between a harmless meeting, a rant against her, or an actual plot. "How are things coming with the ball?"

"The invitations are out, and we've already had quite a few responses.

Chief High Factor Lhanyr and his wife will be here, and so will Seltyr and High Factor Almardyn . . ."

Mykella listened to the others who would be attending, then asked, "Will you let me know what response you get from the First Seltyr? As soon as you do?"

"He won't say no," predicted Rachylana. "Even if he's totally against you, he'll be here."

"Why do you say that? The Seltyrs don't want me to succeed."

"They probably don't. Most of them, anyway, but you've proved you're powerful. Those who don't have good connections in Southgate can't afford to offend you. That's why nine Seltyrs have already said they'll attend. With that many attending, the First Seltyr can't snub you without appearing weak. He'll make an appearance and be very charming. He'll hope that you won't be."

Mykella sighed. "I'll have to be exceedingly charming and warm, then."

Rachylana nodded. "Exceedingly, and you should also have the commander here. If he's not—"

"Some will think that I've lost the full support of the Southern Guards?"

"Or that you think he's beneath you."

Areyst wouldn't like that, Mykella knew, but he'd understand. He understood far more than he ever said. That was another reason why she was attracted to him.

Rachylana laughed.

"What?" asked Mykella.

"The look on your face. I've never seen that expression before. You're actually really interested in him—and not because he's your Arms-Commander."

Mykella realized she was blushing. Then she shook her head. "Only you would see that." *Except you really didn't see it so much as sense it.* That worried Mykella, yet she didn't see any more green in Rachylana's life-thread—or did she?

She wanted to shake her head. So much depended on what she sensed, but she often had no way to cross-check what she felt.

"Is that why you named him your heir?"

"I wouldn't have named him if he weren't trustworthy, no matter how I was attracted to him."

"That's not an answer," pursued Rachylana, with a smile.

"No . . . it's not, but it's the only answer I have."

"You two are like dustcats. Everyone else depends on you, and you're both capable of tearing up everything in sight, and you just keep circling each other."

"Rachylana . . . That's stretching things."

"Is it?"

"Yes, it is."

"Not by much. I'll bet you use the Table to look at him every chance you get. If you aren't, you're wasting an opportunity." Rachylana grinned.

Mykella found herself blushing again.

"Oh . . . you are!"

"I'm not. I didn't even think of that. Besides, it doesn't work that way."

Rachylana just shook her head, then took the smallest chunk of bread and nibbled on it.

"You don't eat anything," Mykella said.

"I can't. Otherwise, I'd look like a cow. It's disgusting how much you and Salyna can eat."

"If you exercised the way she does, you could, too."

Rachylana paused, then said almost mournfully. "I might have to."

Mykella refrained from laughing and finished the remainder of her tea.

After breakfast, she returned to her quarters, then checked the Table. It wasn't any brighter. If anything, it appeared slightly duller than it had the previous day. *Is that really so, or is that just the way you perceive it? How can you tell?*

The problem was that she couldn't, but she was fairly certain that it wasn't obviously brighter.

She stepped up to the mirrored surface and commenced her searches. Cheleyza was in what looked to be a stable talking to an ostler and several officers in cavalry uniforms identical to the one she wore. Former Commander Demyl was donning a white uniform in a comparatively small bedchamber. Areyst was meeting with a group of Southern Guard captains, and his image remained shadowed in silver and green. Khanasyl stood in his factorage, gesturing vigorously at an underling, who was not quite cringing. She could find no image of Duchael—none at all. She wondered what else he had known and who had killed him.

Not that you'll ever know a fraction of what he did or even find his body. She might discover who was behind his murder, but proving it would be close to impossible. The longer she was Lady-Protector, the more she was discovering how little the laws or the Charter meant to the Seltyrs, and yet . . . *You don't want to be like them, but power is all they respect.*

Maxymt was still on the run, looking more haggard than ever.

After a moment, she concentrated on Majer Sheorak. She actually recognized where he was, if only because of the color of the Vyanhills to the east. He was riding north on the eternastone highway that connected Krost to Borlan, and he'd be riding for another two tendays before he reached Dereka. So few people truly understood how large Corus was, and how far apart the larger cities were. It was almost as if the cities had been built first . . .

Her mouth dropped open. *Of course they had been.* The Alectors had placed the Tables first, then built the cities around them and the eternastone roads around them. It was the only way any of that made sense. For a moment, she just thought, but thinking about the past would not solve her present problems.

She let the Table revert to mirrored silver, then dropped into the deeper darkness beneath the palace, but none of the Table markers seemed noticeably brighter. That was fine with her because she really didn't want to travel to confirm the location of the other scepter, not until she had recovered more from her last adventure . . . and she still hadn't had time or energy to look for the silver mirrors . . . if there even were any others.

Then she returned to her quarters and walked to the antechamber to her study, where, as usual, Chalmyr was waiting.

"Have we heard anything from High Factor Pytroven or Zy-lander?"

Chalmyr extended an envelope. "This was delivered less than half a glass ago by a messenger from High Factor Pytroven. His messenger waits below."

Mykella used her belt knife to slit open the envelope. She replaced the knife, then extracted the single sheet, reading it quickly. "He would be pleased to call upon me at the second glass of the afternoon, tomorrow, if that would be convenient." She nodded. "That would be convenient. Would you draft a quick reply to that effect?"

"Yes, Lady. I'll have it for you shortly."

"Have we heard anything about Forester Loryalt's return?"

"No, Lady."

"Thank you." Mykella smiled as warmly as she could and stepped into the formal study, glancing toward the windows and the hazy silver-green sky that suggested neither rain nor warmth.

33

Mykella woke early on Sexdi and dressed in her customary nightsilks. While she was still sore and bruised in spots, she'd had nightmares about the scepters. So she immediately dropped into the darkness and followed the green-black ways to the yellow-orange marker that the soarer had said was Lysia.

When she emerged from the depths, she found herself standing beside a Table, one alternating shades of purple and pink, if ever so slightly. She glanced around, but there was no one in the Table chamber. Nor could she sense anyone, or pick up any feel of the ugly purple that would have suggested an Ifrit was near or had been recently. But . . . there was a faint purplish gray feel . . . somewhere. She stepped toward the Table and concentrated on the idea of the scepter.

When the mists swirled, then parted, they revealed the image of a seal—similar to the one she'd seen when she'd thought of Efra—except there were two crossed scepters beneath a larger silver scepter that glowed purple. The image blanked, to reveal an Ifrit with jet-black hair and purple eyes. Those eyes opened wide, then filled with what Mykella could only have called hatred.

Immediately, purplish arms rose out of the Table.

Mykella stepped back, strengthening her shields, and angled a Talent probe to the nodes of each arm. The arms collapsed, leaving a residue of purple and lingering hatred that she could only sense. The Table surface had returned to a mirror finish.

That didn't help much.

She studied the Table again, trying to sense the same sense of purpleness she'd felt from the other casket, but all she could feel was that it was somewhere near. After several moments, she turned toward the open passageway that led up the stone steps to an upper level. She had taken three steps when she realized that the sense of purpleness was fading, and she turned back to the Table chamber.

Slowly, she walked around the chamber, occasionally looking at the Table. Then she stopped and looked at the stone wall closely. To the left of a light-torch bracket was the faintest line in the stone, just like the one in Dereka, and another line a yard farther left. She reached for the darkness beneath and eased herself through the stone and into the passageway beyond the wall. While there was doubtless some sort of mechanism to move the stone, she saw no point in wasting time trying to figure out what it might be.

The purpleness was far stronger in the corridor that stretched before her some ten yards, lit by another ancient light-torch. She walked slowly to the end of the corridor and looked inside the chamber to the left. Like the room holding the other scepter, the one before her was square and looked to be the same size, roughly five yards on a side. As in Dereka, there was a table-desk positioned against the wall near one corner, with a long-legged chair before it. Farther to the right was a single wide and tall chest of drawers, with the same odd dimensions.

She glanced down at the floor beside the desk. There lay a set of garments, a green tunic trimmed in brilliant purple, with matching trousers, and black boots. All the garb radiated a silver sheen suggesting embedded lifeforce, even after all the years the clothing had lain there.

Lifting her eyes, Mykella could see the closed casket that had to hold the scepter, positioned in a niche in the wall adjoining the one before which the table-desk was set. Purpleness oozed from the casket.

She stepped forward, avoiding the garments, and lifted the heavy chair with legs far too long for her, setting it down before the wall. Again, she almost had to climb the chair to be able to stand on the seat and touch the casket.

Should you open it? How else will you know if it's the scepter?

She had to turn the crystal key before she could ease the heavy lid up slightly, just enough to see the silver and black scepter and the three crystals—and feel the power. Then she quickly but carefully lowered the top. Before easing herself off the chair, she took a deep breath. She did know exactly where both scepters happened to be, for all the good it might do her.

Should you take the keys and lock the caskets? Somehow that felt wrong, almost useless. She had the feeling that if the Ifrits came seeking the scepters, they'd either have their own keys or the tools to force the caskets.

She carried the chair back and placed it about where it had been. She did leave the scepter chamber before she reached out to the darkness to return to Tempre.

Once back in the palace, she ate a hurried breakfast, after Salyna and before Rachylana appeared, then finished dressing and made her way toward her formal study.

Early as it was, Chalmyr was waiting. "There are missives on your desk, Lady."

"Thank you." She smiled, briefly, and entered the study.

Envelopes—almost a score—were laid out on the wood. She sat down and looked at them. Then she took out her belt knife and slit open the first one, and began to read.

Lady-Protector—
I appeal to your sense of fairness and justice. The dye-makers have raised the price of the red and yellow dyes. They say this is because

the Ongelyan traders will not travel farther than Indyor because their faith will not allow them to enter a land ruled by a woman. I must plead that you reduce my tariffs, for with the price of dyestuff, I cannot match the prices offered to the coastal traders by the Seltyrs of Southgate . . .

She laid that one aside and opened the next, reading it quickly.

. . . the storms have ripped the very leaves from every vine in my eastern vineyards . . . cannot pay the tariffs you have set . . .

The next was no better.

. . . penalties imposed by the Forester for the planting of water oaks are a great burden. Those trees were planted a generation ago by my grandfather. Yet the Forester claims I am responsible . . .

She couldn't help but smile when she picked up the fourth envelope, large and thick, and bearing the seal of the Arms-Commander of Lanachrona. For a brief moment, she held an image of Areyst, his blond hair, green eyes, and open face. Then her smile vanished as she considered the weight of the envelope. She opened it and scanned the lines.

. . . training is proceeding well . . . Commander Choalt has developed a special reconnaissance-and-attack company to serve as an advance group and to warn of approaching scouts . . . scattered reports of individual squads of Midcoast troopers, riding the lands and trails near the border, and I have ordered him to send that company to watch the border . . . attached a map with likely routes of attack and support along the main highway . . .

The one line that provided some warmth was that of the closing words, because they departed from the strictly factual.

. . . trust that all is well with you in Tempre . . .

She did smile once more before she turned to the next missive. None of the next dozen envelopes contained anything hopeful. All were pleas of one sort or another for special treatment. She had three left to read when Chalmyr rapped on the door.

"Chief Engineer Nusgeyl is waiting below, Lady."

"Did he say what he wanted?"

"He said that he needed to discuss your instructions."

Doubtless to tell me oh-so-politely that he cannot comply . . . or that it will cost me dearly in golds we cannot afford to spend . . . "I'll see him now."

In what seemed moments, the door opened.

"Lady-Protector." The squarish engineer bowed deeply after entering the study, far more respectful in demeanor than when Mykella had first met him. His jacket was of the same dark gray, but over black trousers, and his wavy blond hair seemed longer.

"You wished to see me, Chief Engineer."

"I did, Lady."

"About what?"

"I received your instructions, and I understand them clearly. I can certainly comply with your most reasonable request that all materials be itemized and approved by you." Nusgeyl smiled politely.

"Then why do you need to see me?" After only a few words, Mykella was getting irritated at the inspector's tactic of making her ask questions rather than merely stating whatever his problem might be.

"None of my crews have ever worked on the towpaths. They have no experience, and it will take much time. They do not have that time because they are working from morning to night repairing the damage to the sewers caused by the recent storm and the overflowing of the rivers."

"Chief Engineer . . . my problem as Lady-Protector is simple. The previous Minister of Highways and Rivers and his assistant diverted large sums from the accounts of the ministry. Nor were all funds wisely spent. While there are sufficient funds to purchase materials, if carefully, and enough golds to pay you and those who work for you, there are no funds to hire outside crews."

"We cannot handle both tasks at the same time, Lady."

"Then repair the sewers in all areas except in the east, where the large mansions of the Seltyrs are. Then repair the towpaths. Only after the towpaths and the sewers along the South River are repaired are your crews to deal with the eastern sewers."

Nusgeyl could not quite conceal his dismay. "Lady-Protector . . . ah . . ."

"The Seltyrs are always telling me that trade is most important. I must take them at their word. That requires that the part of Tempre dealing with factorages and crafts and the towpaths should be repaired first. If anyone should question you, or demand that you do other than I have ordered, you might suggest that they come to me directly. Of course, the sooner you finish with the South River area and the west of Tempre and the towpaths, the sooner you can deal with the lesser problem of the sewers in the east."

"Yes, Lady-Protector." Nusgeyl nodded, almost sadly.

"I will support you, Chief Engineer, if you follow my orders. It might be useful to us both if you were to inform me in writing of any Seltyr who believes he is above the needs of the city as a whole." She smiled. "I do have the right to take justice into my own bare hands, as the late minister discovered."

"The First Seltyr has been requesting that the sewers serving his villa be addressed first."

Mykella could believe that. She also knew that was something Nusgeyl would never put in writing. "I'll inform the First Seltyr that you're carrying out orders I gave you personally and request that he support you in those duties." She smiled. "Is there anything else, Chief Engineer?"

"No, Lady-Protector." Nusgeyl bowed, then retreated.

Mykella could sense both relief and apprehension.

Before she was interrupted again, she picked up the pen and began to write.

My dear First Seltyr,
It has come to my attention that you have expressed interest in various sewer repairs in the eastern part of Tempre. Recently, you pointed out to me the importance of factorages and trade to Lanachrona.

Since trade and crafts are the heart of trade, I have directed the chief engineer to first repair the sewers in the area where trade and factoring take place, then repair the towpaths. Since he is a dutiful and faithful engineer, he is bound to follow that directive. Anything that slows his work or might injure his health, I'm certain you and all Seltyrs would agree, would not be in the interests of trade, nor in your interests as First Seltyr.

At the same time, I thought you would like to know that I have taken your concerns about the need to put my priorities on those matters which bear directly on trade.

Mykella smiled wryly as she set down the draft. Khanasyl wouldn't like it, but Nusgeyl deserved some protection.

"Chalmyr . . ." she called. He could rewrite the draft in his elegant hand while she read the last of the complaints and petitions.

By the second glass of the afternoon, Mykella was restive. Several more requests for tariff relief had arrived before she'd taken a quick lunch and gone over the state of the Treasury—again—with Haelyt. Even with her attempts to restrict spending, the stock of golds was dwindling faster than she had anticipated. She was thankful that they had recovered some of Porofyr's diversions because they well might be needed before the spring tariff payments began to come in.

"High Factor Pytroven, Lady-Protector," Chalmyr announced.

"Have him come in." Mykella stood, hoping that Lhanyr's recommendation was accurate.

The man who entered scarcely fit the image of a High Factor. He was mostly bald, with only a fringe of frizzy gray hair running from ear to ear, and stood but a few fingers taller than Mykella herself. So stout was he that she suspected he weighed more than twice what she did, and his eyes were both deep-set and bulbous. One was green and the other blue, and his life-thread was so light a brown that it was almost yellow. He bowed both deeply and gracefully, despite his significant girth. "Lady-Protector."

"High Factor Pytroven. Thank you for coming." Mykella gestured to the chairs and seated herself.

Pytroven sat down, then cleared his throat. "I'm pleased to be here, Lady. I think I am. I don't have any idea why. I do hope I haven't done anything to offend you." His voice was a pleasant if slightly raspy baritone.

Mykella laughed softly. "If you have, I certainly don't know anything about it. I wanted to hear your thoughts about the Ministry of Highways and Rivers . . . how the ministry affects you, what it might do to improve things for factors . . ." She waited.

Pytroven cleared his throat again. "I can't say I've thought much about the ministry. They keep the towpaths in shape and the highways clear. That's about all I can ask for."

"What about the sewers?"

"They're supposed to do that? I never knew that." The factor fingered his fleshy chin. "They might do better there. The southwest corner off my warehouse. It always stinks. I sent a message to the inspector. He wrote back, said it wasn't a sewer problem."

"Did he say what it was?"

"He called it a compliance problem. He said he'd asked the Ministry of Justice to look into it. I wrote them. Never heard anything back." The heavy factor shook his head.

"That's because the previous Finance Minister told the Justice Minister not to do anything. I've been looking into that."

A puzzled look crossed Pytroven's face, but he did not speak.

Mykella laughed softly once more. "You're being careful, High Factor. Yes, that Finance Minister was my uncle, the usurper. Some of the things he did are the reason why I'm asking factors and Seltyrs here to talk to me. What do you hear about trade and how matters look in the year ahead?"

"I deal most in barrels and kegs and sacking and handcarts, and sometimes wagons. Things that hold goods or carry them. Don't have too many factors and Seltyrs asking for such, except Porofyr and lately Klevytr."

"You have a reputation for quality, don't you."

"I don't mind saying I do, Lady-Protector. If your steward wants the best for you . . ."

"I'll tell my sister. She's the one running the palace these days."

Another puzzled look crossed the factor's face. "I'd heard she was training some women for something . . . for the Southern Guards, I mean."

"That's my youngest sister. My other sister is handling the palace. What have you heard about the women she's training?"

"Some of the womenfolk aren't too happy, I hear. There aren't many sculls to be had. Those that are . . . they want more."

Mykella hadn't thought that removing some threescore women from being harlots or sculls would have disrupted the households of High Factors, not with the tens of thousands of people in Tempre. "What's the daily wage for a scull?"

"Two coppers and a meal. Now, they want three, even four."

"What else have you heard?"

Mykella continued to ask questions and listen for another half glass.

When Pytroven left, she sat back in her chair. The High Factor was honest and most likely a good factor, but he struck her as too open and too direct to be able to deal with Seltyrs like Khanasyl and Klevytr. She hoped that Zylander was better qualified.

She also needed to pay a visit to the less-than-honorable Seltyr Klevytr . . . among other things.

34

Although Mykella had used the Table late on Sexdi to look at Klevytr, at that time, the Seltyr had been talking to his wife, who had not looked pleased. In itself, that meant little, but combined with what Pytroven had revealed, it was suggestive. To keep track of Klevytr—and anyone else—required more and more use of the Table, something that had always concerned Mykella, given its ties to the Ifrits and the additional time required.

When she used the Table after breakfast on Septi, Klevytr was overseeing the packing of a wide range of goods in his factorage.

That was even more indicative, but not exactly proof. She sighed, knowing that she needed to go calling on the Seltyr to forestall his possible desire to depart from Tempre. Not that she cared that much for Klevytr, but she didn't want others to follow his example, and it would be better to use more personal persuasion than direct force.

A quick scan of the others she was following revealed nothing of interest although she did watch Areyst, lingering longer than she should have, as he groomed and saddled his mount, indistinct as his image was. Then she returned in her own fashion to her quarters and made her way to the antechamber, where Chalmyr awaited her.

"More missives and petitions this morning?" she asked.

"Another halfscore of petitions. There is also a report from the chief engineer."

"Thank you. I'll need a squad to accompany me this morning, in about a glass. Please send word to the duty-squad leader."

When she entered her study, Mykella walked past her desk and the envelopes laid out there and went straight to the window. Under the bright morning sun, she saw that the palace gardeners had finally finished cleaning up the park on the *other* side of the avenue . . . but it had required Rachylana's direct orders to the head gardener— and the implied threat of action by Mykella—to take care of that, not that the palace gardeners had happened to be all that busy. The head gardener had protested that it wasn't traditionally part of their jobs.

There are too many people who worked for Father who are protesting that what needs to be done isn't part of their jobs. How did he let that happen? She shook her head. Were soarers and Ifrits and scepters of unimaginable power part of the traditional job of the Protector of Lanachrona? Was trying to prove that a woman could rule part of it?

After several moments, she walked back to the desk and seated herself, starting through the envelopes. Four of them were from factors pleading about tariffs. The fifth was a much smaller envelope with graceful writing. She slit it open and eased out the single sheet of notepaper.

Dear Lady-Protector—

I deeply apologize for my tardiness in thanking you for your selfless actions in saving me and my father's retainers from the brigands who attacked the summer villa. I had meant to thank you in person the next morning, but you had already departed in the depths of night, and matters soon became so unsettled when we returned to Tempre that I have just now realized my oversight and discourtesy in not immediately offering my thanks and appreciation.

Once more, I offer my deepest thanks and admiration.

The signature was that of Kietyra Seltyrsdaughter.

Unsettled? Was the thank-you also a message of sorts?

Mykella set the note and envelope to the side and picked up the three sheets from Nusgeyl, who had listed the work to be done on the towpath repairs and a schedule of materials. The total cost for materials was listed at ten golds with the notation that his accounts currently would cover that expense.

After a fleeting smile, Mykella jotted down a quick approval for Chalmyr to return to the engineer, then read the next missive . . . this one asking for a widow's stipend for a guard trainee killed before he became a Guard. Mykella jotted a quick note to Areyst, then read the last three missives—all tariff-related. Then she stood and stretched before walking out to the anteroom and handing the two notes to the scrivener. "If you would have this one dispatched to Chief Engineer Nusgeyl and this to Arms-Commander Areyst . . ."

"Yes, Lady."

"I read through all the missives. Have the previous Lords-Protector received these sorts of petitions in such numbers?" she asked.

A wry smile appeared on the scrivener's lips. "Only when they first ruled, Lady. Only then."

Mykella nodded. "That makes a definite kind of sense. I'm riding out to visit Seltyr Klevytr. I hope I won't be gone for more than two glasses. I will be back in time to meet with High Factor Zylander."

Mykella walked to her rooms, slipped down to the Table, and called up the image of Klevytr. From what she could tell, the Seltyr was in the study in his factorage. She also looked in on Khanasyl, who was in an ornate library that could only have been in his sumptuous villa off the Eastern Avenue. She returned to her rooms, donned the nightsilk riding jacket and gloves, and made her way down to the courtyard, where Maeltor waited with her gray and a squad of Southern Guards.

"Where to, Lady?" asked the captain.

"The factorage of Seltyr Klevytr." Mykella jump-mounted the gray and settled herself into the saddle. "That is one of the factorages whose location I requested."

Maeltor nodded. "I took the precaution of obtaining the locations of all the High Factors and Seltyrs." He urged his mount forward.

Mykella laughed almost silently as she guided the gray alongside the captain. "You understand my needs well, Captain. Better than do the Seltyrs."

"That will be to their regret," replied Maeltor, his voice matter-of-fact.

Mykella couldn't help but wonder if the Seltyrs ever regretted any-thing but the loss of golds, but she kept that thought to herself as she rode away from the palace.

Klevytr's factorage was a block and a half to the west of the estab-lishment that had been Porofyr's—now officially a possession of the Lady-Protector—and consisted of three warehouses and a counting-house joined by brick walls. Both of the ironbound and weathered timbered gates were open when Mykella reined up before the counting-house.

Klevytr hurried out to the covered porch even before Mykella could dismount. "Lady-Protector," he offered smoothly.

"Seltyr Klevytr," she replied, then dismounted. "I require a few moments of your time . . . privately. Perhaps you have a study."

"Of course. Of course."

While the Seltyr's voice was hearty, Mykella sensed the apprehen-sion behind and beneath the words. She strengthened her shields before she started up the three steps to the porch.

"To the left, Lady," offered Klevytr, stepping back into the small entry hall.

Mykella stepped inside, then to the side to let him lead the way. Neither spoke until they stood in the comparatively small counting-house study that held little more than a desk and chairs and a single bookcase filled with ledgers.

Klevytr closed the door and turned to Mykella. "Are you here to destroy me in the same fashion as you did Porofyr?" His tone was somewhere between light and joking, but there was deep concern behind it.

"Let us not talk of such," replied Mykella. "Porofyr stole thousands of golds from the accounts he managed. He shipped most of them as well as all of his own personal wealth to Southgate, from where I will never be able to recover them without conquering Southgate. That is something I have no desire to do—unless the Seltyrs there force me. You have committed no offenses." She paused. "Or have you?"

"No, I have not."

The truth of those words was clear, for which Mykella was grateful. She cared little for Klevytr, but that was scarcely the point for her visit. "I think it would be far better for you—and your family—to remain in Tempre rather than for you to continue in your attempts to pack up and transfer your wealth, business, and family out of Tempre."

"A prudent man must always be concerned for his future and that of his family. Surely, you would grant such."

"Oh . . . I would indeed. That is why I am here. A prudent man would not uproot his family and change his business, risking great losses—and the enmity of his ruler—merely because he dislikes the idea of a lady ruler. Nor would a prudent Lady-Protector destroy a successful and generally reputable Seltyr merely because he dislikes her."

Klevytr nodded slowly. "It is likely that Lanachrona will be attacked. You are powerful. You will survive, but the Southern Guards is outnumbered. Can you assure me that we will survive as well?"

"There are no assurances in life such as those you seek, Seltyr. I would point out that you are respected and successful here, and that should you leave, you will lose much because, by leaving, you will forfeit all properties and lands. Also, anyone of stature who leaves in the face of difficulty is always known thereafter as one who looks only to his own interests, and such men are considered suspect in all other lands for so long as they live."

"Your thoughts offer little consolation, Lady-Protector."

"I cannot offer consolation, Seltyr. I can only offer advice." Mykella smiled pleasantly. "I will be offering some thoughts along the same lines to the First Seltyr shortly."

"I see."

"How is your daughter faring?"

"She is well, Lady-Protector, and thankful to be so."

"I am very glad of that. She is a worthy daughter, and most courageous." Mykella inclined her head slightly. "I will not take more of your time, but I did wish to make you fully aware of how I feel."

Klevytr inclined his head in return. "I do appreciate your advice, Lady-Protector, and your thoughtfulness in sharing your words with me."

From what Mykella could sense, Klevytr was somewhat angry, yet relieved and more than a little puzzled. Let him be. Still . . . she would have to watch him although she had the sense that he would not leave now . . . unless matters changed.

"You are most welcome." Mykella offered a last smile, then turned and left the study.

Klevytr followed her without speaking and waited on the porch of the countinghouse while she mounted the gray.

"Back to the palace, Lady-Protector?" asked Maeltor.

"No. To the villa of the First Seltyr." Mykella looked to Klevytr and smiled. "Good day."

"And to you, Lady."

The ride across Tempre to the Eastern Avenue and out to Khanasyl's villa took almost a quarter glass. As they neared the double gates in the brilliant white wall, a guard in white appeared behind the enameled white iron grillework. Mykella could sense the man's apprehension as she rode up with the guards behind her.

Maeltor rode forward. "The Lady-Protector is here to see the First Seltyr."

Mykella smiled at the guard, projecting warmth and friendliness.

After several moments, the gate opened; but when she rode past the guard, Mykella could see the nervous perspiration on the man's face.

The lane from the gate joined a paved circle around a small park, rising gently to the villa set on the top of the low hill. Mykella guided the gray to the right. At the front of the villa was a columned portico with a covered area wide enough to accommodate three coaches abreast and two or more with full teams end to end.

She reined up beside a mounting block and called up to the man in a gray and crimson uniform standing at the top of the portico steps. "I'm here to see the First Seltyr."

The functionary looked down at the black-clad Lady-Protector and the squad of Southern Guards. He swallowed. "Yes, Lady-Protector."

Mykella vaulted, if carefully, off the gray and onto the mounting block, then stepped down and started up the three white marble risers, far wider than those of the main entry to the palace. She had just reached the flat stone terrace before the short covered walk to the main entry when the functionary asked, "Is First Seltyr Khanasyl expecting you, Lady?"

"I doubt it, but he will see me. You are?"

"Dobrak, first assistant steward."

"Good," said Mykella, heading toward the entry doors.

Dobrak hurried ahead and held the door.

"Is he still in his study?"

"Ah . . . yes, Lady." After a moment, the assistant steward started across the square entry hall—more of an enclosed courtyard that rose more than two stories, with stepped garden beds set in white marble on each side. She recognized both miniature lime and lemon trees in those beds, as well as two large heating stoves, half-recessed into the raised beds on each side of the courtyard.

At the far side, Dobrak led Mykella through a square arch and down a wide corridor to the left, lit by clerestory windows on the front side of the villa. At the end of the corridor, almost a hundred yards from the courtyard, Dobrak stopped before two double doors, each whitened oak trimmed with hammered black iron.

He rapped on the door firmly, then declaimed loudly, "The Lady-Protector to see you, sir!"

There was absolute silence for a long moment behind the doors.

"By all means . . . have her come in." Even with the double doors between her and Khanasyl, Mykella could sense the consternation that the heartiness of the Seltyr's words covered.

The assistant steward quickly reached forward and opened the door, half bowing as he did so. Mykella concealed a smile at how quickly the door closed behind her as she stepped into the chamber, a library rather than a study.

The walls flanking the double doors were filled with dark wooden bookshelves, and every shelf was close to overflowing with leather-bound volumes. In the center of the wall to her right were a pair of floor-to-ceiling windows, framed by gray-trimmed red velvet hangings. The wall to her left held two bookcases, with a space some five yards across between them. In the open space was a larger-than-life sculpture of a man wearing an antique-looking jacket and trousers and holding a book in his left hand. Facing her was Khanasyl, standing before a large desk piled high with volumes, although Mykella felt that most were ledgers. Behind him was another set of floor-to-ceiling double windows, through which she could see an extensive walled garden.

Walls within walls. More so than even behind the palace.

The floor was of a polished pearly gray stone, bare of carpeting except for the large circular crimson-and-gray-patterned rug, in the middle of which stood Khanasyl's desk.

"Greetings, Lady-Protector . . . I did not expect you . . ."

"I did not anticipate that you would, First Seltyr." Mykella walked toward the Seltyr, stopping on the edge of the carpet.

"Please . . . be seated." Khanasyl gestured to the large leather-upholstered armchair set at an angle to the corner of the desk. "Might I offer you some refreshment?"

"No, thank you. I will be brief." Mykella did not sit in the armchair but perched on the broad left arm, so that she was looking levelly at the tall Seltyr when he settled into the raised and overlarge chair behind the desk. "I just had a visit with Seltyr Klevytr. He had a number of concerns. They were remarkably similar to those you raised when we last met, and he was seriously considering leaving Tempre for good. I pointed out to him that doing so would cost him dearly, and he seemed to understand." Mykella smiled coldly. "Unfortunately, until I did explain matters to him, he appeared unaware of the costs of such an action. Tell me. Are you planning to leave Tempre?"

"No. Of course not. Why would you think that?"

Mykella could read the vehemence and the truth behind Khanasyl's words, and that confirmed one of her suspicions. "Why would I not think that? You said that you were concerned about the future of trade in Tempre. Two Seltyrs with whom you've spent much time both considered leaving."

"I would never do such."

"I'm very glad to hear that." Mykella paused, then added, "It would be unfortunate if word happened to get out that one Seltyr hinted that the wise might leave Tempre . . . and that he or others then acquired various assets at far less than their value."

"That is a rather presumptuous assumption, Lady-Protector."

"First Seltyr, I am not assuming anything. I merely said that such a rumor would be most unfortunate. It would also be unfortunate if word happened to get out that, at the same time, a Seltyr recommended persons for a post who all knew were, shall we say, less than qualified. It might appear that . . ." She paused. "I think you know exactly what it might appear to be."

Khanasyl laughed, warmly, then shook his head. "Such statements . . . who could possibly believe them?"

"No one, I would think," replied Mykella with a light laugh of her own, "if nothing more along those lines happened to surface."

"I can assure you that nothing like that will surface, Lady."

"I can assure you, First Seltyr, that if anything more like that does occur, it will surface, sooner or later. I would be very disappointed if any such words or acts did." Mykella used her Talent to gather light to herself. "Very disappointed," she said softly, letting the light fade away.

After the slightest hesitation, Khanasyl smiled, warmly and falsely,

falsely in the sense that, for the first time, a sense of fear filled him. "I will do my best not to disappoint you, Lady-Protector."

"And I will do my best to make Tempre a very good place for fair and open trade and commerce," she replied, slipping off the arm of the chair and standing directly facing Khanasyl. "I look forward to your efforts in reassuring all the other Seltyrs about my commitments to that. You know, as many others do not, that the Seltyrs of Southgate do not have your best interests in mind, no matter what they say. They never have. The Protectors of Lanachrona may not always have acted wisely in the past, but they did have Lanachrona's interests in mind, as do I." That all Protectors always acted in Lanachrona's interests was probably an overstatement, but one that Khanasyl would not dispute.

"A land's interests may not be that of a Seltyr's," said Khanasyl mildly as he slipped to his feet.

"Over the years, they are the same. A Seltyr who puts this year or this season above good business over time will find himself far poorer and in far worse shape." She smiled. "I am not telling you anything you do not know, but you might wish to point it out to others who have forgotten."

"It is a good thought."

"It is the thought with which I will leave you. Good day, First Seltyr." With a last smile, she turned and walked toward the double doors.

Not surprisingly, the left door opened as she neared it. She did not look back.

The wind began to pick up on the ride back to the palace, and dark clouds scudded out of the northeast, suggesting a cold rain. Mykella only hoped it was not another heavy downpour and that the winds remained moderate.

She had barely gotten back to her study when Chalmyr announced High Factor Zylander.

When the High Factor entered, he bowed, a gesture of respect neither obsequious nor perfunctory. "Lady-Protector. You wished to see me."

Mykella motioned to the chairs before the desk, then sat down, adjusting the square cushion that reminded her, again, that she needed a chair more suited to her. "I did."

As the High Factor seated himself, Mykella studied him. In comparison to Pytroven, Zylander was physically almost nondescript—of moderate height, with mostly gray hair and washed-out hazel eyes above a neatly trimmed square gray beard. His straight nose was neither long nor short He wore a gray woolen jacket and trousers, and his white shirt was of a finely woven cotton but had been worn enough that it was clearly not recently made. He waited politely for Mykella to speak.

"You may have heard, High Factor, that there have been certain difficulties with the Ministry of Highways and Rivers. I have talked about those difficulties with a number of Seltyrs and High Factors. Chief High Factor Lhanyr suggested that I also discuss these matters with you."

"Lhanyr has always been one for including more people in matters." Zylander smiled, almost shyly, it felt to Mykella.

"How do you feel about the Ministry of Highways and Rivers?"

"Without clear highways and firm towpaths, trade will suffer. The least of the factors knows that."

"So does the Lady-Protector. Has the ministry failed in any of this?"

Zylander frowned slightly. "I would not say that the ministry has failed. There are tales . . ."

Mykella nodded, but did not speak, waiting for the High Factor to continue.

"You know the ox pens? Those closest to the Great Piers are kept the cleanest and the driest, and all the bargemasters would wish those. Yet I have often seen them empty for days, until the barges of certain Seltyrs arrived."

"Do all Seltyrs and factors pay the same fees for penning their oxen?"

"They do. A copper an ox for each day. It does not matter which pen is offered."

"You're suggesting that the portmaster makes the offers for reasons other than who might arrive first."

"Not the portmaster. The assistant portmaster who deals with the pens. It is well-known that there are ways . . ." Zylander shrugged.

"How do you think it should be handled?"

"The better pens might cost more, perhaps an additional copper for each pair of oxen. Those who wished the better pens could pay for them."

"And the assistant portmaster?"

"Perhaps he should work for a Seltyr and not for the Minister of Highways and Rivers." Zylander laughed softly, but warmly, and without malice.

"Are there other matters?" prompted Mykella. "Like those."

". . . there may be . . . but I have only heard from others . . ."

"While you tried to obtain the better pens and could not do so? Not without . . . certain considerations?"

"Even such considerations, as you put it, were not sufficient. I was willing to pay for better pens. I would have preferred that they be available to those willing to pay and that such payments go to the Lord-Protector."

Mykella nodded, then said, "Recently, the storms washed out certain parts of the towpaths. I discovered that previous repairs had been less than what they should have been."

"That is not surprising. There are parts of the towpaths where the paving stones do not seem firmly in place when the oxen cross them. That was not so when I took over for my father some years ago."

"What else have you noticed?"

"The river walls along the South River are sagging in places . . ."

Mykella asked gentle questions and listened for almost a glass before she inquired, "Do you think a devoted Minister of Highways and Rivers could improve all that you have noticed?"

"Golds would be required, but those things could be better. They should be."

"I am seeking such a minister. Would you be interested?"

Zylander laughed softly. "Did Lhanyr offer my name?"

"Why do you ask?"

"Because I have mentioned much of this to him, and he has always said that, with all my observations and ideas, I should seek to become Minister of Highways and Rivers."

"He did recommend you. He also said he had not talked to you about that and did not know if you would be interested."

The High Factor nodded slowly. "If . . . if you are willing for me to make changes, I would consider it."

"Some changes are necessary immediately, such as the way repairs are accomplished and the way the oxen pens are offered. Others we would need to discuss as to how they might be done. The Treasury is not what it should be."

"I had heard such." Zylander smiled. "It is said that when a man is offered the chance to remedy all that about which he has complained, he is a fool to accept that chance because nothing is as it seems. Yet . . . I am willing to be called a fool."

"I would not call you a fool, High Factor. Nor would I force you, but I would like you to be minister."

"If it would not trouble you too much, I would request that I not be named minister until just before the turn of spring. I will need some time to go over matters with my son and daughter."

"I can do that." Mykella smiled warmly. "Thank you." She stood.

As he rose, Zylander looked at her shyly, once more. "I had not thought to come with this on my thoughts."

"I know. I could tell."

"You can tell more than most, I fear, Lady-Protector, and that is good for a ruler and her land. It is not so good for you." He bowed respectfully. "By your leave?"

"Of course, High Factor and Minister."

When the door closed, Mykella took a deep breath. She still didn't truly understand why her father had not seen what Porofyr had done and how he had abused his position. At least, Zylander knew what the problems were and had ideas on how to remedy them. All she had to do was hold everything together and come up with more golds.

35

After Zylander left, Mykella spent a quarter of a glass looking at petitions she didn't want to read. Then she stood. She still hadn't investigated the silver mirrors—if they even existed outside the soarers' city—and if she didn't before long, she wouldn't have any time to do so. Nothing else on her desk or from her remaining ministers was that urgent, and she needed to seek out the silver mirrors, if only to see if they offered any way to use her Talent more effectively. Reading another petition and dealing with another spoiled Seltyr's problems could wait. She tried not to think about the fact that Tempre was only one city in Lanachrona and that she hadn't even had a chance to look into what needed to be done elsewhere—and until she had ministers who were both good and trustworthy, that would be close to impossible.

If she needed to, she could come back and read petitions by lamplight, but traveling the dark ways meant she needed light to see where she ended up, and it was only a bit past third glass.

With that, she left the study and stopped in the anteroom. "I have some things to do. I don't know if I'll be back this afternoon."

"Yes, Lady."

As she left, she could hear the murmur of the messenger boy. "Where does she go? . . . say no one can find her . . ."

". . . best to ask the Ancients . . ."

Mykella wanted to shake her head. Already, despite her efforts to be circumspect, events had forced her to reveal too much of her Talent.

She walked quickly to her quarters, where she donned the heavy nightsilk riding jacket and gloves. After walking to the window, close to the granite of the palace, with her Talent she reached out for the darkness, letting herself sink into the greenish black, but not quite all the way to the deep green.

Amid the depths, she searched for lines of silver . . . or amber . . . or faint, faint traces of either. The chill settled around her, but she began to sense . . . silvered amber patches of what seemed like mist. She reached for the one that seemed closest—or was it just the strongest?

Unlike her first attempts with the Tables, the silver, faint as it was, felt more welcoming, and . . . she stood in a chamber with a rounded roof that was so low her hair almost brushed it. She glanced down. Her boots rested on a shimmering surface—a mirror—except it was frosted in places, and it was circular and surrounded by a ring of what looked to be green tile.

A gust of wind like biting ice-mist ruffled her hair, and she looked up. She wasn't in a narrow chamber so much as in a tunnel that opened to show sky and a distant horizon difficult to discern because the sun was low in the west, and its whitish light was almost directly in her eyes. She turned and glanced behind her, but there was nothing except a flush wall of the green tile.

The light wind that gusted into the tunnel made the depths beneath seem warm in comparison. She took several steps forward and away from the silvered floor mirror and squinted out toward the sun . . . and swallowed hard as she stopped in her tracks. The tunnel ended a yard from where she stood, and it overlooked a vast plain, or at least land that was comparatively flat, from a very great height, because she could make out no individual features of the ground far below. She edged forward slightly, enough to see that the tunnel seemed to emerge or end with sheer rock faces on each side.

Where are you?

She edged backwards, not wanting to get too close to the edge. The only place she'd seen or heard of with such a sheer cliff was the Aerlal Plateau, and she'd only seen it from a distance of tens of vingts. But why had the soarers put a mirror in the middle of the enormous stone wall that surrounded the plateau?

Even as she posed that thought, she began to sense a blackish presence or presences.

. . . one has come . . . so long . . .

Mykella turned back from the overlook to see two manlike creatures flow out of the sides of the tunnel, blocky tan figures a head shorter than she was. In the dimness of the tunnel, their skins still sparkled in irregular patches, as if tiny gems or miniature light-torches were embedded there. Their eyes were crystal-like, hard silvered green, and they wore no clothing, but their rough skin showed no breasts or udders or any visible animal or human organs.

Feelings—rather than thoughts—flowed from the manlike creatures, and they exuded a terrible loneliness . . . and a raw desire . . . so crude and direct that her stomach churned.

They moved toward her, purposefully.

Mykella grasped for the darkness and *wrenched* herself into the depths.

Behind her, for an instant, she felt a spear of pain and total despair. *Were those the "others" the soarer had mentioned?*

She would have shuddered if she could have as she hung suspended in the darkness. A second thought occurred. *Did they think she had been a soarer? But why . . . ?*

Within herself, she shuddered again, if only in her mind.

Then she forced herself to try to find another mirror, one somewhere farther from the Plateau, because, if those figures were the "others," the soarer had said that they existed only where it was cold. She focused on one that "felt" warmer . . .

. . . and found herself standing in another low-ceilinged chamber or tunnel, her boots on another silver mirror, save that this one was rectangular in shape and covered in fine dust. It was rimmed in the seamless green tile. The light was far dimmer, so much so that Mykella realized she was sensing more than seeing. Again, the wall behind the mirror was the same green tile and a tunnel lay before her, but less than three yards away was a pile of rock that filled all but the tiniest space through which indirect light sifted.

Can you use the darkness to slip through the rock?

She reached for the green, found it near at hand, and eased herself toward the light, keeping a firm grip on the darkness, just in case this tunnel also ended in a cliff face.

It did, and she found herself hanging in midair, but less than a handful of yards above a field of jumbled boulders, if in the middle of a drizzling rain. The rugged slopes before her were covered in ever-greens, stretching in all directions, with nothing to offer any sign of where she might be.

She eased herself back into the darkness beneath and tried again.

This time, she found herself in total darkness, and she immediately dropped back into the greenish black below, sensing that the tunnel was totally blocked.

A fourth attempt landed her in waist-deep snow in what looked to be a ravine, until she realized that it had been a tunnel, except that something had destroyed the upper part.

Between the drizzle and the snow, she was shivering, and she reached to the green darkness a last time—to bring herself back to her quarters and her own dressing chamber.

There, she changed into dry nightsilks and her other boots.

What were the mirrors for? Except for the one in the city of the ancients, all the others had been in high mountainous locations—and she thought it most likely the one that had been buried had been as well.

Then she thought about the one in the cliff wall of the Aerlal Plateau . . . and shuddered.

After several moments, she drew herself together.

So much for the mirrors' providing help.

She glanced toward the window and the sunset, then turned and headed back toward the formal study.

She could finish the rest of the petitions before dinner. *And you thought that reading petitions was horrible.*

36

Over the rest of Octdi and Novdi, Mykella felt as though she scrambled from one thing to another, just trying to keep up. The Table showed her that Klevytr had stopped packing things away and that Zylander had several talks with a younger man who resembled him, no doubt his son. Cheleyza remained in Harmony, and Areyst was alternating between meetings with officers and conducting training exercises, even in the rain that had fallen across Tempre and Viencet on Octdi. Salyna left a note that said she and the auxiliaries had encountered some difficulty in dealing with the prisoners from Porofyr's factorage, but that she'd resolved matters, and several of the better auxiliaries were helping to patrol the factorage.

Mykella met twice with Haelyt. While the outflow of golds had slowed, it was still occurring. She didn't want to stop payments or even give an order to slow them because that would cause too much concern among the factors and Seltyrs. Someone had been spreading the word, because Elwayt had told Rachylana that some of the herders were requesting payment when they delivered livestock, and even one of the millers had. Although Mykella did have some cushion with the golds from Porofyr's wagon, given the outlays to come, it wasn't that much. Loryalt still had not returned to Tempre, and the rain had effectively stopped any immediate repairs to the sewers and towpaths.

Mykella kept checking the markers of the other Tables but could sense little change. Were the Ifrits somehow watching through the Tables and waiting until she was occupied with something else—such as an invasion by the coastal princes? Or were they biding their time to ready even mightier weapons . . . or for some other reason? She made two other attempts to gain better control over the dark deep greenness, with slightly more success, but not enough to feel truly confident if she had to face Ifrits who could use or draw on the scepters.

Decdi morning, she did sleep late, if a glass beyond her normal waking counted as late. She took a bit more time washing up before she made her way to the breakfast room.

Salyna was sitting silently at one side of the table, slowly sipping tea, letting the steam wreath her face. Dark circles under her eyes made her look even thinner than she was.

"Are you all right?" Mykella reached out with her Talent. All she sensed was fatigue.

"Besides being exhausted? I think so." Salyna looked up. "How do you do it? I'm just worried about sixty-some women."

"You have to do everything," Mykella replied, looking up as Muergya set a pot of tea, steam still issuing from the spout, before her. "I can call on a few people." She turned to Muergya. "An omelet and ham strips and dark bread, if the kitchen has any."

"Yes, Lady." The serving girl hurried off.

Salyna waited for Muergya to leave, then said, "You have to check up on all of them. I've seen that."

"Except for Areyst."

"You'd like to see more of him, wouldn't you?" Salyna smiled.

"Yes," Mykella admitted.

"When will you tell him?"

"Salyna . . ." Mykella's voice contained a mixture of exasperation and humor.

"All right . . ." After a moment, the blonde asked, "What about Lord Gharyk?"

"He's honest enough, but he can't do much until I can replace even more people in the Justice Ministry, and I've been having enough trouble with Highways and Rivers and Finance. I can't afford to be running three ministries myself." Mykella shook her head. "I'm not doing a very good job with two—and that's just dealing mostly with what's happening in Tempre."

"No one else could do any better. You didn't create the problems, either."

"No . . . but I'm not sure that I didn't make some of them worse."

"Did you have any choice if you wanted anything left in the Treasury?"

"Probably not."

Salyna nodded.

Neither spoke, and Mykella sipped her tea, waiting for Muergya to return with the omelet and ham strips, when Rachylana entered the breakfast room, stifling a yawn. Mykella realized that it was the first time in days that the three of them had eaten together—after years of always doing so.

"It looks like the rain has finally stopped," said Rachylana.

"It's still drizzling," replied Salyna glumly. "The exercise grounds are slop and worse."

"It will be clear by this afternoon," predicted the redhead, slipping into her place.

"That may be, but it will be days before things dry out."

Muergya returned and set a platter before Mykella, as well as a basket of dark bread. "I'll have an omelet for you in a moment, Lady Rachylana."

"Thank you."

Salyna took several bites of her breakfast, then looked at Mykella. "I've been having the auxiliaries use the people they know to find out anything of interest that might help you. Seltyr Seniel, Seltyr Klevytr, and Seltyr Whaerel have been looking into buying additional wagons and dray horses, and High Factor Scalyn has bought a barge and a team of oxen."

"Klevytr was the one whose summer villa was attacked, wasn't he?" asked Rachylana.

Salyna's look at the redhead was a tired glare. "You know that."

Mykella spoke quickly. "I appreciate the information. I've worried about Klevytr, but I hadn't heard anything about the others. I'll have to keep a close eye on all of them." Mykella decided to say nothing more because she wanted all the information Salyna could provide, and saying she already knew was likely to give the impression that she really didn't need more information. In fact, the limitations of the Table and her own time were becoming more and more obvious, and she could use any and all information her sisters could provide.

"I'll see what else they can find out."

"Good."

"What are you wearing to the ball?" Rachylana asked Salyna.

"The ball? I haven't given it a thought. Training the auxiliaries is taking all my time right now. They try hard, but there's so much they don't know . . . so much." Salyna sighed.

"You will be there, won't you?"

"Yes. I'll be there." She paused, as if about to say something, then shook her head.

Mykella could almost read what Salyna wanted to say as if she had. *I'll be there, but I have better things to do than to go to functions.*

"Balls serve a function, too, you know?" observed Rachylana.

"Such as allowing Mykella to get a better idea of whom to trust and whom not to? Or parading women like cattle up for bidding? How many young daughters will accompany their fathers, in place of their mothers, so that other Seltyrs can observe them?"

It could be worse ... so much worse, and I'd never thought that. Mykella repressed a shudder, taking another sip of tea.

"Right now," returned Rachylana, "I'd judge about eight."

"How do you know that? They only respond that they're attending."

"There are three widowers, and they won't bring their mistresses, and there are a High Factor and a Seltyr who haven't appeared with their wives in years ... and I'm guessing that two or three others will have wives who are suddenly indisposed."

"The poor girls won't even see the men to whom they might be matched," Salyna said.

"Is that much better than for us?" asked Rachylana. "The men who might seek matches with us won't do it if they have to come to Tempre."

"Not yet." Mykella's voice was tart. "They will." *One way or another.*

"Is that a promise or a prophecy?" countered Rachylana.

"It will happen."

"If you succeed, they'll have to, and if you don't, we'll all end up matched or dead. Is that it? Or do you know something you're not saying?" The softness of Rachylana's last words muted the repressed anger in the first.

"Cheleyza is likely to accompany the Northcoast forces. Many of the golds Joramyl stole went to Northcoast to build a cavalry force. She wears that uniform all the time now. They will attack. That doesn't mean they'll win."

"You're holding something back," Rachylana said. "Does it have to do with the reason why you're green again?"

"She's not green ..." Salyna's words trailed off. "Why can you see that, and I can't?" She turned to Mykella. "Do you know why? You must."

Mykella shook her head. "Some people can. Some can't. I don't know why it happens that way." And that was true. She knew which people could, it seemed, because of the green in their life-thread, but not why some people had the green and not others.

Muergya reappeared and set a platter in front of Rachylana. "Your omelet, Lady."

"Thank you."

"What are you going to do this afternoon?" asked Salyna abruptly, her eyes on Mykella.

"I'd thought I'd take a ride through Tempre to see how things are going. After all this rain, I'd like to get out. Do either of you two want to come?"

"I can't," said Salyna.

"I will." Rachylana speared a ham slice.

Mykella understood why Rachylana would accompany her—and that was another worry.

"I need to go." Salyna rose and hurried out of the breakfast room.

Because she didn't want to answer Rachylana's questions immediately or avoid them directly, Mykella finished the last of her breakfast quickly and rose. "I have to answer more petitions and missives."

As she walked from the breakfast room, she wished she didn't have to finish the petitions waiting in the Lady-Protector's study; but there would be more on Londi, and she'd get behind if she didn't finish what she could.

Still . . . she would take that ride later in the afternoon—even with Rachylana. It had been too long since she'd made a ride through Tempre . . . and one thing she had resolved was that she would not become isolated from the people in the way her father had.

No . . . you won't make the same mistakes he did. You'll just make different ones.

At least they'd be her mistakes, and not inherited errors, not that the realization was any great comfort.

37

Mykella could tell that Rachylana truly wanted to ride. The redhead was already mounted and waiting in the rear courtyard with the Southern Guard squad, led by Zhulyn, when Mykella stepped into northwest courtyard slightly after the second glass of the afternoon. She mounted quickly, glancing skyward and noting that a brisk breeze blew out of the southwest and that the southern half of the silver-green sky was clear and crisp.

"Where to, Lady-Protector?" asked the squad leader.

"Out to the Great Piers, then south on the west side of the South River." Mykella urged the gelding forward.

Rachylana immediately rode up beside her sister, and a pair of guards rode around them and took the lead on the way out of the courtyard and onto the avenue.

"It's getting warmer," said the redhead. "It usually does when we get a south wind."

"And snow comes from the north or northeast, and rain from the northwest."

"Except in the depth of winter, when the light powdery snow comes from the northwest."

"Like Cheleyza," said Mykella dryly. "She looks so fragile, and she's anything but delicate. Then, Salyna would say that a killer saber looks delicate compared to a broadsword, but the sabers are more effective in battle."

"Some would say that about you," Rachylana pointed out. "You're not that tall."

"No one would ever call me delicate," rejoined Mykella. "On a good day, they might call me slender." Her eyes went to the north side of the pavement, where the stone gutters were still carrying water, if not quite up to the edges.

Rachylana nodded, then ventured, "You know Salyna can't see the green, or the purple, and it really bothers her." She eased her chestnut closer to Mykella's gray.

"I know. That's why it's better if we don't talk about it."

"I shouldn't," said Rachylana in a low voice. "I know that. But . . . sometimes, she gets so . . . uppity, about arms and her scullery women. I just want to remind her that there are things she can't see or do."

"Why? That just upsets her."

"What about me? You're the Lady-Protector, and you have some of the powers of an Ancient. She's better with weapons than most of the Southern Guards, and she knows it, and they know it. All I can do is look pretty and arrange entertainment and season-turn balls."

"You're running the palace as well."

"Any woman can do that." Rachylana snorted.

No . . . just any intelligent, well-brought-up, and responsible woman who understands how palaces work. Mykella kept that thought to herself because she understood exactly what Rachylana had meant, even if her sister hadn't quite said it. "What else do you want to do?"

"I don't know. I just don't want to be matched and sent off."

"I said that was up to you." Mykella also refrained from pointing out that a season ago, Rachylana had been most interested in being married off, if only to her worthless cousin Berenyt.

They rode more than a hundred yards without speaking, nearing the eastern end of the Great Piers, still almost empty, with but three barges and two rivercraft tied there. One barge looked to be riding low, as if it had taken on water, but Mykella didn't see anyone bailing or pumping out water.

Finally, Rachylana said, "Mykel the Great was like you, wasn't he? Having Talent like a soarer, I mean?"

"From the stories and the records, he could do more than I can. He was also a great battle leader, and the Seltyrs listened to every word he said."

"Mykella . . . you're still young."

"I know that." *Too young to be a truly effective ruler . . . at least in the eyes of most of the Seltyrs in Tempre. Most probably still think of me as a child.*

"Who knows what you'll be able to do?"

If I can survive Ifrits and invasions and intrigues . . . and doubting Seltyrs and factors . . . and who knows what else. "It gets harder in some ways. The more you learn, the more you realize that what you *can* do isn't always what you should do, much as you want to."

"Is that a polite way to tell me that reminding Salyna what she can't see isn't a good idea?"

"I wasn't thinking of that. I was thinking about being polite to that overstuffed First Seltyr. Or to that idiot Klevytr . . ."

"Oh . . . Mykella." Rachylana shook her head. "They're only men."

"They can still make things hard on people." *And they act as though they're so superior even when they've done something stupid.*

As they headed up Factors' Street past several two-story dwellings that had seen better days, Mykella noted that more windows were boarded up than had been the last time she had ridden this way. Ahead, several youngsters crowded onto the rickety balcony of a dwelling almost without stain or paint on its gray and weathered siding. One pointed toward the riders.

Mykella used her Talent to try to hear what the three were saying.

". . . those are Southern Guards . . ."

". . . two women . . ."

". . . little one is the Lady-Protector, I'd wager . . . wearing black . . . say she always wears black . . ."

". . . say she's part soarer . . ."

Mykella tried not to wince at that, especially recalling her encounter with the "others."

". . . too big to be a soarer . . ."

". . . how would you know?"

". . . I know . . ."

"No, you don't . . . don't know anything . . ."

Mykella smiled at the last part of the interchange as the three forgot the riders and began to argue more furiously among themselves.

Rachylana glanced at Mykella, then back toward the balcony that they had just passed. "Did you hear what they were arguing about?"

"Some of it. Each of them was trying to prove she was right."

"Was that why you were smiling?"

"Yes. I can remember when we argued like that."

For a time, Rachylana was silent. Finally, she said, "Maybe we don't argue because we're each right in our own way."

Right in our own way? "What do you mean?"

"We don't see things the same way. You see things in terms of Talent and golds. Salyna sees them more in terms of arms. I see them in the way people manipulate each other."

I certainly see the manipulation . . . "I think you're talking about what motivates people to try to get their way. How do you see things differently?" Even from the street, looking to her left, through the lanes leading to the South River, Mykella could see that the South River was running near flood stage but not high enough to overtop its banks. Most likely there would be even more destruction where the towpath had already been damaged . . . and greater repair costs.

Two laborers lugged pails of what looked to be water and mud up a set of cellar steps from the side door of a tinsmith's shop. *How many cellars were flooded? Did that happen when the gutters overflowed because the sewers needed repairs?* She needed to ask Nusgeyl about that.

"Most people aren't like you and Salyna," Rachylana said. "You have power. People have to react to you. Salyna has a different kind of power. People want to make you look bad because they can't challenge you directly. They start rumors; they try to steal things in ways that they won't get caught to get golds because that's another kind of power. Or like Cheleyza . . . they set things up so you look bad. She tried to get you to wear a ball gown that would have made you look ridiculous. Then she pretended you'd hurt her when you rejected her 'help,' and Father made you apologize to her. That made her feel superior."

"I'm sure it did. I hated having to do that. She gloried in it, and we both pretended it was nothing, and she gloated the whole time behind that false smile of the concerned aunt."

"She was always false, but she wasn't weak." Rachylana shook her head. "She could manipulate Uncle Joramyl and Berenyt. That's a kind of power. Me . . . I don't have that kind of power, or power like you or Salyna."

"You're as strong as Salyna, and you ride every bit as well as she does."

"I'm not as interested in intimidating men."

Mykella turned in the saddle and looked at her sister. "So far as I can see, women who aren't strong tend to end up as worn-out floor mats. Why do you think so many women wanted to become auxiliaries? They didn't have our advantages."

"Our advantages? What . . ." Rachylana broke off as she looked at Mykella. After a moment, she said, "When you look like that . . ."

"What?"

Rachylana shook her head.

Just as you think she's beginning to understand . . . We do have advantages that other women don't. Not the advantages that men have . . . Not yet. Mykella squared herself in the saddle ever so slightly.

She still needed to see what other damage the latest storm had done.

38

Although Mykella had spent much of Decdi, before and after her ride, writing replies to petitions, she'd also studied maps of western Lanachrona and wrestled with the dark green of the depths, with slightly greater success—in that she began to be able to channel the darkness, not just the lighter green that glowed but the darker green, upward and around her as far as the Table chamber. The surprising aspect was that, as she had gotten more proficient, it was less tiring. Then again, Salyna had said that working with blades got easier as skill improved.

Her first task on Londi morning, after dressing, was to check the Table. There was little notable about what most of those she surveyed were doing . . . except for Cheleyza. Her aunt was riding, wearing the dark green cavalry uniform. To her right was her brother Chalcaer, and to her left, also in uniform, was Paelyt. Chalcaer's face was expressionless, but Mykella felt that the Prince of Northcoast was less than pleased. *Or are you seeing what you want to see?*

Mykella concentrated on trying to get an image from farther away and was rewarded with a view of part of a column of riders following the three. From the light and the shadows, the column was riding south on an eternastone highway through an evergreen forest. That— and the fact that Mykella's previous observations on Decdi had not shown Cheleyza riding, but in her chamber—suggested that the Northcoast forces were still fairly far north, possibly only having left Harmony that morning or sometime late the day before.

When she reached her study after breakfast, Mykella immediately wrote Areyst about Cheleyza and Chalcaer. She also added a separate missive saying that she very much looked forward to his presence at the season-turn ball, as she was certain did most of the Seltyrs. Then she summoned Maeltor, informed him of what she had learned, and gave him the two messages to be sent to Areyst in Viencet.

Before long, she'd received another message from Engineer Nusgeyl, this one noting that the rains of the previous tenday had resulted in more damage to the sewers, especially to the storm drains, and that towpath repairs would be delayed for likely a week—unless he could hire another crew. That would likely cost fifty golds.

Fifty golds you can spare more than having the towpath unusable now that season-turn and the time of more traders on the river is approaching.

She sent back a message telling him to hire the crew.

Then she looked at the master ledger again, not that she hadn't known already how tight matters were getting. She'd had to advance Salyna more golds for additional weapons, supplies, and mounts, but those had come from her "personal" funds as Lady-Protector. Most would have thought her foolish for letting Salyna train the women; but something told Mykella it was anything but foolhardy, although she wouldn't have wanted to explain why. But then, for the moment, she didn't have to.

Cerlyk hadn't heard from Forester Loryalt, but the assistant forester insisted that Loryalt would be in Tempre before long because he always stayed close to his schedule. Mykella forbore asking what the Forestry Ministry meant by "close."

Abruptly, Mykella stood and walked to the window. From there, she looked out across the courtyard, beyond the park, at the roofs and streets and lanes of Tempre. There was so much to do . . . and doubtless so many things she didn't know enough about to know they had to be done—from the management of forestry lands to the Southern Guards.

At that thought, she walked back to the study door, opened it, and stepped out into the anteroom, looking at Chalmyr. "I'd like to see Captain Maeltor . . . at his earliest convenience."

"Yes, Lady."

Less than a half glass later, the captain stepped into her study, inclining his head respectfully. "You sent for me, Lady?"

Mykella could sense wariness behind the pleasant words.

"I did. I wanted your thoughts about several matters. Please sit down."

Maeltor's concerns did not abate as he settled stiffly into the middle chair of the three facing the desk, sitting on only the front half of the seat.

"Captain . . . I assume you have been watching, at least part of the time, the training and the progress of the auxiliaries."

"Yes, I have, Lady-Protector."

"While it is early, I would be interested in your thoughts about how that training is progressing."

Maeltor offered an embarrassed smile. "I have never attempted to train women, Lady."

"You don't think the training is going well, then?"

"No . . . it is not that. In the Southern Guards, the first weeks of training are handled by a senior squad leader with great experience. Your sister—Undercaptain Salyna—is doing the direct instruction. She asks many questions of the two squad leaders who are assisting her, but she decides and leads."

"And?"

"It is different." Maeltor shook his head. "None of the women object or even put off chores or hateful duties. They all do the exercises—"

"All of them?"

The captain smiled. "On the first day, two women objected. The undercaptain picked one up and threw her into a pile of manure, then told her to leave. The other pretended to obey, then tried to use a pitchfork as a lance. The undercaptain disarmed her and slit her throat."

Mykella swallowed. That was a side of Salyna she'd thought might have been there, but she'd never seen it.

"She was right to do that. She had to, because assaulting an officer merits death, but that is one reason why senior squad leaders handle the training of Southern Guard recruits."

"How did the other guards take that?"

"Undercaptain Bursuin asked Undercaptain Salyna to spar with him with sabers. He is somewhat taller, a good stone heavier. She disarmed him quickly. No one has said anything since."

"You said that the training was different."

"The undercaptain has the women working more glasses, and they spend more time on physical exercises. That is wise, because, with the exception of your sister and four or five women from herding or laboring families, most do not have the strength in their arms and shoulders that is best for handing weapons. She does not drill them as much, and she started them on riding work on the second day. The undercaptain works harder than any junior officer."

Mykella nodded.

"You do not look surprised, Lady-Protector."

"What Southern Guard officer would respect her if she did not do so? She would be regarded as not having earned the rank and having been given it because she is my sister."

Maeltor smiled. "That was what the Arms-Commander said."

"I don't believe you answered my question about how their training is coming along."

"It is too early to say." Maeltor paused. "If they continue as they have, they will be of great value to the Guards. Some, perhaps more than a few, show signs that they could hold their own in battle; but part of that would depend on how well they fight as a unit."

"Fight?" asked Mykella.

"The undercaptain is training them to fight as well as for other duties. We will be outnumbered if all the coastal princes attack. I think the undercaptain would have the auxiliaries prepared for all possibilities."

"How do the other guards feel about that?"

"Many doubted until they watched the undercaptain. Now they just watch. The senior squad leaders will say nothing. They never do until recruits survive their first skirmish or fight."

"And you?

"I hope that the undercaptain is successful. One can never have enough trained troopers when one goes into battle."

"Diplomatically said, Captain," observed Mykella.

"I fear not, Lady. It is only what I believe."

"Do we have enough brimstone?"

"We could use more, but we always can because there is none to be found in Lanachrona, and the factors are not always reliable in obtaining it."

"Are there certain factors who usually provide it?"

"Seltyr Thaen and the First Seltyr obtain most of it."

Not exactly what you wanted to hear. "Is there anything else needed?"

"I am certain that Arms-Commander Areyst would know that far better than I, Lady."

Mykella laughed. "You're both loyal and diplomatic." She rose. "Thank you very much for your observations. I could have seen everything you have seen and still not known what it meant."

Maeltor was on his feet before Mykella had finished the first two words. "I'm pleased that I could be of service."

"You've always been of service, Captain, long before I even knew who you were, and I do appreciate it. I won't keep you longer."

"Thank you, Lady." Maeltor flushed slightly, but bowed, then turned and left the study.

Mykella stood there for several moments, thinking.

What the captain had said about being outnumbered brought home again the fact that the Southern Guards was too small to effectively protect Lanachrona against a coalition of enemies. Had it always been that way . . . and just not recognized? Were the times changing? What could she do about it? Significantly higher tariffs would weaken the land as much as a Southern Guards that was out-numbered.

More important . . . what could she do personally?

She walked to the window, once more, and looked out, not really seeing anything.

39

Mykella looked up from the master Finance ledger as Chalmyr rapped on the door. She'd canceled the ministers' meeting. What was the point when she was acting minister for two ministries, when Areyst was gone, and Cerlyk had little to report? She'd spent the morning checking the Table in more detail, then dealing with petitions, and questions of disbursements with Haelyt, and she still felt behind.

Chalmyr opened the door slightly. "Lady-Protector, this just ar-rived by Guard messenger. It's from Arms-Commander Areyst."

"Thank you." Mykella rose and took the sealed envelope from the scrivener.

Once Chalmyr had closed the study door, she smiled. Unlike some ministers, Areyst was prompt. Here it was early on Duadi afternoon, and she had a reply to her message of the day before. Abruptly, she frowned. Was it? She was assuming . . . Quickly, she slit the envelope and extracted the single sheet, beginning to read the spare but ele-gant script.

Lady-Protector—
I am in receipt of your message of Londi, eightweek of spring, with the information on the progress of the forces departing Harmony. It would appear unlikely that those forces could reach the border of Lanachrona before the second week of summer. If you discover anything that would change that date, I would greatly appreciate knowing it.

I will be returning to Tempre on Quattri afternoon. I trust we will be able to meet then to discuss the situation. I look forward to seeing you.

He'd written that he looked forward to seeing her rather than looking forward to the meeting. Was she reading too much into the last line?

Possibly, but you'll know when he shows up. Exactly what she'd know . . . that was another question.

She replaced the message in its envelope, then slipped it into the flat and narrow left-hand drawer of the desk. Then she looked at the petitions, including several more from the Vyanhills area, doubtless from vintners who had suffered a late frost the previous spring. If they were like the other petitions, the vintners wanted their tariffs reduced. She had problems with that, because their tariffs were based on their production and income—and if they hadn't produced and sold as much, their tariffs were already going to be lower. None of them seemed to care that they still wanted the services of the Lady-Protector but not to pay as much for them. How did they expect her to provide the same services with fewer golds?

She sighed. Of course, they were like everyone else. They really didn't care about anyone else, just about what impacted them. She'd known that, but it was a truth that was driven home harder every day that she was Lady-Protector.

After a long moment, she opened the next petition and began to read.

More than a glass—and ten letters, pleas, and petitions—later, Chalmyr rapped on the study door.

"Lady-Protector, Forester Loryalt is here to see you."

"Have him come in."

Loryalt was a small and wiry man with a deeply tanned face and short-cut jet-black hair shot through with streaks of white. His bow was somehow both compact and courtly. "Lady-Protector . . . Much has changed since I departed Tempre."

Mykella gestured to the chairs. "It has indeed. Cerlyk has been most helpful in your absence, but I did wish to hear all that you learned from your tour and inspections."

"I cannot say that my news is good." Loryalt's smile was wintry. "I will provide you with a written report shortly. By Octdi, I would judge."

"Given what I have already discovered, I did not expect your news to be the best. My uncle, the would-be usurper, diverted . . . thousands of golds from the Treasury." Mykella had almost said "tens of thousands of golds," but had caught her words. "That included some of the revenues from the early cuts."

"I had recommended against those cuts. I can show you copies of my recommendations if you wish."

"Cerlyk didn't mention those." *And I wonder why not.*

"He didn't know I'd presented them to your father."

"They weren't in the records for the Forestry Ministry," Mykella said. "Or in the Lord-Protector's files."

"That may be. I did present them to your father, but he told me he needed to consult the Finance Ministry. I then received letters signed by your uncle, as Finance Minister, declaring the need for greater revenues and stating that the cuts were necessary. I have kept those copies safe."

Mykella sensed the absolute truth of the Forester's words. "I do not doubt that in the slightest. What did you do after that?"

"I told your father that he would be hard-pressed to gather much in the way of timber revenues from the lands he held for several years to come. He told me that he and the Finance Minister had discussed it and that the revenues were needed." The wintry smile reappeared. "There was little I could do then."

"What about tariffs on private timber sales?"

"There will be some. How much I cannot say, but they will be lower because so much was cut this past year from your lands that no one will cut until they have to because the prices of logs and lumber have declined so much."

Mykella kept the wince to herself and decided to change the subject. "I've received two petitions so far from landowners protesting levies you laid upon them for excessive numbers of water oaks on their lands."

Loryalt sighed and shook his head. "Every year there are some. Water oaks are called such because they resemble oaks. They are not. They also require much water, and their roots drain it from other trees . . ."

Mykella nodded although she knew much of what Loryalt was telling her.

". . . stunts forest growth around them. They grow much faster, and their wood is softer, almost as soft as that of the southern pines. For that reason, timber stands must be thinned of water oaks while they are young. No more than two trees in a hundred should be water oaks. Landowners who have excessive numbers of water oaks face higher tariffs. They complain because they said that their timber sales are already lower. They fail to take into account that with too many water oaks, less water runs off the land and into the streams and rivers, and less water means fewer crops can use the river water. Also, timber growth on lands lower on the slopes that may belong to others is hurt."

"Who determined all that?" asked Mykella, fascinated by how the trees affected the rivers, something she had not thought about.

"The Alectors of olden times, but Mykel the Great affirmed that policy soon after he became Lord-Protector. He said that not all that the Alectors had done was evil. At least, that was what my grandfather's grandfather said."

Mykella laughed softly. "Tell me more. Tell me what every Protector should know about the forests that most don't know."

Although Loryalt nodded politely, Mykella could sense the astonishment at her words.

"Lady-Protector . . . I do not know where to begin . . ."

"Wherever you wish . . . I need to know as much as I can."

Loryalt frowned. "Cerlyk said . . . it was as though you can tell if a man tells you falsehoods . . ."

"I usually can . . . Unless he lies to himself as well."

For a moment, the Forester was silent. Then he began to speak. "The forests of Corus are old, and the oldest trees are those that can live in the coldest climes . . ."

Mykella listened.

40

Tridi had not been much better than Duadi, and the first glasses of Quattri appeared to be turning out no better, although Mykella had not refrained from smiling when the Table had shown her the Northcoast forces riding through a severe rainstorm. The disturbing aspect of that had been that the storm had seemed to slow them very little. Then she had gotten a report from Nusgeyl that the additional damage to the towpath west of the Great Piers—caused by the second storm—would require more material and time to repair, even with the additional men. And almost at noon, she was reading a particularly obnoxious missive from one Seltyr Chuylt.

Lady-Protector—

It is with great regret that I send this missive to you, for I know that you must deal with many matters both significant and less significant. However, since the storms of over a week ago, the area around the villas to the southeast of that of the First Seltyr has been covered in a fog of stench arising from damages to the sewers, or possibly from deficiencies in their construction that were undiscovered until the present. . . . Even so, it would appear disconcerting, if not intolerable, that almost two tendays after this damage, some repairs and relief cannot be afforded . . .

First, Seltyr Pualavyn had tried to bribe Duchael to repair the sewers serving the Seltyrs first, and now Chuylt was complaining—but none of them thought anything really wrong with plundering the Treasury to their own benefit if they could get away with it, and all of them complained about paying tariffs. Still . . . Mykella kept on reading to the bottom of the second page, when she gathered together the sheets and the envelope and walked out into the anteroom.

"Yes, Lady?" The faintest hint of a smile lay behind Chalmyr's words.

"Please draft a long, an exceedingly long and terribly courteous reply to Seltyr Chuylt explaining that the Ministry of Highways and Rivers is working hard to make repairs and that we have employed extra laborers to do so, and that, on the advice of the First Seltyr, we are repairing those areas that affect trade and commerce first."

Chalmyr nodded as he accepted the Seltyr's complaint.

Mykella left the antechamber and made her way to the breakfast room, where she forced herself to eat a midday meal before hurrying back to her study, only to find Lord Gharyk waiting. She motioned for him to join her, then closed the door behind them and sat down behind the desk that she still felt dwarfed her. "What do you have in mind?"

"I had thought to bring this matter up in the ministers' meeting, but the more I have discovered, the more that I thought you would like to hear about it earlier and privately."

Mykella waited.

"As you know, I have not been pleased about the situation with Head Gaoler Huatyn, but the responsibility for the deaths of offenders in custody is difficult to prove." Gharyk smiled apologetically. "On the other hand, the Seltyrs are more interested in . . . the misuse of golds."

"What have you discovered?"

"Huatyn's brother has been the one supplying the gaol in Tempre with the victuals for the prisoners. Victuals might be too good a term for their food, but the costs charged to the Ministry of Justice have recently increased twofold. What is most interesting is that the number of prisoners has decreased by a third, and the costs of food in the markets is little higher. I requested an explanation for the increase in costs, and I received this in return from Head Gaoler Huatyn." Gharyk handed several sheets across the desk to Mykella.

She took them and began to read. One phrase immediately stood out.

". . . reviewing the supplying of victuals as a result of your inquiry, and I am most certain we can reduce the costs without depriving the prisoners . . ."

She raised her eyebrows. "That's almost a confession, a statement that you've caught him doing something wrong."

"He won't see it that way, but . . ."

"Keep his reply safe, and tell him you expect the quality and quantity of the fare not to decline."

"I had thought to do so."

How long could she put off dealing with the gaol problems? Mykella wondered.

After Gharyk had left, Mykella had another session with Haelyt before Chalmyr announced the arrival of Areyst, and the chief clerk slipped from the study.

Mykella stood as the Arms-Commander entered. For the briefest of instants, before he bowed, his eyes met hers, and she sensed a wave of warmth. She managed to keep a pleasant smile on her face although she felt she already showed too much.

"Lady-Protector." Areyst smiled, a touch more than pleasantly.

"Arms-Commander." She paused, then added, "I'm glad to see that you have returned safely and, I hope, without incident."

"I have, Lady, although I would wager that you have faced far, far greater dangers than have I."

"There have been a few . . . incidents." Belatedly, she motioned. "Please do sit down." She took her own seat behind the desk.

"Thank you." He laid a folder on the corner of the desk. "Here is my report on the condition of the Southern Guards and a general plan for dealing with any invaders, should it come to that. In the simplest form, we would use Commander Choalt's special company, and other companies as necessary, to harass them until they are well into Lanachrona. We would tell the people of the first three towns along the highway to leave. All are small towns . . ."

"They won't like that."

"No . . . but the terrain there is too flat and open, and that favors the larger force. The towns are not large."

Mykella understood, unhappily. "I will read it with interest. If I have questions, I will let you know." After another moment of silence, she said, "The Northcoast forces rode through a heavy rainstorm this morning. It did not seem to slow them. They appear to be north of Arwyn."

Areyst nodded. "From Arwyn to Hieron is almost two hundred

fifty vingts, and from there to Salcer more than three hundred. It will be the end of the first week of summer before they reach our border . . . if that is their intent." He smiled ironically. "I cannot imagine any other intent unless they wish to attack Prince Skrelyn."

"They would not attack him now. They have already persuaded him to join in the attack on us, with the implication that the army she and her brother command could always be used otherwise, and with the promise of wedding him. It might be an unspoken promise."

"If Chalcaer is good at battle planning and scheming, he will work to have Skrelyn's forces take the heaviest casualties."

"If he isn't, Cheleyza will advise him."

"She was wise to flee you," Areyst observed.

"Do you think I'm that evil?"

He shook his head. "You're not evil at all. If anything, you may be too even-handed. It's not evil to put an end to evil."

"If you know what evil is," she replied softly. "The problem is that everyone thinks what they do is right. Or they believe their acts are justified by what they believe others have done to them. Cheleyza believes she has every right to attack and kill me because I killed her husband and his son, and that they should have ruled Lanachrona because my father was weak and his weakness was destroying the land." She offered a sad smile. "They were right about that. His weakness was hurting Lanachrona. Every day I discover something else."

"Did they help him, or did they encourage his weaknesses?"

"You and I both know the answer to that."

"Unlike all of them, you see what is," he said quietly. "You do not shy from changing it."

"Trying to change it," she corrected.

"You have already wrought change."

Not enough but more than most want. "There will have to be more if Lanachrona is to prosper."

"Even the Seltyrs know that."

"Oh . . . they know it." She laughed softly. "They just want someone else to pay for it."

"As it ever was." His eyes rested on her.

She couldn't help but sense the admiration—and attraction, but she managed to keep her thoughts—mostly—on what she needed to say. "You will be at the season-turn ball, as my escort and heir." Mykella watched him closely as she finished speaking.

"Lady, you know that I would not be your heir . . . and not as Arms-Commander."

"We have no choice. You are the best choice for Arms-Commander, and your presence as my heir keeps the Seltyrs in line."

"Your power keeps them in line."

"It does," she admitted, "when they are near me. But they know that, should anything happen to me, you and the Southern Guards will oppose them. Your designation as my heir also protects my sisters."

"Perhaps for now." Areyst smiled. "Undercaptain Salyna is well on the way to protecting herself."

"I'm afraid she's more interested in protecting me," Mykella found herself saying. "That's not good for her."

"If people don't want to protect you . . . the ruler, then the land faces great troubles."

Mykella realized what he meant, and that, once more, warmed her. "You're kind, Arms-Commander, but I fear there are many who would not lift a finger to protect me."

"In time, there will be many."

If we survive the next year. "We can hope." She smiled at him.

For another long moment, he was silent. Then he cleared his throat. "You understand that it would not be for the best were I to remain in Tempre until season-turn. I had thought to return to Viencet on Novdi afternoon."

"I had not thought you would remain. If you could return with a company for the season-turn parade, perhaps on Septi or Octdi of tenweek."

"You think that the parade should be held as usual." Areyst's words were not a question.

"Don't you?"

"I would judge that would be for the best, but that decision is yours."

"Then we are agreed?" Mykella found her eyes looking into his, and his linked to hers.

For a moment, neither spoke.

After a silence, Areyst looked at the pile of letters and petitions on the side of her desk. "You are reading and answering all of those?"

"Who else knows what I'm thinking?"

"At the least, you should have another scrivener to write out your responses."

Half the time I don't even know what they'll be. "In time . . . in time. Right now, it's faster for me to scrawl something and have Chalmyr rewrite it diplomatically for my signature."

He nodded. "You need more assistants."

"Finding assistants I can trust would take more time than I have." *And untrustworthy assistants helped do in Father.*

"Everyone can be tempted, Lady. Fear and respect inspire trust even in those who are most tempted."

"You're saying I have to be willing to be ruthless."

"Am I telling you what you do not already know?"

She wanted to laugh, not out of humor, but because he had caught her out . . . and he'd done so gently but firmly. "You already know me well."

"I know little about you, Lady."

He might as well have said that he wanted to know more because those unspoken words hung between them. After a moment, Mykella said, "You will come to know more, Commander, whether you will it or not."

"I would will it, Lady." His eyes met hers again.

Mykella forced herself to stand, but her eyes remained on him for a long moment.

He stood quickly, and bowed. "If you have any questions"—his eyes went to the report—"you only have to let me know."

"I will."

Again . . . their eyes locked for a moment. Then he offered a pleasant smile, behind which was concern, affection, and embarrassment.

After Areyst had left, Mykella just sat behind the desk. *Was Rachylana right? Are we like cautious dustcats circling each other?* She shook her head even as she had to admit there was truth in the observation. But she wasn't ready to ask him to be a consort, and he wasn't in a position to ask her.

A quick rap on the door was followed by Rachylana's entrance. The redhead shut the door quietly but firmly, and marched up to the desk, where she sat on the corner and looked down at Mykella. "I saw the Arms-Commander leaving the palace . . ."

"You *just* happened to see him?" Mykella raised her eyebrows.

"I was looking," the redhead admitted. "I wanted to see what he did." She grinned. "He looked back toward your study several times, and he was smiling—the happy kind of smile, not the calculating kind."

"How could you tell that?"

"I can tell." Rachylana paused. "You can always tell, can't you? I'm not that good, but I could feel it."

Mykella studied her sister—and her life-thread. Was Rachylana's embedded green thread thicker—or brighter? "How did you manage to get a key to the Table-chamber lock?"

Rachylana's mouth dropped open. "How . . . ?"

"How?" Mykella's voice was cold iron.

"I just told the armorer that the palace was my responsibility and that I needed a key."

"Just?"

"Well . . . I did say that I hated to bother you for a written authorization."

"I imagine you were very persuasive."

"It wasn't that hard."

Mykella frowned. "You pressed Talent on him, didn't you?"

"Just a little . . ."

Mykella offered an exasperated sigh.

"Don't tell me you haven't done it, Mykella. Don't you dare."

Abruptly, Mykella laughed. "But only on Seltyrs, not poor armorers."

"I had to. I had to see if I had real Talent."

That, Mykella understood. "Can you see things in the Table?"

"It's like you said—only people I know. I've been very careful. Anytime I sense anything dangerous, even a hint of purple, I leave right away, and I won't go in if I feel it. That only happened once." Rachylana paused. "I can feel your shields, you know . . . or sense them. I can't do anything like that. I don't think I ever will be able to."

"You don't know that . . ."

"Mykella . . . you figured out shields in weeks. You had to have. I've had weeks, and I can sense things, and I can persuade people a little, but I'll never have the power you do."

"We'll have to see."

Rachylana shook her head. "I know what I know, and you know it, too. Don't you?"

"I know you can't right now. That could change."

"The Vedra could flow back to the Aerlal Plateau, too."

Mykella wasn't about to argue. "Don't go to the Table chamber until I can go with you."

"When? Next week?" Rachylana didn't disguise the edge in her voice.

"Tomorrow, midmorning. That's a better time to see what people are doing, and we'll see if I can help you with more."

"You will? You really will?" Rachylana paused. "Why are you changing your mind?"

"I'm not. If you can use the Table, you can help me . . . if you would. I can't spend all my time looking. Neither can you. With two of us, at different times, though . . ."

After a moment, Rachylana nodded. "That makes sense." She slipped off the corner of the desk. "When are you going to ask Areyst?"

"I don't know."

Rachylana shook her head again. "At least you're admitting that you will."

"Not until after we deal with Cheleyza."

"Why?"

"Because I have to prove that I can rule through trouble without a man at my side." *Because no one will believe I can unless I do.*

The redhead nodded slowly. "You're probably right about that."

Why does it have to be that way?

That question lingered in Mykella's mind long after Rachylana had left the study.

41

At midmorning on Quinti, rather than earlier in the day, as she often did, Mykella went to the Table chamber, this time with Rachylana and by foot. Rachylana wore heavy riding clothes, as Mykella had requested. She let Rachylana unlock the door but let her own Talent enter before her. There was no feeling of purpleness beyond that of the Table, and she stepped into the chamber, followed by Rachylana.

Once they stood before the Table, Mykella said, "Try to find Cheleyza."

The mists appeared, then swirled away, revealing Cheleyza riding along an avenue, her brother besides her, with people lined up on each side, between the gutters lining the eternastone roadway and the shops fronting the sidewalks.

"That has to be Arwyn," observed Mykella. "They can't have reached Salcer by now."

"How good is that?"

"It gives Areyst more time to train the recruits and Salyna more time with the auxiliaries, and that will free more guards. Now . . . see if you can find someone you know that I don't."

Rachylana looked down into the mirrored surface of the Table, and the mists appeared, then slowly cleared to show a Southern Guard undercaptain riding along a dusty road behind two guards, and beside a squad leader.

"Who is that?" asked Mykella.

"Undercaptain Muirgun. I met him once with Berenyt." The image faded as Rachylana turned. "There aren't that many people I've met that you don't know."

Mykella nodded. "Let's see what Commander Demyl is doing."

The commander was in the white uniform, standing beside two other officers. All three were looking down at a map table.

"Where is he?" asked Rachylana.

"Southgate, from the uniform."

"Traitor . . ." murmured Rachylana.

After that, the two quickly scanned others, including Maxymt, who was walking a lane in a small hamlet, and Khanasyl, who was talking to two other Seltyrs Mykella did not recognize in his elaborate study. Mykella avoided looking for Areyst.

When the Table returned to its mirror finish, Rachylana turned to Mykella. "You didn't look for Areyst."

"With you at my shoulder?" That wasn't the reason, but the fact that Areyst would be hard to see. Mykella didn't want to explain that yet.

Rachylana raised her eyebrows.

"Let me have some illusion of privacy," added Mykella.

"For now."

"Longer than that, please."

Rachylana smiled, then asked, "How do you use the Tables to travel?"

"I started by standing on the Table and thinking about the darkness beneath. I found myself dropping through the Table into the darkness. I was scared, but I focused on one of the faint markers—they're colors in the distance. I tried several of the markers. The first was Blackstear, and it was winter. I almost froze to death before I got back. I don't know where all of the others are, but one is where the building collapsed over the Table. I got a lump on my head there. Another one might be under a hill or mountain because there are empty tunnels but no way out, not that I could find—"

"You explored these all alone?"

"What was I supposed to do? The soarer said I had to master my Talent, or the Ifrits would come through the Tables and take over Corus again." Mykella didn't want to talk about the foolish things she'd done. "Have you tried anything except looking through the Table?"

Rachylana looked down.

Mykella waited.

"I tried standing on it and thinking about going somewhere. Nothing happened."

Should you really try to teach her more? Mykella had asked Rachylana to wear riding clothes for that reason, but she still wondered if it were wise to try. After a moment, she put out a hand and vaulted onto the Table, then gestured for Rachylana to join her.

The redhead clambered onto the Table, less gracefully than Mykella. "Now what?"

"Hold my hand. I'm going to try to take you to Blackstear. It's cold, but it should be safe. Think of the darkness and of a black triangle marker."

Mykella grasped her sister's hand and concentrated on the darkness and upon the dark marker that was Blackstear . . . and she was in the depths . . . with no sense of Rachylana. At the same time, she could sense that the yellow and orange marker that was Lysia was "flashing," enough to catch her attention when she hadn't even been seeking it.

Immediately, she focused on the blueness of the Tempre Table and found herself standing beside her sister on top of the Table.

"You . . . you just slipped away," Rachylana finally said.

"I'm sorry. I was trying to get you to sense what it was like."

"I just felt a wave of green and black . . . and you were gone."

"That green and black is what carries you."

Rachylana shivered. "Salyna was right."

"What do you mean?"

"Sometimes, you scare me, Mykella. You step onto the Table, then turn into a mist and slide into the stone . . . and you take it like it was nothing at all."

"It takes getting used to. The first time it happened, I felt smothered by stone, and I wouldn't try it again for days."

"But you did."

"I felt like I had no choice. I had to do something."

Rachylana shook her head. "I don't think . . . I don't know."

Mykella eased off the Table. "I'm not about to push you. I hope that gives you a better feel. Just don't try it if there's any hint of purpleness around."

"I won't. I promise."

"I have to go. Something's happening in Lysia."

"Why do you have to go? That's on the other side of Corus."

"Because if the Ifrits get a foothold, they can spread across the land using the Tables. They're weaker when they first arrive." That was a guess on Mykella's part, but so far it had seemed to be true.

Mykella pulled her gloves out of the pocket of her riding jacket and slipped them on. She hadn't wanted to wear them when she'd been trying to see if Rachylana could use the Table because she'd thought that holding her sister's hand, flesh to flesh, might help. Then she vaulted back onto the Table, not that she had to, and sought the deeper darkness.

As she emerged in the Table chamber in Lysia, she felt as though she had to break through a wall of purple—without her shields, because she had never been able to carry them and use the darkness—or the Tables—to travel. She took two unsteady steps on the stone flooring before she caught her balance. She immediately began to re-create her shields, even before she caught sight of the massive black-haired and white-faced Ifrit standing on the Table, as if he had just emerged from the depths—or from Efra.

The Ifrit turned, still standing on the Table, and leveled a massive pistol-like weapon at Mykella. The bluish flame-bolt slammed into her incomplete shields and threw her—and her shield—against the wall of the Table chamber. Her feet went out from under her, and her head cracked against something.

Another weapon-bolt struck her shields, and fire burned through her shoulder.

. . . die . . . vileness . . . Talent bitch . . .

Mykella didn't move, but concentrated on strengthening her shields and trying to draw power from the green beneath. A second bolt from the pistol flared away from her shields, and the fire that penetrated was more like a brief flash of pain.

As the green rose around Mykella, the Ifrit's face contorted, and a pair of purplish arms began to rise from the Table.

Mykella stood but did not move forward, instead concentrating on sending a green Talent probe toward the nodes of the advancing massive purple arms. She had trouble finding the nodes, and the arms were pressing against her shields when she managed to use the Talent probe to twist apart one node . . . and then the other. The arms sagged, then collapsed into purple dust that vanished.

Two more blue flame-bolts slammed into Mykella's shields, but she scarcely felt them as she Talent-reached for the Ifrit's life-thread node. He began to fade, as if he were trying to use the Table, but he wasn't quick enough. Mykella ripped his node apart, and another cloud of purple dust flared and vanished.

Mykella could sense that the Table was still pulsing, more brightly than ever.

Is that a sign that another Ifrit is about to arrive? She wondered, because she'd never sensed that sort of pulsing when she'd used the Tables. *Or is it only when an Ifrit is coming from another world? But why would that be?*

Mykella waited . . . and waited.

The flashed purple-pink pulses grew shorter and more intense, as well as so frequent that the "light" was almost continuous.

She had no idea how long she waited although she had to flex her knees so they wouldn't stiffen.

Then another shadowy and massive figure appeared, beginning to solidify upon the Table. Mykella could see what looked to be a weapon in the Ifrit's still-indistinct hand and immediately began to extend a Talent probe.

Just as the violet and green of tunic and trousers came into sharp focus, Mykella finally sensed the life-thread and node—and struck.

The Ifrit barely had time to look surprised before she staggered forward and flared into purplish dust.

Mykella frowned as she stood alone in the Table chamber, knowing something was different but not what. Then she realized what it was—the Table had stopped pulsing, and had reverted to a dullish purple-pink.

There aren't any more coming. After a moment, she amended that thought. *Not yet.*

She waited a bit longer before reaching out to the darkness and sending herself back to Tempre.

She'd barely appeared in the Table chamber in the depths of the palace when Rachylana blurted, "Are you all right? You were gone almost half a glass. I tried to see what you were doing in Lysia."

"Did you see anything?" Mykella's voice was ragged.

"Nothing. Well, there were flashes of green and purple and blue intersecting, then there was only green."

"There were two Ifrits, and they appeared on the Table with weapons ready. I was late, and the first one was already there. That took longer."

"They're dead?"

Mykella nodded.

"Just like that."

Just like that? Mykella said nothing.

Rachylana stepped forward and looked at Mykella, closely. "I'm sorry. You've got more welts, but they're not as bad as before."

"I'll also have a bump on my head. A weapon pushed me into a stone wall."

"Are you all right?" Rachylana asked again.

"I'll be sore in a few places, but I'll be fine."

"Do you know why I couldn't see you?"

"The stronger the Talent, from what I can tell, the less the Table shows."

"The . . . Ifrit . . . it had Talent? I couldn't see anything."

"I don't know if they have Talent themselves or it's part of the weapons and tools they carry. Maybe it's both, but they can use Talent as a weapon."

"And you stopped it?

Mykella nodded. "Both of them."

"Will there be more?"

"Not for a while, I think." Mykella tried to moisten dry lips. "We can leave the Table. I need something to eat and to drink before I go back to the study."

Rachylana was very quiet on the walk back up to the top level of the palace, for which Mykella was thankful. She had the feeling that the next time the Ifrits tried, they'd bring more and better weapons if they could. She also had the feeling that they'd be coming back to the Table at Lysia.

The rest of Quinti was a long day, one filled with details, and included two meetings with the clerks in the Ministry of Highways and Rivers and with reading and studying Areyst's report and general plan for dealing with the forces of the coastal princes. In addition, Mykella approved more golds for sewer and towpath repairs, gratefully received the news that some hundred golds in assorted barge tariffs had trickled into the Treasury . . . and read more petitions and requests. When she checked the Table later, it showed nothing new or interesting although the Northcoast forces were riding through mist or fog.

42

As was happening all too often, Mykella awoke on Sexdi bruised in places she didn't remember bruising, and with a throbbing headache, one that she hoped a large mug of tea would soothe to some extent. She made her way to the breakfast room, where, from the crumbs on one side of the table, Salyna had left earlier, and asked Muergya for a pot of strong tea. She was sipping the last of the first mug, waiting for her breakfast, when Rachylana appeared.

"You look purple and purple," offered the redhead cheerfully.

"Thank you," replied Mykella dryly.

"Do you have any other—" Rachylana broke off as Muergya appeared with a platter that she set before Mykella.

"Tea and whatever you fixed for her, please," requested Rachylana.

The serving girl nodded and slipped toward the stairs down to the lower-level kitchens.

"You were saying?" prompted Mykella.

"Whether you have any other Ifrit problems and whether you can recover before something else happens."

"The Ifrits will be back. They'll bring stronger weapons. Much stronger, the soarer told me. I don't know when, but it will likely be at the worst possible time."

"Can I do anything else to help?"

Mykella had thought about that. "Yes, you can. Would you be willing to check the Table several times a day? And let me know if you see anything of note . . . or danger?"

Rachylana smiled. "I'd be happy to."

"But don't go in there if there's any hint of strong purple. Just let me know."

"Do you want me to keep some sort of notes?"

"If you would . . . about Cheleyza and any of the Seltyrs here."

"I can do that."

"How are the undress uniforms coming?"

Rachylana grimaced. "We . . . we have some things to work out. Salyna thinks all women should look boyish."

"And she thinks that you want to make them all look too . . . womanly?"

"Something like that."

"Split the difference. They shouldn't be mistaken for boys, and they shouldn't turn the Guards' thoughts to their sex."

"We agreed on that, already," said Rachylana. "The problem is that we have different ideas on what's boyish and what's . . . womanly."

"Go more toward boyish than you'd like, but not so much as Salyna wants."

"Can I tell her that?"

"You can tell her I suggested that, and if you two don't agree on something, I'll decide." Mykella smiled, knowing that neither of her sisters cared much for her fashion sense or taste.

"We'll work it out."

"Good."

After breakfast, Mykella skipped using the Table and headed to her study, glad that her headache was only dull pressure that seemed to be easing.

"You might wish to read this first, Lady," offered Chalmyr, as Mykella stepped into the anteroom. "It came by courier from Southgate."

Trouble of some sort. "Thank you. I will."

When she entered the study, she found another nine missives stacked on the left side of her desk. She ignored those and slit open the envelope that bore a white and black wax seal. She smoothed the two sheets and began to read.

Lady-Protector—
Greetings to you from the Seltyrs' Council of Southgate, and with our best wishes for a continuation of the warm and open relations that have characterized the interactions between Southgate and Lanachrona over the past several decades . . .

Warm and open relations? The very words suggested to Mykella that her predecessors had been too generous in dealing with the Seltyrs of Southgate. She continued reading.

. . . and our hope that rumors that have recently reached Southgate are distortions and not rooted in fact or policy. Some have suggested that Lanachrona is embarking upon an expansion of its ability to wage war and that excessive tariffs are contemplated in anticipation of such action. The Council has disparaged such reports, believing that no ruler would embark upon such a course immediately upon ascension to authority, but would appreciate greatly your confirmation that the continuation of past policies and practices is indeed your determination so that such unfounded rumors can be expeditiously laid to rest.

Trade and commerce, particularly between Lanachrona and Southgate, have laid much of the foundation for the long and peaceful state of affairs in the west of Corus for many years, and we trust that you share our belief that any change in the terms of such trade would be adverse to all and perhaps even to peace and stability in Corus. Certainly, we of Southgate are pledged to continue the past policies, and we reaffirm that determination as proof of our good-will and friendship, and trust that you will do the same . . .

The remainder of the communication comprised flowery nothings. Mykella read the missive again. The second reading left her more uneasy, and she stood and walked to the study door and out into the anteroom.

"Chalmyr . . . would you see if Lord Gharyk and Forester Loryalt would both be available in a glass?"

"Yes, Lady."

Mykella returned to her study and began to read through the other missives. She'd finished three when the door opened, and Salyna stepped inside. She wore almost-shapeless gray trousers and tunic. "Do you have a moment, Mykella?"

"At least half a glass. What is it?"

Salyna closed the door and sat down in the chair nearest the corner of Mykella's desk. The circles under her eyes remained dark, and her hair had been cut to neck length.

"Your hair's shorter," observed Mykella.

"Longer, and it gets in the way. Rachylana would say that I'll never attract a match that way, but by the time any suitor is ready to come here, I'll have time for it to grow. Besides, he'd better appreciate me for more than my hair. That's the smallest of my problems."

"What can I do?"

"One of the small problems—the frigging undress uniforms. We need to decide, so that they'll be ready when the training's over. Rachylana wants the women to look like Seltyr's daughters playing at being guards, and I think they ought to look like guards . . ."

"She mentioned that this morning."

"What did you tell her?"

"I told her the uniforms ought look more boyish or masculine than she wants, but not so boyish as you want, and that if you two can't agree, I'd decide. Has she talked to you today?"

Salyna shook her head. "Would you really decide?"

"Only if you two can't work it out." *And I'd rather not.* "Is there anything else you need?"

"Not so far. Commander Areyst has been very helpful since he returned. He did send Bursuin to Viencet."

"He was the one you disarmed in sparring? Was he being difficult?"

"More like quietly making things harder to accomplish. He cited rules that hadn't been used or enforced in decades. Even Zhulyn was rolling his eyes."

"I suspect Areyst transferred him to work under Commander Choalt. Did he?"

"That was what Zhulyn said. How did you know?" There was an edge to Salyna's words.

"I didn't. I guessed. From Commander Areyst's reports, I gathered that Commander Choalt doesn't put up with nonsense." *And Jeraxylt said so seasons ago.*

Salyna stood. "I need to go. Thank you for talking to Rachylana. I probably won't see you until Novdi or Decdi."

Less than a quarter glass after Salyna had left, Gharyk and Loryalt appeared together, both bowing and taking seats before the desk.

Mykella handed the missive from the Council of Southgate to Gharyk. "I've just received this. I'd like each of you to read it. Then I'd like your thoughts."

Gharyk read through the two pages and handed them to Loryalt. The Justice Minister's brow furrowed as he waited for the Forester to finish.

Loryalt finally handed the sheets back to Mykella, then looked to Gharyk. "You're better with the fancy words."

Gharyk cleared his throat. "They're aware that they've received favorable treatment in terms of tariffs and road charges, and they don't want things to change."

"Road charges?"

"They charge a silver a wagon at their way stations in Zalt, or the two outside of Southgate, and any outland trader or factor who doesn't have a countersigned waybill faces a gold in fines and the loss of a fifth part of his wares or merchandise."

Mykella frowned. "A silver isn't much at all, and there aren't that many Seltyrs who make the trips. Why would they bother?" She paused. "Do they require a copy of the waybill?"

"I believe so."

"From their own traders coming to Lanachrona as well?"

Gharyk nodded.

"Is there a fine or penalty for misstatements on the waybill?"

"It used to be a gold or a twentieth part of the goods, whichever was greater."

"So if the Council studied and added up all the items on the waybills, they would know what goods came from Lanachrona and what we needed from Southgate. Also . . . they could, if they wished, dispute waybills and punish Seltyrs or factors individually."

"I suppose so," said Gharyk.

"We had some trouble with hardwoods five years back," interjected Loryalt. "Landowner on our side of the Coastal Range ran wagons down there. They claimed he understated the number of logs when he got to Southgate. They took a wagon's worth and burned the logs."

"Why did they burn them? Do you know?" asked Gharyk.

Loryalt shook his head.

Mykella handed the sheets to Gharyk. "I'd like you to compose a reply that thanks the Council of Southgate for their concerns and assures them that we will keep their words in mind, and that we will do our best to follow the examples set by Southgate, although some changes might be necessary, given our differences in geography and size. Please do not write it so concisely as I have said and make it far more flowery and elaborate."

A faint smile crossed the lips of the Justice Minister. "I will endeavor to draft a document that meets your requirements, Lady-Protector."

Mykella stood. "Thank you both."

After they left, she pondered the matter of the burning of the logs. *Why would they burn good hardwoods when they could sell them for golds, or even silvers . . . or ship them to Dramur?*

Once again, each tenday brought a new conundrum of some sort—if not more.

Areyst was scheduled to arrive at the second glass of the afternoon, but a good half glass before that, Mykella was standing at the window; looking eastward in the direction of the Southern Guards, not that she could see the complex from her study windows.

She walked back to her desk and reread the last petition, one unlike all the others.

> Most graceous Lady Protectir—
> Please look to the towpath drovers. We get but a copper for ten vints, and it takes two tendays from Hieron for two of us. Drovers on the coast get a copper for five vints. Please help.

Under the shaky script was an "X."

Mykella couldn't tell from the missive whether each drover got a copper for ten vingts or whether the pair split the fee. Either way, it seemed a poor wage, but she was well aware that she didn't know enough to judge just how poor.

She set the letter down and walked back to the window. Still no sign of Areyst.

When she finally saw him ride into the front courtyard of the palace, she forced herself to walk to her desk and sit down. Even so, it felt like almost a glass before the study door opened, and he walked in and bowed.

"Lady-Protector."

"Commander." Mykella gestured to the chairs.

Areyst took the center seat and sat erect, not on the front edge, as did Maeltor, but not all the way back, as did the indulgent Seltyrs. His green eyes seemed more intense as they rested on her, and the hint of a smile lurked in his eyes and the corners of his mouth.

Mykella sensed his amusement but not the reason why. Finally, she spoke. "I read your report and recommendations for dealing with the coastal forces."

Areyst nodded politely but did not speak.

"You didn't say anything," she finally said

"You did not ask me anything, Lady." The hint of amusement remained behind his eyes.

Mykella wanted to tell him that he was being impossible, but that would have made her seem too . . . predictably feminine. "You're right. I didn't. I was offering you the chance to say anything you might wish, though."

"Do you have any questions about the strategy? Was there anything you found unclear?"

"I did not find anything unclear." And she hadn't. Areyst wrote clearly. "I do have some questions. Why do you think that the coastal forces will advance quickly?"

"There is nothing worth taking with a large force until they near Viencet, and even if they ransack the three towns near the border, they will obtain few supplies. They may choose to hold back the main body and take the first towns with a company or two, then press on with all forces. In that case, Commander Choalt's special company will deal their advance forces heavy losses, and they will bring all their forces to bear. That is why we will move into position well west of Viencet."

"Your maps show that there is a wide flat valley from the east end of the foothills of the Coastal Range and that it stretches some twenty vingts to the low hills separating the first valley from the one that holds Viencet. You plan to attack partway into the hills just west of Viencet, not at either end?"

"They will expect an attack to be more likely at either end. Also, if necessary, there is a back road that returns to Viencet. It is shorter than the highway, but steeper. We can reach the attack point without being seen by scouts, whereas the main highway is open to view for vingts. We could regroup by the back road as well, if necessary."

"How far is the attack hill from the highway, and how far is the highway from the center of the hills south of the Vedra and north of the highway?"

Areyst frowned, and his eyes narrowed. "The hill where we would wait and begin the attack is less than a half vingt from the highway. The southern rises of the hills to the north end perhaps two vingts from the highway, no more than three."

"Could you attack from the northern hills?"

"One could attack from anywhere, but we would lose all surprise. The hill I have chosen looks as though it is unsuitable for an attack."

"What if they discover your force?"

"They would likely stop and take position on one of the hills to the west. Then they would decide how to attack us directly because they could not advance toward Viencet or Tempre without moving into a position that would favor us. If they take a hill position, then Commander Choalt's special company has some tactics and devices that are suitable for harassment without great losses on our part."

"You plan to harry and harass to reduce their forces as much as possible before you fight a pitched battle."

"Yes, Lady."

"What of supplies . . . ?"

Mykella discovered she did have more than a few questions, and it was almost a glass later when she finally said, "I have no more questions right now."

Areyst smiled. "You asked more questions than most of my majers."

"They know more than I do."

"Many of your questions were better. I will have to consider changes because of points you raised."

"You flatter me, Commander." Mykella managed to keep her tone light.

"I know that you know when I do not tell the truth. I dare not flatter you falsely."

"Tell me, Commander. Are you good at knowing when your officers or men are not telling the truth or the whole truth?"

Areyst shrugged, an almost-ironic gesture. "So it is said, and I would like to think so, but thinking so might well let a man deceive himself."

Or a woman. Mykella laughed, softly. "That's a very good observation. I'll have to keep it in mind. You're leaving on Novdi, you said?"

"Yes, Lady, if that is agreeable to you."

"It is agreeable, but only if . . . you make a last visit here before you depart." There was the briefest pause before she added, "I would like to know your thoughts and any changes you may have considered before you return to Viencet."

"Would a glass before noon on Novdi be suitable, Lady?"

"It would."

"Then I look forward to seeing you then."

Mykella stood, reluctantly, she realized, and while Areyst rose quickly, she sensed his reluctance as well. "Good day, Commander. Take care." The last words were fractionally softer.

"As I can, Lady. Thank you." He bowed, then straightened.

Their eyes met . . . and neither spoke.

Mykella tried not to swallow.

Areyst inclined his head slightly, again, then turned and left the study.

Mykella looked at the door as it closed. *You might as well have blurted out that you're interested in him.*

But she couldn't help but smile as she walked to the window so that she could watch him ride from the palace.

43

Septi morning turned out to be comparatively quiet. That gave Mykella time to make changes to Gharyk's reply to the Council of Southgate and have Chalmyr redraft it in his elegant hand. She signed and sealed the response, and had it dispatched to the Southgate courier who had been quartered in the Southern Guard barrack for two days, awaiting a reply.

After that, she read through the handful of petitions, the number of which seemed to be dropping off, and drafted short instructions on how to answer each to Chalmyr. Then she did her daily survey of the master ledger and made a quick visit to the main level of the palace to check on the clerks of the Ministry of Highways and Rivers, wishing that Zylander had been able to become minister sooner.

Later that morning, she studied Areyst's plans and maps—trying to calculate how close she might be able to get to the battle area through the dark ways. She'd looked at the maps so many times, but just before she was about to close the folder, she paused and turned to the map that showed all of Corus under the Alectors. There was something about it that bothered her, more than a little. Outside of the vanished cities of Elcien and Faitel—*destroyed in the Cataclysm with weapons that Ifrits might bring back*, she worried—none of the cities were all that close together. Even the distances between smaller towns were not insignificant. Some of the distances were vast indeed, such as the nearly one thousand vingts from Dereka to Dekhron. Without the rivers and the eternastone highways, she doubted that there would have ever been any travel, trade, or communication between Lanachrona and Deforya. Even with Chalcaer and Cheleyza wanting to conquer Lanachrona, they'd have to ride their forces five hundred vingts to reach Salcer and another three-hundred-odd vingts to the borders.

Had the Alectors located all the cities so far apart to make wars or conflicts between lands difficult? All the lands had been one under the Alectors. It had to have been for another reason.

Was that distance why Father and Joramyl let the Southern Guards dwindle in size, believing no one would ride an invading force that far?

She shook her head. Speculating on why matters had come to be would have to wait.

Septi afternoon, after eating as much as she could, she repaired to her quarters, where she donned her nightsilk riding jacket and gloves. Then she reached for the greenish darkness far beneath the palace and slipped downward through the stone to the depths.

In moments that seemed endless, she was sightless and in chill, trying to sense where she was as she moved westward beneath the ground. When she thought she was near a point north of Viencet, she eased her way upward into the sunlight. She emerged in a rocky clearing, surrounded by large-trunked pines, startling a hare that bounded away and barely evaded a fox that had been stalking it. The air was clean, and cool, with a hint of dampness that suggested recent rain.

From the clearing, on the north side of a hill, Mykella could see nothing but tree trunks and, through them in places, tree-covered hills and rocky outcroppings. So she strengthened her grasp on the darkness and slowly lifted herself upward until she was above the treetops. She looked northward, and finally caught a glint of water, then a bit more of a line of silver that had to be the Vedra. To the northeast was a narrow valley and a clumping of houses that she thought she recognized although she didn't immediately recall the name of the hamlet.

Turning, she began to move southward and uphill until she hovered above the crest of a ridge that held more rocks than trees. To the south was another line of hills. The highest point on the hill directly south looked to be somewhat more than a vingt away. To the southeast, over the hills before her, she could make out the outlines of a town. From her previous explorations, she recognized it as Viencet. She turned her eyes to the southwest, trying to find the line of hills that Areyst had mentioned and the map in the battle plan had shown.

Slowly, she moved southward until she hovered above the southern line of hills. While the strength of the darkness below had weakened, she could still draw enough to hold her height above the trees and survey the land. To the southwest, she could make out rolling rises, rather than what she would have called hills. South of the hill below her, the forest thinned to scattered pines and red clay and rock and high grasses and bushes. A vingt or so of mostly wild grasses stretched from the foot of the hill to the eternastone highway. On the south side of the highway, another half vingt of grasses and bushes led to the rolling rises described by Areyst.

At least, the locale seemed to fit the area Areyst had described.

And what exactly will you do when the time comes?

Mykella had no idea, only that she needed to be there. She just hoped she could figure out how to be effective . . . somehow.

As she thought about returning to Tempre, a shadow passed over her, then something slammed into the back of her head, leaving a line of fire across her skull. She threw up both arms and hands and turned, barely warding off a large iron gray bird—a ferrohawk—as another swept down and past her. The first ferrohawk climbed and dived back at her, but the nightsilk of her jacket sleeve kept the bird's claws from ripping her skin. Then the second bird climbed above her and came down in a high-speed, high-angled stoop. Mykella blocked the attack with her arm, but the impact was enough to jolt her, and the ferrohawk tumbled away before regaining stability.

Flailing her arms to keep the two away—doubtless a nesting pair that saw her as a predatory intruder—she slowly descended between the trees, mostly pines, toward the darkness.

As she slipped downward through the stone toward the chill, she couldn't help but think about the ludicrousness—and seriousness—of what had just happened. The ferrohawks had brought home—again—her vulnerability when "soaring" because she couldn't soar or use the dark paths and maintain shields at the same time.

The chill of the depths numbed some of the pain—until she emerged in her quarters.

Cleaning the wounds in her scalp and getting the bleeding to stop took almost half a glass. Then she searched for and finally found an unguent that was supposed to keep shallow wounds from festering. Applying it was more than awkward, because she had to hold a mirror with one hand and angle it so she could use the dressing-table mirror to see where to place the unguent. After that she tried to get the greasy oiliness out of her hair, except where it was near the claw marks, and comb it so that the wounds weren't that obvious.

She also checked her arm, more than certain that, despite the nightsilk, there would be bruising by the morrow. All in all, it took her more time to deal with the result of the ferrohawks' territorial protectiveness than it had to seek out and scout Areyst's planned battle positions.

Is that a lesson of some sort? Or just the perverseness of the world?

She hoped she had the courage of the ferrohawks when she faced adversaries of greater power and size.

Finally, she finished cleaning herself up and made her way from her quarters back to the formal study and the waiting missives, ledgers, and mounting claims on her Treasury.

44

As Salyna had predicted, Mykella did not see her youngest sister on either Septi or Octdi . . . or at breakfast on Novdi morning. Surprisingly, Rachylana was already seated in the breakfast room when Mykella entered.

"You're early," offered Mykella as she took her place.

"I couldn't sleep."

Muergya brought two platters, setting one in front of each sister, then returned with a pot of tea for Mykella and a basket of warm bread. She frowned as she stepped back from Mykella.

Mykella could sense her concern and suspected the serving girl had glimpsed the marks in her scalp even though she'd tried to comb her hair over them.

"When did you last check the Table?" asked Mykella, pouring her tea.

"Late yesterday afternoon. Cheleyza and her forces were still riding through forests. They hadn't reached that part of the highway where it goes through the Coastal Range north of the River Vedra. Anyway, the maps say that it does, and they're riding through forested low hills." Rachylana took a small morsel of a large egg, a duck egg, making a face as she swallowed it.

Mykella looked at the duck egg, boiled, and took a bite out of one of the ham strips, followed by a sip of her tea. "What else?"

"Khanasyl has been meeting with a number of Seltyrs. Most of them I don't recognize. None of them look happy. I can't find any sign of that fat lizard Maxymt."

"When you can't find people, it's because you don't know them, or they have Talent, or they're dead. You were able to see him before, weren't you?"

"For the past few days. He was always looking over his shoulder."

"Then he's most likely dead. What about Commander Demyl?"

"He's still in Southgate. He doesn't look happy. I don't think he's a commander there."

"I'd doubt it. He might be a majer, but that would gall him."

"Good." Rachylana reached for the bread.

Mykella handed her the basket.

"You got hurt again, didn't you?"

"Why do you say that?"

"The way you moved your arm."

"It's bruised, and I've got some other scratches. I interrupted a pair of nesting ferrohawks. They weren't happy."

Rachylana shook her head. "No one would ever guess what you do and where you go."

"I hope not. How are arrangements for the ball coming?"

"As well as one could hope, with no envoys or distinguished visitors in attendance."

Before long, Mykella finished and made her way to her formal study, where, for once, all that waited her was a pair of petitions and a report from Engineer Nusgeyl indicating that the western sewer repairs were completed and that the towpath and eastern sewer repairs would be finished by nineweek—provided there were no immoderate storms.

Promptly, a glass before noon, Areyst stepped into Mykella's study.

"Lady-Protector."

"Commander . . ."

"As you requested, I am here before departing for Viencet." After straightening from his bow, Areyst's eyes caught and held Mykella's.

She did not look away but concentrated on sensing what he felt. Then she had to struggle not to flush. "Commander . . ." she said gently, gesturing toward the chairs.

"You did request my presence," he said with a smile after sitting.

"I did." She paused. "You may understand why. Tell me about your upbringing."

Areyst nodded, almost solemnly, yet he seemed relieved by her question as he began to speak. "I was born and raised in Krost. There my family had created a glassblowing shop and later a factorage. The crystal sands are most suitable for all manner of glass. I am the youngest of three, and the least suited to either glassblowing or factoring. I found I lacked the . . . ability to create beauty in molten glass. Oh, I could turn out quite workmanlike bowls and tumblers, and even goblets—often perfect copies if I had a model to follow. But my own creations were uninspired. I was similarly unsuited for haggling over the costs of sands or colorants or for knowing when to hold fast against a determined bargainer."

At that pause, Mykella interjected. "That seems surprising. You read people well."

"I should not have said 'knowing.' I always knew exactly what someone would pay or not pay. What I did not know, for I was young, was that it is never wise to push for the very last copper. In time, people come to hate and avoid you, and it became clear to my parents and brothers that no one would bargain with me. They would leave if they had to deal with me, or find an excuse to talk to anyone else." Areyst's smile was almost one of embarrassment.

"How did you come to join the Southern Guards?"

"I was good at fighting, even as a boy. My father paid for me to be trained as a rider, a marksman, and with the use of blades. He arranged for me to be given a provisional commission as an undercaptain. He said—if I had to fight—that I should be an officer."

"You have done well."

Areyst laughed. "It was not always so. I served two tours as a provisional undercaptain. Had I not been foolish enough to lead a squad against Ongelyan nomads who threatened a local factor in Indyor, I would probably have been sent back to Krost in disgrace."

"A local factor?"

"His youngest daughter had married the captain."

Mykella laughed. "And that made your commission permanent?"

"It did. It also resulted in my spending almost ten years in outposts subject to raiders and nomads, with a few seasons in Viencet and here in Tempre."

"You have no sisters?"

"One older sister. She married a vintner and lives in Vyan. Once in a while, I get a bottle of very good wine."

"You must have other talents besides reading people and being an outstanding officer."

"My talents in the arts are the same as those in glassblowing. I cannot write verse. I write directly. Too directly, Commander Choalt has said. Nor can I sculpt or paint. I can use tools but to repair and replace."

"Men will follow you," Mykella observed.

"They will. They know I do my best for them. Good soldiers appreciate that."

"And you make sure that the poor ones do not remain in the Guards."

"First, I try to make them into good soldiers. Sometimes, I have succeeded." After the briefest pause, Areyst asked, "And what of you, Lady-Protector?"

"I am not artistic. I have a head for figures. You know that."

"A very good head for numbers. You were correct about the use of rifles because of the powder shortages you deduced."

"Thank you."

"You also do not like manipulating people or letting others take the blame for your acts."

"And how did you deduce that, Commander?"

"When you had your brother escort you to see the Seltyrs, and I was about to remonstrate with him, you stepped in. You urged your mount forward so that I could not even speak directly to him."

Mykella didn't recall going quite that far. "I didn't want to manipulate him, but there wasn't any other way to find out how much was being stolen."

"How much was stolen?"

Mykella shrugged. "So far, we've been able to track close to ten thousand golds. My calculations suggest that more than twice that amount is missing, but it's difficult to prove you've lost what never reached the Treasury. We've recovered less than ten thousand."

"How much of that, if I may ask, have you spent personally?"

Mykella frowned.

"It is impertinent, I know, but if you would indulge me . . ." His voice was soft.

Since Mykella could discern no calculation, she finally answered. "I gave a hundred golds to Salyna to pay for uniforms for the auxiliaries, and I will be paying for a ball gown because both my sisters insist that I need a new gown for the season-turn ball."

Areyst laughed, warmly and openly. "You worry about buying one gown in a season, as Lady-Protector, when Lady Cheleyza must have bought fifty in a year as the wife of the Finance Minister. That says much."

"Oh? And what does it say?" Mykella regretted the words even as she spoke. "Please don't answer that. I shouldn't have asked."

"You're ashamed to ask a compliment of me? You, who have risked your life for Lanachrona more times in a season than most guards do in their entire lives?" There was both admiration and sadness behind his words.

"How do you know that?"

"I have seen the signs, Lady, and I have listened. I have seen bruises that powder did not cover, and soreness and stiffness that care and posture did not completely disguise. I know you have ridden roads and byways that no Protector has seen in generations. You have dared depths and places that would have killed others and that you did so not knowing if you would prevail."

"And there were too many times where I overestimated my abilities, Commander. That was not courage, but false pride and stupidity."

"Saying so is honesty, my Lady."

The way he said those words shocked her because she realized that, even if she had not chosen him in her mind, she still would have been his Lady. For a moment, she could say nothing. "You are more kind than I can say. Far more kind."

He shook his head. "I strive to be honest and fair, but few would ever call me kind."

He believed that, Mykella realized. "Few are likely to call me such, either. In that, we may well be alike."

"Perhaps in more ways than that," he replied.

"Perhaps." She smiled, then let the expression fade, with regret, she hoped. "I must raise a question about your plan before you depart."

"Yes?"

"I noticed that there is an expanse of grass to the north of the highway opposite where you plan to stage your attack."

"You worry the enemy could flee through those grasses to the woods? Or to flank us? Did you walk the grasses?"

"No. I saw them from the hillside above."

"You would find that those grasses conceal very uneven ground. There are gullies and ravines that one cannot see until it is too late— even when mounted."

"The entire grassy area is like that?"

"Some of it is worse. Much worse."

"I should have known you would have considered that."

"How would you know without asking? I am pleased that you asked."

And he was, she felt. *Why? Because he wasn't looking for blind approval?* She smiled again. "I need to ask. There is much I must learn, and little time to do so."

"Is that not true for all?"

"Most likely," she admitted. Mykella wanted to hear more, but asking more at the moment was not for the best. *You should learn more each time he comes . . . and let him see and sense more of you.*

She stood. "I will not keep you longer, Commander. I would that you take care, and I will be looking for you on your return to Tempre."

"I will report to you once my men are situated back in the Southern Guard barracks. It will be my duty . . . and pleasure."

Their eyes met again.

After several moments, Areyst bowed, then straightened. "Until then, my Lady." His words were polite and formal. The feelings behind them were not. He turned and left.

Mykella swallowed hard as the door closed. *Seeing him leave is getting difficult.* Yet she knew that to say more than she had so far was neither wise, nor for the best. *Not yet.* At the same time, she didn't want him to feel she was playing with him. She hoped his ability to read people revealed that much in her.

Again, she watched from the study window as Areyst rode back away from the palace.

45

Salyna entered the breakfast room on Decdi, a good two glasses after dawn, started to seat herself next to Mykella—and stopped. "Mykella! The back of your head . . ."

Mykella set down her mug. "They're ferrohawk claw marks. A nesting pair. They caught me from behind."

"You can protect yourself, I thought . . ."

"There are times I can't, and I thought I was safe where I was. I wasn't."

Salyna's eyes narrowed. "There aren't any ferrohawks near Tempre." She glanced across the table to Rachylana.

Rachylana looked back innocently.

"It happened near Viencet. I was scouting the approaches to the town."

"That's the job of the Southern Guards, not the Lady-Protector." Salyna slid into the chair beside Mykella and helped herself to cooling bacon slices from the platter in the middle of the table, and then to one of the small loaves in the basket.

"I can do things the Guards can't, just like your auxiliaries will do what the Guards can't or won't."

"But . . ."

"If you say anything to that, Salyna," interrupted Rachylana, "you'll undermine what you're doing, such as it is."

Mykella winced, but neither sister was looking at her.

"You couldn't do what these women you call sculls are already doing. You couldn't even do the exercises." The scorn in Salyna's voice was palpable. "If you want a challenge, come and help me train the auxiliaries. Of course, that is hard work, and . . ."

"And what?"

Salyna shrugged. "We sweat a lot."

"That's not what you meant," Rachylana persisted.

"What did I mean?" replied Salyna innocently.

"You know very well what you meant."

"I'm sure I haven't the faintest idea." The corners of Salyna's mouth curled upward ever so slightly.

"When do you begin . . . in the morning?" Rachylana's voice was cold, her eyes far colder than her voice.

"The top of the first full glass after dawn."

"I have some . . . chores here . . . that I still have to do." Rachylana looked to Mykella.

"We'll work it out," said Mykella, puzzled as to why Rachylana would consider training with the auxiliaries, even after Salyna's obvious baiting, when the redhead had heretofore steadfastly resisted such comments.

"I'm certain we can do without you for a few glasses," Salyna added.

"I'll be there."

"I'm sure you will be."

Mykella winced at the implication behind Salyna's reply and the unspoken words along the lines of "when you're not arranging balls and other meaningless things." She forced herself to take a sip of tea. "Now that you two have that settled . . . could we get on with breakfast?"

The two younger sisters exchanged glances.

"How much arms training do you think Cheleyza has had?" Mykella asked quickly, coming up with the first question she could find to defuse the simmering antagonism.

"What?" Salyna looked puzzled.

"She rides well. She's been directing cavalry. She wears an officer's uniform."

"Oh . . ." Salyna frowned. "She's from Northcoast. Most women there get weapons training of some sort. As the sister of the prince, though . . ."

"She'd either get more or less," interjected Rachylana. "Not the same as other women. Since she seems so at home in uniform, I'd say more."

"I'd never have guessed it from her wardrobe," mused Mykella.

"But she rode a lot, and she was always thin," added Salyna.

"There's always something you don't know about people," offered Rachylana. "Even when you've grown up with them."

Salyna glanced across the table, then decided against saying anything. So did Mykella as she passed the teapot to Salyna.

After eating quickly, Salyna rose.

"You're not leaving so soon?" asked Rachylana.

"This is late for the auxiliaries. We're trying to get as much training in as possible before season-turn."

"Should I—" began Rachylana.

"Tomorrow morning would be better. It's a regular day. I'm improvising today." With that, Salyna hurried off.

Rachylana looked to Mykella. "She didn't seem that angry at the end."

"She wasn't. She was just rushed. You could sense that, couldn't you?"

"I thought so . . . but sometimes . . ." Rachylana shook her head.

"Why did you—"

"Unless I do, she'll never understand. Right now, there's no way to prove that what I do is also of worth."

For all her Talent, Mykella wasn't sure she understood all that went on between her sisters . . . or why Rachylana suddenly was concerned about proving something to Salyna.

"Oh . . . as soon as you finish, you need to check the Table with me. I think . . . well . . . it would be better . . ."

"What?" Mykella managed not to snap.

"It's hard to explain."

"Then . . . let's go down, and you can show me." Mykella stood. *If it's not one thing . . . it's another.* "Do you have your key?"

"Yes." Rachylana took a long swallow of tea, making a face. "I'll be glad when we can get fresh cider again." Then she stood.

The two walked silently from the breakfast room and down the main staircase, back along the silent west corridor, then past the corridor guard and down the narrow staircase to the lowest level of the palace, then back along the north corridor to the Table chamber.

Rachylana used her key on the heavy lock on the iron shutters, then opened the door.

Mykella sensed nothing amiss and stepped into the chamber, with her sister following, then gestured toward the Table. "If you'd show me . . . whatever it is . . ."

The redhead stepped up to the Table, looked down, and concentrated.

The scene that came into view when the mists cleared showed Cheleyza standing before what looked to be a large stable.

"I think they have to be in Hieron," Rachylana explained. "They were riding across one of the bridges built by the Alectors this morning. It had to be across the Vedra. I couldn't believe they were riding so early. I checked the maps you gave me. That's the only bridge across a big river anywhere near where they could be. But I wanted you to see for yourself."

"They're farther south than we thought, then."

Rachylana gestured toward the Table, now showing Cheleyza striding across the packed earth of a stableyard. "She looks angry. She does often, I've noticed."

"It could be that she always was." *Except she hadn't felt that way the few times you met with her before. She gave off a feeling of being superior.* "Or at least since she left here."

"I think it's because she's thinking more and more of what she lost. She wanted to be the wife of the Lord-Protector." Rachylana paused. "No . . . she wanted to be the one controlling the Lord-Protector. Behind that charm, she was always a bitch."

Except you didn't see it then. "She's always wanted her own way, I think." Mykella paused. "You were right, but I'm glad you wanted to show me. I'll need to send a message to Areyst. I'd like you to look more frequently today. I'll look several times tomorrow so that you don't have to leave the auxiliaries on the first day you're working with them."

"Salyna would be happy if I left."

"Not happy. Self-justified."

"That's why I won't."

"You both have good qualities, but they're different. You can't be each other, you know?"

"I know that, but Salyna looks down on anyone who doesn't have 'practical' skills. She could accept your Finance clerking because that involved saving golds. Arranging balls and running the palace—those are things any woman can do."

"They're not, but you won't convince her of that," Mykella added quickly and smoothly, "We can't do much more here at the moment"—she knew there was little more she could do right then to smooth the friction between the two—"and I do need to get word to Areyst."

The two turned from the Table, and the image faded into mists that quickly dispersed, leaving behind a blank and shining mirrored surface.

46

The first days of nineweek of spring passed quickly—and without incident, even as the Table showed Cheleyza's forces riding steadily toward Lanachrona. Mykella began working out a new tariff schedule with Haelyt. She'd have to be most careful in how she approached the factors and Seltyrs, and she wasn't about to do so until after she dealt with the attackers. If she weren't successful, the tariff changes wouldn't matter, and there was no sense in upsetting the factors and Seltyrs unless she proved Lanachrona could stand on its own under a Lady-Protector.

On Quattri morning, since she had heard nothing from Zylander, she sent a message requesting a meeting with him on Sexdi or Septi morning, then settled down to consider how long before Cheleyza and her forces reached Salcer.

At that moment, Chalmyr announced Lord Gharyk, who entered the study and bowed. "Lady-Protector."

Mykella gestured to the chairs. "Do you bring me news about matters at the gaol?"

"No, Lady. This is another matter. As I indicated I would do some weeks ago, I have been working to untangle the legalities of your succession, as it applies to your properties and interests, and while they look to be close to being resolved, there are certain problems."

"What are those problems?"

"Were you aware that your father gifted the villa on Eastern Avenue to your late uncle?"

Mykella stiffened. "What? That's always belonged to the Protector. Father never said anything about that."

"There was a deed registered last summer."

"It had to be forged."

"I had thought so, myself, because he never brought the matter before me or my clerks, but the document was registered by your uncle, and the signatures and seals appear legitimate—"

"I can't believe that. Father never would have—"

Gharyk lifted a hand. "The property is not a problem. In all senses, both legal and political, you are the sole heir. I have filed the proper documentation to return it to your ambit."

"Then . . . what is the problem?"

". . . several factors have lodged claims against you—through the property, of course—for damages, Lady-Protector . . ."

"Why? Has the Treasury failed to pay them for goods?"

"It appears as though your late uncle failed to pay them, and as his direct blood heir . . ."

"The debt is mine?"

"It is." Gharyk cleared his throat. "In many cases, the obligations of a debtor are discharged through repudiation, either through repudiation of all inheritance, which is a mere formality for most people, because they inherit little or nothing, or through repudiation on the grounds that the debts were incurred through fraud, deception, or other means outside the law. You could do that, in view of your uncle's acts, and no one would contest that repudiation."

"You don't think that's a good idea, I can see."

"In these times—"

Mykella sighed. "I agree. It's a very bad idea." *Practically and politically.* "What are these debts?"

Gharyk removed a sheet from the folder he carried and extended it across the desk to her.

Mykella read through the listing, her eyes widening. "Ninety-seven golds for seamstresses, a hundred golds for various victuals, sixty-seven golds for horses . . ." The total was close to a thousand golds. She lowered the list and sat there. Somehow, the golds for seamstresses, for all those gowns and dresses, bothered her more than the other expenditures, not that she liked the idea of paying any of them in the slightest.

"Lady . . . if it is a problem . . ."

"No . . . I'll pay. These people have a right to be paid. It's just . . . on top of everything else . . ." She paused. "If I give you the golds, you'll take care of the payments and whatever documents are necessary to show all the debts have been paid?"

"Yes, Lady. It will take a day or two to draw up the documents."

Mykella rose. "Thank you. Let me know when you are ready for the golds."

Gharyk stood and bowed. "I will. My apologies for having to bring this before you."

"You weren't the cause. I do appreciate your resolving it. Thank you again."

Once Gharyk had left, and she was sure he was nowhere near, Mykella left her study and walked to her apartments, still smoldering inside. *Not only did they kill Father and Jeraxylt and gut the Treasury, but they left debts that you have to pay . . .*

Because she wanted to be alone, Mykella made her way, through the darkness, down to the Table chamber. There she checked the Table, but it was neither brighter nor duller. Then she slipped into the depths and studied the other Table markers, but she could detect no changes there, although there was . . . something . . . about the orange and yellow of Lysia, and that meant she'd have to watch that even more carefully in the tenday ahead.

Next she called up an image of Cheleyza and found her aunt again still riding southward, although on a different mount, it appeared. Khanasyl was inventorying goods in a warehouse, and Klevytr appeared to be unpacking goods, which did relieve Mykella to some degree. Zylander was explaining something in a ledger to the younger man who was likely his son.

At that moment, Mykella heard a click behind her. She turned and saw the chamber door open.

Rachylana stood there, her mouth opening. "Mykella . . . how . . . ?"

"There's a back way of sorts, with Talent."

"The way you travel places?"

Mykella nodded. *The less said, the better.*

"I came back to check the Table. Salyna is giving the auxiliaries a break of sorts. They're working on learning their letters."

"I'm glad you're here. I can't tell you how angry I am!"

"At me? Or Salyna?"

"No." Mykella shook her head. "I'm going to have to pay nearly a hundred golds to seamstresses for dresses that Cheleyza had made. That doesn't count hundreds more in the expenses for mounts, victuals, and other supplies that weren't paid by Joramyl."

"Why? He was the one who bought it all."

"I'm his heir, and I never repudiated . . . well . . . I can't. I could repudiate those debts, Gharyk tells me, without prejudice . . . if I didn't accept the inheritance, or if I insisted that the debts were incurred through fraud."

"What inheritance?"

"The villa and its lands."

"I don't understand. What is there to inherit from Joramyl? That was Father's, not Joramyl's."

"Father gifted it to him last summer. Gharyk discovered that and the debts filed against the property."

"That bitch! That scheming, murderous . . . it had to be her."

"You see why I'm angry?"

"Oh, Mykella. . . ."

Rachylana stepped forward and hugged her sister.

Much as she appreciated the hug, Mykella couldn't help but wonder why the debt for the dresses had upset her as much as the gifting of the villa. Was it just because so many dresses seemed so frivolous? Or because Cheleyza was so contemptuous in leaving them behind after spending so much on them?

47

Mykella stood by the study window at midmorning on Septi, looking out at a hazy spring day that might well turn into the warmest day of the year. The day before, reluctantly, she had signed thirty-one documents and transferred nine hundred eighty-four golds from her personal accounts to those of the Ministry of Justice to cover the debts Gharyk had uncovered. The Justice Minister had promised that all the claimants would be paid by the end of the day on Sexdi. Paying golds for Joramyl's debts, especially for Cheleyza's gowns, grated on her. But then, the amount of stolen golds and greed and selfishness she'd uncovered over the past two seasons grated on her. After a last look at the park, where the bushes were in bloom, and a few flowers had begun to show colors, she turned and walked back to her desk—and the master ledger.

At the second glass of the afternoon, Zylander appeared.

"Lady-Protector, you requested my presence?"

"I did. I wished to discuss with you a number of matters so that you can consider certain decisions before you take the position of Minister of Highways and Rivers." She nodded toward the chairs and waited until he had seated himself. "As you may know, when the indiscretions of the former minister became known, the assistant minister fled and has not been seen or heard from since. It is most likely that he will never appear again in Lanachrona." *Or anywhere else.* "You will need to seek an assistant minister, someone you can rely upon and trust. Before you appoint him, he must meet me and obtain my approval."

"I would not have it any other way, Lady."

"I do not wish you to choose someone because you think I will find him or her pleasant or agreeable but rather capable and honest. There are also other matters that you should address, beginning with changes in the priority of repairs to the sewers and towpaths . . ."

Mykella gave a brief summary of the past difficulties. "You will also need to work with the Minister of Justice to develop better ways of making sure that all who manufacture or craft within Tempre—and other cities—comply with the rules for sewers and for the handling of wastes. This has been neglected in the recent past . . ."

All in all, Mykella spent almost two glasses with Zylander who, thankfully, began to ask detailed questions and showed more than a passing understanding of the problems.

Once the minister-to-be had left, Mykella repaired to her quarters and donned the nightsilk riding jacket and gloves, then slipped into darkness and through the stone of the palace to the depths of deep green . . . and then, with concern, to the Table chamber in Lysia.

When she emerged, she immediately threw up full shields, but the chamber was empty, and she advanced the several steps to where she could look down at the Table. The mirrored surface showed nothing. Then she studied the Table with her senses and Talent, finally noticing the slightest variation in the basic purple that infused the Table.

Is that the way it begins when the Ifrits are getting ready to appear? Or do the Tables vary ever so slightly all the time, and you haven't noticed?

Not for the first time, or even close to it, she wished she had more understanding and experience in dealing with the Ifrits and the Tables.

Finally, she dropped back into the darkness and returned to the Tempre Table. There she called up images of Cheleyza, Demyl, Khanasyl, Lhanyr, and others, including Areyst, who was leading a squad through the rolling rises where he planned to encounter the coastal forces.

After that, what with one thing and other—including petitions, another discrepancy in the ledgers for the Ministry of Highways and Rivers, a request for another hundred golds from Chief Engineer Nusgeyl, supported by three detailed pages of explanation—it was well after sunset before Mykella returned to the family dining room and a cooling fowl pie . . . and a scowling Rachylana, who was drinking, rather than merely sipping, a red wine. She had been drinking for a time, if the empty carafe happened to be any indication.

"How has the week gone?" Mykella seated herself. "With the auxiliaries, I meant?"

Before Rachylana could reply, Muergya appeared with another carafe of red wine and a basket of warm bread. Mykella filled her goblet, then, after Muergya slipped away, looked to the redhead. "You were saying?"

"The exercises aren't bad, the ones to strengthen arms and shoulders. I don't really need those. Arms practice is hard."

There was more behind those words. "Salyna expects more out of you?"

"It's worse that that. I have to spar and practice with her."

"Because she says that no one else will press you?"

"How did you guess?"

Mykella could have heard the irony in Rachylana's tone from three chambers away. "She had the same problem when she was learning weapons years ago. She also wants you to be good because you reflect on her."

"I have bruises everywhere."

Mykella raised her eyebrows. She didn't feel that sympathetic. It seemed that not a week had passed since she'd met the soarer that she hadn't ended up with more bruises and injuries.

"It's not the same. You're fighting Ifrits and raiders . . ."

"And ferrohawks." Mykella lifted the carafe to fill her goblet, then set it down as she realized the goblet was still mostly full.

"It's different when your own sister enjoys catching you making mistakes and can use that to punish you."

"You don't have to train with the auxiliaries," Mykella pointed out, spooning out a healthy helping of crust-and-fowl pie onto her platter.

"I don't have your Talent," replied Rachylana, not quite belligerently.

"I wouldn't do as well with arms as do either you or Salyna," temporized Mykella.

"You don't have to."

"No." Mykella offered a laugh. "I don't. I have to deal with finding ministers who will be honest and capable in a city where most are looking to fill their strong rooms as quickly as possible. I have to pay for the gowns of the scheming wife of an uncle who poisoned our father. Sooner or later, I'll have to have children, whether I want to or not—that is, if I can deal with Cheleyza, Chalcaer, and Skrelyn . . . and another group of invading Ifrits . . ."

"You won't even let me indulge in a little self-pity," snapped Rachylana. "You and Salyna."

I just did . . . but not for long. Stifling a sigh, Mykella pressed a feeling of concern toward her sister . . . lightly. "We all have worries. I'm sorry Salyna seems to enjoy being hard on you."

"That's easy enough for you to say."

"It doesn't make it any less true. Besides, don't you think she's trying to force you to get better quickly? You should be able to sense that."

Rachylana opened her mouth, then closed it. After a long moment, she finally said, "That makes it worse in some ways. She's right, and she can justify it."

Mykella nodded.

"Is that all you have to say?"

"What can I say? She's trying to train you in arms, quickly, and she likes being superior. There are three ways to deal with it. Ignore her. Get better as fast as you can, or choose not to train with the auxiliaries. I can't make those choices for you."

Rachylana drained the wine in her goblet. "I don't want you to. I just want her to care a little more."

"Why don't you tell her that? Tell her you know she's better. Tell her that you know you need to learn, and then ask her if she really has to enjoy it quite so much, because it's not the bruises that hurt, but that it seems like she enjoys hurting you, as if she has to prove a point."

"She'll get mad."

"She might."

"Still . . . I just might tell her." Rachylana pulled the casserole in front of her platter.

Mykella repressed a sigh, hoping for a quiet remainder of the meal.

48

Late on Novdi morning, Chalmyr entered the study and handed Mykella an envelope with a blank seal. "This arrived a few moments ago, Lady."

"From whom?"

"A public courier delivered it to the palace."

"Thank you." Mykella took the envelope and studied it with her Talent, but it held none of the shades that indicated poison. She finally opened it and began to read.

Lady-Protector—

I have received the long-overdue payment for two fine mounts purchased by the previous Lord-Protector. The golds I received do total the amount owed. I did not receive any compensation for the time when I had not the horses or the payment. That amounted to one full season. I understand that you are not responsible for paying interest on debts incurred by another in the matter of inheritances. These are difficult times. Some recompense would be most welcome . . .

The signature was that of Dustayk, Factor in Livestock.

Mykella shook her head. She'd honored the debts incurred by Joramyl, even after he'd plundered her father's Treasury and the kingdom, in a spirit of goodwill . . . and the good factor Dustayk wanted interest on a debt she probably wasn't even obligated to pay—except as a gesture of good faith?

What is it with people? You do your best to be honorable, and they want more.

She shook her head, then blotted the dampness from the back of her neck. For all that the windows were open, not a hint of a breeze moved the warm damp air. She set the petition or plea or whatever it might be called on the corner of the desk, then stood and walked to the windows. Even standing before them, she could not feel the slightest breath of air.

She hadn't ridden through Tempre in days. A ride would be cooler, and she could also see—or smell—the results of the sewer repairs. After sending word to the duty-squad leader, she drafted a reply to Dustayk, noting that, while she had not been obligated to pay the debt, she had done so in good faith, and for Dustayk to expect her to pay interest on a debt which was not hers was stretching the limits of good faith. She handed the draft to Chalmyr, then stopped by her apartments to get her riding jacket and gloves before making her way down to the main level.

Maeltor was mounted with the escort squad that awaited her when she stepped out into the rear courtyard of the palace.

"Captain . . . I'm honored, but this is merely a ride through Tempre." Mykella jump-vaulted into the saddle of the gray, then squared herself in the saddle.

"I hope you do not mind, Lady, but I have not ridden as much as I should recently."

"I do not mind in the slightest, although your nose may protest. I need to ride up the west side of the South River from the Great Piers, then through the metalworking quarter."

"We are at your command, Lady." The captain smiled.

Mykella returned the smile and urged the gray forward.

Even though it was Novdi, when Mykella rode up the boulevard just to the west of the South River, she could see the telltale grayish smoke rising from the low buildings within the walls of the rendering yards. Despite the smell, she led the squad down an alley to the river wall so that she could see whether the large fired-clay pipes were still in use. The same brownish gray fluid oozed from them into the river, but she said nothing as she turned her mount back toward the boulevard.

A half vingt farther south, past the low hill, she rode across a narrow stone bridge to the east side of the river and headed south through the smoke and haze of the metalworking quarter. There, too, an oily residue continued to bubble up from where the covered pipes from several buildings entered the water, creating the same bluish sheen on the water she had noted earlier although she thought the shimmer held a hint of purple as well.

She was relieved to find, south of the metalworking buildings, the odor of human wastes so pronounced on her earlier rides had vanished. She also saw no piles of night soil.

At least there's some improvement.

She turned to Maeltor, riding beside her. "How does it smell now, compared to the last time you rode with me?"

"I did not smell much change to the north, by the rendering yards and the metalworkers, but here it is much more pleasant."

Mykella nodded. "I thought so, but I wanted your opinion." The discharge pipes from the metalworking shops, the rendering yards, and the tanneries still concerned her.

Mykella ended the part of her "inspection ride" at the square where the boulevard and avenue crossed, slowing as she turned the gray past the Traveler's Rest Inn on the southwest corner. She did note that the shutters sported a new coat of varnish, in addition to the porch railings she had observed earlier. While she could not be certain, it seemed to Mykella that the number of people on the streets was less than usual.

When she finally rode in through the open gates to the palace, she studied the building, struck by two aspects of its construction that she had never fully considered before. First, the stones were sharp and crisp, as if they had been laid in place less than a year before— except for the addition on the west side that held the kitchens. Second, every single window was of the same size and shape, and the spacing between windows was precisely the same. So far as she could recall, there were only two structures in all of Tempre with those attributes: the palace and the Southern Guard complex.

Why had the Alectors built them that way? For what purpose? She might guess, but she doubted she would ever know for certain, and that bothered her.

Once she was back at the palace, she checked her formal study. Although Chalmyr had left, there were no petitions or other documents on her desk. From there, she dropped into the darkness and made a quick transit to the Table chamber in Lysia, but the minute variation in the Table pulsations did not seem to have changed. The rest of the day she spent following Cheleyza and others in the Table before returning to wrestle with the ledgers and projected expenses for the remainder of the spring season.

When she finally entered the family dining room that evening and looked at the platter of cold sliced fowl and pickled cucumbers and beets, with the faint odor of vinegar in the heavy air, Mykella glanced from Salyna to Rachylana and back to Salyna. The two stood at one side of the room, and Salyna stopped talking and turned toward Mykella.

Mykella didn't sense any overt anger between the two, but she felt something. Her eyes went back to Rachylana and caught the faint bruise on the left side of her sister's face, above the jaw and forward of her ear. "Dare I ask how matters are with the auxiliaries?"

"Well enough," replied Salyna dryly. "I think the auxiliaries should ride in the season-turn parade. Their undress uniforms are ready—or they will be by Sexdi—and you're only bringing a company back from Viencet. If the auxiliaries ride, along with the headquarters group, that will make the column longer. It won't be as long as in the past, but it won't be that much shorter. I think that's important."

"Is that what's important, or showing Tempre that there will be women in the Guards?"

"Both are, don't you think?"

"What does Captain Maeltor think?"

At that, Rachylana leaned forward slightly but said nothing.

"He said that the matter was between you and the commander," replied Salyna.

Mykella laughed softly. "He's being diplomatic."

"He's being smart," added Rachylana.

"That, too," said Mykella. "I will agree, but only if the commander agrees as well, and you can only tell everyone that the commander and I will decide when he returns."

Salyna nodded. "That's fair enough, but I still think it's a good idea."

Mykella saw no reason to say more. Her eyes strayed back to Rachylana's face.

"One of the auxiliaries got somewhat familiar with Rachylana," Salyna said quickly, as if glad not to be discussing the parade.

"And?"

"We ended up settling it," replied Rachylana.

"How, might I ask?"

"It happened during blade practice." Salyna looked to the red-head. "You can explain better since I only saw the last part."

"I was practicing with one of the women. We were using wooden blanks, and she said something about not wanting to take orders from a woman who'd been raised in privilege. One thing led to another . . ." Rachylana shrugged, an attempt at innocence.

"They don't know who you are?" asked Mykella.

"They think I'm some factor's daughter who might end up a squad leader. I asked Salyna not to say more. Saying I was a factor's daughter was necessary because I have to do things at the palace and because I have the privilege of getting bruised by Salyna more than the others."

"That's because you have a feel for blades," interjected Salyna. "It's like you can sense where they're going to strike."

"No one even guessed—" Mykella stopped. "Of course not. They wouldn't expect two of you there, and very few people see any of us closely—except for some of the Southern Guards. What about them?"

"Most of them haven't looked that closely, either," Salyna said wryly.

"So what happened?"

"I knocked the blank out of her hand, and she started to yell at me," replied Rachylana. "I told her to be quiet, and she grabbed a hay rake. I dodged most of it. I had to knock her down with the blank."

"Actually, she knocked her out," said Salyna. "That stopped all the muttering."

"Out loud, anyway," said Rachylana, with a sideways look at Mykella.

"Will that be a problem?" asked Mykella.

Salyna shook her head. "The Guards is about discipline, and some-times that discipline has to be administered by force. After she woke up, I put her to mucking stables every night for the next two weeks—if she wanted to stay in the auxiliaries. She didn't complain."

"I'll still have to watch her," said Rachylana.

Both Mykella and Salyna nodded.

49

On Duadi, the minister's meeting was longer than Mykella liked, largely because she had made the mistake of asking Loryalt for an explanation of the future impact of the excessive number of water oaks in private timber stands. That had led into revenue projections and questions about her concerns, leading to her "admission" that there was a strong likelihood the coastal principalities were considering military action against Lanachrona, but that so far, no forces had entered Lanachrona. Nor had either prince made demands or declarations. She had eased out of that discussion by promising a fuller talk on the Southern Guards the following Duadi, when Commander Areyst would have a chance to be present.

Then, after dealing with petitions, requests for appointments, and other matters, Mykella had eaten a quick noon meal before making her way down to the Finance Minister's study.

"Good afternoon, Lady," offered Haelyt, as Mykella closed the door behind her.

"Good afternoon. I do hope it's good, or promising. What do we have in the way of tariff payments for spring. They're due on Octdi, are they not?"

"That they are, Lady."

"And?"

"Only Seltyr Almardyn, Seltyr Klevytr, and High Factor Zylander have paid their spring tariffs, Lady," replied the chief clerk.

"Is this normal?"

"No, Lady. Tariffs are due on the Octdi before season-turn. Most factors and Seltyrs pay late on Octdi or early on Novdi. Almost all the crafters wait until Novdi morning. A few crafters, Seltyrs, and factors pay on the following Londi morning. In past years, perhaps as many as ten have paid early in the week, by now. No Lord-Protector has ever assessed penalties for Londi payments, but all have extracted penalties for those paid on Duadi of oneweek . . . and later."

"So we're not doing well on receipts?"

"The three who have paid did so handsomely, but . . ."

"The others are waiting as long as they can."

"It would appear so, Lady."

That didn't surprise Mykella. "I'll check later—"

A series of quick and hard raps on the Finance study doors were followed by the figure of a Southern Guard bursting into the chamber. "Lady-Protector!"

Mykella recognized the man—belatedly—as Casaryk, the duty-squad leader. "Yes, Squad Leader?"

"Four men dressed as factors entered the Justice chambers and tried to kill Lord Gharyk."

Mykella stiffened. "How is he? How badly hurt is he?"

"He's wounded, Lady, but he's awake and having the wound tended. It does not appear mortal. He asked for you immediately."

Mykella turned to Haelyt. "We'll finish later."

The chief clerk inclined his head, but Mykella was already out the door, trailed by Casaryk. As she hurried toward the main staircase, she checked and strengthened her personal shields. "Do you know how it happened?"

"No, Lady. Fiendyk was on corridor duty. He heard someone yell for a guard, and he ran to the Finance study. He called for backup. When he reached the study, one man tried to escape, and tried to use a dagger. Fiendyk put a blade through him. The fellow died on the spot."

Let there be some witnesses so that I have a chance of getting to the bottom of this. If I even can.

Mykella did not voice the thought, not when the Southern Guard was there for protection, rather than trying to find out who was behind attempted killings.

One of the stair guards joined Casaryk, and the two escorted Mykella through the score of scattered crafters and factors and others with business on the main floor of the palace. Another pair of guards flanked the main-floor entry to the Justice Ministry chambers, but one stepped back, and the other, on the left, opened the door for her.

A Southern Guard, presumably one with healing training, was looking at Gharyk's bare shoulder and holding a dressing there. A man dressed in a linen jacket and matching gray trousers and well-polished black boots was tied to a chair and gagged. A bruise and scrapes across his forehead suggested that he'd encountered a blunt object with considerable force. Two other well-attired figures lay sprawled on the stone-tiled floor of the outer chamber, both faceup, and both with considerable blood across their shirts and jackets.

"Lord Gharyk!" Mykella called.

"Lady-Protector." Gharyk nodded slightly.

"How deep is the wound?" she asked, sending a Talent probe toward the minister.

"Not deep enough to cause heavy bleeding," replied the Guard healer. "It looks clean, and the weapon was good steel. I've flooded it with tincture . . ."

Mykella's own probe showed—she thought—much the same. "What happened?"

"The four of them appeared here," replied Gharyk. "Two presented themselves as advocates from Vyan with concerns about the handling of justicing there. I have had some concerns about that very matter, which whoever sent them obviously knew." Gharyk winced as the healer's needle went into his shoulder. "But their choice of words concerned me, and their garments were not so dusty and worn as those of travelers. I managed to distract them enough to get to my blade and call for assistance." Gharyk smiled. "Wystan was quite effective with a chair, and Zekael managed to trip one of them and summon the corridor guard."

The Southern Guard standing to the side—presumably Fiendyk—cleared his throat. "Begging your pardon, Lady-Protector, Lord, the minister killed the one in the blue there after taking that thrust in the shoulder."

Mykella turned to the captive in the chair and gathered light to her, a cold and menacing green light, and projected terror and power. "Remove his gag."

Fiendyk did so.

"What is your name?"

The captive swallowed, then quavered, "Gualyn, Lady."

"Who hired you?"

"I can't say . . ."

Mykella pressed her shields against his face so that he could not breathe. After letting him twist and turn against his bonds, and turn red, she released the shields enough to let him take several gasping breaths. "Who hired you?"

"Can't . . . kill me . . . anyway . . ."

Mykella reapplied the shields, this time holding them until she sensed he was close to passing out. "I can keep this up until your lungs are so raw you'll be coughing up blood. Then I'll block your mouth and let you breathe your own blood."

Gualyn swallowed and blurted, "Caenoral . . . everyone knows he's the one you go to if you want trouble removed."

"He hired you?

"Yes, Lady."

"Do you know who hired him?"

"No, Lady. He never tells us. Honest . . . he never does."

Mykella sensed both the fear and truth behind the words.

"I could ask others, but I'd prefer to get a quick answer." Mykella smiled coldly. "So would you. Where would I find Caenoral in the next glass?"

"They'll kill me."

"They might. Do you think I won't . . . if you don't tell me?" Mykella pressed the shields across the man's chest.

"No . . . West Lane . . . he's got a shimmersilk factorage . . . two blocks south of the Great Piers . . . at the end of the lane . . . looks like an alley."

"And I will find him there?"

"He's usually there, Lady . . ." The plea behind the words was obvious.

Mykella looked to Casaryk. "When I'm done, put Gualyn in with the other prisoners at the Southern Guard complex. For now, anyway. He wouldn't last the night in the gaol." Her eyes went back to the captive. "Would you?"

He shook his head.

"Lord Gharyk," asked Mykella, "what is the name of Gaoler Huatyn's brother?"

Gharyk frowned. "I do not see . . . do you think . . . ?"

"I don't know, but it might be useful."

"He has two. Kluatyn is the one who supplied the gaol, and Lhuatyr is the youngest."

Mykella had watched the captive with senses as well as eyes while Gharyk spoke, but Gualyn showed no sign of recognition of either name.

"Casaryk . . . if you'd come with me for a moment?" Mykella moved to the door of the chamber and lowered her voice. "I want a squad to accompany me to Caenoral's factorage, and another to cordon off the gaol. They have my permission to use all necessary force to keep anyone from leaving the gaol."

"Yes, Lady."

Even so, it was almost half a glass later before Mykella was riding westward on the avenue toward the purported factorage owned by Caenoral. Maeltor had joined the force and rode to her left.

"Lady . . . what do you intend to do with this Caenoral?"

"Find out what he knows."

"He will not be as easy as the captive you questioned in the palace."

"Then . . . neither will I." Mykella sensed Maeltor's almost-concealed wince, and added, "Captain, some people respond only to power. If that is the case, I will use what is necessary to protect Lanachrona and my people." *Whatever is necessary.*

As the captive had said, West Lane was more like an alley than a true lane. A single narrow structure stood at the end, looking as though it had been built to block the lane. Dirty yellow bricks composed the front, and the space where there had been two windows flanking the narrow ironbound door had been bricked up as well, long enough ago that the grime on those yellow bricks matched the others. The three upper-level windows were shuttered, and there was a narrow space on each side of the building between it and the rear walls of larger factorages. Through the passages, Mykella could see light, presumably from the other part of West Lane, or whatever it was called there. West Lane itself was empty, although Mykella had the feeling it had not been so for long.

When Mykella and Maeltor reined up before the door, with only a single wide stone for a stoop, the captain gestured to one of the guards. "See if anyone will answer."

The ranker dismounted and stepped up to the door, where he pounded vigorously, then waited before pounding again. After several times of doing that, he turned. "The door is locked, and no one is answering."

"Be difficult to break it down," offered Maeltor.

"There may be another way." Mykella dismounted and handed the gray's reins to the captain. "Just have everyone wait for a moment." She walked into the north passageway, looking for a door. There wasn't one. She kept walking, noticing, surprisingly, that the passageway was well swept and clean of all trash or debris. When she emerged onto the lane on the far side, she found it, too, vacant. The west side of the building was a duplicate of the east face, even to the bricked-up windows. She rapped on the door. Again . . . no one answered.

Then she walked the north passage. There was no door there, either. She retreated until she was close to the bricks of the wall of the purported factorage, and well back from the Southern Guards before she called to the darkness. She was close enough to the Great Piers that it rose to enfold her, and she slipped through the wall and into a small chamber filled with small bolts of shimmersilk suspended between posts.

While the chamber door was closed, it was not locked or bolted, and she opened it, stepping into a hallway. She sensed two men to her left, in the anteroom behind the east door, but no one else in the building. She walked as quietly as she could toward them.

Both were looking at the barred and bolted door. One stood, the other sat behind a narrow counter on a stool. Neither turned when she stood in the archway behind them.

"That won't do you much good," she said calmly, gathering light to her.

The first man whirled and flung a knife at her. The blade bounced off her shields and clattered on the brick floor.

"You must be Caenoral," Mykella said. "I'd suggest that you open the door. Be polite to all the Southern Guards there. Don't run, either."

"You . . . you're the Lady-Protector." A greasy smile crossed the man's face. "You have a way of surprising a man."

"Shouldn't any woman, especially one in my position?" Mykella replied. "And your friend? His name?"

The man on the stool looked to Mykella but said nothing. His eyes seemed wide.

"If you wish to open the door, you may certainly do so," said the first man.

"Thank you." Mykella stepped toward him, then to the side, knowing what he had in mind.

He lunged—but hit her shields so hard that he staggered back and ended up on his buttocks.

With three swift movements, Mykella lifted the two bars and tossed them into the lap of the man she thought was Caenoral, then slid the bolt back and opened the door, stepping back as it swung inward. "Guards!"

The man behind the counter dropped from the stool.

"Don't!" snapped Mykella, forcing Talent command into the single word.

The counterman froze.

She looked to the crouching man who had tossed the bars aside. "You, too."

"You can't do this," he said, slowly rising to his feet.

"Are you Caenoral?" Mykella pressed.

She could sense the answer before he said, "What does it matter?"

"Thank you. It does matter, because you're the man people go to in order to make trouble go away."

"I'm just a shimmersilk factor, nothing more."

At that moment, Maeltor entered the factorage, saber at the ready. He inclined his head. "Lady."

"I found an open door. The one in front of the counter is Caenoral. The one behind the counter hasn't said a word. It would be helpful to tie them both up. Caenoral threw the blade on the floor at me, and the other one tried to escape."

"Our pleasure, Lady."

Another knife appeared in Caenoral's hand.

Mykella stepped in front of the captain and moved forward, extending her shields and pressing Caenoral against the wall. The other man bolted for the door, only to be knocked to the floor by the flat of Maeltor's saber. Mykella pressed her shields tightly across Caenoral's face, taking care to anchor herself to the stone.

A short time later, the purported factor slumped, and his fingers released the weapon. Mykella eased back on her shields. Caenoral gasped for air.

The two guards who had bound the hands of the still-staggered second man behind his back quickly bound Caenoral.

She smiled. "How much were you paid to clothe and send four bravos after Lord Gharyk? Ten golds?"

The contempt she felt was enough to prompt another figure. "More like fifty, then."

Caenoral's brows knit.

"Say . . . forty plus what one might call expenses."

She could see the sweat beading on his forehead.

"Who paid you? Kluatyn?"

The blankness in the eyes of the would-be factor, and the sense of noncomprehension provided a sense of an answer.

"So it was Lhuatyr, then?"

Mykella sensed fear from both men. "I thought as much."

"I never said that was who it was," protested Caenoral. "You can't prove anything."

Mykella smiled again. "I don't have to. You drew weapons on the Lady-Protector twice." She turned to the other bound man. "You didn't. You might end up in the workhouse or quarries for life. Did Lhuatyr say why he wanted Lord Gharyk dead?"

"No, Lady. . . ." The man's voice trembled. "He didn't say nothing, except it had to be quick, before season-turn."

"I could tell you lots of things, Lady-Protector." A wheedling oily tone infused Caenoral's voice. "But I couldn't if I was dead."

"That's true. But would I want to hear them?" She turned to the captain. "Bring them both along with us. Later, they'll join the others.

"Lady . . ." Maeltor began . . .

"I know. I'm taxing the resources of the Southern Guards. It won't be for that much longer. This part of it, that is. We need to get to the gaol. Leave three men to guard the place for now." With that, Mykella strode from the factorage and jump-mounted the gray.

". . . how'd she do that . . ." came a murmur from back in the squad.

Mykella doubted the question referred to her mounting style.

A quarter glass later, Mykella and the remainder of the squad reined up before the gaol—a squarish two-story building of the same gray stone as the justicing building beside which it was set. The gaol was on the west side of the justicing building that fronted the south-Tempre market square, while the building housing the inspectors and other functionaries was on the east side.

A small crowd had gathered in the square—all watching the gaol. Most heads turned as Mykella reined up.

Casaryk rode forward. "Just before we got here, two fellows tried to ride away. We caught an assistant gaoler. He said the one who escaped was Lhuatyr."

That figures. Mykella nodded. "He's the one who arranged for the attack on Lord Gharyk."

"I'm sorry, Lady, but his mount was much faster."

"You did what you could. We'll have to deal with him later." Mykella dismounted. "I need to have a talk with Gaoler Huatyn."

"Ten guards should accompany you, Lady," offered the squad leader. "The rest of the assistant gaolers are gathered in the front hall. They've barricaded it from the rest of the gaol because someone opened the cells."

"I'll talk to the assistant gaolers first. We need to take down their names." She turned to Maeltor. "If prisoners try to escape . . . capture those you can. Try not to kill them, but don't risk any guards."

The captain nodded, then raised his voice. "First five ranks! Dismount and accompany the Lady-Protector. Sabers at the ready. All others! Rifles ready!"

Once the ten Southern Guards formed up, flanking Mykella, she walked toward the front entrance of the gaol, where four Southern Guards already stood, rifles aimed at the door.

Why do you always end up walking into things? She wasn't certain she had a good answer to her own question. So she kept walking, checking her shields.

One of the guards escorting her stepped forward and opened the door. "The Lady-Protector!"

Mykella again gathered light to her as she stepped from the bright sunlight of a spring afternoon into the comparative dimness of the gaol's receiving hall. She'd expected perhaps a score of people, but just eight men stood in the space, all holding long truncheons. A stone staircase at the back of the hall extended up to an iron grate, locked and barring access to the archway and corridor beyond. To the right of the staircase, against the rear wall, was a similar archway, its grated door also locked. Mykella heard voices from both upper and lower levels.

Mykella moved forward until she was well inside, with the guards still beside her. Then she waited several moments. "Where is Gaoler Huatyn?"

There was no answer.

Mykella increased the light around her, then pointed to the burliest of the men. "You! Where is Huatyn?"

The man squinted, then mumbled, ". . . didn't see him come out . . . started unlocking cells on the upper level."

"Are the cells on the lower level still locked?"

". . . think so . . ."

"You think so, Lady!" snapped one of the guards.

"I think so, Lady," the man parroted.

"Is that the only way into the upper level?" Mykella pointed to the staircase.

"Yes, Lady . . . all the windows up there are barred."

"Who down here has the keys to the grille door up there and to the cells?"

After a moment, an older balding man with wispy gray and red hair stepped forward. "Guess I won't be needing these any longer, Lady."

One of the guards moved out and took the key ring, then passed it to Mykella.

Mykella turned to the nearest guard. "I'm going up. Have someone get the names of everyone here."

"Yes, Lady."

Holding the keys, Mykella started up the stairs. At the top, she had to try three keys before she discovered the one that opened the grille gate. Then she stepped through the archway.

Two men jumped at her and staggered back from her shields.

"Stand back!" she ordered, anchoring her shields to the stone beneath her.

Another man launched himself at her, with a bar of some sort in his hand, only to crash to the floor. She moved forward enough to allow the guards to hurry through the archway, before she turned and relocked the grille.

Mykella glanced past the men bunched before her to the end of the long corridor, past the rows of cells. Another grate barred access to a ladder leading up to the roof—except the gate was locked, and behind it two figures were scrambling up the iron ladder.

Mykella turned and pointed to the guard at the rear. "Run down and tell the captain that Huatyn and Kluatyn are trying to escape off the roof!" Belatedly, she handed him the keys. "Lock the grille behind you and bring back the keys as soon as you can."

"Yes, Lady."

Mykella walked toward the mass of prisoners, letting greenish light flare around her. "It's time to return to your cells."

"No!" A huge shambling figure a yard taller than Mykella lunged toward her, brushing aside the guard who tried to stop him, as if the guard were little more than a straw figure.

Mykella anchored her shields and pressed a Talent probe against the man's life-thread, trying to exert just enough pressure to drop him. But the life-thread parted, and the man plunged forward, slamming into the worn stone floor. Mykella held in the wince. She hadn't meant to kill him, but she'd wanted to stop him before he hurt another guard.

"It's time to return to your cells." She kept her voice calm, but boosted it with Talent, moving forward and around the fallen man, then pointing to the first open cell. "Whose is this?"

"Mine, Lady." A bearded young man stepped forward, smiling ingratiatingly.

Mykella frowned, then shook her head. "No, it's not. Do you want . . . ?"

The young man paled. "It's a good cell . . . can't blame a fellow for trying."

"It's old Dissak's," came a voice. A man emerged from the mass of prisoners, leading a frail white-haired figure with blank eyes. "He's a longtime duster. Doesn't think much anymore. They pick him up now and again, just out of pity."

Mykella waited until the duster was inside the cell, then had to wait until the Southern Guard returned with the keys before she could lock it.

One by one, she locked each cell after returning the prisoners, sometimes one, sometimes two. When she finished—at the far end— she glanced up at the open trapdoor to the roof, then shook her head and turned to the guards. "Two of you stay here, just in case those two try to come back down."

Then she walked past the celled prisoners.

". . . something to remember anyway . . ."

". . . not everyone gaoled by the Lady-Protector . . ."

Mykella managed not to smile as she made her way to the grille gate, which she unlocked and left unlocked. She started down the stairs.

Maeltor met her at the bottom. "Huatyn and his brother jumped off the roof, trying to escape. The brother landed on his head. He's dead. Huatyn broke one leg, it looks like, and maybe his arm."

"Good. I'm glad he's alive. He has a lot to answer for." So did she, but she wasn't about to say so publicly.

"What are you going to do about the gaol?"

"Detail one of the senior squad leaders advising Undercaptain Salyna . . . to act as gaoler. Have him tell the other gaolers that if anything goes wrong, I'll be back, and I won't be happy."

Maeltor offered a wry smile. "That might work . . . for a while."

"You and the commander and I will have to work something out when he returns at the end of the week. I think that from now on, I'll need to interview anyone who is considered for the head gaoler." *Another headache, but who else can sense what lies behind smiles and promising words?* She paused. Rachylana was getting a better sense of people. In time . . .

That would have to wait. For now, Rachylana needed more work with Salyna.

"Give these to the senior squad leader when you can." She handed the keys to Maeltor, then began to walk across the hall toward the open door.

When she emerged into the light, she saw a crowd of more than a hundred people watching from the square. She squared her shoulders, then said, using Talent to boost her words. "Everything is fine. The prisoners are in their cells, and those who have used the gaol improperly are in custody—or dead."

Then she waited as a Southern Guard led the gray to her, and she mounted—barely making it. She was light-headed, and her hands were shaking. She definitely needed to return to the palace and get something to eat.

As she rode back northward, she realized that she had more questions than answers. Who had been paying Huatyn? How many were there? Would she be able to find out once his injuries were treated? Or would she just have to close that ledger?

There was also the question of why a Southern Guard healer was stationed in the palace? Had that been Areyst's doing? When he returned later in the tenday, she just might ask.

There wasn't much she could do about the missing Lhuatyr. She'd never met him, and she couldn't use the Table to find him. About all she could do was offer a reward for his capture, something like ten golds alive, five dead. At the very least, trying to evade capture might send him packing from Tempre. All of the mess around the gaol pointed out—again—why it was unwise to let anything slide. Things always seemed to go from bad to worse.

How can you do everything at once? You don't have enough golds and enough trustworthy people.

For those shortages . . . she had no immediate answer.

50

On Tridi morning, Mykella rode over to the Southern Guard buildings to try to get more information from Caenoral and Huatyn. She learned little new from Caenoral simply because she didn't have enough information to ask questions pointed enough to sense his reactions. Caenoral had been especially insufferable, in his polite and greasy way, promising to reveal everything he knew in return for clemency and exile. In the end, Mykella left him without committing to anything.

Huatyn had just been resigned when she had stopped outside his cell.

"How much did Porofyr pay you?"

"I never met Minister Porofyr."

"Was someone connected with First Seltyr Khanasyl the one who had you kill the man who fired the warehouse of High Factor Hasenyt?"

"I don't know. Fellow gave me ten golds to keep him quiet. Never saw him before."

Most of her inquiries elicited a similar frustrating, if truthful, response. One did not.

"Did you tell Lhuatyr to have Minister Gharyk killed?"

"No! He's always been a hothead. Gharyk couldn't have proved anything except substandard fare. No reason at all to go to Caenoral." Huatyn shook his head. "Frigging son of a poisoned sow . . . I told Kluatyn not to tell him . . ."

That had seemed all too true. In the end, Mykella rode back to the palace in a thoughtful mood. Caenoral knew literally where all-too-many bodies were buried, but to give him clemency? Or to have to spend days and days learning enough to ask decent questions? And how could she justify letting him go with all that he'd done? She had the feeling she'd be better off letting him be executed, information or not.

When she returned to the study, Chalmyr was, as always, waiting. "Lady . . . the announcements are ready to be dispatched."

Announcements? Then she recalled—the letters to various functionaries, not to mention Khanasyl and Lhanyr, about her appointment of Zylander as Minister of Highways and Rivers. "Thank you. Please dispatch them. Make sure that Lhanyr and Khanasyl get theirs first."

"Yes, Lady."

Mykella retreated to her too-warm study, where only a light breeze intermittently fluttered through the windows.

Just before the second glass of the afternoon, Chalmyr announced, "First Seltyr Khanasyl to see you, Lady-Protector."

Mykella managed not to smile. She could sense that the old scrivener had used her full title to remind Khanasyl where he was. "Have him come in." She did stand.

The large, if not overlarge, Seltyr entered the study and offered a bow that was precise in respect, despite a certain amount of concealed anger. "Lady-Protector . . ."

Before he could say more, Mykella gestured to the chairs and seated herself, then waited.

Khanasyl slipped into the middle chair and offered a wide and insincere smile. "Lady-Protector," he began again, "I have just received your announcement of the appointment of High Factor Zylander as the new Minister of Highways and Rivers."

Mykella nodded but did not speak.

"I must say that I find your choice somewhat perplexing. Minister Zylander will be the first factor to hold the post in many, many years."

"You wonder how I could appoint a 'mere' High Factor rather than the traditional appointment of a Seltyr?"

"I must say that the choice has raised more concerns about your interest in trade."

"Why should it? The last Seltyr to hold the post stole from the Treasury and tried to flee to Southgate. At least one other Seltyr considered the same. I have not seen any factors attempting either. They seem to be quite interested in commerce and trade . . . and in remaining in Tempre."

"Still, it is unusual . . . and I did offer several names for your consideration."

"Yes, you did. You might recall that I asked for those recommendations, First Seltyr. You offered me three. None was suitable. I asked the Chief High Factor for his recommendations. One was suitable, and has great understanding of commerce and trade. All have pressed me to appoint a minister. How would you have proceeded?"

Khanasyl frowned. "All those I recommended understand trade."

"I am certain they do, but I caught one trying to bribe an assistant minister, another with a temper so violent that none wish to work with him, and a third who dislikes me intensely, so much so that he almost left Tempre."

"I could not speak to those matters."

"You do not have to, First Seltyr, but I must." Mykella smiled. "Unlike my predecessors, I cannot assume that merely because a man is a Seltyr he will be knowledgeable, loyal, and trustworthy. As we both know, there are good Seltyrs and those who do not have the best interests of Lanachrona in mind. The same is true of High Factors, of course, and even crafters."

"You would not . . ."

"No. I would not, but a minister must consider the needs of all."

"This is most unprecedented . . ."

"That is because the times are unprecedented, First Seltyr. When I make future appointments, I will again ask for your recommendations, and should you present someone as qualified and devoted as did the chief High Factor, I will certainly consider him with great care." Mykella rose. "I am so glad you came to see me, and I do look forward to seeing you at the season-turn ball."

Khanasyl rose quickly. "And I you, Lady."

Mykella remained standing after the study door closed.

She knew she had been brief with Khanasyl, but she had been

pleasant, and she had conveyed that she was certainly open to his recommendations of qualified Seltyrs. Even so, she was still fretting slightly by the time she walked to the family dining room that evening, not just about Khanasyl and the attack on Gharyk and all the other nagging items that she seemed unable to fully resolve but about the likely attack on Lanachrona itself

With all her pondering, she found herself stepping through the archway close to a glass later than normal. Yet she was the first one there although, after she seated herself, Rachylana hurried in, breathing heavily.

"I thought you'd already be eating," offered the redhead as she slid into the chair across the table from Mykella.

"I was late, too." Mykella poured amber wine from the carafe into her goblet.

Muergya set two platters on the table. "We tried to keep the cutlets warm, Lady."

"Thank you." *With this weather, that shouldn't have been hard.* Mykella turned back to look at Rachylana. "I wasn't sure either you or Salyna would be here."

"I don't have to eat all the meals with the recruits, now that I'm an officer trainee. Salyna and Maeltor decided that she needed someone else below her in the chain of command. I'm better at blades than she thought, and I can ride well."

Mykella just looked at her.

"I'm not that good at attacking with a saber . . ."

"But you can sense others, and that gives you an advantage."

"And there are many things I didn't have to learn."

"So you're a provisional undercaptain or something?"

"Something," Rachylana admitted. "It won't be decided until they talk it over with you and Areyst."

"That does make sense. Have they told the other auxiliaries who you are?"

"No." Rachylana took a long swallow from her goblet, then looked directly at her sister. "I want to know something."

"What might that be?"

"What prompted you to choose Areyst as Arms-Commander and

as a possible match? You scarcely knew him when you made him your heir."

"All the officers whose judgment I trusted, and even some whose judgment I didn't, all agreed that he was a good field commander. I could tell that he was honest and that he respected the position of the Lord-Protector. No one else did—except possibly Commander Choalt—and I've never met him."

"That explains why you named him Arms-Commander. You've already explained why you named him heir, and I understand that." Rachylana paused and took another, smaller, swallow of her wine. "Why did you consider him as a possible match—the only possible match, it appears—when you knew so little about him?"

"Whoever I match and wed has to be for more than attraction," Mykella said. "If I wed any suitor from Southgate or the coastal principalities, it would be a disaster. I'm the ruler, but they're all raised to believe that women are subject to their men. I can't have that, and neither can Lanachrona. I might wed the Landarch's son, without those problems, because they, or at least their envoy, believe I'm descended from the Ancients, but that would create another problem because Deforya and Tempre are so far apart that he'd end up having to rule there, and I'd end up ruling here, and that's not the way I want a marriage to be. That leaves marrying someone in Lanachrona." She offered a sardonic smile. "From what you've seen and heard about the available sons of Seltyrs . . . can you see why I don't care for that."

Rachylana laughed, a sound with an undertone of sarcasm. "That's a very good argument, Mykella. It's very, very good. I don't believe a word. You thought that out after you'd decided."

Mykella smiled, ruefully. "You're right. I went on my feelings, but that doesn't mean they were wrong."

"I had feelings, too." Rachylana did not quite snap.

"Are they the same feelings that you have now?" Mykella looked straight into her sister's eyes.

After a moment, Rachylana shook her head. "They were still feelings."

"There are feelings, and there are feelings. I can look back and point out what I just said. Is what I said wrong, even if I started from a feeling?"

"No." After a moment, the redhead said, "You were fortunate. I wasn't."

It was more than fortune. "I can't turn away, even if it happened to be fortune, can I? Should I?"

"You make it sound so cold . . . so calculating."

"It's not . . . quite that way," Mykella admitted. "It isn't for him, either. You know that. You've said as much before."

"Then . . . why don't you show it?" A hint of testiness emerged in Rachylana's voice.

"I can't. Not yet. He knows that, too." *You hope he does.*

"You and Salyna . . . you have to prove everything."

And you don't? "I have to prove it to the Seltyrs and High Factors, or I'll be using my Talent every moment of every day for the rest of my life and ruling by sheer power. I don't want to do that."

"You may, anyway."

"I have to try."

"What about Areyst? How will he feel about it all after he discovers who you really are?"

"That's another reason why he has to succeed as Arms-Commander before anything can happen."

"What if he doesn't?"

"Then . . . it doesn't matter . . . because I won't be Lady-Protector, and he won't be Arms-Commander."

Rachylana looked across the table. "Oh . . . Mykella . . ."

The redhead didn't need to say more.

51

By early afternoon on Septi, Mykella found herself walking to the study windows and looking out. The air had cooled with the arrival of high clouds and a westerly breeze, but she still felt warm and constricted in the study, and it was all too clear that summer was likely to arrive with a vengeance. Her quick trips to Lysia and into the darkness helped cool her, but the effect did not last long. The pulsations of the Table at Lysia were slightly stronger, but not strong enough that she could sense them from Tempre itself.

When she returned to her desk from another walk to the windows, she picked up the missive that had arrived that morning from Almardyn and scanned the lines again.

> . . . while you did not pick the most popular of candidates, few would be willing to argue that you picked a man who is not qualified. Zylander is highly qualified. That may make him less desirable to many Seltyrs and factors, but that is of value to the Protector of Lanchrona . . .

Interesting that he'd now rather refer to the "Protector" than to the "Lady-Protector." A brief smile faded as another thought struck her. *Are matters so bad that you have to reread the favorable missives?*

She set down the missive and walked out into the anteroom. "I'm going to the Table chamber."

"Yes, Lady."

Mykella could have gone to her apartments and called the darkness, but for some reason, she felt like walking. That meant, of course, that one of the stair guards accompanied her from the base of the main staircase to the guarded doorway to the smaller staircase in the northwest corner of the palace. Since the lower corridor was empty, she didn't bother with unlocking the iron-shuttered doors, but used the greenish darkness to slip through the walls into the Table chamber itself.

The Table itself remained the same dullish unseen purple to her senses, but more like a dull black stone to her eyes, except for its mirrorlike surface. She stepped up to it and concentrated on Cheleyza, only to find that the image that appeared after the mists swirled and cleared showed her aunt riding down a broad stone-paved avenue, with long shadows falling across the avenue, suggesting tall buildings on one side.

"It has to be Salcer . . ." There weren't any other cities close enough for Cheleyza to have reached.

After that, she went through another series of searches, but none revealed anything but scenes of routine activity, nothing untoward, and she made her way back up to her formal study.

Shortly after the third glass of the afternoon chimed, she saw Areyst ride into the palace courtyard. She remained at the window, trying to remain calm and composed, until Chalmyr rapped on the door.

"Lady—"

"Have the commander come in." She found herself blushing, and she took a slow breath before walking deliberately toward her desk.

The door opened, and Areyst stepped into the study, then bowed.

"Commander." Mykella tried not to look too long into his eyes as he straightened. She failed, if not too obviously, but that didn't matter . . . much . . . because, as she looked away, he lowered his eyes.

"Lady. I am here as requested."

She could sense a hint of . . . something. Attraction, concern, or both?

"I'm glad that you are." She seated herself and waited for a moment. "How was your trip from Viencet?"

"Hot and without problems." He leaned forward, ever so slightly, in the chair. "As soon as I arrived, Undercaptain Salyna appeared."

"About the season-turn parade, I presume?"

He nodded.

"What is your honest opinion, Commander?"

"I have always been uneasy with the idea of women being used as troopers in combat, and I fear this is a step toward that."

"The Alectors did so."

"And they perished."

"Not for that reason. Do you doubt women would be helpful, especially now?"

Areyst shook his head. "That is the problem. They would be helpful. Even without full training, I can see how they have kept headquarters in better shape. Yet . . ."

"Is their progress too slow?"

"Captain Maeltor has sent reports on the auxiliaries. Your sister—or sisters—have been more effective than he imagined possible."

"Then . . . do you think they should ride on Novdi?"

"I must admit that I see the advantages, but you realize that will not sit well with many in Tempre."

"I know that, but I have seen that matters must change. Now we have a reason to make that change. It would be harder if we tried later."

"Then I will agree that they should ride, but as a secondary group before the main headquarters party."

"That would be for the best."

He smiled. "You are also persuasive and effective. That seems to be a trait you all share."

"How effective has Salyna been?"

"According to Captain Maeltor, most ride as well as any ranker after initial training, and they behave like guards. Some are still a little awkward with sabers, but all can use a rifle and get the bullet into a target. Most can do so from the saddle. Provisional Undercaptain Rachylana has made exceptional progress."

"Oh?" Mykella wasn't surprised but wanted to hear more.

"She insisted on additional sparring with the captain, on the grounds that no one else could teach her. He noted that she was exceptionally . . . fierce, but disciplined." Areyst smiled wryly. "I fear she may have impressed him too much."

"Have I impressed you too much?" Mykella asked quietly.

Areyst froze for an instant. Then he let an embarrassed smile appear. "It would be useless to protest that. You can sense all that I feel." He paused. "I can only say that—"

"Commander," she interrupted him quickly, "your conduct has been exemplary, and your devotion to Lanachrona and your duties has been equally outstanding. You have my greatest admiration." She paused but momentarily. "Unhappily, as Arms-Commander, the situation you face is also the greatest challenge encountered by any Arms-Commander in generations, and that must concern us both before anything else is considered or decided."

She wanted to smile wildly at the hope that flared behind his eyes even as he replied in an even tone, "I understand that fully, Lady."

"Earlier this afternoon, I used the Table to discover that Lady Cheleyza and the Northcoast forces were riding through Salcer."

Areyst frowned. "Our scouts have solid reports that a good ten companies of Skrelyn's forces have stationed themselves at Areyka. They have been there for several days."

"That's the last sizable town in Midcoast, is it not?"

The commander nodded. "Skrelyn cannot be trusting enough to have all his forces ready on the border."

"So a larger force will likely accompany Chalcaer and Cheleyza?"

"I would judge so." He fingered his chin. "Can you determine that through the Table?"

"I can try. Sometimes. They won't leave Salcer today, though, I wouldn't think."

"That is unlikely."

"I'll look later, and in the morning. What have you done about Thesma? It's less than ten vingts from the border."

"We have warned the villagers. I would like to tell them more, but . . ."

"You think I should offer recompense for lost goods?"

"If it is possible. It is a very small village."

Mykella shook her head. "If we are successful, I will offer recompense afterwards. Should any mention of that occur before, the claims will mount to three times what they should be." She sighed. "I will have to . . ." Then she smiled. "That is a task for a certain undercaptain in the auxiliaries."

Areyst returned the smile. "You are already finding tasks for them."

"I cannot do everything. That has become most apparent." She cleared her throat. "Did Captain Maeltor inform you about the difficulties with the gaol?"

"He did. The arrangement you suggested will work for a time, possibly a season, but . . ."

For the next glass, Mykella was most careful to keep the conversation on the needs of Lanachrona and the Southern Guards.

Finally, Areyst said, "I have nothing else to report, Lady. Do you have other questions?"

"When Lord Gharyk was attacked, even before I reached his study, there was a Southern Guard healer present and attending to his wound. You never mentioned that."

Areyst smiled, but there was a certain embarrassment behind his expression. "I knew that the palace healer had betrayed his trust and that you had not replaced him. I thought it . . . prudent . . . to place a healer nearby."

"What else have you arranged . . . in the nature of prudence?"

"A few extra guards in and around the palace. They are not so much for your protection as for the protection of those who serve you loyally. They appear to be more . . . vulnerable than are you, and your sisters are amid Southern Guards much of the time."

"Your thoughtfulness is much appreciated. It is also welcome . . . and necessary." Mykella rose. "I do appreciate your reports and your presence, and I look forward to observing the season-turn parade and seeing you afterwards at the ball. As the heir, you will escort me personally."

Areyst sprang to his feet. "Lady . . . you know how I feel about that . . ."

"Yes, Commander, I believe I do." *And I hope you continue to feel the other ways that you do after we make our way through all that lies before us.* She pushed away the other, more disturbing, possibilities that faced them and offered a pleasant smile. "Until later."

He bowed again.

When he lifted his eyes to hers, for a moment, neither moved nor spoke.

Mykella felt as though she did not take a breath until the door closed behind him.

52

Late on Novdi morning, a glass before noon, Mykella had finished studying the Table. For the past two days, she had been trying to manipulate the images displayed in an effort to determine what Areyst and she needed to know—the size of the Midcoast force accompanying Cheleyza and Chalcaer—but, finally, that morning, after almost a glass of working with the Table, she had finally mastered a better way of focusing the images. That hadn't given her all the information she wanted, but the images had revealed a long column of riders, the first half wearing the maroon of Midcoast and the last half the dark green of Northcoast.

The other matter that concerned her was that she could sense clearly the growing pulsations and brilliance of the Table in Lysia—all the way from Tempre. She'd made a quick transit there but sensed that the pinkish purpleness around that Table had barely increased—so far. She had no doubts that would soon change.

Then she'd had to return to Tempre to hurry and dress for the season-turn parade. In the end, at a half glass before noon, she dismounted at the foot of the small reviewing stand placed for the season-turn parade at the base of the Great Piers, equidistant from the ancient green towers at either end of the piers. Accompanied by Squad Leader Casaryk and two Southern Guards, she climbed to the topmost level, where the three remained as escorts. Lord Zylander and his wife were already there, standing on the second level, and before long, they were joined by Lord and Lady Gharyk, followed by Forester Loryalt, who was unaccompanied.

Waiting in the stand in the damp and too-warm weather, Mykella was glad that she only wore a nightsilk shirt and a light silver shimmersilk vest. She would have boiled in even a light jacket. Her eyes surveyed those in the reviewing stand below her, catching sight of Cerlyk, as well as High Factor Hasenyt. She could also sense more than a few pair of eyes covertly scanning her, and she maintained a pleasant smile.

Farther to the south, along both sides of the avenue, were a number of women, many of them in worn and frayed holiday finery. Mykella did not recall such a group at previous parades, but had that been because she had not been looking at the bystanders all that closely?

Before long, the mounted guards would ride northward toward the piers along the great eternastone highway that had become the avenue inside Tempre. Once they passed the reviewing stand, they would follow the turn in the avenue and head due east past the palace itself, then to the Southern Guard compound. Areyst had brought Fourth Company from Viencet rather than returning either First, Second, or Third Company—those usually stationed in Tempre—doubtless because the troopers in the first three companies could use more training.

A wistful smile crossed Mykella's lips as she thought of her mother's words about the need for the tradition of the parade. Given how many traditions her own presence as Lady-Protector had upset, she certainly hadn't wanted to destroy another one by canceling the first season-turn parade since she had become Lady-Protector.

To the south, she saw the four Southern Guards bearing trumpets riding toward the stand. Others did, too, and most eyes turned. At that moment, Mykella began to gather light to herself, not a blinding glare, but what she thought was just enough to highlight her presence in the reviewing stand—not enough to cause people to turn but enough for them to notice if they looked in her direction.

When the trumpeters reached a point even with the southern edge of the reviewing stand, they raised their instruments. A crisp but lengthy fanfare filled the avenue, and when the trumpeters passed Mykella, they lifted the trumpets in salute. Behind them some fifty yards or so rode the standard-bearers of Fourth Company, followed by the company officer and his squad leaders, then the company rankers.

As she had seen so many times before, when the company standard bearer passed her, he lowered the company ensign in a salute, holding it at a forty-five-degree angle all the way past the stand before snapping it back erect.

After Fourth Company, another fifty yards back, came the headquarters contingent, led by a standard bearer—and followed by Salyna in the riding undress uniform of the auxiliaries. At first glance she looked no different from any other young junior officer, and Mykella noted that she had swept her blond hair, never that long, up under the officer's cap. Rachylana rode behind Salyna by several yards, and her red hair was also up, as was that of every auxiliary.

Muted cheers rose from the workingwomen south of the reviewing stand as the auxiliaries passed. Mykella smiled slightly more broadly.

Given all her worries about Salyna's project, Mykella was relieved. The women looked as though they belonged in their new uniforms, and she saw no obvious lapses in formation or in bearing. Part of her feeling was confirmed by the fact that the murmurs from those in the reviewing stand and along the avenue did not even begin until the auxiliaries were almost in front of the stand, and the standard-bearer dipped the headquarters ensign.

"... women ... in uniform?"

"... uniforms a little different ..."

"Some of the riders in uniform are women ..."

"... expect that from a Lady-Protector ... a bit much ... don't you think ..."

"... needs all the men to fight ..."

At least someone sees a reason behind it.

Following the auxiliaries came the male guards of the headquarters group, only about a score in all. Then came a rider bearing the banner of the Arms-Commander, another touch Mykella did not recall.

Mykella used her Talent to project an aura of light around Areyst as he neared the stand, and the faintest link of light between them. Riding beside Areyst was Captain Maeltor, and behind them four Southern Guards with drums, keeping a low beat and signifying the end of the column.

The standard-bearer for the Arms-Commander lowered that ensign early, and as Areyst neared the point where he was almost abreast of Mykella, he removed his visored cap, held it across his chest, and bowed in the saddle in her direction. As he straightened, his eyes met hers, if but for an instant. Then he replaced the cap. Only then did the Arms-Commander's banner rise again.

A series of low murmurs rippled through the crowd, and more eyes focused on Mykella.

". . . is the heir, you know . . ."

". . . handsome enough . . ."

". . . just for show . . . be a match to the Landarch's son . . . what else can she do?"

". . . women in the Guards . . . Arms-Commander as heir . . . not the way things used to be . . ."

As the various functionaries and their spouses or guests who had been invited to be on the reviewing stand began to step down and disperse, Lady Gharyk—Jylara—turned, looked up at Mykella, and offered a nod and a knowing smile.

Mykella kept smiling as she prepared to leave the reviewing stand just after the others.

Once she returned to the palace, she'd have to ready herself for the evening ahead . . . and the ball, where every word and gesture would be scrutinized for some meaning.

53

"It's . . . like the other, Lady." Wyandra, the dressing maid Mykella utilized mainly for seeing that she had clean nightsilks, stepped back after fastening the last button of Mykella's new ball gown.

Mykella surveyed herself in the bedchamber mirror. The gown ordered by Rachylana almost matched the darkly bright green of the depths, and Mykella wondered if, in using the Table, Rachylana had ever seen that shade. The gown's cut was both conservative and daring, with a high neck and sleeves that tapered almost skintight at

Mykella's wrists. Above the low waist, the green shimmersilk fitted her figure tightly, but not enough to hamper her movement. The quarter-full skirt, a touch longer than ankle length, allowed her easy movement as well as to wear her formal boots rather than dancing shoes.

"I like it." Mykella picked up the green gloves from the dressing table, a pair that matched the dress perfectly.

"It looks wonderful on you," replied Uleana, standing behind Wyandra.

Wonderful? I doubt that. "Thank you both," said Mykella, nodding to the pair, then turned and walked toward the family parlor to meet her sisters.

She also needed to tell Areyst what she'd discovered that morning about the coastal forces, not that a few glasses made that much difference, but, when she'd tried to reach him after the parade, according to Maeltor, he'd been inspecting the Southern Guard compound and conducting an additional review of the auxiliaries, and in neither duty had she wished to intrude.

Before she even reached the door of the parlor, Rachylana stepped out into the outer corridor, wearing a scoop-necked gown of a pale but intense blue that highlighted her mahogany-red hair, with a shawl of the same shade. Salyna followed, wearing the same gown she'd worn at the last ball, one with a square-cut neck in a rich but muted blue that brought out the color in her face. She did not wear a shawl, but a new matching jacket with three-quarter sleeves.

"I don't know how you do it, Mykella" observed Rachylana. "It shouldn't look that good on you, but it does." She offered a knowing grin to her older sister.

"It's that shade of green," Salyna said. "It makes her look more alive."

"That was the idea," replied Rachylana. "I had a hard time getting the dyers to come up with exactly the right shade. The rest was easy, because Wyandra and the seamstresses just followed the pattern of the other green dress."

Mykella looked to Salyna, about to ask her about Areyst's review, when she heard the sound of boots behind her. She turned.

Elwayt was leading Areyst toward them. The Arms-Commander wore the full-dress dark blue and cream uniform of a Southern Guard officer.

By the Ancients . . . he is handsome. Mykella managed not to stare or gape.

At almost the same moment, Areyst's eyes fixed on Mykella, and his purposeful stride faltered—if but for an instant.

From behind Mykella's shoulder, Rachylana whispered, "The way he looked at you any woman would die for."

"I'd rather live for it," murmured Mykella, barely moving her lips, before returning Areyst's warm smile.

The Arms-Commander bowed, then extended an arm to Mykella. "Lady-Protector?"

Mykella took it. "My pleasure, Commander."

Mykella and Areyst led the way down the main staircase of the palace and along the back corridors—cordoned off by the Southern Guards in dress uniforms—to the north entry to the ballroom. Slightly behind them followed Rachylana and Salyna.

The ballroom itself was just north of the southeast corner of the main level of the palace. Created centuries before by merging a series of chambers, it was narrow, with windows only on the eastern and southern walls. An ancient parquet floor had been laid over the stone floor tiles, and the wall hangings were the traditional dark blue and cream.

The receiving line was far shorter, of necessity, than at past balls, with Salyna at the front, Rachylana next, followed by Areyst, then Mykella as Lady-Protector—the first time ever that the position of power at the end had been claimed by a woman. Elwayt stood before the receiving line, announcing the names.

Because invitations to the ball were limited to those of import in Tempre, such as her ministers and the High Factors and Seltyrs—or envoys—Mykella had expected the number of attendees to be smaller; but Rachylana had earlier informed her that, in the end, the number attending was likely to be higher.

Out of curiosity, and nothing less.

The very first person in the line was Assistant Forester Cerlyk, accompanied by a younger black-haired woman. "Lady-Protector . . . my wife Shalyana."

Mykella could sense the young woman was expecting, although the cut of her gown did not reveal it. "It's good to meet you, Shalyana. Your husband has been of great service."

"Thank you, Lady."

"You're welcome. Do you have any other children?"

"Ah . . . we have none," said Cerlyk. "We have hoped . . ."

Mykella smiled. "It may be that your hopes have been answered."

Shalyana beamed and squeezed Cerlyk's arm. As they left, Mykella heard her murmur, ". . . told you so . . . is an Ancient."

Areyst glanced at Mykella but said nothing.

After Cerlyk came Lord Gharyk and Jylara.

"Lady-Protector," offered Gharyk, smiling slightly nervously.

"Lord Gharyk, Lady Jylara, you are always welcome here. I trust your shoulder is better," she said to the Finance Minister. "If it should trouble you . . ."

"It's no trouble at all, Lady."

From the feelings of Jylara, that was not precisely true, and Mykella looked to her. "Do take care of him."

That did bring a smile to Jylara's face. "I'll do my best, Lady."

Then came High Factor Rhavyl and his daughter, Xyena, followed by Seltyr Almardyn and his wife, a graceful and slender gray-haired woman, who smiled warmly at Mykella. Then came Forester Loryalt and his wife.

Before long, Zylander appeared, with a woman who could almost have been his sister. "Lady-Protector, my wife Lexyla."

"Lord Zylander, I'm pleased to see you both." Mykella smiled warmly.

Zylander's return smile was shy, and he eased past Mykella.

"You have asked much of him, Lady. Do not cast him aside on a whim," Lexyla murmured.

"Your husband will be a good minister, and whims are bad ruling, Lady Lexyla," replied Mykella softly, impressed by the woman's quiet directness.

Lexyla offered a nod in response.

After a procession of Seltyrs and High Factors whom Mykella knew by name and little else, Khanasyl and his wife appeared.

The First Seltyr looked to Areyst and smiled. "It's good to see you here, Commander."

"I'm here by the power and grace of the Lady-Protector, First Seltyr. It is unwise to disregard either." Areyst smiled politely.

Khanasyl bowed to Mykella. "Lady-Protector. Perhaps a dance and a word later?"

"Of course." Mykella inclined her head.

As Khanasyl and his wife eased away, Areyst glanced at Mykella.

He's actually a bit jealous. She reached out and squeezed his wrist gently, even as she turned to greet Seltyr Pualavyn.

Before long, after High Factor Barsytan and his daughter, a stocky wide-eyed young woman, came Seltyr Klevytr, with his daughter, surprisingly to Mykella.

"Lady-Protector, my daughter Kietyra, whom you met in less pleasant circumstances."

"Less pleasant, Seltyr, but she comported herself with character and poise."

Kietyra flushed as Mykella turned to her. "Lady-Protector, I cannot thank you enough . . ."

"Your safety and your father's presence in Tempre are thanks enough."

"You are kind, Lady-Protector," murmured Klevytr.

"To those who support Lanachrona," she replied even more quietly.

Somewhat later among those entering were High Factor Hasenyt and his wife, and even later, Seltyr Thaen and his wife, both very quiet and subdued, in contrast to his reputation.

When the last of the guests had presented themselves, Mykella and Areyst walked toward the low dais on which the orchestra players were seated, a permanent platform set against the midpoint of the long inner wall of the ballroom. Salyna and Rachylana followed, and the four stopped below the orchestra.

"Everyone was most formal and polite," offered Salyna, dryly. "Not a word less or more than proper. With a few acceptable exceptions."

"You didn't see what happened at the other end of the line, did she, Commander?" asked Rachylana.

Areyst smiled. "I would defer to the Lady-Protector."

"Wise man," replied Salyna. "That also means that Mykella conveyed warnings without speaking."

"I was most polite to everyone," said Mykella demurely.

"Polite can be . . ." Rachylana stopped and looked to her right, from where Khanasyl approached Mykella.

The First Seltyr bowed deeply. "Lady-Protector, if I might have this dance?"

"Of course, First Seltyr" Mykella wasn't thrilled about dancing with the tall Seltyr, but she did want to know exactly what he had in mind and what new concerns had roused him to request the dance, and her questions of Salyna and talk with Areyst could wait a bit.

Khanasyl took her hand, barely touching her, as if she were both fragile and deadly, as he guided her into those already dancing. "Might I ask what you intend of the commander since you have informally named him your heir?"

"Must I intend anything beyond that? I designated him as heir so that everyone would know that, in the event of the unforeseen, a strong Protector would follow."

"Yet you had him beside you tonight."

"Exactly where the designated heir should be."

"Then I must needs be more direct, Lady. Do you intend to wed?"

"At some time, that will be necessary, but questions of matching and marriage, First Seltyr, must wait until all Corus is satisfied that a Lady-Protector can rule effectively . . ."

"That might be a long time, Lady . . ."

"The way many now think in Corus, the matter will be settled within the year, I believe, and then, if you have questions, we shall talk once more."

Mykella could see, past the First Seltyr's shoulder, Areyst dancing with Rachylana, and her sister apparently asking a question.

"You seem most confident, Lady."

"All the past Lords-Protector have been confident. For some, that confidence was justified. For others, it was not. Seldom were the predictions of those observing all that accurate. So we shall see."

"Your words and actions have doubtless angered both Southgate and the coastal princes. Do you honestly believe Lanachrona can stand against all?"

"Anger and actions are not the same," Mykella pointed out. "Prince Skrelyn has already forced out most of the Seltyrs, has he not?"

"So it is rumored."

"Southgate does not have enough armsmen to attack Lanachrona. Would the Council of Southgate ally itself with Skrelyn? They may not be pleased with Lanachrona, but a Lanachrona controlled by Midcoast and Northcoast would be far less to their liking—or their purses."

"That suggests you can prevail against the two coastal princes."

"If they choose to attack, we will defend. If not, we will trade."

"Lady-Protector, I would that your actions be as effective as your words, but how are we to know?"

"Acts are decided by actions, and for a ruler who has just come to power, no words will suffice in the minds of the doubtful."

Khanasyl laughed softly and ironically. "I do not think you have answered me."

"In time, you will see that I have. Wait and see how I act before you do, First Seltyr."

"I have no choice, do I?"

"No other wise choice," replied Mykella with a smile she hoped was enigmatic.

As the music of the dance faded, Khanasyl had almost guided Mykella back to where they had begun. "My thanks for the pleasure of your company and your words, Lady-Protector."

"And for your words," replied Mykella.

Mykella waited as Areyst and Rachylana returned to join her and Salyna.

"That was interesting," observed Salyna. "What did the First Seltyr want?"

"He wanted to know how Lanachrona would stand against Southgate and the coastal princes. I told him that Southgate wasn't about to attack us, and they won't."

"They won't?" asked Rachylana, looking to Areyst.

"No," replied the commander. "They are not equipped to ride or travel long distances. They have no way of supplying such a force, and our towns and hamlets are spread too far apart for raiding to support a force until they are well inside Lanachrona."

"That didn't make him happy, I'd wager," said Salyna.

"He's the type that's seldom happy," observed Rachylana.

As the orchestra began to play another melody, Areyst turned and bowed politely. "Might I have this dance, Lady?"

"You might." Mykella inclined her head and smiled. The smile was anything but perfunctory or forced.

Areyst took her right hand, placing his left hand at waist level on her back, guiding her gently into the flow of dancers. His fingers felt warm to Mykella even through her gloves.

"The last time we danced, Lady, I believe we talked of numbers and ledgers, and I observed that was an unusual preoccupation for the daughter of the Lord-Protector. I had no idea how wrong I was, for it is certainly necessary for a Lady-Protector."

"Necessary, but not always followed by all Lords-Protector," replied Mykella. "That failure, I fear, led to my father's undoing. Golds tell far more than glib words."

"What do the golds tell you now?"

"That the Seltyrs still doubt but fear me enough to pay their tariffs although it appears that most will wait until the last moment. That many of the golds diverted from the Treasury went to pay Northcoast to increase its cavalry."

"Can you prove that enough to convince the Seltyrs?" Areyst guided her past another couple. The woman eyed Areyst speculatively.

"No. That matters little because we face what is, not what might have been."

Areyst laughed. "So few understand that. They worry about what they might have done otherwise when that but wastes time and effort."

"I tried to find where you were this afternoon, to tell you what I discovered in the Table, but Captain Maeltor said you were occupied with the auxiliaries. What did you determine?"

"I was about to ask the same of you."

"Indulge me," said Mykella with a smile.

"The women are better trained than I could have hoped for the time they have been under discipline. The Southern Guard squad leaders who have watched say that Undercaptain Salyna is merciless, but not quite impossible, in her demands of them. I fear that she will insist on bringing them to Viencet as support."

"Fear? Would that not allow every Southern Guard in Viencet to oppose the invaders?"

"It would."

Mykella understood what he meant . . . all too well. "It may be a risk we must take. It took me almost two days, but I did determine that the Midcoast forces accompanying Cheleyza and Chalcaer look to be equal to those of Northcoast."

"Could you tell how many companies of each?"

"It is hard to tell with the Table. I would guess fifteen of each."

Areyst frowned, if momentarily. "With ten companies already on the border, we will be outnumbered by more than two to one."

"Are your troops not better trained and more experienced?"

"For the most part, I believe so."

"How long do we have before the princes enter Lanachrona?"

"They have moved more quickly than they might have. In his last dispatch, Commander Choalt estimated that they would reach Thesma a week from the coming Octdi, if not before. Your information suggests it may be sooner."

"Isn't that hard on the mounts?"

"They stockpiled grain along the highway south, and they had sent spare mounts south to just north of the Vedra weeks ago."

"They had to have planned some of this well before . . ." Mykella didn't finish the sentence.

"Well before you became Lady-Protector. It would appear that way." Areyst smiled ironically. "I do not think that they are using those mounts for what was once planned."

"Joramyl and Chalcaer planned to attack Midcoast and split it between them? I've thought so for some time."

"You never said anything, Lady."

"I had one torn scrap of paper that suggested it. Nothing else. Who would believe that? Besides, it's better to let people believe that we were the target all along. Otherwise, Southgate and even Deforya might think that the Lords-Protector—and now the Lady-Protector— have aims of great conquest."

Areyst looked directly at her, his pale green eyes fixing on hers. "You would unsettle any man or woman, Lady."

"I believe you told me that when last we danced, Commander," Mykella replied dryly.

"It is no less true now."

"Do I unsettle you?" Mykella's question was direct, if softly offered.

"Might I be honest?"

"Please."

His eyes again sought hers. "You unsettle me more than I thought anyone ever could. Yet"—he took a not-quite-deep breath—"I would rather be unsettled by you than pleased by anyone else."

What do you say to that? Her fingers tightened slightly around his, and her other hand squeezed his shoulder. "Thank you."

For another few moments, they danced without speaking, before the music died away, and Areyst escorted her back to the position before the orchestra and her sisters. As he did, Mykella could tell he was worried that he had offered too much or perhaps exceeded his position.

She was about to ask him to dance when Chief High Factor Lhanyr approached.

"Might I ask for a dance, Lady-Protector?"

"You might." Mykella glanced toward Areyst, who immediately turned to Salyna.

Lhanyr was definitely not the dancer that Khanasyl had been, and Areyst was. Mykella paused mentally. *Was Areyst that good a dancer, or did you enjoy dancing with him so much that you really didn't notice?* Areyst certainly wasn't a bad dancer; but the rest hadn't mattered, she realized.

"Zylander said that you have been most supportive in allowing him to pick his own assistant minister."

"So long as I approve of his choice," Mykella said lightly. "Some of the assistant ministers in the past have been less than satisfactory."

"How can one tell before the fact?"

"One cannot tell about exactly how well they will do, but one can tell if they are honest and willing."

"You can tell that, Lady. I do not know that others can." The freckles on Lhanyr's face stood out more when he smiled . . . or they seemed to.

"We all have talents."

"Some are more valuable than others."

Mykella merely nodded.

"You know that the Seltyrs are displeased with your choice."

"I am certain that they are, but none of those recommended to me were satisfactory. If a Seltyr of ability and probity had been suggested, I would have considered him. I do not have time to meet with every Seltyr in Lanachrona to determine if he happened to be interested and if he had the ability for the position. I must rely on you and the First Seltyr. You offered better men."

"Had I not?"

"I would have asked you and the First Seltyr for other possibilities."

Lhanyr nodded thoughtfully, then eased her through the other dancers back to her position before the orchestra dais.

Mykella surveyed the dancers, catching sight of Salyna and Areyst, then turned to Rachylana, who she found talking to Kietyra.

"Oh . . . Lady-Protector . . . I didn't mean to intrude . . ."

"You're not intruding. It is a ball. Please keep talking."

Kietyra swallowed.

Mykella looked to Rachylana.

"You were asking what it was like to be raised in the palace," Rachylana said. "If we hadn't had sisters, it would have been very lonely."

"But . . . my sisters and I . . ."

"Don't always get along?" asked Mykella with a laugh. "We didn't either. Sometimes, we still don't. But we're still sisters." She shifted her weight from one boot to the other. She was already glad she wore formal boots. She couldn't have imagined how she might have felt wearing dancing shoes.

As the music for that dance faded, Areyst reappeared with Salyna.

Mykella looked to him—blond, green-eyed, and handsome—and said, "I believe the next dance is mine, Commander."

"It would be my pleasure."

Rachylana had kept glancing to the far side of the ballroom. Abruptly, she looked away and back at Kietyra. "I'm sorry. You were saying that your sisters . . ."

"They all think they know so much more because they're older."

"We have had that . . . discussion," said Salyna. "I'm the youngest as well. That was one of the reasons I took up arms training."

Kietyra's mouth opened. "You . . . you were the one in the parade." Her eyes went to Rachylana. "Both of you."

Rachylana put a finger to her lips. "Talk about Salyna, not about me. She is the accomplished one."

Mykella glanced to one side, where she saw another officer in a formal uniform moving toward them. She frowned for an instant but said nothing as Maeltor appeared and bowed to Rachylana as the music swelled once more.

"If I might, Lady."

Rachylana offered a polite smile, one that seemed false in a different way to Mykella, and replied, "You might."

Mykella stepped toward Areyst, who immediately took her hand.

"The Lady-Protector asked him to dance . . ." Mykella could hear the marveling tone in Kietyra's voice as Areyst guided her away from the others and into the dancers.

Areyst had also heard those words, because he looked down at Mykella and murmured, "She knows you little, Lady, for no man would refuse such an invitation."

"Many would, were I not Lady-Protector."

"I would not," he replied.

The truth Mykella sensed behind those words made the next moments the best of the evening . . . and of the ball.

54

Despite how late it had been before Mykella retired on Novdi evening after the Ball, she woke early—and hungry. After dressing, she hurried to the breakfast room. Salyna was already there, and Rachylana quickly followed Mykella, scrambling into a gray auxiliary working tunic even as she entered the room.

Muergya arrived with two large pots of tea. "Be back with ham-and-egg casserole, Ladies."

Mykella took her seat and immediately poured the tea into her mug. "I think we avoided any real problems last night."

"You might say that," offered Salyna. "In the near future, anyway."

"Mykella, you looked happy when you were dancing with the commander," said Rachylana. "I don't know as I've ever seen you look that way."

"Love will do that," suggested Salyna.

"It's not love." *Not yet.*

"You could have deceived us," retorted Rachylana. "Will you marry him?"

"He has to agree, and I haven't asked him. There's no point in it until after we deal with Chalcaer, Cheleyza, and Skrelyn. I told you that."

"After last night, I wondered if you'd changed your mind." Rachylana grinned.

"What if he says 'no' when you ask?" A mischievous smile followed Salyna's question.

"I won't force him."

"As if you'd have to with the way he looked at you before the ball." Rachylana laughed.

Mykella looked back across the table at Rachylana. "I didn't know that a certain captain was on the invitation list."

"Yes," added Salyna. "How did that happen to come about?"

Rachylana returned Mykella's look with one perfectly guileless—even if Mykella could sense both embarrassment and amusement behind the innocent expression. "The two most senior officers of the Southern Guards in Tempre are always invited. Commander Areyst is the most senior, and, at present, Captain Maeltor is the next most senior."

"Very convenient," suggested Salyna.

"He was very impartial. He asked both of us to dance the same number of times."

"You kept count?" Salyna raised her eyebrows.

Mykella couldn't help herself. She began to laugh.

After a moment, so did the other two.

The laughter died away as Muergya returned with a single casserole dish and a basket of bread. Mykella lifted her mug, then set it down at the insistent rapping on the outer door to the main palace corridor.

The three glanced at each other.

"Yes?" Mykella finally said.

"Squad Leader Casaryk, Lady. Commander Areyst wishes a few moments of your time before he departs for Viencet."

"I'll be right there." Mykella rose and walked toward the outer door.

"What is it?" asked Rachylana.

"It can't be good," replied Mykella, looking back. "He wasn't supposed to leave until tomorrow." She opened the door.

Casaryk had already retreated, and, some twenty yards away, Areyst stood at the top of the main staircase, wearing his undress blues, his visored cap in his hand.

Mykella walked toward him, stopping a yard or so away.

"Lady-Protector." He inclined his head.

"Commander. I take it we face some unforeseen difficulties?"

"Not so much unforeseen as occurring earlier than anticipated. The Midcoast forces crossed into Lanachrona yesterday morning and attacked Thesma. The villagers had hidden all their grain already. They fled into the forests to the north. Skrelyn's men put the empty village to the torch." Areyst shook his head. "They won't get supplies that way, but it's going to be hard on the next two villages, one way or the other."

"They'll flee, won't they?"

"Baryma has close to four hundred crofters and growers."

Mykella understood. Short of burning their own grain and supplies, and driving their livestock into the woods where reclaiming it would be difficult if not impossible, the villagers had no feasible way to deny some of those supplies to the Midcoast forces.

"When do you want the auxiliaries?" she asked.

"Not before Tridi. Quattri would be better. I have already told all the headquarters staff to accompany Fourth Company. Captain Maeltor will accompany Undercaptain Salyna and the auxiliaries. She will have to leave half a score to keep the quarters and buildings, and those dealing with the gaol. Maeltor will leave those recovering from their injuries and a few others."

"They will leave on Quattri, then. Do you think that this is designed to stir us up and that their main forces will regroup and rest before attacking?"

"That is possible. It is also possible that they feel an early and strong attack is more likely to be effective. I cannot tell from what has happened so far. I will send dispatches daily."

"You do not—"

"I know you can see much, but there is much you cannot."

Mykella had to grant that although she was beginning to feel that she should have spent more time working with the Table, distasteful as the proximity to the pinkish purple felt. "I will be there when it is necessary."

"Lady, you should not . . ." Areyst broke off his words.

"I should not do what?" snapped Mykella.

"I am only concerned about you," he said quietly.

"Concerned?" Mykella was about to say more except that she couldn't but help sense the depth of feeling behind his words. She said nothing more, instead looking at him steadily. "I will be fine. If I do not stand for my land, how can I ask anyone else to do so?" *Especially when you have shields and they do not?*

"You will send word?"

"If and as I can. I would be there with the auxiliaries, except there are . . . signs that the Ifrits may also be about to try something, and I would like to be near a Table until I am needed."

"Lady . . ." More unspoken concern lay behind the single word.

"Commander, we each will do what we must." Although she wanted to reach out and touch him, at least take his hand, she did not—not with Casaryk and the stair guards watching, if from a distance. "I will join you as I can." *That is a promise in more ways than one.*

The faintest hint of a smile crossed his lips, and he inclined his head. As he straightened, he murmured, "I look forward to that."

Then he offered a last smile, turned, and headed down the main staircase.

Not wishing to seem too concerned—or lovestruck—Mykella also turned and walked back to the breakfast room.

Both sisters looked to her as she closed the door behind her and returned to her place at the table and her uneaten breakfast.

"What was that all about?" asked Salyna.

"Skrelyn's advance forces put Thesma to the torch yesterday morning. Areyst got the courier message early this morning. He's returning with Fourth Company and the headquarters group, most of it anyway."

"Mykella . . . you know we're outnumbered," began Salyna.

"Yes, you can. I don't like it. Neither does Areyst, but we'll need every man."

"What do you mean?" asked Rachylana.

"Salyna is going to take the auxiliaries to Viencet to handle all the support duties. That will free what . . . another company?" Mykella looked to her youngest sister.

"More like a company and a half. Perhaps two." Salyna paused. "He didn't come to me . . ."

"Captain Maeltor will accompany you. Commander Areyst asked me to tell you because of the press of time. Remember . . . he just found out a glass or so ago." That wasn't quite what Areyst had said, but in spirit it was true enough, and the fact that he had not said so directly told Mykella that he was worried indeed.

55

For the remainder of Decdi and all of Londi, Mykella saw Salyna and Rachylana only in passing, as both busied themselves with the coming transfer of the auxiliaries from Tempre to Viencet— excepting the handful or so aiding with prisoners and the gaol. Mykella did have to expend several hundred more golds for supplies and three wagons, in addition to almost another thousand golds to the Southern Guards.

On Duadi, after breakfast, Mykella made her way to the Table chamber to check on the progress of the coastal forces. When she entered the chamber, she could immediately sense that the purplish pink glow of the Table was brighter, not greatly, but noticeably; but that glow was not pulsing.

She forced herself to concentrate first on Cheleyza and Chalcaer. When the mists swirled away, she could make out the dark-haired figure of her aunt, mounted and reined up, seemingly on a rise or hill-top. Mykella fumbled mentally for a moment, then managed to refocus the image from a greater distance and some height above Cheleyza, showing her and her brother on a rise to the north of the road.

After several more attempts, she finally obtained a view that showed almost the entire column, clearly more than several vingts in length, riding along a stretch of the great eternastone road that looked to be similar to that in western Lanachrona. By raising her viewpoint, Mykella could just barely make out sparsely forested hills to the north of the road and a line of silver that was likely the River Vedra.

She blotted her forehead and let the image lapse.

After a moment, she let herself drop into the darkness, not so much because she intended to travel anywhere but to obtain a sense of what might be happening with the other Tables. Almost immediately, she could feel a difference in the orange and yellow that was Lysia, and she gathered more of the deeper darkness to her.

Recalling her past follies, the instant she emerged in the chamber in Lysia, she re-created full shields. She needn't have done so because the room was empty. Even so, the Table was not only brighter, but the pulsations were stronger, yet she could determine no increased sense of the ugly purple pinkness that heralded the pending arrival or presence of an Alector. Finally, she dropped her shields and surrendered herself to the green darkness to make her way through the depths back to Tempre.

Frost billowed off her riding jacket as she emerged in her own personal chambers. From there, after doffing the nightsilk riding jacket and gloves, she quickly walked to the Finance study to see Haelyt and learn how the tariff collections had fared. Then, ledger in hand, she hurried back up to her study, arriving just before the glass to find Gharyk, Zylander, and Loryalt all waiting in the anteroom for her. With a smile and a gesture, she invited them in, then settled into place at the cherry conference table.

"Before we begin, Lady," said Loryalt, "might I ask if all the Southern Guard has left Tempre? Last Duadi, you mentioned that we would hear more about the ambitions of the coastal prince and that Commander Areyst would be here."

"I did promise that, it is true. Unfortunately, my concerns and Commander Areyst's predictions have turned out to be accurate. Prince Skrelyn and Prince Chalcaer look to be mounting an attack from the west. Arms-Commander Areyst has been quietly gathering the Southern Guard companies from all over Lanachrona for the past season and readying them for this possibility. He is mounting a defense to the west of Viencet."

"That is well within Lanachrona. You did not suggest we would be fighting on our land." Loryalt's tone was mildly accusatory.

"Until Decdi we did not know for certain that an invasion was imminent. Commander Areyst received a dispatch that a Midcoast force had put the town of Thesma to the torch. He had warned the townspeople, so that there was little loss of life."

"He warned them, but you did not defend them?"

Mykella looked directly at the Forester. "Because my predecessors gravely neglected the Southern Guards, we are outnumbered. While

Commander Areyst has done his best to recruit and train more men, large increases in the Southern Guards cannot be accomplished in less than a season, and Commander Areyst recommended against losing men unnecessarily in defending a small town in terrain unfavorable to us. He is taking a stronger position to the west of Viencet, and he is using almost all available Southern Guards. Some of you may have noticed the women auxiliaries in the season-turn parade. They were organized and trained to undertake those duties that do not require men in order to free another two companies of Guards to fight."

Gharyk nodded, and so did Zylander.

"With the situation you faced, Lady," offered the Justice Minister, "that would seem prudent."

"But there is no one here to protect Tempre . . ." Loryalt said.

"If Commander Areyst succeeds, there will be no need. If he does not, one or two companies would not avail against thirty or more."

Loryalt swallowed.

"I have said little because I did not wish to alarm people. I also did not wish to accuse other lands of acts unless they so acted. Now that they have acted, so will we."

"Might I ask . . . ?"

"You may, but I cannot answer, because Commander Areyst is the one in charge of defending Lanachrona. I will commit that I will be present when he and his forces meet the enemy." *Somehow . . .* But she had the strong feeling that the coastal attacks and the next Ifrit incursion were going to be simultaneous . . . or as close to that as the Efran Ifrits could manage.

"You . . . ?"

"You were not here, Forester," interjected Gharyk, "but you might recall that the Lady-Protector is not without certain skills that might prove useful in battle."

"Ah . . . I had not thought . . . recent Lords-Protector . . ."

"I will aid our forces as I can," Mykella said smoothly. *And that certainly is true.* "Now . . . since we can do little here to aid Commander Areyst, I would like to report on the situation with regard to tariffs and revenues. According to the figures available last night, all Seltyrs and factors owing tariffs have paid, with the exception of five, one of whom died last tenday, the most honorable Waoffl . . . collections are less than last year . . . and with the additional costs incurred by the Southern Guards . . . and the five hundred additional golds required for repairs of the sewers and the towpaths . . ." Mykella went on to give a quick summary of the finances of the Treasury. When she finished, she nodded to Gharyk.

"As all of you know, I suffered certain indignities last tenday, as result of my investigation into irregularities involving the handling of the gaol in Tempre . . ." Gharyk reported on the gaol situation, and the temporary use of stipended squad leaders and auxiliaries. ". . . are looking for a new gaoler and assistant gaolers."

Zylander brought up the drover's petition that Mykella had referred to him, noting that the decline in barge trade might possibly be partly because drovers preferred to work the coastal section of the River Vedra rather than the area between Hieron and Tempre.

After some discussion, Mykella concluded by saying, "After we deal with the coastal princes, I think we'll need a meeting of Seltyrs and factors about the drovers and the costs of maintaining the towpaths and other services provided to the Seltyrs and factors."

After the ministers filed out of the study, Mykella remained at her desk, thinking. Many of the problems she had faced had resulted from greed and corruption. They, in turn, had resulted from lack of knowledge and oversight by her father, and even by Joramyl. Oversight required either more effort or more people, if not both, but more people required more golds in tariffs to pay them. Even fear of the Lady-Protector was useless, as she'd determined in the case of the purported factor Caenoral, when she didn't have enough knowledge. But higher tariffs meant people were less prosperous . . .

She frowned. *Which people?* If some of the tariffs went to pay people who kept things running better, wouldn't they buy more, enough to offset the increased tariffs? But would they?

She had to admit that she didn't know. Yet the way her predecessors had run the Treasury and the land hadn't been working all that well . . . and she certainly didn't have a Southern Guards of a size necessary to discourage attacks.

Finally, she stood and walked to the window, still thinking.

56

Well before her normal breakfast time on Quattri, accompanied by four Southern Guards from the single squad remaining in Tempre, Mykella rode her gray into the quadrangle in the middle of the Southern Guard headquarters. There, Salyna and Rachylana were supervising the outloading of the auxiliaries. From where the sisters had reined up beside a supply wagon, both turned in surprise at the arrival of their older sister.

"Mykella, what are you doing here?" demanded Rachylana.

"I shouldn't come to see you off?"

"We can take care of ourselves—and the auxiliaries," declared the redhead.

"I'm well aware of that," Mykella replied with a soft laugh.

"You didn't see Areyst off," Salyna offered, with a smile. "Not from here."

"Areyst isn't my sister." Mykella looked squarely at Salyna, then at Rachylana. "I want to make one thing clear. You are *not* to take the auxiliaries into combat."

"What if we're attacked?"

"Only if you are attacked, and you are *not* to place yourself where you will be attacked."

Salyna did not quite meet Mykella's eyes.

"I mean it. If things don't go as planned, one of you could be heir to Lanachrona. It would be good if there were an heir."

"What about you?" asked Rachylana.

"I'm going to have to balance dealing with Ifrits and the coastal forces. I will be there before battle begins. Don't make me worry about you two."

"Shouldn't you be more worried about you?"

"I have shields. You don't."

"Why—" began Salyna.

"You're more worried about the Ifrits, aren't you?" interrupted Rachylana.

"Yes." Mykella saw no sense in dissembling. "I have the feeling that somehow they're using the Tables to see what's going on and that they'll attack in force about the same time as Skrelyn and Cheleyza."

"But . . . you can't do that. With the Table, I mean." A puzzled expression crossed Rachylana's face.

"In the last few days, I've been able to do more, but I'm learning by trial and error. They built the Tables, and they've had thousands of years' experience."

The two younger sisters exchanged glances, and Mykella could sense that neither had considered that aspect of matters.

"I'm asking you to be careful," Mykella repeated.

"We will," promised Salyna.

"More careful than that," added Mykella.

Even after she watched the auxiliaries finish forming up and ride out onto the avenue, Mykella had her doubts about just how careful Salyna would be. Still . . . Mykella would be in Viencet before any attacks. *You hope you will be.*

In the meantime, she needed to get back to the palace and check on the various Tables and the progress of the invaders . . . and to see how Areyst was organizing his defenses . . . and if they were located where he had indicated in his proposed battle plan.

57

Quinti and Sexdi passed with little change, except that Cheleyza and her forces were clearly in western Lanachrona, where their rate of advance had slowed. Was that to rest their mounts, to allow supply wagons to catch up . . . or for some other reason? From the Table, Mykella could not tell.

Then, Septi morning, while in the Table chamber, just before she began to study the coastal forces, she felt what she could have only described as a pinkish flash. Immediately, she called the greenish blackness and dropped into the depths, searching for the cause of that flash if that were what it happened to be.

Three Table markers were clearly brighter, the maroon and blue of Dulka, the sullen red that she thought might be Soupat, and a pink marker that she had never seen before, or not that she recalled. The orange and yellow Table marker of Lysia did not seem brighter, but that might have been because the others were far brighter than they had been.

Now what?

Did she have any choice—except where to go?

She knew that the sullen red Table mattered little except in support of other Tables, because that Table was the one buried in stones, timber, and rubble, and if she hadn't been able to move there, certainly no Alector could, nor would their weapons be of much use against all the stone. That left Dulka, where she had never been, and the pink Table, whose physical location she knew not at all.

Mykella pulled on her gloves and fastened up the nightsilk riding jacket, then dropped into the depths, angling toward the pink marker. When she neared it, though, she discovered that it felt surrounded by a web of pinkish threads. The threads recoiled away from her, and she felt as though she was breaking through a silvery barrier . . .

A stone-walled chamber surrounded Mykella. The illumination came from one lone light-torch remaining functional from the two sets of double light-torches set five yards apart in bronze brackets on each side wall. Beside the Table itself, the only object in the chamber was a black oak chest slightly over a yard in height and set against the north wall, equidistant between the light-torches. The only exit to the Table chamber was through a square arch at the west end of the chamber, from which stone steps led upward from the chamber. The walls and ceiling were all of polished red stone, a material Mykella had not seen in any other Table chamber.

She looked at the Table, gaining immediately a feeling of immense age as she neared it. The mirrored surface was cloudy beneath the shimmer, something she had not seen with any other Table. More out of curiosity than anything, she concentrated on seeing Salyna—and was rewarded with an immediate image of her sister directing some sort of mounted drill, flanked by a white-haired Southern Guard.

She let the image lapse and studied the ancient Table, but could not find any sense of an Alector—only a feel of growing purplish pink. That disturbed her, but there did not seem to be anything that she could do. Finally, she walked to the archway and started up the steps, only to find them blocked at the top by a wall of what looked and felt like polished black onyx—except the stone was neither warm nor cold to the touch.

She turned and walked back down to the chamber and tried to reach the darkness, harder than from other Table chambers, but soon she was in the chill depths, flashing toward the blue and maroon Table. This time, she emerged without difficulty in an empty Table chamber. At one end of the chamber was a statue of a single figure, close to three yards in height. Mykella could see that the statue was a representation of an Alector, apparently life-sized. That gave her a visceral feeling of just how large the Alectors had been . . . and still were. The stone figure held a silver scepter topped with glittering blue stones arranged to simulate a flame. While a dozen light-torch brackets graced the walls, only five light-torches provided any illumination.

There were decorative hangings on the side walls, holding angular and unfamiliar designs. Between the two hangings to Mykella's right was an archway and a stone-walled corridor beyond that appeared to end at a wall. She sensed no one near, nor could she detect any sign of an Alector although the Table definitely radiated the same purplish power as had the "pink" Table.

The frost boiling off her jacket into a foggy mist reminded Mykella of how far she had traveled, and that suggested the pink Table was far closer to Tempre.

After several moments, she strode into the corridor toward the wall—except it was a screen wall, with passages on each side around the central screen. All the walls had been finished with blue ceramic tile, except for a single course at the edge, done in maroon. She could sense a large hall beyond the screen wall, with a platform overlooking it—seemingly identical to the hall near the amber Table she had visited more than a season earlier. She stepped onto the platform beyond the wall into an amphitheater in whose size the light of a handful of light-torches was lost. Sensing no one, and no exit, Mykella turned and hurried back to the Table chamber.

From there, she traveled to Lysia. The Table there might have been brighter, and it was still pulsing, slightly more strongly. Again, there was little she could do, and she eased herself into the depths and back to Tempre.

When she again stood in her own Table chamber, she couldn't help thinking, *What if all this is a distraction, a way to tire and send me everywhere?*

Yet . . . what else could she do? If large numbers of Ifrits arrived and escaped from the Table chambers, it wouldn't matter what happened between the coastal princes and Lanachrona—and, outside of her sisters and Areyst, she really couldn't tell anyone.

After taking a deep breath, she stepped up to the Tempre Table and sought out Cheleyza.

Again, the Table showed an image of the immediate area around Cheleyza, which appeared to be a clearing or a space just below a pine forest. Mykella forced a Talent probe into the Table, trying to get the Table to display an image from higher, as if from the eye of a ferro-hawk.

That probe was halted by a purple wall that she had not even sensed before, and the feeling of someone watching from a great distance. She pressed harder, and the presence—and the barrier—vanished.

Mykella finally focused an image in the Table that satisfied her, from high in the sky, that showed the coastal forces in a camp on the north side of the highway and some twenty vingts west of Viencet . . . and perhaps five east of a blackened area that was likely the town of Baryma. By then, perspiration was oozing from her forehead as well as down her neck.

But when she tried to gain an image of Baryma itself, without thinking of Cheleyza, the Table blanked. Even with the images from the sky, there had to be a link to someone Mykella knew. *Why?*

She had no idea, but when she then concentrated on Salyna,

straining for an image from the sky, the Table rewarded her with a picture that showed the auxiliaries riding in an exercise formation on the flat ground just west of Viencet.

Mykella let that image fade and used the darkness to reach her personal chambers, as well as to cool herself. She immediately stripped off gloves and jacket, belatedly realizing that she should have done so when she had first returned to Tempre. She still ended up having to wash up again and change to another set of clean nightsilks.

Then, with thoughts still on what was happening farther to the west, Mykella walked from her apartments to the anteroom, where Chalmyr was waiting, an envelope in hand. "Lady . . ."

"Oh . . ." Mykella almost jumped. "I'm sorry. I was thinking."

"A messenger brought this from the First Seltyr."

"Thank you." Mykella took it and walked into her study, closing the door.

She used her belt knife to slit the envelope. Then she removed the single sheet and began to read.

Lady-Protector—
It has come to my attention that there are effectively no Southern Guards remaining in Tempre . . .

Mykella scanned the letter and set it aside, laying it on the desk. First Seltyr or not, she really didn't want to respond although she knew she would, just not at that moment.

All any of them care about is whether they're protected, not whether the people are, or whether Lanachrona will prosper . . . She snorted and walked to the window, glad for the scattered clouds and slightly cooler breeze that came through the windows.

She could not have stood there for more than a tenth of a glass when there was a rap on the study door. She turned. "Yes?"

"Lady, you have a dispatch from Arms-Commander Areyst," Chalmyr announced.

"I'll take it." Mykella hurried toward the study door, practically snatching the envelope from the scrivener's hand as he extended it. "Thank you."

She forced herself to wait until Chalmyr had closed the door before she opened and read the dispatch.

My Lady-Protector—

I regret to inform you that three companies of Midcoast cavalry raided and fired Baryma. Commander Choalt's special company attacked them as they departed the town, and the body count suggests that almost half the raiders were killed or severely injured. Those severely injured did not survive. The townspeople appeared and killed them. Majer Choalt lost but ten troopers.

Our scouts have not caught sight of the main coastal forces, but it is likely that they are near.

The auxiliaries have arrived. They have promptly taken over all routine duties. This has afforded a mixed blessing, since some of the supply troopers are unused to weapons practice. Overall, the results are good.

Undercaptain Salyna has insisted on some mounted practice for the auxiliaries, but has only done so after assuring that all maintenance and support is accomplished. The food has improved in just the days since Undercaptain Rachylana and her staff took over the cooking. That improvement alone suggests that the auxiliaries will likely have a permanent position in the Guards, but even the auxiliary cooks take arms practice. Undercaptain Rachylana insists.

Any information you can supply regarding the coastal forces would be most useful.

The only thing below the body of the report was Areyst's signature, not that she had really expected more than that.

Mykella smiled as she reread the salutation, and the single possessive pronoun that suggested more than formality. The smile faded as she considered all that she had discovered that morning, especially the hidden presence of an Ifrit and the power building in the Tables.

Still . . . she could write out what she had discovered in the Table and dispatch that information immediately, although Choalt's scouts might well discover that before the courier arrived.

Another thought occurred to her. If she had set up a relay post to the north of Viencet, with mounts there, a place she could easily reach through the darkness . . .

She shook her head.

She hadn't considered that because she hadn't wanted to reveal all that she could do, and now there wasn't time to deal with all that it would involve, especially since she had to keep watching the Tables. And it would take more troopers.

Mykella snorted. *Everything* took more people and more golds.

58

Over Octdi, Novdi, and Decdi, Mykella watched and visited the three tables she had been monitoring two and sometimes three times a day, yet while the sense of power built, she could find no way to block or channel it away from the Tables, and there were never any Alectors around. Yet she knew from what she had seen and what the ancient soarer had revealed that the Ifrits could not move easily from world to world without the Tables, not in the way that she could move across the dark webs, and that they were limited to traveling from Table to Table on Corus. That meant they could not travel to Dereka, where one of the scepters happened to be, and that suggested an attack on the Table in Lysia was a certainty—but she had no idea exactly when.

She had worked with Chalmyr to write replies to the handful of factors and Seltyrs who had requested an explanation of why the Southern Guards had been pulled out of Tempre, politely pointing out that leaving Guards in Tempre was neither wise nor effective. No one responded to her reply, not to her, in any case, although she was most certain that some of those Seltyrs and factors were doubtless less than pleased.

On Londi, before noon., Mykella had just finished checking the three Tables and following the coastal forces—now less than fifteen vingts from where Areyst meant to engage them, but moving slowly—and returned to the study when Chalmyr announced that Chief High Factor Lhanyr needed to speak to her most urgently.

"Have him come in." At least, Lhanyr had always appeared reasonable. Mykella stood to welcome.

"Lady-Protector . . . I did not know if I would find you here . . ."

"For now, Chief High Factor . . . for now." She gestured to the chairs and seated herself.

Lhanyr took the middle chair. "It is said you will be with the Southern Guards . . ."

"If I am needed." Mykella smiled politely. "But I am sure that is not the matter which brought you here."

"No, indeed. It is a matter of import, but not of quite that which you face with the coastal barbarians." The freckle-faced High Factor cleared his throat. "We had talked at the ball about the assistant minister of Highways and Rivers. I have been approached by a number of factors who claim that the First Seltyr is pressing every Seltyr to write you on behalf of one Jharyd, the son of Seltyr Thaen, on the grounds that, if a High Factor is the minister, then his assistant should certainly be from a Seltyr background . . ."

Mykella did not hear the next words because, somewhere beneath the palace, the green darkness *screamed* . . . and for an instant, she could sense the searing brilliance of three Table markers—pink, blue and maroon, and sullen red.

". . . not be a problem in itself, save that young Jharyd possesses all the faults of his sire and none of the virtues . . ."

Mykella stood. "I beg your indulgence, Chief High Factor, but a matter far more urgent has just occurred . . ."

Lhanyr's face showed consternation.

"I will explain later—if I am here to explain. If not, you will understand why."

With that, she hurried to the door and out through the anteroom, not quite running to her chambers, where she threw on the nightsilk jacket and gloves, then dropped through the darkness toward the pink Table. As she did, she realized she'd left the door to her quarters ajar—but there was no help for that.

Again, almost belatedly, she sought the deepest of the green, immersing herself in it as deeply as she could, letting it infuse her before she rose toward the web of pink that surrounded the Table that was her first destination.

The pink threads writhed away from her, but with a vehemence that somehow sent waves of pressure through the green darkness with enough force that Mykella felt battered and bruised when she emerged in the polished red stone chamber. She barely managed to raise her shields before a bolt of purple-blue flame slammed into them, driving her back against the stone.

Strengthening her shields, and locking them to the stone, she straightened.

Two Ifrits stood on the Table. Between them stood a device on a tripod whose blue crystalline barrel was aimed at Mykella.

Another bolt of blue flared against her shields, and a dagger of fire lanced into her shoulder . . . as did another.

. . . keep firing . . . don't let it . . . recover . . .

It? It? Mykella extended a Talent probe toward the nearer Ifrit.

Another blue bolt rocked her and her shields, but her probe lurched forward, first brushing, then tightening around the cablelike life-thread of the massive Ifrit, a thread that vanished into the Table itself.

As bolt after bolt struck her shields, and unseen fire-knives cut at her, leaving no trace but pain, Mykella fumbled her probe around the life-thread node. Finally, the node parted, and the Ifrit started to scream—except he vanished.

The rate of fire from the weapon slowed as the second Ifrit struggled with Mykella's second probe. Then . . . node and Ifrit vanished.

For several moments, Mykella just stood there, breathing deeply. As she did, she could sense the Table reverting to a duller . . . "quieter" state. Even so, she had to get to Dulka . . . but the Ifrits would be waiting. Then she realized that she did not have to appear in the Table chamber itself. That had been her habit, and that habit had almost been her undoing. In Dulka, and off most Table chambers, there was a tunnel.

Mykella made a special effort to drop into the deepest green on her transit to Dulka. Unlike the pink Table, the Table at Dulka was not excessively pink-webbed, and she managed to emerge in the tunnel behind the screen wall finished in blue and maroon ceramic tiles.

The purplish feel of Ifrits was overpowering, although she was a good ten yards from the Table chamber itself. She did nothing until her shields were in place and strong. Then she raised a concealment shield before her and began to ease her way along the dimness of the torch-light-illuminated tunnel, barely able to make out a handful of the words spoken by the pair with the terrible weapon.

. . . someone . . . here . . . somewhere . . .

. . . cannot be . . . sealed . . . has to appear on the Table . . .

. . . know that? . . . no one seen . . . ancient . . .

Mykella almost smiled at that. Except for the one or perhaps two Ifrits who had seen her by using the Table from Efra, none of those who had encountered her had returned to Efra. She stopped short of the end of the tunnel and used her senses to slip a Talent probe toward the pair.

The first one dropped without knowing what had struck her.

The second one unleashed the weapon, firing blue-purple bolts everywhere, yelling as he did. *. . . ancient! . . . unspeakable evil . . . degraded . . .*

Several bolts ricocheted off the polished gray walls and struck her shields before Mykella was able to untwist his life-thread.

Her forehead was damp, and she felt vaguely dirty all over. The two had really never had a chance. She stiffened. *If they succeed, no one here will have a chance to live without being farmed like nightsheep or cattle. Cattle . . . that was the very word they use.*

Still . . . she felt dirty, but there was no help for it . . . and there was one Table left to deal with, although she wasn't certain how, given the lack of space there.

Mykella had no sooner dropped into the depths, half-wondering if she really needed to go to the buried Table that was sullen red, when an ugly purplish wave vibrated all through the pink web—the one that linked Table to Table. For a timeless moment, Mykella strained to discover the source . . . before she realized from the rapid fading of the sullen red Table marker that the wave had to have started there.

Her thoughts went no farther, not when the convulsions created in the greenish darkness by that wave slammed into her, striking her with alternating blows of ice and fire, fire and ice, leaving her reeling, if figuratively, in the chill depths, stalled in the cold.

She had to get back to Tempre . . . she had to . . .

Concentrating on the deeper green, she struggled toward the blue marker, as if swimming upstream through a torrent, forcing herself around the Table and, eventually to her own quarters. That . . . she'd had to do, because the Table chamber was locked.

For a moment, she stood beside the window of her bedchamber— she thought it was her bedchamber, but nothing was as it seemed— before her knees folded.

"Lady . . . Lady . . . what happened?"

A face hovered over Mykella, one she did not recognize immediately..

"Who . . . ?"

"It's me . . . Uleanna . . ."

At least, she was definitely back in Tempre.

That was the last thought she had before the burning darkness swept over her . . . except through that blackness ugly pink embers flared down and burned, like red-hot pokers jabbing into her body, her face . . . and every so often coolness bathed her, coolness that became ice, until she shivered . . . and was again singed and burned once more.

How many cycles of fire and ice followed before she woke, she did not know, save that she lay in her own bed with Uleanna and Wyandra looking at her.

"Lady . . . are you awake?"

For a moment, Mykella could not speak, as if she had forgotten how.

"I'm . . . awake," she finally croaked. "Thirsty . . ."

"You should drink this," said the dressing maid, offering a beaker.

Mykella eyed the amber liquid.

"It's watered ale. It helps more than water."

Mykella didn't argue. As Uleanna helped her sit up and propped her up with pillows, she sipped the watered-down bitterness.

Later, as she lay back, her face still burning, she wondered, *How long can you keep doing this? Every time it gets harder . . . and worse.*

That was another of the questions for which she had no answer, and she was so tired and weak that she could only hope that the coastal forces continued to take their time in advancing toward Viencet.

59

On Duadi, weak as she was, Mykella did not leave her apartments although the reason was not so much exhaustion as her appearance. She hated canceling the ministers' meeting by note, but having them see her the way she was would have been worse. By Tridi morning, she was strong enough to sit up and move without feeling too light-headed.

She couldn't help but feel trouble was heading toward Lysia, and she felt angry, more than anything, because she could hardly move. *Why do you have to be so small? Why didn't you think more before you entered the pink Table chamber?*

So many things she'd had to learn the hard way, and she was running out of time and strength for that. Yet every move she made hurt, and her entire body radiated heat, despite all the watered ale she had drunk.

As she sat on the end of her bed, her eyes moved to the dressing-table mirror and her reflection there. Irregular dark blotches were scattered across her face. They were also distributed across most of her body. The skin of her face was close to bright red, as if she'd spent days in the summer sun without a hat, and it radiated heat hotter than any sunburn she'd experienced as a child. The warm muggy air that came through the windows didn't help that, either.

Isn't there anything you can do?

She nodded. There was something she could do . . . she thought. Slowly and gingerly, she rose to her feet and took slow step after slow step toward the window. When she was finally close enough, she touched the stone of the casement . . . and called out to the darkness, the deepest and greenest of those depths.

After a long, almost-endless moment, the deepest greens of the depths enfolded her, almost caressingly, cooling the heat yet not chilling her. In time, they dropped away, retreating to the deepness from which those greens had risen.

What Mykella noticed first was that the insufferable heat had vanished. So had the pain.

She turned her head and looked at the mirror. Even from across the bedchamber, she could see that the redness to her face had vanished— but her skin was dry and flaky and peeling, and she was again so terribly weak and light-headed that she found herself swaying so much that she had to put out a hand to the stone casement again just to steady herself.

The four steps from the window to the bed were so exhausting that she could not even reach for the coverlet before the darkness rose . . . but it was a comforting and refreshing darkness.

She surrendered, hopefully, to sleep.

60

When Mykella woke again, it was just after dawn on Quattri. She stretched, and no stabs of pain shot through her shoulders or elsewhere in her body although she was aware of soreness in her upper arms and abdomen. She stood and walked to the dressing-table mirror, studying herself. Most of the dead skin on her face had flaked off, but there were still a few patches . . . nothing that unguent and powder could not disguise.

She did take her time washing up and dressing in the clean

nightsilks that someone—doubtless Wyandra's assistant—had washed, let dry, and folded. By the time she had eaten breakfast, one of the size Salyna usually wolfed down, and made her way through the darkness down to the Table chamber, she felt decently refreshed. Not wonderful, but far better than she had before she had called to the depths.

Given the resulting exhaustion from using the green of the depths, though, it was clear that seeking such aid had its own dangers. *Doesn't everything?*

Holding her shields, Mykella approached the Table, then immediately sought out the location of Cheleyza and her forces. Again, manipulating the image took effort, enough that her forehead was damp when she finally looked down on the coastal forces—encamped just to the west of the rolling rises where some—but not all—of the Southern Guards were stationed.

Why are they taking so long . . . after they moved so quickly? Or is it because they need to rest their mounts and men after pressing them so much?

Mykella found Salyna in a small chamber, where she was talking with Areyst and another older officer, presumably Commander Choalt. Mykella didn't recall ever meeting Choalt although she might have seen him in a season-turn parade when she was far younger.

Just before she was about to release the last image, she felt . . . something . . . that distant sense of presence she had sensed once before, but it vanished instantly, and as much as she probed the Table and manipulated the image, she could find no remaining trace of that Ifrit.

Before she left the Table chamber, she dropped into the dark greenness slightly, trying to sense what was occurring with the Table in Lysia, especially after the presence incident with the Tempre Table. While she could sense pulsations, the Table in Lysia was not that much brighter.

She still did not understand why the Ifrits had not attacked again during the previous two days when she had been unable to do much of anything. Then . . . she frowned. She could not sense them through a Table—unless they were using it.

Could that also be true for them?

Was that why she'd felt that distant presence?

Even so, why had they not followed up on the earlier attacks? She was thankful they had not but was convinced it would not be long before they did.

Knowing there was nothing else she could do, she returned to her apartments, then walked down the upper palace corridor toward her study. When Mykella walked into the anteroom of the study, Chalmyr bounded to his feet, a smile of relief on his face.

"We are most glad to see you, Lady. There were . . . stories . . . you were most ill . . ."

"Injured," Mykella said dryly. "When this is all over, matters will become clearer. We are fighting more than one enemy." She straightened. "Are there any messages, any dispatches?"

"Yes, Lady . . ." He handed her four envelopes. "This one is the latest. It arrived less than a glass ago."

"I'll read it immediately." She paused. "Was the Chief High Factor too upset at my departure the other day?"

Chalmyr shook his head. "He was puzzled, I believe, but he said something about it being unwise to doubt you."

"And the ministers?"

"None ventured a word."

That could mean anything. But Mykella did not pursue it. There wasn't anything she could—or should—do about it at the moment. "If you would please draft a note conveying my apologies . . ." Mykella looked at the old scrivener. "You already did, didn't you?"

Chalmyr smiled. "It is on your desk. You may need to change it."

"Thank you." Mykella carried the four envelopes into the study, warm and damp, despite the open windows. She immediately opened the latest dispatch and began to read.

My Lady-Protector—

Mykella smiled at the salutation and then continued reading.

As you may have gathered from your own observations, the coastal forces have moved slowly since they entered Lanachronan lands. Our scouts have observed them, at times from less than half a vingt. From the look of their mounts, they are resting them and feeding them on our spring grass and crops. I can only surmise that this was necessary because of the speed with which they rode to Lanachrona. It is also possible that they feel that we cannot maintain our position without great costs and that we will have to attack them before long from a position of disadvantage. I do not plan to do such. Instead, we have begun to implement the tactics we last discussed using Commander Choalt's forces and two other excellent companies. Before long, I believe, they will tire of losses and resume their initiative. If there is any reason why we should not employ this strategy, it would be best if you so informed me at your earliest convenience . . .

In short . . . let me know quickly. Mykella smiled briefly.

We have at most three days, I would judge, before our enemies begin to bring the battle to us. Then we will see how well we have prepared.

That was all, except for his signature.

Two of the remaining envelopes were also addressed in Areyst's hand, and she opened them and quickly scanned them. They conveyed nothing she had not gathered from the Table or from his last dispatch.

That left one envelope, and she recognized that clear but functional script even before she slit the envelope and spread the single sheet out before her.

Dear Mykella—
I do not know what the commander has conveyed, but the scouts I have talked to tell me that we are outnumbered, by as much as two to one. It may be more.

I know that all the officers will claim that no one person can change what happens on a battlefield. I also know that you may be the only one able to do the impossible. I can only hope that you are able to deal with whatever keeps you in Tempre quickly and join us before too much longer.

The signature was a simple "S."

Mykella set down the letter. She had no doubts about the accuracy of both Areyst's dispatch and Salyna's letter. Yet . . . if she left Tempre, she would lose all ability to follow matters with the Table. If she went to Viencet, she would not even be able to check on what was happening in Lysia without a ride of at least half a glass—and then she would be out of touch with the Southern Guards.

If you don't deal with the Ifrits, none of us will have lands to worry about before long. Did she know that in all certainty?

While that question echoed in her thoughts, images flooded through her mind—the first Ifrit who had tried to take over her mind and body through the Table, the three who cut down Southern Guards and Klevytr's helpless retainers, those who had appeared in Blackstear . . . and the latest two pair with a weapon that would have cut down hundreds of Southern Guards—or Northcoast cavalry—in instants.

Had a one showed any concern for a single individual out of all those they had killed?

From what she had seen in the Table that morning, it would be at least another day, more likely two, before the coastal forces were ready to attack. Then . . . then she would have to decide.

In the meantime, she would watch from the Table . . . and keep observing and visiting the Table chamber in Lysia.

What else could she do?

61

On Quinti, Mykella overslept, not waking until the sun actually crept into her room, rather than rising at dawn. For the few moments after she opened her eyes, she just lay there, glad that she felt better. Then, thinking about Tables and battles, she threw herself out of bed and began to wash up. She dressed in her night-silks and headed to the breakfast room. It didn't matter that the egg-and-ham scramble was almost cool, as was the bread. She ate quickly and returned to her apartments, from where she dropped through the darkness-infused stone to the Table chamber.

Her first thought was to locate the coastal forces. They had moved their encampment to another rise, one less than three vingts from the Lanachronan position, but the cookfires were still burning, and she didn't see anyone forming up . . . not yet.

When she checked on Salyna, however, she was dismayed to find that the auxiliaries were not in Viencet but encamped on the rise to the east of that occupied by the main body of the Southern Guards. She was still considering that when, once more, she felt that sense of distant presence through the Table. Again, it vanished before she could do anything.

She pulled on her gloves and dropped through the darkness to the Table chamber in Lysia, making an entry beyond an archway and at the foot of a set of steps seemingly carved out of solid stone. Then, shields in place, she eased back toward the Table, now markedly brighter, with stronger pulsations.

She just looked at it for a time. She didn't like the idea of remaining in Lysia. Something might happen in a glass—or not for days.

Finally, she called the darkness and made her way back to Tempre . . . directly to her own apartments, from where she walked to the study. There she drafted several letters, her mind still on Lysia and on Viencet, wondering which conflict would happen next. She signed the final version of the apology to Chief High Factor Lhanyr and walked to the window, from where she looked out on a hot, hazy morning.

Abruptly, she turned and left the study, walking back to her quarters.

There she donned the nightsilk riding jacket and gloves and dropped through the darkness to the Table chamber, where she immediately called up the image of the coastal forces.

They were definitely beginning to form up.

She could travel the dark ways to get close enough to the battle so that she'd only have to walk a vingt or two . . . and that would be far faster than riding. She squared her shoulders and prepared to depart.

At that moment, the Table flooded with pinkish light—and the image she'd been viewing vanished. Even without trying, she could sense a wave of power surrounding the yellow and orange of the Table in Lysia.

Frig! Frig! Frig!

Yet she had no real choice. The world she knew would vanish if she did not deal with the Ifrits. Her eyes burned. She swallowed and called the darkness.

She did not rush, but let herself drop into the very depths of the deepest green, letting it infuse her and surround her before she reached Lysia. There, she emerged near the rubble blocking the top of the staircase, where she restructured her shields, weaving within them threads of the deep green, then layering on top of them a concealment shield.

The stone stairway was empty. So, she sensed, was the Table chamber, yet the area was infused with the ugly purpleness of Ifrits and an odd pink glow. She eased her way down the steps, slowly, carefully, and quietly. When she reached the archway at the base of the staircase, she could see that the Table chamber held two Ifrits, again with the same weapon that she had encountered in Dulka and at the pink Table. They wore identical uniforms of green trimmed in purple. They were not on the Table, and they had the weapon aimed at the area right above the Table, as if they expected her to appear there. While one glanced in her direction, he saw nothing, and his brilliant violet eyes quickly returned to the Table.

Mykella remained by the archway, silently extending a Talent probe toward the nearer Ifrit's life-thread node, this time deftly untwisting it. The Ifrit gave but a single short gasp and staggered, then dropped sideways.

. . . Ancient   one . . . fieldmaster . . . here! . . . somewhere . . . The remaining weaponeer loosed a series of purple-blue bolts across the top of the Table.

Where?

. . . [unseen] . . . [—] dead . . .

More purple-blue flame-bolts flared against the wall beyond the Table.

Mykella had another Talent probe moving toward the weaponeer.

Spray the corridor . . . Now!

So fast did the Ifrit swing the weapon that a flurry of fire-missiles smashed into Mykella's shields, forcing her back several steps before she locked her shields to the stone. She lost momentary control of her Talent probe and had to re-form it, much more slowly against the barrage of flame-bolts that rattled her shields, and sent darts of unseen fire through her shoulders and chest.

Hold it . . . almost have the scepter ready . . . Those mental words came from somewhere Mykella could not see, but they had to be from within the hidden wall chambers holding the scepter.

Slowly, against the pressure of the weapon's bolts, Mykella forced the Talent probe forward until she could finally reach the life-thread node of the remaining Ifrit weaponeer.

His shriek was piercing and short, as he toppled.

Mykella paused for an instant, unlocking her shields from the stone, still half-astounded to see the figures of the two Ifrits turn purplish gray, then begin to disintegrate.

Without having to fight against the weapon, she moved more quickly, but carefully, into the Table chamber. There she saw an open archway, where there had been none before.

As she turned toward it, waves of pink-purple light flared from that opening, rolling out in eye-searing waves, so bright that, beyond the once-hidden archway, Mykella could see nothing. That did not mean that she could not sense the approach of another Ifrit.

Your concealment avails you nothing. The words rolled at her mind like a boulder rumbling down a slope at her, or an avalanche crashing down the side of a mountain as massive as the Aerial Plateau.

Behind the words, she felt a probe, one purplish, ugly, and powerful, and she called up more of the greenness from the depths, erecting a barrier.

The Ifrit's probe recoiled, and Mykella could sense anger of a sort as well as a cold and calculating determination.

A different Ancient are you . . . a throwback from the distant past? That will only prolong your existence a few moments.

The thought that she could not have power unless she had been a distant ancestor of the soarers . . . that angered Mykella, and she raised shields of green behind green, pressing them forward toward the swelling purple pinkness trying to force its way toward her.

Because of the shields, or her very will, Mykella could at last make out the figure standing just inside the stone passage that led to where the scepter had been hidden and safeguarded.

To her eyes and senses, the Ifrit towered more than three yards, with legs as big around as the small casks that held fine brandy. His shoulders looked to be a yard and a half across. In his right hand, at waist level, he held the scepter, the source of the brilliant, eye-searing pink-purple light that filled the stone chambers, leaving no traces of shadows.

Not even you, little Ancient, can stand against the power of the scepter.

Mykella did not speak, but kept channeling, almost begging, or pleading for more and more of the green from the depths that was simultaneously brighter than the sun and darker than black.

Nature is not enough, little one.

The scepter rose in the Ifrit's hand so that the brilliant jeweled tip pointed in Mykella's direction. Yet she noticed that for all the size and strength of the massive white-faced and black-haired Ifrit, his arm trembled slightly.

Immediately, she launched an arrow of green toward his huge violet eyes.

The scepter lifted, and purple flared from it. The chamber roared with the impact of purple and green.

Before the Ifrit could aim that scepter at her, Mykella created another green bolt, this one aimed at the Ifrit's knees.

Purple and green again met, and the stone walls of the chamber seemed to shake.

The Ifrit stood a step from the archway into the chamber, using the power of the scepter to press Mykella and her green shield back.

A purple bolt from the scepter crashed into her shields, and she was forced back another step, even as she tried to draw more green from the depths.

Another series of bolts, and she again had to retreat.

Before the Ifrit could summon another bolt, she unleashed her own flurry of green arrows. While they halted his progress, she was unable to make him retreat, and she was forced back another step with his next attack.

From somewhere in the back of her mind, she heard a voice, a memory . . . *channel the green against the device* . . . Trying to ignore the purple bolts that felt as though they were shivering her shields, Mykella began to channel the green from the depths, not through her, but up through the stone directly under the scepter, trying to build up a massive concentration of the green that she could direct to clamp around the scepter all at once.

As she built up more and more green beneath the stone, she found herself moving backward more and more quickly. Soon, she would be against the wall.

With a wide smile, the Ifrit raised the scepter. *Farewell* . . . *Ancient* . . .

Mykella clamped all the green around the scepter—just as a massive surge of purpled pink flared from the jeweled tip of the scepter.

Holding her shields, she flattened herself on the stone floor as waves of power collided, and so much sound and force exploded around her that she saw and heard nothing.

The absolute quiet woke Mykella.

She opened her eyes. She couldn't have been out that long because the last purple shining dust motes were flicking out of existence around her.

Lying on the stone floor, Mykella lifted her head, yet reverberating from the explosion that had engulfed the chamber. A shroud of greenish black still encircled her, dimming her view. Just inside the Table chamber, less than a yard from where the huge Ifrit had stood and aimed all the power of the scepter at her, the scepter lay, appearing like a plain silver and black scepter, nothing more.

There was not a single sign of the Ifrit.

The Table had vanished as well. Had that been part of the massive explosion?

Mykella could not believe it. Nothing could damage a Table. What power had the combination of green and purple Talent forces unleashed? Or had they been amplified by the scepter and the apparent explosion of the Table. The very walls of the chamber had been splintered and broken . . . and thin stray rays of early-afternoon light arrowed into the chamber through cracks in the stone ceiling, providing a twilightlike illumination.

Those walls had taken punishment from the huge flare guns and from time itself—and had held . . . but not against the scepter and the power of the green depths.

Mykella slowly rose to her feet, exhausted, looking around the chamber. All that remained of the Ifrits and the Table was fast-vanishing purplish dust. Yet the scepter remained untouched, undamaged.

You have prevailed. You must return the scepter to its case. Now!

Mykella sensed the arrival of the Ancient, but she was so spent that she could not even turn her head at that moment.

All she could do was pant from all the exertion. She looked at the scepter, lying on the stone less than two yards away. She wondered if she could even lift it, given how hard the Ifrit had struggled with it. Yet she *knew* that if she picked it up, it would seem like a feather. She tried to stop panting but couldn't. Her lungs were starved for air. So she just waited.

So did the soarer.

"Why now?" Mykella finally asked.

Every moment that it is outside its case, it unbalances the [????]. All

Corus suffers . . . before long . . . in places the earth will begin to tremble . . .

Mykella looked at the soarer. "That's not true. You're afraid of something else. What will keep them from coming back, time and time again?"

There was no answer, only the sense of a smile, not that Mykella could see it, only feel it.

"What?" Mykella would have snapped, had she not been so tired.

You have destroyed the Table. They will be unable to locate the scepter from their world if it is replaced in its case. Nor will they be able to travel to this point on Corus without a Table, only by foot or mount, if they can even find it from afar.

With what the soarer said, Mykella realized that the Ifrits would not be able to reach the scepter in Dereka, for there was no Table there, either. "So why must I replace the scepter?"

So that it cannot be found. More of import, it does unbalance all that lies beneath Corus. In time, the very land will twist.

"But . . . things won't change that fast, will they?"

No. The admission was like lead. *But before long the last of us will die, and in time, so will you. Few like you are born. No one will be left to guard the scepter or replace it.*

The stark honest desperation of that cut through Mykella. "But I could be very powerful with it?"

Not any more powerful than you could be without it—if you work at mastering your Talent. Drawing from the scepter is easier, but you would come to look like them. Worse, you would begin to act as they do.

Yet, without even asking, Mykella knew she would live longer, far longer . . .

She looked at the scepter.

All will fear you. None will enter your heart. You will cease to be who you are. The scepters corrode the strongest of wills and Talents. Even the Ifrits feared using them except to maintain the pink Table web. Why do you think they were so protected and cased?

"Without a Table . . ."

Neither scepter is near a Table, and that absence will weaken their web and protect the world—if you replace the scepter.

After several moments, Mykella took one step, then another.

Behind her, the green-shrouded figure of the Ancient did not move.

Mykella bent and lifted the scepter. It was not so heavy as she recalled. Was that because only a trace of purpleness remained.

It will rebuild its force, and soon. Replace it.

The last words were not so much command as plea.

Mykella walked slowly to the last chamber. There she had to set the scepter on the strange table-desk and move the chair so that she could climb up to the still-open case that had held the scepter. Then she eased the scepter into position so that it rested against the proper brackets and fittings.

Only then did she take a last look at the seemingly harmless silver and black scepter and close the heavy cover, making sure that it was firmly in place. What about the key?

After several moments, she turned it, but left it in place.

If any Ifrit can get here now, the key would make no difference. Besides, if you change your mind, you can always come back and remove it.

Then, for the second time, she returned the chair to where it had been, before walking back to rejoin the soarer.

Close the door.

"How?"

Twist the light-torch bracket back to its proper position.

Mykella almost laughed. She did not, fearing the sound would come out close to hysterical. Such a simple matter, and she'd never even considered it. She had to stand on tiptoes to do so, then watched as the stone slid into place, showing no sign that an archway had ever graced that stone wall.

In turn, she looked at the vacant depression that had once held a Table. She couldn't even see what was happening in Viencet. Had the fighting begun. Was it over? Were they all still positioning themselves.

She turned and looked to the soarer.

The old Ancient looked back at the young Ancient.

62

Mykella looked to the soarer. "I've saved your world—"

It is more yours than ours . . . and will be more so in the ages to come.

"I've saved the world, but I need to save my land." *If I can.* After a moment, she added. "You can at least guide me to the point on the black paths closest to where the princes have massed their forces." Guidance would save her strength somewhat for what was to come. She hoped.

We can do that . . . and more . . .

We? wondered Mykella. "You know where they are east of Viencet?"

Not knowing is your shortcoming. Ours is different. Gather as much of the green to you as you can. Hold it to yourself.

"I thought I was supposed to channel it."

Now that no longer matters, Lady [???].

The term that followed the word "Lady" made no sense to Mykella, but it conveyed a certain respect. Grudging respect, Mykella suspected. She did not argue, but tried to draw more deeply of the green and bind it to herself. As she did so, her tiredness diminished. *But at what price later?*

Two other soarers appeared, superficially the same as the one Mykella "knew." Yet they were different, and one felt much younger—and somehow sadder, although neither communicated anything through "word" or gesture.

Think of where you wish to be.

Mykella obliged, concentrating on the rolling hills to the south of the eternastone highway and west of Viencet where doubtless two forces were drawn up facing each other—unless the fighting had already begun, or worse, she feared, ended.

Please let me arrive in time . . . please. She did not even know to whom or what she addressed that plea . . . or what exactly she would or could do once she joined the Southern Guards forces.

Then they dropped into the depths, or the depths rose and carried them downward. The chill felt welcome, refreshing, and Mykella was almost sorry when she sensed they were rising.

They emerged above a line of hills, with a soarer on each side of Mykella and one above her. Barely beneath them were the tips of trees, mainly evergreens,. She glanced back, seeing the thin line of silver that was the River Vedra, then looked forward once more to realize that the air around her shimmered a faint green, doubtless the effect of being transported by the soarers.

The day was no longer afternoon either, but morning, late morning.

"It's not afternoon."

Lysia is far to the east.

Mykella should have realized that, but she'd never traveled that far—not when she'd been able to see the sun.

As they crossed another half-treed rill, Mykella caught sight of the eternastone highway no more than a few vingts away. Were there forces formed up on the south side?

. . . only a little more . . .

Even Mykella could sense the strain as she could feel and see herself descending into an open space. When her boots touched the reddish rocky ground, amid clumps of grass and creosote bushes, with but a few low and scattered pines here and there, she looked to "her" soarer.

We can carry you no farther.

"Thank you."

We repay as we can, Lady-[???].

Then the three faded into the hillside as they also headed back northward, toward the lifeweb of greenish black that bound the world together. Even after they were nowhere to be seen, though, the air around Mykella seemed to hold a faint greenish tinge. She shook her head. The green remained.

All that dealing with the green must have affected the way you see.

She looked to the south, searching for what she had thought she had seen from the air. From where she stood, across the grass and its scattered piñons and junipers, Mykella could make out the two forces on the rolling rises on the south side of the eternastone highway. To the west, all across a low ridge, spread the combined armies of North-coast and Midcoast, although the green and yellow of Northcoast seemed twice as numerous as the maroon of Midcoast. To the east was the much smaller body of the Southern Guards, occupying a slightly higher—and smaller—rise. She judged that she had not quite two vingts between where she stood and the edge of the highway, and half a vingt beyond that, if up a gentle slope, to the edge of the coastal forces.

She began to walk, quickly. Running would only leave her ex-hausted, and she would need all the strength she could muster when she reached the enemy. She hoped she could reach the forces of the princes—and Cheleyza—before the battle broke out.

She had covered about a hundred yards through the grasses when she came to a ravine, almost concealed by the grass. She had to walk westward for a good fifty yards to find a place narrow enough that she could jump across. That took far less effort than using Talent when she could not easily draw upon the darkness.

Dealing with Cheleyza and the coastal forces would be so much easier if they'd been kind enough to attack where you could do that.

Of course, she could have let them attack Tempre—but that would have resulted in hundreds, if not thousands, more deaths and de-stroyed Lanachronan power in another way.

She turned toward the southwest again, angling back in the direc-tion of the northern flank of the enemy forces. After traversing two smaller ravines and ground more uneven than it had seemed when she started walking, she was finally within a few hundred yards of the highway and breathing more heavily. Areyst had been right about the grass concealing uneven terrain, but the last hundred yards was rela-tively level.

She was less than fifty yards from the highway when she caught sight of three lancers, riding quickly toward her. Belatedly, realizing she hadn't even raised her shields, she did so, but kept walking, if more slowly, to catch her breath.

The mounted lancers rode toward her, then stopped on the stone pavement a good ten yards away, their eyes wide.

"An Ancient . . ." murmured one.

The second looked to the first, as if puzzled.

"Leave her . . . if she is, we should do nothing. If she is not, we need do nothing."

"But—"

"Leave her."

The second rider glanced at the third, who nodded. All three remained where they had reined up.

Mykella did not look at them but continued to walk, crossing the stone of the highway, trying not to wince at the intrusiveness of the Ifrit purple that bound the stone and somehow burned at her feet even through the soles of her boots.

She continued up the north side of the long ridge, aiming her steps at the center of the green-clad formation—where Cheleyza and Chalcaer had to be. The hill seemed steeper than it had looked before she had begun to hike up it. Ahead was a small contingent of foot troopers, and beyond them, the mounted forces.

Until she was within yards of the foot troopers, most seemed not to have noticed her, or, if they had, they ignored her presence. Then, several men on the north end of the formation moved back, leaving a space for her, lowering their rifles slightly. Mykella did not acknowledge the movement or look to either side, but kept walking.

"Hold that line!" bellowed a voice.

An angular squad leader—from the insignia on his shoulder—hurried forward, brandishing a blade. "You! Get out of here!"

Mykella kept walking.

The squad leader moved toward her and jabbed the blade at her, not a killing blow, or even one meant to hit her, but it struck her shields and rebounded slightly. The trooper flushed, raising his blade. "You stop, or you'll die!"

Mykella ignored the command and continued onward.

The squad leader ran after her and slammed his blade against her shields.

Without looking back, Mykella reached out with her Talent and undid his life-thread node. The squad leader pitched forward onto the matted spring grass and bushes.

She kept walking uphill.

As murmurs preceded her up the gentle slope, and a handful of rankers rushed toward the fallen squad leader behind her, the remaining footmen parted. Beyond the foot soldiers, some two hundred yards from the center of the formation, she encountered the first of the heavy cavalry.

"Little woman! You don't belong here!" called a voice.

Mykella ignored those words, boosted her shields slightly, and kept walking.

A rider reined up directly in front of her.

Mykella stopped and looked up, then gathered a trace of light to her, except it came out greenish, rather than gold or white.

The squad leader paled. "You can't do this . . . Ancient."

Mykella said nothing and kept looking at the squad leader in his green uniform.

"Squad Leader! What's the problem?"

The second rider was a green-clad Northcoast officer, a captain, Mykella judged, who reined up beside the squad leader. The squad leader said nothing but pointed to Mykella.

The captain frowned. "What was she doing?"

"Walking up the hill."

The captain pursed his lips, looked at Mykella, and finally said, "There's going to be a battle here. Even you could get hurt."

Mykella said nothing.

The two men exchanged looks.

Finally, the captain turned back to the squad leader. "Escort her where she wants to go. See if she'll just walk where she's going. They haven't started an attack yet. I'll talk to the majer and tell him about her." He paused. "From what the legends say, if you don't harm them, they don't harm you."

"Yes, sir."

Both men eased their mounts from Mykella's path, and she resumed walking, angling her path toward the center of the formation, where she felt Cheleyza had to be. She did not question that feeling, accepting it.

The squad leader rode to the side and just behind her.

They had only covered another fifty yards when an undercaptain moved his mount forward. "Squad Leader! What are you doing?"

"Following orders, sir. The captain told me to escort the Ancient through the formation before the easterners attack. What I'm doing, sir."

Mykella gathered a touch more light to herself but did not stop walking.

The undercaptain looked at Mykella, then back to the squad leader. Then the junior officer swallowed. "Carry on."

There are some advantages to military discipline ... and legends, Mykella thought, continuing onward, now moving across the level ground of the ridge crest where the hill grasses, those that had not been trampled down, moved intermittently in the light breeze. While she was warm in the nightsilk jacket and gloves, it was early enough in the day that she was not feeling overpowering heat. *Not yet.* She didn't want to take them off because, before everything ended, she'd need their protection. She could only do so much when she could not draw on the darkness. *Even there, you can only do so much. It's just more.*

The space around the riders in the middle of the formation showed where she would find Cheleyza and Chalcaer, and she gradually turned toward them, worrying that the squad leader who escorted her might protest or raise an alarm.

He did not, even as Mykella neared the first guards of the command group.

"Who's that, Squad Leader?" demanded an officer with gold bars and star on his collar.

"It's an Ancient, sir. I was ordered to escort her out of the formation, sir."

"An Ancient? Don't they soar?"

Mykella could sense the doubt from the senior officer.

Another rider pressed forward, out of the formation.

"That's no Ancient! That's the so-called Lady-Protector!" Cheleyza turned her mount and urged the mare toward Mykella, pulling out a saber as she did.

Mykella stopped and linked her shields to the rock below the surface, marveling at the grace of the other woman's movements. Salyna had suggested Cheleyza would be skilled, but it was another thing to experience such skills.

The mare slammed into Mykella's shields. Neither shields nor Mykella moved.

The mare's legs crumpled, and Cheleyza flew over Mykella. Surprisingly, to Mykella, Cheleyza rolled and staggered to her feet.

Mykella reached out with her Talent and rip-unraveled Cheleyza's life-thread. After a moment's hesitation, she unraveled the second thread, although she doubted the unborn child would have survived her mother's death. Still, she wasn't about to allow any possibility of fighting another war based on the child.

She turned to see Paelyt raise his rifle and fire.

"Die, you cursed Ancient! You worthless, deceptive bitch!"

Slowly, she walked toward the mounted officer, who kept firing. Each bullet that slammed into her shields was like a needle, not like the knives of the Ifrits' firebolts, but painful.

As she neared Paelyt, she again extended her Talent and unraveled his life-thread. He slumped in the saddle.

Beyond Paelyt, Chalcaer turned, his face paling as he watched Mykella walk toward him with slow, deliberate steps.

He yanked a rifle from its holder, aimed, and fired.

Other riders began to fire, and the darts of fire, now like wasp stings, needled her chest and shoulders. For some reason, the nightsilk did not protect against those stings.

She kept walking. Chalcaer fired again, and once more, then slammed the rifle into the saddle sheath and drew his saber.

Mykella Talent-grasped his life-thread and twisted. Chalcaer's mouth opened, but no sound issued forth as he slumped forward in the saddle, and his saber slipped from his lifeless fingers into the matted spring grasses.

The riders beside the fallen prince charged, and Mykella linked her shields to the stone beneath. One rider crashed into the shields, he and his mount suffering the same fate as Cheleyza and her mount, and the others began to circle her, as if uncertain as to what they could or should do.

In the distance to the east, she heard a trumpet triplet, the signal for the Southern Guards.

"Re-form! Re-form!" came a command from somewhere.

As riders milled around her, she knew she had to get to Skrelyn, a prince she did not know and had never seen. All she could do was trust her feelings. Despite the welter of pain and the reddish haze within her shields, she unlocked the shields from the stone and put one foot in front of the other, moving across the top of the hill between riders who scarcely saw her now that they moved to repulse the Southern Guard charge.

More than once she and her shields were knocked to one side or another, and several times she had to regain her feet.

"There's the evil one!"

Mykella turned to see an entire squad riding toward her. In the second rank was a man in maroon and gold. That had to be Skrelyn, but in the press of riders, there was no way even to think about reaching his life-thread.

Instead, she hurled herself three steps to the left, almost directly in front of the charging mounts and, standing erect, with her shields again linked to the rock below, took the force of the charge. Horses piled up before her, and men were flung from their saddles.

Mykella concentrated on Skrelyn, who had tried to rein up, then angle sideways, before his mount was pinned between two others.

In that moment, Mykella struck, yanking his life-thread apart.

After that she just stood, amid the wounded and dying mounts and men, trying to hang on to her shields. She did turn, slowly, back to the east, watching as the dark blue uniforms surged uphill and into a far larger mass of riders.

Then, when a second wave of Southern Guards appeared to the south and charged the flank, the maroon-clad riders broke.

More mounts and men, some in green and gold, and some in maroon, rode past and around Mykella, seemingly ignoring her.

From the north, Mykella heard a familiar triplet, and she turned.

Riders in undress blues—auxiliaries—in a wedge formation— galloped up across the hillside, apparently from the northwest into the rear corner, such as it was, of the remaining Northcoast forces.

From the northwest? Mykella remained standing, puzzled.

"They're everywhere!" yelled someone.

Mykella wondered, trying to make out what was happening through eyes that tried to dim on her.

The remaining Midcoast riders scattered as the blue-coated auxiliaries rode closer. Mykella tried to count—there were so few . . . far less than a score . . .

In spite of her determination, Mykella found herself sinking to her knees amid the packed mass of downed horses and men, amid the groans, the blood, and the feel of death, and the worse agony of dying. She kept trying to hold her shields . . . trying to hold on to anything, hoping that the blue-clad auxiliaries—or the Southern Guards—could reach her before she totally collapsed.

A red-haired figure in blue and cream reined up. "Mykella! Mykella!"

Red hair . . . should be blond . . . But Mykella could not even utter her sister's name before the reddish haze merged with green and darkness . . . and the odors of blood, the feel of death, and the sadness of greed and treachery.

63

Mykella swam out of red pain and black heat to find someone blotting her forehead with a damp cloth. Her eyes watered, and she had to squint to make out Rachylana. After a moment, she could see more clearly. She was on a narrow pallet in a small room. She was still wearing nightsilks, but not the riding jacket or gloves.

"You're awake! It's been more than a day." Relief flooded from Rachylana. Her eyes were red, although she was no longer crying, and Mykella could sense the sorrow.

"Salyna . . . Areyst?" Mykella's voice quavered.

Rachylana shook her head.

Mykella shuddered.

"Not . . . Areyst . . ." Rachylana said quickly. "He'll heal."

"Salyna?"

"She was . . . too brave. I felt . . . what you were doing. When I told her, she . . . she said the only chance we had was to attack from the flank when no one was looking. She waited . . . broke through . . . made me take the second squad. I just . . . kept them together . . . followed the green to you . . ." Rachylana swallowed. "Areyst led the Guards . . . He saw, more than I did, the green on the other rise. He told me . . . later . . . it had to be you. When the shooting started, he ordered the charge. He led it himself."

"Why?" Mykella thought she knew.

"Against a larger force . . . he had to." Rachylana offered a sad smile. "He had to for other reasons, too."

Unhappily, Mykella understood that as well. "How badly . . . is he hurt?"

"A broken arm, but the bone didn't splinter and come through the skin. Cuts and bruises." After a pause, Rachylana went on. "Areyst . . . the Southern Guards, they couldn't have done it without you. We were outnumbered three to one."

"They were waiting for reinforcements? That was why they didn't attack earlier?" Mykella's voice was raspy and hoarse. "What . . . happened?"

"They broke . . ." Rachylana shook her head. "Then it was awful . . . too many bodies to bury properly . . . thousands . . . The captives . . . they're still digging . . . mass graves . . . be another few days. They weren't trained all that well, for all their numbers . . ."

Mykella let out the breath she hadn't realized she was holding.

"They found the bodies—Cheleyza, Chalcaer, and Skrelyn. How did you do it? There wasn't a wound on any of them. I don't mean killing them . . . but against all the others?"

"I had help." That was a safe answer. "Can I see him?"

"He's asked the same of you."

Slowly, Mykella sat up and put her bare feet over the side of the pallet bed. She decided not to stand. She was still light-headed.

Behind Rachylana, the rough plank door swung open.

Areyst, his right arm bound to his body in a tight sling, stepped forward. His face was drawn, and his left cheek was a mass of barely scabbed cuts.

Mykella looked at him. She could hardly believe he stood there.

"Lady-Protector . . ." Broken arm and all, he knelt, his eyes on her.

She had only thought she'd paid for becoming Lady-Protector when she'd ascended that last step of the palace a season before. Rachylana had been right about romantic tales. They never mentioned the true costs . . . the thousands of dead, the lost hopes of the Ifrits from a dead world, the deaths of forty-odd half-trained women . . .

. . . and the loss of a sister who had given everything.

She and Areyst had much to repay. Some could never be repaid. As for the rest . . . they did have years in which to do so.

"Just . . . just your lady," she finally said.

64

Mykella had spent all of Sexdi and most of Septi recovering in Viencet. Only late on Septi did she and Areyst ride back to Tempre with two companies of Southern Guards. Choalt followed with the remainder of the Guards and the captives late on Octdi.

Decdi morning, Mykella met in the formal study with Areyst. Both were bruised in more places than Mykella cared to think, and Areyst had scrapes and cuts on the left side of his face, in addition to his bound and splinted right arm. As he sat in the chair across the desk from her, she could sense his discomfort.

"You're still determined to ride in the memorial procession?" she asked gently.

"You are," he pointed out with a crooked smile.

"I'm not slashed up with a broken arm."

"I will ride."

Mykella knew better than to pursue that. "How many of the Guards did we lose? You couldn't tell me yesterday."

"Choalt had to wait for the casualty reports from each company. More than eight companies' worth, and forty-one out of the sixty some auxiliaries. We'll lose more in the next few weeks from their wounds."

Nearly a thousand . . . and Salyna.

"What about Northcoast . . . Midcoast?"

"Choalt didn't show any mercy at the end. With all the losses we'd already taken, we couldn't afford it. Anyone who didn't surrender immediately we cut down. He didn't count closely, but they had to dig mass graves. It took three days with the men we could spare and all the captives. The best estimate was over five thousand men. We still have some four hundred captives, and probably two thousand survivors fled west. Most of the survivors were from Northcoast. Skrelyn's forces took the brunt of our attacks." Areyst shook his head, then winced as the movement jarred his arm.

And for what? Merely to keep things as they were, with all of us poorer?

"Do you plan to conquer Midcoast, Lady? You could, you know?"

"Conquer it? We could. But could we afford to hold it and govern it? I don't think so. We'll send an envoy with a full company of Southern Guards with simple terms, first to Hafin, then to Harmony."

Areyst raised his eyebrows.

"Leave us alone. Allow our factors and Seltyrs to trade unhampered, without tariffs and harassment, and pay us ten thousand golds for damages."

"That won't . . ."

"Cover the costs? No, but they can pay it, and it won't destroy Midcoast. We'll send similar terms to Northcoast."

"The Northerners might balk at that. They know we won't ride over a thousands vingts to attack them."

"We'll suggest that any ruler who does not abide by those terms will not remain long a ruler, just as Chalcaer and Skrelyn did not."

"You . . . can do that, can't you?"

"Yes. I could get close enough to walk into Harmony unseen." *Although it might be a long, long walk.* "It would mean some planning and some time away from Tempre. I'd rather not, but I've already done worse that I didn't want to do. Besides, Joramyl siphoned off that much from our Treasury, if not more. We deserve it back."

"Who do you want to send as envoy?"

"What about Commander Choalt and his picked company, with reinforcements?"

"That would be my inclination," Areyst admitted, his eyes resting on her.

Mykella let herself enjoy his appreciation of her—for a moment. "We need to get ready for the memorial parade."

"The Seltyrs wanted a victory parade," he said.

"We won, and everyone lost. I'm not about to celebrate that. I want them to see how many empty saddles there are. Besides, when they get next season's tariffs, if we had a victory parade, they'd complain even more."

"You're breaking tradition, you know?"

"By escorting Salyna's caisson? I've broken a few already, and there will be more. She deserves it." *And so much more.* "In a way, even if I didn't recognize it then, she was the one who made me realize what I could be."

"I thought that was the soarer." Areyst smiled, an expression with just a hint of teasing.

"The soarer *told* me. Salyna *showed* me." Mykella stood, then waited for Areyst to rise before walking around the desk and taking his good hand. She leaned forward and brushed his cheek with her lips. "And you encouraged me by accepting who I am."

"You give me too much credit."

She smiled. "You've earned it."

After leaving her study, she returned to her quarters to prepare herself for the ordeal of the funeral procession and memorial service. She had no uniform to wear, unlike Areyst, and to wear one would have would have set the wrong impression. Instead, she wore her best nightsilk blacks, with a black-edged blue mourning sash of the kind that would be worn by the Southern Guards. She did add, in the sole gesture to tradition, the black shimmersilk headscarf that had been her mother's. It was too hot for a cloak, and, besides, she did not wish to hide herself from her people.

A knock on the door to her apartments, and Mykella opened it to see Rachylana standing there, wearing the undress uniform of the auxiliaries, as well as a mourning sash.

"Are you ready?" asked her sister.

Mykella nodded.

"They're waiting in the courtyard."

"Then we should go," agreed Mykella.

As they started down the staircase to the main level of the palace, Rachylana said, "I'm staying with the auxiliaries."

"You said that before. You don't have to."

"No. I have to. Salyna was right." Rachylana's laugh was short, hard, and brittle. "I wish she could have heard me say that. Things have to change, and they won't if I don't help them."

"You'll do well with the auxiliaries."

"Did you know that yesterday, twenty more girls appeared at Southern Guard headquarters wanting to join?"

"No, I didn't. That will help greatly."

"Salyna would be pleased."

"Yes . . . she would. She believed in the auxiliaries."

Although she said nothing more, Mykella couldn't help but reflect on how much the redhead who had loved flirting and balls had changed.

Once she reached the courtyard, Mykella mounted the gray gelding and checked her Talent shields. She hoped she wouldn't need them, but for the rest of her life, she intended to raise them in any public appearance. Three of the auxiliaries formed up before Mykella and Rachylana, and three followed as they headed out of the courtyard and turned westward on the avenue leading to the Great Piers.

As they passed the reviewing stand where the crowds were already beginning to gather, Rachylana said, "It will seem strange for none of the family to be in the reviewing stand before the palace."

"I asked Lord and Lady Gharyk to represent us on the top level, and the First Seltyr and the Chief High Factor to join them."

Rachylana nodded. "You need to be in the procession. Without you . . ."

"Without Salyna, without you, without Areyst, without Choalt, without thousands of guards and auxiliaries—it wasn't just me," Mykella said firmly.

"But you held them all together."

"Isn't that what a Protector is supposed to do?" *And what some, including Father, failed to do.*

When she neared where the procession was forming up, Mykella surveyed the first ranks. At the front of the funeral procession were three riderless horses, side by side, each led by a Southern Guard. One horse represented the rank-and-file guards lost, one the officers, and one Salyna. The saddle of each riderless horse was draped in the dark blue of the Southern Guards, with a black wreath across the front of the saddle. Behind the three horses rode the command staff, followed by Choalt and Areyst, and finally the Southern Guard companies that had fought at Viencet, company by company, beginning with First Company. All the officers and men wore the black-edged blue mourning sashes.

The funeral procession would be long because it was a memorial for all the fallen, and not just for Salyna. Each company would ride past the palace, their ensigns draped in black, and for every man who had fallen, there was a riderless horse in formation. Obtaining enough mounts had been a challenge, but Areyst had managed it, although many had been Northcoast and Midcoast mounts before the last battle.

Accompanied by Rachylana and her escorts, Mykella rode slowly to the end of the procession, a good vingt southwest of the Great Piers. There she reined up behind the remaining auxiliaries, led by Rachylana, and beside the black caisson and ceremonial casket containing the urn with Salyna's ashes, a caisson pulled by four black horses. Behind the caisson were two Southern Guards and two auxiliaries.

As she looked at the caisson and casket, Mykella's eyes burned, and she looked down for a moment, and swallowed. Then she straightened in the saddle and waited.

At the turn of the glass marking noon, a trumpet fanfare announced the beginning of the procession. Even so, it was a good half glass until the last company before Mykella and the auxiliaries began to move.

At that moment, she drew upon the darkness beneath Tempre and created a transparent pillar of pale greenish light that rose from her and one of deep and dark translucent green that rose from the coffin, twisting them together midway between her and the caisson and rising some ten yards into the sky before dissipating.

"Ohhh . . ."

Mykella had expected no less than an involuntary reaction from even the scattered bystanders south of the Great Piers.

Thousands of people lined the avenue, all the way from the Great Piers past the palace to the Southern Guard compound to the east. Despite the heat of midday, the area across from the palace and reviewing stand between the low wall that comprised the northern edge of the public gardens and the edge of the boulevard was packed so tightly that as Mykella neared the palace, she could not see how any of them could move.

When the crowd saw the pillar of light and darkness, the murmurs died away, and many bowed their heads. Others just gaped.

Mykella turned her eyes, but not her head, to observe the reviewing stand. Below Lord and Lady Gharyk, Khanasyl, and Lhanyr were the other Seltyrs and High Factors of Tempre and their wives, not all of them, but enough so that every space on the stand was taken and other Seltyrs and factors spread away from the stand on both sides.

Just before Mykella and the caisson neared the reviewing stand, Mykella drew more upon the lifeweb darkness beneath her and Tempre and intensified both light and greenish darkness around her and the coffin, enough, she hoped, to emphasize for those in the reviewing stand the link between her and her sister. As she had done at her father's memorial parade, she projected respect and honor, but that honor was for Salyna and all the fallen Southern Guards.

She could hear the sobbing from all sides.

The procession continued to the Southern Guard compound, as did Mykella and the caisson, rather than ending at the palace, because

Salyna would have wanted it that way, to be treated as a Guard officer and not as the Lady-Protector's sister.

A good glass later, as Mykella, Areyst, and Rachylana rode back toward the palace with an honor guard—and the urn that held Salyna's ashes, the remaining bystanders on the side of the avenue seemed to freeze as the riders passed them.

"Your procession silenced the entire city," Areyst said. "I've never seen anything like it."

"Some of the Seltyrs wept," added Rachylana. "They never cry."

"They should weep. They should weep in shame," Mykella replied. "Too many of their golds were paid for in blood."

"Would that more rulers understood that," said Areyst quietly.

Mykella only nodded, thinking about the coming private memorial service for Salyna.

LESS THAN A GLASS AFTER RETURNING TO THE PALACE, MYKELLA, Rachylana, and Areyst met Lord and Lady Gharyk, First Seltyr Khanasyl, and Chief Factor Lhanyr on the main floor of the otherwise deserted palace. From there, an honor guard of two auxiliaries and four Southern Guards escorted them through the plaza in front of the palace, then through the rear courtyard and the rear gate to the memorial garden around the private mausoleum—to the north and uphill from the regular palace gardens.

Once Rachylana carried the urn to the granite presentation table under the front arch of the mausoleum, and everyone had assembled facing the small outer rotunda, Mykella began the ceremony.

"We acknowledge that Captain Salyna, an officer of the Southern Guards and sister of the Lady-Protector of Lanachrona, has died. She died in defense of her land, her people, and her sister." Mykella had to pause so that she did not choke up. "Her efforts helped save our land, and she gave unselfishly of herself when no one would have thought less of her for not doing so. She sacrificed the hope of a long and happy life for us. We are here to mourn her loss and offer our last formal farewell in celebration of her life." With that, Mykella stepped back and nodded to Rachylana.

The redhead stepped forward, still wearing the uniform of the auxiliaries. She paused until there was absolute silence before the mausoleum.

"Our sister was the youngest daughter of the Lord-Protector of Lanachrona, but she was more than that. She was a woman who fought to prove that women could do all that men could, and she did so effectively and courageously. She began to change Lanachrona, and she gave her life to save me and my sister, the Lady-Protector. Like our father, she believed most deeply that the principal goal of the Protector of Lanachrona, and the Protector's family as well, was to protect the people of Lanachrona. She drove herself harder than anyone could have believed in all her efforts, and set an example that any woman—or any man—would be hard-pressed to emulate. We will miss her, and so will Lanachrona."

Tears streamed down Rachylana's face, but her voice was steady and strong, and she did not lower her eyes when she finished.

After another silence, Areyst delivered the blessing. "For an honored and accomplished officer, in the name of the one and the wholeness that is, and always will be . . ."

Mykella listened intently, sensing the effort Areyst had to make to keep his voice firm.

When Areyst finished the blessing, the honor guard re-formed below the steps of the mausoleum to escort the small memorial party—just the seven of them—back to the palace.

Mykella did not wipe away the tears that flowed.

65

In the entry hallway of the palace in late afternoon, after the four others who had been at the memorial service had departed, Areyst looked to Rachylana for a moment, then to Mykella. "If you would have a moment later? I need to check with Commander Choalt. . . ."

"Please . . . I'll be here. You can stay for dinner as well."

"I would like that." For a moment, his pale green eyes rested on her.

Mykella realized that not only was the green of his life-thread more pronounced, but so was the intensity of the green of his eyes . . . and those eyes held both love and respect.

"Don't . . . be too long."

"Only so long as it takes, my Lady." He inclined his head, then straightened and smiled, before turning and leaving.

Mykella watched him go, then looked to her sister. "He wasn't telling the truth . . . about Choalt."

"No, he wasn't. That's because he was trying to be tactful," replied Rachylana.

"He thought we needed time together. Why didn't he . . ." Mykella shook her head. "He knew he would have sounded arrogant by saying we needed time together without him. He was right, though." She offered a rueful smile. "Let's go upstairs."

Rachylana nodded.

The two found their way up the staircase and to the family parlor. Mykella sat down in one of the armchairs, and Rachylana took the one across from her. Neither spoke for a time.

"Why did it have to end this way?" Mykella finally asked, adding, "For Salyna?"

"Because she was who she was, and you're who you are, and because Father couldn't bear the burdens of being Lord-Protector any longer." Rachylana's voice was soft, but not bitter.

"You two saved me. I couldn't have held my shields any longer."

"She saved me," added the redhead. "She knew where to go and what to do. I just followed."

"You did more than that."

"At the end, I had to. She told me to find you." Tears seeped from the corners of Rachylana's eyes. "If I'd stayed . . ."

Would it have made any difference? Mykella wondered, but didn't ask the question because she feared the answer.

"If I'd stayed, I couldn't have saved her," said Rachylana, "then . . . I would have lost you both."

"Oh . . . Rachylana . . ." murmured Mykella. Her eyes burned once more, and tears she had already shed so many of that she wondered if she had any left to flow spilled onto her cheeks.

Again . . . neither spoke for a time.

Finally, Rachylana cleared her throat. "You were right about not having a victory parade."

"I don't know about that. I just know I couldn't have done it. Maybe people needed a sign of victory . . . but with everything . . . and Salyna . . . I just couldn't. I couldn't."

"I'm glad you didn't."

"So am I." Mykella paused. "Do you remember when she went hunting . . . and killed the boar with arrows when Jeraxylt couldn't with his rifle . . ."

". . . or when she took the duty guard's mount and rode into the Preserve," replied Rachylana. "She couldn't have been over five . . ."

The two of them sat for close to a glass, sharing memories.

Then Rachylana stood. "Areyst should be here before long, and I do need to check on the auxiliaries."

"To let them know you're still available?"

"Something like that . . . and . . ."

Mykella understood the unspoken words. *. . . and Salyna would have.* She rose from the armchair. "I'll walk down to the courtyard with you."

"He'll be down there by now, talking to the duty guards."

"You think so?"

Rachylana raised a single eyebrow, that skill that Mykella had once derided even as she'd tried in vain to duplicate it. "You think not?"

Mykella laughed.

The two walked quickly, but not hurriedly, down the steps and back along the west corridor to the rear door. As Rachylana had predicted, Areyst was talking to the duty squad leader when the two sisters stepped out into the palace courtyard.

He turned. "Lady . . . Captain Rachylana."

"I need to check on the auxiliaries," said Rachylana. "Might I borrow your mount?"

"Of course."

Rachylana glanced at Mykella. "I *will* be back in time for dinner."

Mykella found herself smiling at the glint in her sister's eyes. "We'll wait for you."

"You'd better."

Mykella smiled at Areyst. "Commander . . . would you mind escorting me?"

"Not at all, Lady.'

Not only did Areyst open the door with his one good arm, but he offered it to Mykella, and they walked along the west corridor and back up the main staircase.

"Where are we going?" Areyst's tone was amused.

"To the family parlor," she replied.

"That sounds ominous," he said gently.

"I have my reasons." She kept her voice light.

"You always do, Lady."

After they reached the upper level of the palace and entered the parlor, Mykella closed the door and turned to him. "You called me your lady . . ."

Areyst swallowed.

That was the first time, ever, she had seen—and sensed—his being less than perfectly poised. She also realized that she'd never . . . ever . . . risked telling him how she felt. She'd given signs but never said anything.

Slowly, she reached out and up . . . and let her fingers touch his cheek, drawing the deep darkness from deep beneath the palace and letting its chill enfold them both. When the chill receded, his skin was flaky, but the scars and scabs were gone.

His eyes widened.

"How is your arm?"

"The worst of the aching is gone."

Tiny flashes of light filled Mykella's eyes, and she dropped, rather than sat, into the nearest armchair.

Worry filled Areyst's face as he stepped over and leaned down. "Are you all right?"

"I'm . . . not as recovered as I thought," she admitted. "I wanted to do that earlier, but I knew I couldn't."

Areyst stepped back, then carried one of the straight-backed chairs over next to the armchair. He sat down and looked at her.

Mykella could sense that he was almost as exhausted as she was, and for several moments, they were silent.

"Using the darkness of the Ancients to heal . . . is tiring. I don't think it would work for near-mortal injuries because it uses the body's own strength."

"You always surprise me," he said.

"I hope . . . I always will." She paused. "Do . . . you still want me to be your lady?"

The rush of hope, desire, and love that followed her words left her speechless, even though his words were simple. "I do."

The embarrassed smile that followed was almost painful to her, and she leaned forward before he could say more. "I so hoped you would." She swallowed and held up her hand so that he would not speak. "When I thought you had died in the battle . . . my heart almost stopped. Rachylana could tell you . . ."

His good hand reached out and touched her hair, then traced the line of her cheek before dropping to take her right hand. "I thought I saw . . . I didn't know, but I worried so." He shook his head. "I kept thinking it was foolish of me to hope, but from the day you stood up to me after commandeering an entire squad, I kept looking at you. I hoped you didn't notice."

"Yet you hoped I would," she said, not quite teasingly.

"I did."

"Rachylana won't be back for a while . . ." Mykella smiled gently and took his hand in hers. "Tell me more, dearest."

EPILOGUE

At ninth glass on Octdi, at the end of the first week of Harvest, Mykella stood in her study, looking at those seated around the conference table—her ministers, including Areyst, who wore a lighter splint around his right arm, and First Seltyr Khanasyl and Chief High Factor Lhanyr. Loryalt appeared worried, as did Zylander, while Gharyk's lips occasionally curled into a faint smile. Behind Areyst's professional smile lurked greater amusement. Khanasyl and Lhanyr radiated puzzlement, clearly wondering why they had been summoned.

"Now that the envoys from both Northcoast and Midcoast have arrived," Mykella began, "we will receive them in the lower reception chamber shortly. They will protest, because they have been instructed to do so, but each will present a signed agreement of surrender and formally turn over the sum of the settlement agreement required, in gold. We already have received the golds, but a formal ceremony is required, and that ceremony will be witnessed not only by the ministers and Arms-Commander of Lanachrona, but also by you, First Seltyr, as representative of the Seltyrs, and by you, Chief High Factor, as the representative of the High Factors. I am charging you both with the duty and responsibility of conveying the facts and terms of the agreements to all Seltyrs and factors."

"Might I ask again why there was no celebration of our victory?" asked Khanasyl.

"We prevailed and, against far greater numbers, destroyed the power of both Midcoast and Northcoast. Given that our triumph, if one could call it that, cost us close to half the Southern Guards and annihilated close to nine out of ten armsmen of our enemies, I did not feel that such a result merited any public celebration. Given that it occurred because of the failures of my predecessors and yours, for us to celebrate would have been arrogant and self-deluding. We have much work still ahead to rebuild Lanachrona. That work is proceeding, and I do appreciate greatly the current cooperation of both Seltyrs and factors . . . but a celebration of escape from such disaster would seem . . . shall we say . . . presumptuous." Mykella smiled politely. "Do you think it otherwise, First Seltyr?"

"I would call it . . . traditional."

"You might indeed, and tradition is often appropriate. When the cost to a land is so high, and so many still mourn, tradition merely for the sake of tradition is inappropriate. We can and will celebrate when we have returned Lanachrona to its former greatness."

The First Seltyr nodded, as did the Chief High Factor.

Mykella could sense that Khanasyl actually agreed, and that he had raised the question to receive an answer he could give to others. That was encouraging, because it reflected an acceptance of her position as Protector, not merely her power. *Except power created that acceptance.* "After we receive the envoys from Midcoast and Northcoast, we will all assemble back here to discuss other matters."

Khanasyl frowned. "Might we ask—"

"You may, but the nature of those matters will wait until after we deal with the envoys." Mykella smiled warmly and cheerfully, projecting good humor. "If you will all take your places below, I will join you shortly, then the envoys will be ushered in, one at a time."

After the six had left the study, Mykella walked over to the open windows and looked out across the plaza courtyard toward the gardens across the avenue. Most of the trees had recovered from the damage of the spring storms. *As Lanachrona will recover.*

After a knock on the door, Chalmyr peered in. "They're ready for you, Lady."

"Thank you." Mykella crossed the study, then the anteroom, and walked to the staircase.

The lower level of the palace had been cleared glasses before, and as she paused at the top of the ancient steps, a short trumpet fanfare echoed from the entry foyer below. Mykella walked down the steps alone, between the Southern Guards stationed at the top and bottom in their dress uniforms of cream and dark blue. Once past the two trumpeters, beside the staircase, Mykella turned right until she reached the doors on the west side of the wide corridor.

Two guards opened them, and she walked through the double doors into the small receiving room off the grand dining hall, whose doors were closed. Before those doors was a low dais with four chairs on one side for the ministers and two on the other side for the First Seltyr and the chief High Factor. Set in the middle of the dais and forward of the other chairs was a tall high-backed chair, not quite a throne, covered with pale green shimmersilk, placed there to set off the nightsilk blacks she wore.

Mykella nodded to the ministers and to the Chief High Factor and First Seltyr before settling into the high-backed chair.

The receiving room doors opened, and a man not all that much older than Mykella stepped into the chamber, bowed once, then walked forward, stopping a yard short of the dais, where he bowed again.

"Lady-Protector."

"Greetings, Lord Dhevan. Welcome to Tempre. I trust your journey was uneventful." Mykella projected a feeling of welcome.

"It was refreshingly so, Lady."

"You have come to formally present and acknowledge the terms of the agreement between our lands. Is that not so?"

"Yes, Lady. I have presented the signed and sealed agreement to your Minister of Justice."

"You have indeed." Mykella looked to Gharyk, who stood and, lifting a gilt-edged leather folder, opened it to display a signed and sealed document.

"Lady-Protector . . . Prince Karolyt has agreed to the terms, but I must note as a matter of fact that we had no choice."

Mykella could sense the young lord's unease, but she needed to impress him in a way he would never forget. "You're correct, Lord Dhevan, you had no choice. None. Your former ruler attacked Lanachrona without provocation. His acts cost us thousands of lives and destroyed three towns for no real reason other than the fact that they refused to turn over all their harvests and goods to him. Defending ourselves against this unprovoked aggression cost us dearly. The plots in which your former ruler was involved also cost me my father, my brother, and my uncle, and the war cost me my sister." Mykella smiled. "I was exceedingly generous in requiring you pay a mere ten thousand golds. Will you and Midcoast be a loyal friend and hold to the terms of the agreement? Or do you wish me to march into Midcoast and tear down Salcer, then Hafin, stone by stone? You have no forces remaining to stop me, as you well know, and whatever forces you may gather in the future will not suffice." She projected absolute power and assurance.

Dhevan swallowed, paling slightly.

"I am not trying to make Midcoast a part of Lanachrona. I am simply requiring a partial repayment for great wrongs." Mykella's voice turned cold and icy. "Do not be foolish enough to make me require a full repayment from Midcoast."

"Yes, Lady."

"You have brought the golds required, and the agreement" Mykella nodded at Gharyk, who closed the gilt-edged case and seated himself. After a moment, she continued. "We will honor that agreement in good faith, as witness the fact that we have neither invaded nor attempted to tariff Midcoast beyond its means." Mykella let her voice warm. "We are far better as a friend than as an enemy, Lord Dhevan. Please convey that to Prince Karolyt."

Dhevan nodded. "Yes, Lady." He bowed deeply.

Mykella could sense he was shaken to the core. *Good.*

Once Dhevan had left the chamber, the two Southern Guards opened the doors, and a tall and lean man in the green and gold of Northcoast strode in, his entire posture and being radiating arrogance.

Mykella did not speak but merely looked at him, this time projecting both power and withering contempt. She watched as the arrogance evaporated under the unseen Talent assault.

The Northcoast envoy stopped several paces short of where Mykella sat in the tall chair. He offered a bow, then straightened. "Lady-Protector. I bring you greetings from Northcoast and Prince Dalcaer."

"I trust you have brought more than greetings, Envoy Keseyn," Mykella replied dryly. "Or have you forgotten that you have an agreement signed and sealed by Prince Dalcaer?"

"Ah . . . yes." After a moment, the envoy continued. "We have presented it to your Minister of Justice."

At Mykella's nod, Gharyk stood once more and displayed a document in a green leather case.

Mykella nodded again, and Gharyk seated himself.

"We trust that Prince Dalcaer had no problems with the agreement."

"Prince Dalcaer has no choice . . . but being a man of great and goodwill . . ."

Mykella again smiled coldly, letting the greenish light flood from her. "It is not a question of his goodwill, but of mine. Given all the wrongs done to Lanachrona by the late Prince Chalcaer, I am showing exceeding goodwill by not wiping out the entire lineage of your ruling family. I am requiring ten thousand golds and a pledge of good faith. Your prince has provided those golds. Now all he has to do is to keep his word. He fails, and his life is forfeit. It's very simple."

"Lady . . . you are most powerful . . ."

"Could the Ancients not reach every land in Corus? Do not try me, Envoy Keseyn. Nor should your prince. His predecessor plotted against my sire and helped steal thousands of golds from our Treasury to build his army. I destroyed him and that army. Ask any of those who survived that battle what I did . . . if you dare. Because Prince Dalcaer is new to his throne, I am being generous and showing goodwill by my limited requirements of him. Do you understand?"

Keseyn's forehead was damp and his face pale.

"You might also tell your prince that I am inclined to become vindictive if he is the kind to punish envoys and messengers for news he does not wish to hear. For that reason, I would request that you not depart Tempre until I provide you with a missive that stresses to your prince my interest in your continued good health. Now that I have met you, I will know if anything ill befalls you."

"You . . . are . . . most kind, Lady."

"I am not necessarily kind, Envoy Keseyn. I do try to be fair and just. It is anything but fair for a ruler to punish an envoy or a messenger for the faults of another. As you please, you may carry my words to Prince Dalcaer. He might recall the fate of his sister and his elder brother."

"Yes, Lady Protector."

Mykella smiled, then projected warmth and softened her voice. "Take care on your journey home, Keseyn."

"Thank you, Lady."

When Keseyn was well out of the palace, Mykella led the six men back upstairs to her study. She remained by the door, trying not to look at Areyst, who managed to keep a politely professional smile on his face. She wasn't certain how he could do it.

"There's no need to sit down. This will not take long. I'll be back in just a moment for the last matter." She stepped back into the anteroom and closed the door behind her.

Rachylana had entered the anteroom and was waiting. This time, she wore the dark blue and cream dress uniform of the auxiliaries, a uniform she had designed, with captain's bars on the collar. "I don't know why . . ."

"Because you're my only surviving relative, because I wouldn't be here without you, and because I refuse to make the announcement myself."

Mykella stepped back into the study, followed by Rachylana.

Rachylana closed the door, and Mykella nodded to Areyst, who stepped forward to stand beside the Lady-Protector.

Mykella could see immediate comprehension on Gharyk's face and a dawning understanding among several others. "I believe you all know my sister, Captain Rachylana. Because she is my sister, and because she served with distinction in the Battle of Viencet under Arms-Commander Areyst, I thought she should be the one to make this announcement."

Rachylana didn't bother to hide a wide smile that was almost a mischievous grin. "I never thought this day would come, but I would like to tell you all of the matching betrothal of Mykella, Lady-Protector of Lanachrona, and Arms-Commander Areyst. The wedding will take place on the afternoon of the ball for the turn of fall."

As Rachylana spoke, Mykella reached out and took Areyst's left hand. Then, after the momentary silence, she looked to Khanasyl. She said nothing.

The tall Seltyr smiled, then laughed, shaking his head and looking to Areyst. "You're a braver man than I, Commander, and more fortunate." Then he looked to Mykella. "Lady . . . we all are grateful for your perseverance, courage, and strength. We wish you both the greatest of happiness together."

Is true happiness always purchased with pain?

Mykella squeezed Areyst's hand, and the return pressure of his fingers—and the joy behind that pressure—coursed through them both. And this time, her tears and Rachylana's were for hope and love.

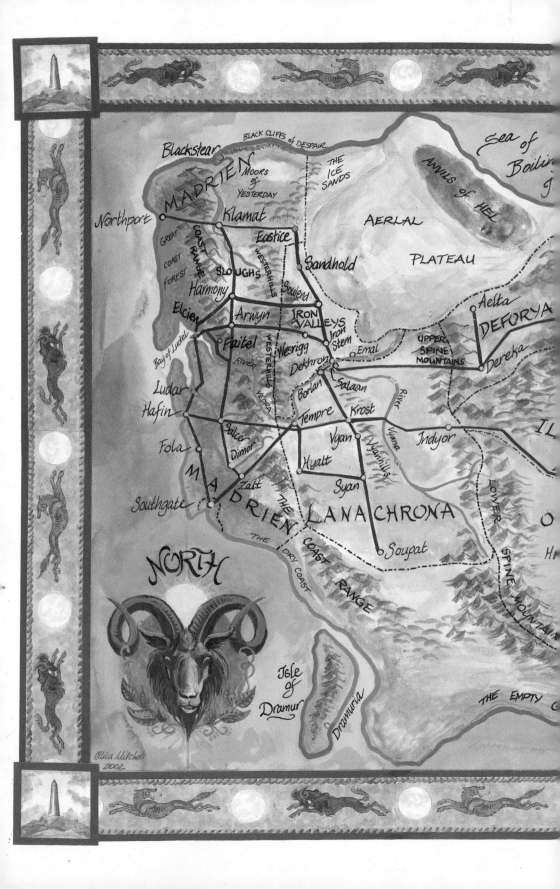